BLOOD
APPEAL

VIGILANTE - A SPECIES OF COMMON LAW

BOOK THREE IN THE PALATINI SERIES

LYLE O'CONNOR

BLOOD
APPEAL

VIGILANTE - A SPECIES OF COMMON LAW
BOOK THREE IN THE PALATINI SERIES

LYLE O'CONNOR

PO Box 221974 Anchorage, Alaska 99522-1974
books@publicationconsultants.com—www.publicationconsultants.com

ISBN 978-1-59433-596-9
ISBN 978-1-59433-597-6 eBook
Library of Congress Catalog Card Number: 2016933352

Manufactured in the United States of America.

Dedicated in love for my Grandchildren—

Kasydi
Ava
Kaydence
Cheyenne
Shiloh
Raegan

Blood Appeal is a work of fiction. All names, characters, places and incidents are products of the author's imagination or are used fictitiously. Any resemblance to actual events or persons, living or deceased, is entirely coincidental.

OTHER BOOKS BY LYLE O'CONNOR

Due Process

Lawless Measures

Acknowledgements

*"The man with insight enough to admit
his limitations comes nearest to perfection."*
—Johann Wolfgang von Goethe

I would like to thank a few people who have made
my limitations less pronounced.

My longtime friend, Walter Allen Grant, author,
and content editor of the Palatini Series.
His guidance continues to provide a vital role in my writing.

A very special thanks to BJ Wood whose generous
collaboration on this novel has brought greater depth to the
characters and strength to the story.

Finally, a shout-out to Danny Crabb for usage
of his southern vernacular in this work.

The Beatles made famous the lyrics,
I get by with a little help from my friends.
I wouldn't have it any other way.

Chapter 1

*"Don't ever think the reason I am peaceful is
because I've forgotten how to be violent"*
—Unknown

Shell Knob, Missouri
April 1, 2003

"9-1-1 dispatch, what is the nature of your emergency?"

"Hey there y'all, this here be Cletus Forbes ov'rin Whiskey Gulch. I has a body layin' out here, and she's a lookin' deader 'n' hell."

Barry County's Sheriff Dispatcher, Emma Lathrop, kept Cletus on the line while she relayed information to two patrol deputies with the added comment, "Check out the validity of the report."

Deputy Bart Delford, a ten-year veteran of the force, picked up the call and responded, "Be near half-an-hour till I get there." It wasn't Delford's first trip to Whiskey Gulch. Cletus had a long, and less than favorable history with Barry County's finest. If the report turned out false, which Delford assumed it was, he'd haul him off to the hoosegow again.

Reporter Jay Landers, a young, energetic newcomer to the local grass-roots weekly newspaper in Barry County, had likewise picked up Lathrop's dispatch over his portable police scanner and wasted no time calling dispatch to verify the report. Landers had never met Cletus, but he soon found himself on the road heading southeast toward Whiskey Gulch to meet the man he knew only by reputation.

In the rural communities of Barry County, any news, legitimate or otherwise, traveled like wildfire. It wouldn't be too far from the truth to say the story grew with every conversation, certainly faster than I'd grown accustomed to in Portland's urban area. I'd been told that everyone knows everyone in Barry County, but it wasn't true. There wasn't anyone who knew everyone, but everyone knew someone, which caused a chain reaction on the local phone lines. They sizzled when there was news to spread. I recalled seeing the process in action in early March. Table Rock Lake was the scene of a horrific boating accident that set off a flurry of phone calls in this tiny community. The informal phone tree activated when the first caller sounded the alarm. Everyone was notified at least once in the first couple of hours, and by day's end it was anybody's guess how many times the word had gone around.

The local newspaper Landers worked for was, at best, an added value to breaking news in the region. The weekly edition hit the shelves every Wednesday and usually validated local phone tree events. Follow up articles and filling in the gaps was the primary impact of the newspaper's mission. Country folk might come across as simple-minded, but they weren't, not like some people think, or portray them. Their human nature dictates the importance of details like anyone else. Precisely the reason Landers hoped he'd landed a scoop.

According to the dispatcher's log, it was five-thirty-three Tuesday morning when Cletus made his call. For Landers, it was an extraordinary stroke of luck in timing. If the report was genuine, and he hurried, he'd have the story copy ready by press time the next morning. If he missed the evening deadline, it would be seven more days before he'd have another chance. By then, the story would have taken on the usual staleness of an update, not a breaking news story. A few days later, Landers told me, "If it had turned out differently, and Cletus didn't have a body, it was okay. I would have caught an early breakfast, and made a human interest story about 9-1-1 calls."

"Good thinking," I said. "It's always worthwhile to have a backup plan."

Landers had managed to reach the Forbes residence in Whiskey Gulch before anyone else had arrived. Again, he wasted no time. He contacted Cletus, introduced himself, and did what reporters are most notorious for; he stuck his nose in where it didn't belong. Up until now, Shell Knob residents had given Cletus little credit for his IQ or common sense. But it would appear he had redeemed himself to some degree when he refused to allow Landers onto his property or to contaminate the crime scene before the responding agencies had arrived. Landers told me, "At that point I was sure it was a ruse."

Cletus referred to himself as a farmer and called his parcel of land a farm, but neither was true. He hadn't tilled the soil or used his acreage to plant crops, at least nothing legitimate. But, he did have a few honeybee hives and a drainage ditch full of blackberry brambles that grew wild. These provided him with a little cash on the side, but in my book it didn't constitute a farm.

I remembered having been on a narrow winding dirt road through Whiskey Gulch and to the best of my recollection the entire valley was a maze of thick brush. In an odd quirk, I distinctly remember thinking a guy could hide a lot of bodies in the Gulch, and they'd likely never be found. If Cletus found a body, then I'd obviously been wrong.

Landers made his deadline. Wednesday afternoon copies of the Cassville rag flew off the shelf at the local retail outlets, enough so that the managing editor ran a second print the following day to meet demand. I didn't find the quest for more information terribly strange behavior for a small community. Fear and morbid curiosity have always had tremendous draw power, even to the best of people. Not only was the community ablaze with gossip, but Landers had also successfully filled in a few of the gaps with his word for word account of Forbes 9-1-1 call and his subsequent interviews. His article had a personal flair. "We were leery it was another prank call. It wouldn't have been funny, but it never stopped ol' Cletus in the past," Lathrop said. Landers pointed out there was good cause to question a call from Cletus at five-thirty-three in the morning. He had a well-known history in Barry County for all the wrong reasons. According to the rumor mill, he had the finest moonshine in the vicinity of Table Rock Lake, bar none. He'd been known to personally taste-test every new batch from his still. A fresh batch of 'shine had also corresponded with many of his previous run-ins with the law.

In an unusual confession to a newspaper reporter, Deputy Delford said, "I was reluctant to go out there at first. It was April Fools' Day, and I figured he was probably playing a joke on us." At one point, Delford told Landers, "It'd been a long and quiet night on patrol. I'd planned to give Cletus a piece of my mind for pulling a stunt like this here one. Then I'd haul him in."

When Deputy Delford arrived, he directed Landers to stay at the house. Forbes pointed and said, "She be over thar." Forbes escorted the Deputy in the direction he'd indicated. Landers reported that Bart, who he'd become friends with since moving to Cassville, and Cletus had walked a couple hundred yards from the house before they disappeared from view. A few seconds later a crackling radio transmission came over the portable scanner confirming the worst, "Dispatch, this here is Delford—we got us a body."

Landers headline the following day landed him top billing for the front-page slot in the publication. In bold type, it read "Young girl's body found in Whiskey Gulch, face down and naked." It was a massive caption filling a quarter of the page. He had his scoop. In other corners of Missouri such as Kansas City or St. Louis, it would've been old news in a day. In Shell Knob, it was likely to be a front-page article for a month. If Landers worked it right, he could keep it in the news longer. Details were sketchy. The victim's identity remained unknown. Delford made a couple of educated guesses. "The girl ain't been dead too awful long and it's a crime scene sure enough. Foul play is expected as the cause of death." An autopsy had been scheduled. The information determining cause and time of death would likely be swift. A Sheriff's Department spokesman released a statement, "We have not received any recent missing persons' reports and there are no local reports of runaways which match the victim's general description." For some, this would signal a relief.

Nothing like this had ever happened in quiet and peaceful Shell Knob; population two-thousand, more or less. There had been deaths from vehicle, swimming, and boating accidents, but not a brutal, cold-blooded murder like this, at least not that any of the townspeople could remember. The unincorporated community of Shell Knob was spread across either side of the northwestern corner of Table Rock Lake along State Highway 39, and smack-dab in the middle of the Mark Twain National Forest's Ava district. In my mind, there was no safer place on earth to live. Apparently I had been mistaken.

Throughout the night, prior to Cletus' Forbes 9-1-1 call, I'd been awakened multiple times in cold sweats. My recollection of dreams was that of blood pooling on the ground. As disturbing as this might have been, what followed was worse. Spine chilling screams echoed in the breeze, followed by eerie moans as if a wolf howled outside my cabin door. I pulled my handgun close to my side and lay in the dark, waiting and watching until I'd fallen back to sleep again. Abruptly, the cycle started over with blood seeping up through the ground, always with blood.

It was through a strange twist of fate that I had arrived in Shell Knob a few months earlier. I'd been traveling from Buffalo, New York to my home in Portland, Oregon when I veered off course. I'd stopped in to check on an acquaintance and then found no need to resume my journey. There were a lot of things to enjoy in Shell Knob. My lady friend, Joyce Farmer, was one of them.

Frankly, I didn't feel like I belonged in Shell Knob, although I had deeply entrenched roots in a similar environment. I had lived on a cattle ranch in the Chenoweth district of The Dalles, Oregon and spent many days and nights hiking and camping in the rolling foothills of the Cascade Mountains. Life was laid-back and peaceful amongst the hills and alfalfa fields of the Columbia River Gorge. It was the kind of upbringing and life most city people only dreamt about but never experienced. However, there came a time when duty called and off to war I went for God, country, and mom's apple pie. Except I didn't find any of those things we'd been fighting for in the rice paddies of a foreign land. Saigon fell to communism, and my commitment to military service ended. I'd sought to do the right thing, but my countrymen disdained the sacrifices that we'd made. I returned to the workforce an empty and unfulfilled person. My compassion for humanity was all but nonexistent. With country living in my rear view mirror, I set my sights on a career. As with many of my friends, the well-trodden routes led to big industrialized cities. My path ended in Portland.

I despised every aspect of urban living, especially the level of crime. It was everywhere. Co-workers at the aluminum factory were ambivalent to the rising crime statistics and avoided the issue as if it would disappear on its own. By their behavior, you would have thought it was an accepted fact of big city life to be contended with—I didn't see it that way.

The abundance of crime, coupled with the lack of interest others demonstrated, made a negative impact on me. Reaching my lowest point, and overwhelmed by victims sufferings, I changed my outlook from thoughts to actions. A kaleidoscope of dreams and ghostly apparitions attached themselves to my obsession. It was a deadly mix. My fixation over the mistreatment of victims of heinous crimes brought me to the breaking point of sanity. Some might even say I broke, but I didn't share their opinion.

I kept to myself and minded my own business. I enjoyed my regular workout routine until crime seized the opportunity to pay me a visit. I didn't ask for it, but I wasn't one to shy away either. One day, fate guided me to Destiny on the bike path near my Portland home. I had frequently pondered what course of action I'd pursue if faced with a violent criminal attack. Mentally I'd prepared for such an event. But I learned I wasn't ready because it seldom goes down the way a person imagines. I witnessed a female fighting for her life and being dragged from the bike trail into a wooded area. I'd armed myself months earlier with a .38-caliber Smith & Wesson revolver for my protection while hiking the urban trails. I reasoned at this time my intervention was necessary. I drew my weapon and interrupted what I believed to be a rape and possible murder in progress.

In the midst of the chaotic scene, a shining spirit-apparition appeared before me. In a demonstrative way, the ghostly female figure urged me to kill the attacker, but I hesitated. It was quickly apparent that neither the victim nor the perpetrator could see her. After the police and ambulance had left with both victim and bad guy, I was once again joined by the apparition. Through her guidance, a path was chosen for me to walk. Forever illuminated as the passage to righteousness, I proceeded steadfastly in The Way. I named the spirit Destiny. She was my friend and closest ally.

As I followed my calling, I factored myself in as a lethal consequence through vigilante justice. My campaign of terror against the vilest of criminals caught the eye of a journalist, Anna Sasins, who led me to a secret society known as Palatini. They were those who represented a knighthood of the resurrected order of freelance assassins—I was knighted "Scythian," one who wields a scythe as the Grim Reaper. The name has served me well. Wisely, I'd hidden my birth name so that it might never be known. Through my façade as a freelance reporter, I am known as Walter Eloy Goe.

Palatini knights existed for a single purpose, to right the wrongs committed on the innocent, as did our medieval predecessors who'd fought crime and tyranny in their day. Our mission was one of guardianship of the people. We lay no claim to being superheroes, but we didn't call 9-1-1 either. We took care of business our way—the vigilante way. We fought our most recent Palatini project along the New York-Canadian border. I'd been called upon to assassinate a couple of Mob targets who were pimping underage girls in their brothels. I was more than happy to lend a hand. The project should have been routine, but it didn't turn out that way. It was my opinion that we'd compromised our principles to bring the bloodshed to an end. Making a deal with the mob was like making a deal with the devil, and I conveyed that message clearly. Other Palatini operators didn't feel the same way. We'd reached our project's primary goal through a pact with another mobster faction who'd agreed to end the human trafficking. I doubted any such agreement would stand for long. They were not honorable men. The dominant opinion prevailed that it was in our best interest to let the mob fix the mob or we'd end up in an endless battle.

My contrary position put me at odds with the Palatini. I came across as disgruntled and as if I distrusted those I was in league with, but it wasn't true. My beliefs were framed with the simplest of principles to guide me. When it came to dealing with lawyers, politicians, and mobsters, I found the adage, "If their lips were moving they were lying," apropos. To my way of thinking, all mobsters were the epitome of evil, as were lawyers and politicians. In the end, I couldn't come to grips with anything the mob promised, and cast the only dissenting vote among Palatini. The project was tied off, and each of us went our separate ways.

Joyce Farmer, my acquaintance, and lady-friend, lived east of Shell Knob on Highway 39. I had a hand in helping her leave the Mob-infested work environment of Toronto, and back to her childhood home in Missouri. Upon my arrival, she gave the impression she was happy to see me again and invited me to stay if I liked. I liked a lot, and we've spent the past three months informally cohabiting.

Joyce had moved back to Shell Knob for her young boys' safety and to help her aging parents run their small family resort on the edge of Table Rock Lake. I understood her reasons for returning to her childhood home. A country lifestyle, free of crime, and closer family ties appealed to her. For Joyce, the straw that broke the camel's back was when her co-worker at Toronto's Musolino's Osteria had been shot-to-death in the restaurant's parking lot. She told me she'd had her fill of big city life and planned to leave as soon as she found a way to finance her return home.

I've kept my life a secret from Joyce. I would've liked to have been up front with her, but I've found my passion difficult to explain. Especially challenging would be where I shot her co-worker to death. Doubtful she would have understood why he deserved termination with extreme prejudice. She would've been less understanding of how, in a roundabout way, the mobsters I killed had donated her funds to move to Missouri. To finance Joyce's relocation, the Mob money we'd intercepted was funneled through Gladys Mitchell, a woman known for her hospitality and generosity to young, disadvantaged women. A sense of rightness prevailed when word trickled back she'd made the commitment to move her family to Shell Knob and away from the criminal elements in Toronto. Meeting up with Joyce again was never part of my plan.

When the project wrapped up, I saddled up for a lengthy road trip to Oregon. Without a reason to rush my jaunt to Portland, I capitalized on the opportunity to see the fruits of my labor and ended up in Shell Knob. For the time being, there was no way around my dilemma; the dealt hand was the hand I played, and I played it smart.

My immediate concern with the finding of the body was the backlash this tiny community would have in response to a brutal murder. My fears were not unfounded. I'd seen it all before, firsthand, in John Day, Oregon, when I killed a pervert that needed killing. In the big cities, people put an extra chain or bolt lock on their front doors for protection from the evil. In small communities, they loaded both barrels of their trusty shotgun and hunted down wickedness as if it were a ravenous wild dog on the prowl. Neither Landers' article nor Barry County's finest would be able to satisfy the locals. All they understood was "lock 'n' load."

Similar to mountain militia's, scores of men, women, and children, climbed into pickups and hopped on four-wheelers to scour the hillsides and ravines. In some cases, people hoofed it from one house to the next to check on neighbors and look for signs of anything suspicious.

Joyce reacted too. Upon receipt of her first phone call, she called her boys in from outside and had them play in the house for the remainder of the day. For the weeks that followed, Joyce and her family kept unusually close tabs on the children.

The report of the killing served to remind me of who I was, and what I'd been called to do. Evil lurked everywhere.

Typically, crime in Barry County was the result of moonshine, meth-amphetamines, or domestic violence. Shocking to the community was the death of an unknown young girl whose body had been found dumped as if she were a bag of garbage. Residents were frightened at the existence of an unknown menace. No one spoke of the possibility the killer was a resident. That was too difficult to fathom. Their concern focused with an outsider, likely a drifter, who had moved in amongst them. Their refuge had been eviscerated by a terrifying act and fear; one that had stolen peace from their community. With their isolated-backcountry way of life having been shattered, suspicion and distrust prevailed.

It was my luck—bad luck—to still be considered an outsider around these parts and not one of the good ol' boys who was above suspicion. Any questioning of my presence in Barry County by the Sheriff's Department would be uncomfortable or worse—revealing.

The resort, where I've had my residency for the past three months, was owned by Joyce's parents, Sue Ellen, and Harlan Farmer. The main two-story, bed and breakfast style resort, was nestled in a picturesque tree lined setting near the lake. Behind the larger structure on the lake's edge sat four rental cabins, quiet and quaint. I'd rented cabin number four. Joyce had offered to rent me a room in the main house next to hers, but I declined. I had to have privacy.

Cassville was the County Seat and sat twenty miles from the east end of Shell Knob. Located between Cassville and the Farmer's resort was Cletus Forbes place. The nearness of Whiskey Gulch to the resort was potentially problematic. I couldn't escape the fact I lived in proximity to the murder. As the crow flies, the resort was less than five miles east from where they'd discovered the girl's body. From the resort's location, all I had to do was pass over Table Rock Bridge and hang a left from Highway 39 towards Ledgerwood Hollow. From there, you had to know where you were going. Whiskey Gulch didn't have a sign.

I saw the writing on the wall, and it spelled danger. I expected an uncomfortable closeness to develop with law enforcement. Knowing I'd be considered a suspect, my interest was galvanized. Self-preservation and a higher calling forced my hand to take a proactive approach. I had to work my sources to see what they had for information. Since my intentions had been to stay off the radar, my pool of people to draw from was limited.

Reporter Jay Landers and I had become quasi-friends. I'd become acquainted with him at a charitable function for kindergartners at the elementary school where Joyce's eldest son, Trey, attended. Landers had taken an interest in me, more than I had in him. I surmised his attraction toward me was based solely on my being presented as a seasoned journalist. Landers was a relative newbie to the media circus while I enjoyed the veteran status of my facade. By regurgitating a few things that my old friend Harold Horn had covered from the crime beat for the Portland Trumpeter-Gazette, and passed them off as my own, I'd convinced Landers that I was the real deal. I told him that to protect myself against the possibility of some bad guy seeking revenge, I'd used a byline. When you lie, be specific and don't flower it up too much. You might forget how you told it, and get caught in your own trap. Most of the time, I chose to avoid the subject of reporting on crime scenes lest I blundered, and he'd become suspicious of my claims. Creating a problem where one didn't exist didn't make any sense to me.

Friday morning I placed a call to Landers. I'd left a message on his office answering machine and held out a degree of hope he'd be able to get back with me soon. As a local reporter, Landers had access to Barry County's Sheriff Department, making him my best and only resource. I needed to know what he'd dug up. My mind spun a hundred miles an hour as I determined the best course of action to take.

Contemplation has been known to require an investment of time which everyone knows down South, is best served by a comfortable stump. Having located such, a gnarly old chunk of a log, I dragged it to the water's edge in front of my cabin. Of course, no viable meditation was possible without the proper accompanying beverage or two while I dangled my feet in the lake water. I brewed a fresh jug of coffee, grabbed a clean cup, and walked fifteen yards to the water's edge. I marked my spot on the ground with the jug and scanned the area for potential shade if the sun grew too warm.

My lounging on the gnarly log lasted but a few minutes before I opted for a more comfortable folding lawn chair. I eased my feet into the lake's warmer water at the edge and poured the coffee. Leaning back, I absorbed the peaceful view and drank while listening to the birds declaring it to be a beautiful day. But my mind ushered back the bloody dreams and bone-chilling screams from the previous nights, until the message sunk in deep. It wasn't a beautiful day for the dead girl. Somewhere in the not too distant future I had the responsibility to ensure it wasn't going to be a beautiful day for those who had committed the murder—I'd see to it personally.

It was early afternoon before Landers returned my call.

"Walter, this is Jay Landers."

"I'll bet you're busy with the scoop on that dead girl?"

"I'm trying brother; I'm trying. I'm finding a lot of hurry up and wait for information from agencies."

I laughed. "Been there and done that." Then I laughed again as I prepared to make inroads. "Just wanted to tell you, you're doing an excellent job with the story. This type of reporting can be hard, but I have a few ideas that I'd like to run past you which might make it a little easier."

"Walter, I know you've covered a few of these cases, I'd appreciate any insight you can provide. Are you available later today?"

"Sure, let's hook up at Carole's Restaurant?"

"How's four-thirty for a cup. I'll buy."

"Sounds good to me. I'm not one to turn down free Java."

Over the past few months, Joyce and I had developed a close relationship. I found her attractive and desirable, but there was an underlying current that plagued our relationship. I wasn't foolish enough to compare what I had with Anna to what Joyce and I shared. I'd been ready to commit my life to Anna, and emotionally I was nowhere near that with Joyce. Anna haunted my memories. Knowing what I had and what I might have had was a burden. Anna was everything I dreamed of in a woman. Stunningly beautiful, a Palatini, and she wielded a knife like a ninja. My life was complete with her in a way that was impossible with Joyce. I could be myself with Anna—a vigilante. I had kissed a future with Anna good-bye when I left Toronto because I was too foolish. I allowed a bad reaction to create a wrong decision. It was the final nail in the coffin of our relationship.

Joyce was an attractive woman too with an embedded beauty throughout her character. Her depth of devotion to family was commendable, as well as her home baked cookies. Joyce's lifestyle was refreshingly simple in all the right ways. I adored that about her.

Joyce sent all the right signals for our bond to blossom. All I had to do was ask, and she'd be mine. But, who's would she be? The person I've shown her, a benevolent and caring Walter, or Walter the assassin who eradicates evil? The fact was she couldn't know either of us, not in any real way. I could see only pain in our future together. How long could I hide being a Palatini before she found out I was something she hated. She would never understand my reasons to kill. She hated violence as did I, but our approach was as different as night from day, and yet, night and day come together twice within every twenty-four-hour period. Doubtful we could find that much common ground. Evil would never be overcome by running away. It had to be challenged and defeated by force.

There was more to consider in our relationship. Joyce had two boys, Trey and Brody Alden. Joyce had met Perry Alden while he vacationed at Table Rock Lake. She was twenty-four years old, and life in Hicksville had lost its appeal. Perhaps worried she'd be an old maid and with notably few choices available in Shell Knob, she took a chance to get out of the town. She spent the next ten-plus years trying to find a way back.

Perry, a Canadian citizen, had money and the drive to secure a great future for his family. But he made unwise choices in his business dealings and was weak in character. Disgruntled, he abandoned Joyce with her two babies and followed the path of least resistance. Perry might've returned to British Columbia, but she wasn't sure, and no longer cared. She filed for divorce, took back her maiden name, and found herself stranded in Toronto waiting tables to make ends meet.

I was not the stabilizing force she or her kids needed in their lives. I never could be. I'd been aware of the difficulties a relationship with Joyce might cause from day one. I longed to be different than what I'd become, but with the dead body showing up, my instincts called to me in my sleep. My heart ached over my concern that I might hurt Joyce. She didn't deserve it. The sooner I left, the better for everyone involved, but how was I to slip away when suspicion was everywhere?

Chapter 2

"The human body can bear immeasurable pain and yet recover.
Wounds can heal. But once your spirit is broken, everything falls apart."
—*Palden Gyatso*

Jay Landers and I met at Carole's Restaurant as planned. He was excited to share his groundwork with me. I let him talk for the first forty-five minutes as he recapped the story from what he had for a beginning to the present status.

"Walter, I don't have any experience at this level of crime reporting, and I know you have covered a few in the past. How would you follow up?"

The fact was Landers didn't know me or anything about me. What he had heard was hearsay from Joyce and lies I'd told him. He hadn't checked his facts and maybe he should have before he acted on assumption.

I responded, "Police interviews and known forensic details. Focus on these two areas first. Stay close to old Cletus and don't dismiss any plausible story lines. I'm not saying trump up stuff. I don't buy into that sort of journalism. But if the facts are coming out thin, then come at the story from a human-interest angle. People eat it up. What do you have on the dead girl?"

"Photographs."

Jay reached underneath the table, pulled out a soft leather satchel and removed a manila folder with staples on either end. His eyes shifted from side to side with a look of guilt. He slipped the envelope to me.

"Take a look for yourself."

I opened the top of the folder and looked inside at the contents. One by one I removed each picture, examined it, and placed it back into the pouch. He'd secured more than a dozen photographs taken at the scene on the first day. Guilt was replaced by pride as Landers smiled ear to ear. I took my time and went through each one carefully before commenting, "Well done my friend. I suppose it's not common knowledge you have these in your possession?"

"Yeah, not exactly. The body was in a ravine not far from the road. I saw the direction Cletus had taken Delford and how quickly he called the body into dispatch. It had to be near the ravine."

"Good deduction."

"I hiked up the opposite side of the ravine, stayed close to the brush and used a telescopic lens to pull it in close."

"Where was Cletus and the deputy while you were taking the shots?"

"Delford was busy walking Cletus back out of the crime scene. When they had moved far enough away, I made a move that could have gotten me in trouble, but I wanted to get closer. I was able to get a couple angles on the body. Not as good as I would have liked, but better than nothing."

"Risky. Daring, but risky. Good job."

"Where would you go from here?"

"I'd use a photo you haven't taken."

Landers scratched his head as he thought, "Like?"

"Like an area shot with the yellow crime scene tape. That would make good copy for the front page next week."

"Okay."

"You never want the photos too graphic. You want to stir the community with curiosity. In general, people are sick and morbid. Use your pictures to make the readers hungry for details not to satisfy their desires. You want them to keep coming back for more."

Jay shuffled through the photos. "What are you looking for?" I asked. Jay shrugged with frustration and allowed a picture to drop on the table top.

I pointed at the photo, "What do you see?"

"A dead girl."

I waited for a more judicious answer.

"Nakedness—I don't know what you're asking me. What am I supposed to be seeing or looking for?"

"The photograph is graphic. She doesn't have a stitch of clothing on her person."

"I just said that." Jay's lips thinned as his jaw muscles tightened.

"Or near her body." I let him process what I'd said. Jay wasn't a dimwit. He was capable of understanding the clues. "Were there any signs of clothing that you saw or in your pictures?"

Jay shuffled back through the photos looking carefully at each. With his last picture in hand, he looked in my direction shaking his head.

"If the investigators don't find a single piece of clothing this may not be the murder scene. It might be a dump site instead." I let it sink in for a minute.

Jay's eyes widened, "The actual crime scene could be anywhere."

"Not anywhere but elsewhere. I think it has to be considered."

Eager to absorb the new found value in his labor he said, "Depending on the time of death, forensics will be able to estimate the distance she was transported to the dumpsite."

"Unfortunately, time of death has too many variables in most cases. Rigor mortis and lividity will likely define the ballpark guess."

"I'll keep an eye out for forensic reports that indicate any clothing found at the scene."

"Notice the posture of the body. This has more to do with profiling the killer's thought process than reporting on the crime. Insight provides a reporter with leads to speculate. In the photo we see the scene was not staged. The body wasn't left in a grotesque pose or sexual exhibition. I'd say the killer in this case intended for the corpse to decompose. He made a poor attempt to hide it, but I'm guessing the killer didn't expect it to be discovered. Exhibitionist killers like their work admired."

"I can tell you've had years of experience with crime scenes, Walter."

"I think it's reasonable to say, I've seen my fair share of crime scenes." If Landers knew the depth of my knowledge, he would've run for his life. "What else do you have on the victim?"

"I spoke with the Sheriff's Department spokesperson. He is waiting for the autopsy report from the coroner's office before a statement is released. But, I have it from a good source the victim was ten to twelve years of age, physically abused, and sexually assaulted."

"Cause of death?"

"Asphyxiation evidenced by strangulation. She had ligature marks on her wrists, ankles, and around her throat."

"That's another clue to consider. Whatever happened to this girl took place elsewhere and not at the dumpsite. With that much damage to her body, you would expect to find notable signs of struggle."

"Any Identification on the girl?"

"Nothing yet. She was brownish skinned with shoulder length black hair. Hispanic would be my guess."

"For your article, make sure you don't go out on a limb with your speculations. You'll lose credibility. You also can't tell the whole truth. Society prefers a whitewashed version. You'll see it, from your editor when he or she cuts into your story and changes what they consider to be offensive. In the big cities, they often de-emphasize the victim being a young child unless it fits their agenda. That's why you'll need to follow-up with an emotionally charged human interest story. Focus on the victim and you'll win your audience."

Jay leaned slightly forward and onto his right elbow as he cradled his jaw between his thumb and index finger. His eyes glazed over as he looked inside the envelope at the stack of pictures. He was silent. Slowly he stroked his jaw. He was formulating the story he'd write. I called to the waiter, "Check, please."

Jay snapped out of his trance, "I was going to get that, Walter."

"Let me buy this time Jay, and let me mention one more thing."

"Yeah sure, you have already given me new ideas for the story."

"This scenario is potentially dangerous. It wasn't the perfect murder—not by a long shot. With her being discovered quickly, there'll be forensic evidence to be processed, and that takes time. Putting emphasis on the murder might put you in the killer's crosshairs. You've made yourself the central collection point for what becomes public knowledge in Barry County. The killer might think you're the only one pushing the story. If you don't tread lightly, you might find yourself stepping on his toes. I'd bet a buck the killer is a trusted member of your community and not some drifter. If I'm right, he won't appreciate you keeping the story alive. He might try and shut you up. Only serial killers like the limelight. Front page revelations make enemies."

Jay nodded. "Thanks, maybe we can get together again?"

"I'd like that, Jay. I see strengths in you that are uncommon among young reporters. I believe you'll get the story told if for no other reason than for the little girl's sake."

"You got it, Walter."

As I drove back to my cabin, I questioned why someone dumped the body at Cletus' place? Table Rock Lake was a massive body of water and a far better place to hide a body. If the killer just wanted to dump the girl's body, there were a lot of side roads with short bridges that would've been more conducive for a quick dump. The killer chose to pack the body through the brush, possibly in the dark, for a hundred yards or more from the roadway. From experience, I could say the killer had to be comfortable with a dead body slung over his shoulder and the risk of being seen during the exposure. It was a lot of extra effort to go through to dump the body. There had to be an ulterior motive as to why they chose Cletus's place.

Cletus was an undesirable sort for any community and not above suspicion in this matter. Landers had caught him in a couple pictures he'd snapped the day he responded to his shack. He had a grungy John Deere ball cap cocked back on his head. Straggly white hair hung out the back of the cap almost to his shoulders in places. His blue bib coveralls had missed one or two washings. What impressed me the most was the amount of saggy, wrinkled skin that was exposed where his coveralls didn't cover. He didn't smile for the pictures. He spared us that ugly display. I had my doubts this good ol' boy had the physical ability to carry out what had been alleged. If he was responsible, he wasn't alone. Landers said his friends referred to him as, "Chicken Charlie," rather than Cletus. I didn't ask.

Until a better lead developed, he would remain a person of interest for the Sheriff's Department. Having a person under wraps was essential to the stability of the community. It reassured locals that the County Mounties were on top of the case and translated into a false sense of safety and security. However, I saw Cletus as a pawn, and determined law enforcement leaned toward the same idea. Cletus might have been a miserable wretch, but not necessarily the product of a low IQ. It would have been incredibly stupid on his part to leave the body close by his house and then call dispatch. It didn't make sense. Why not let it rot amongst the brambles? According to Delford, the girl's body hadn't been there long. In my playbook, the killer wanted fingers pointed at ol' Cletus. The likelihood of an out-of-towner setting Cletus up as a fall guy was zilch. Unless forensic evidence proved otherwise, I leaned toward a frame-up.

While I mulled over the questions, law enforcement was busy rounding up drifters and passersby for a friendly chat. It was their priority. I had no doubt I'd be on the list. I wasn't only new to the community, but I had an obscure history. If the law dogs sniffed around enough, they might discover my hidden identity.

With a sketchy plan to hit the trail in the morning, I wanted to turn in early. Maybe Landers had gathered a fresh lead to share and further investigate.

I pulled my Avenger onto the resort's gravel parking pad and killed the engine. Next to my car sat Duke Dixon's '69 Ford pickup with its woodland camouflage paint job. It was too late to escape; I'd been seen. I wasn't a fan of forced intermingling, especially with the likes of Dixon.

The only person I knew that was impressed by Duke was Duke. I found myself constantly battling the urge to thump him. He was a pompous blowhard who shot his mouth off to scare women and sound tough to frail men, but never delivered on his threats. Having had the inclination to straighten out his personality defects had become a complicated matter. Duke had been Joyce's boyfriend throughout high school, and he'd married her best friend. Secondly, she concerned herself with my safety. She was afraid I'd be severely beaten by Duke. It was a learning environment that helped me understand the practical nature of being stuck between a rock and a hard place.

Duke Dixon was a quick study. In the local community, he held the prestigious position as Chairman of the Vigilance Committee, a quasi-paramilitary law enforcement outfit for the good of all humanity in Barry County, or so he said. That fact alone should have paved the way for our relationship as friends. He was my kind of people, but I couldn't stomach listening to his pompous and lengthy delusions of grandeur. Duke was a local boy, born and reared in the hills of Shell Knob. He was a truck driver by trade, an avid outdoorsman, gun range owner, Second Amendment activist, and survival skills instructor. What I saw was all talk and no action. His big mouth and bigger ego ensured he and I would never be friends.

Seeing people amassed on the front porch, I put my attitude in check, and with a smile on my face, I made my way to the goat rope. Joyce, Duke, and his wife Minnie, sat in a semi-circle holding pint sized mason jars filled with sun-made ice tea. Duke stood and stepped forward to greet me. He extended his hand and said, "How in-the-heck are you doin' there, Stud."

"Stud...is not my name...Ace."

However appropriate; my response was perhaps interpreted as less than congenial. It was no secret to Duke that I didn't care for his brand of friendliness. I'd straightened him out before when he'd addressed me as Stud, but I surmised he was a slow learner and in need of further instruction. In the spirit of cordiality, and since Minnie and Joyce were present, I'd let it go—again.

Duke was three or four inches taller than me and carried two-hundred-fifty-pounds on a muscular frame. His behavior was more than a friendly gesture when he stood to shake my hand; it was his cocky attempt to intimidate. I noted his sly smile as it crept up the right side of his cheek and rose slightly higher when he spoke. He'd learned to use his size to the best of his ability. As he shook hands, he turned his right side in my direction and tightened his grip. It was always a hand-squeezing competition whenever we met.

I leaned toward Joyce as my hand swept across her lower back and nudged her closer. Our lips opened simultaneously as we kissed. I held the kiss longer than Joyce had expected. When we separated, her neck and cheeks revealed a light blush. Duke's face was red too, a deep, full-bodied red that filled his face. Turning toward Minnie I waved and gave her a down-home greeting that I'd picked up since I'd arrived. "Hey girl," I said with a wink. She immediately looked away, but I saw the smile. Her head drooped as she cast her eyes toward the tongue-n-groove floor of the porch. I caught a glimpse of Duke's eyes as he focused on her response. Duke's vibes toward Minnie were a mystery. I didn't care for the behavior, but I'd grown so used to his presence and tolerant of his bluster.

Minnie might have been a likable sort of person if she had a discernible personality. Joyce had warned me in advance of my first meeting with Minnie that she was introverted. Joyce's description was a gross understatement. Minnie wasn't shy; she was timid. I suspected her behavior had been learned and not a natural shyness exhibited by reclusive people. I likened her behavior to that of a severely mistreated and abused animal. We referred to those animals displaying timid traits as having had their spirit broke. Minnie had one of those type spirits—

broken. I didn't know her personal history, but the signs were evident and etched into her face like ancient hieroglyphics.

It was possible those closest to Minnie couldn't see her condition. She was married yet all alone and lonely. How could those in her circle of family and friends overlook such a travesty? Joyce was of the opinion no one wanted to get involved. It wasn't anyone else's business. I disagreed. I was the type of guy that took care of that sort of business. No one stood up to Duke when he bad mouthed Minnie and tore apart her self-esteem. As the man-of-the-house, Duke saw his verbal assaults as his right to rule his kingdom, but shared none of the power, authority or respect with his Duchess. Minnie had been relegated to the position of a servant and treated poorly. Duke's behavior bothered me to the point my heart went out to Minnie. I had to play it smart and not react to my gut instinct.

Joyce wanted to clue me in on how she saw her lifelong friendship with Minnie. They had attended school together from the first grade through high school. "We were best friends most of our childhood." There was something in Joyce's choice of words that caught my attention. "Most," was possibly a Freudian slip. I had to challenge her.

"Not all your childhood?"

"What?"

"You said 'Most' of your childhood. I was questioning what happened to your friendship?"

"Um—uh," her eyebrows squished together as she stuttered. Her puzzled facial expression spoke volumes. "Minnie was pregnant our senior year. She quit school to be a stay-at-home mom, I guess."

"Why would you have to guess? You were best of friends."

Joyce's puzzled look morphed into a blank stare. She searched for an answer she should've known. Perhaps this was the first time in a long time she'd taken into consideration why they were no longer best friends. A few moments had passed before she let out a sigh that blew a dozen strands of hair from her face that had fallen forward. "The baby's daddy was Duke. I didn't see her much after that."

"Ahh, the plot thickens."

"It's all water under the bridge, now."

"Let me get this straight. Duke, your high school sweetheart, got your best friend pregnant. Let me guess, it was while you two were still together?"

"It was a long time ago and doesn't matter."

It was a simple answer to a complex issue—too simple. I waited while she mulled over her thoughts. Her foot tapped the floor lightly under her chair as she sat in front of the window overlooking Table Rock Lake. She drifted into an awkward silence, lost in time and space. I was left hanging while she traveled a long way back on memory lane. I let the questioning rest, but unexpectedly, she continued her answer. "All Shell Knob was aware I was back from Toronto. Minnie called and asked to get together. That's when I noticed the change. The Minnie I called my friend was gone." She paused as her countenance saddened. It was a look that made me want to save her from the pain, but I was powerless to help. She continued, "Maybe it was the loss of her son that destroyed the girl I remembered. I don't know."

Composed, I intuitively shot from the hip. "The loss of a child is a devastating experience. The level of pain is unexplainable, and the effects can be insurmountable."

Joyce stood and walked to where I was standing. Her eyes grew heavy with an ocean of tears. She wrapped both arms around my neck and hung her head to one side of my chest as the tears flowed freely. "I didn't think you would understand."

Joyce had no way of knowing my understanding was from the head and not the heart. "Give her leeway. She needs someone she can confide in, and Duke's never going to be that person. She needs someone she can call her friend. She needs you." I didn't like being disingenuous and superficial, but it was the only way I'd learned to communicate feelings. In the recess of my mind I doubted Minnie could be repaired. Joyce's efforts would go down in flames, but she had to try.

Joyce whispered, "I'd like you to get along better with Duke. It's the only way I can help Minnie." I disliked Duke, and the longer I was around him, the less I cared to be around him. To top it off I wasn't big on commitments, but I conceded to her request. "I'll cut him some slack—more than he deserves."

Shortly after Joyce returned to Shell Knob, Duke had frequently visited her or found an excuse to stop at the resort. More often than not it was without Minnie in tow. Joyce didn't consider his behavior particularly odd, but she had confessed there were times when he visited her alone that made her uncomfortable. She didn't give me the details, and it was just as well because he'd racked up a lot of dislikes with me.

Duke didn't live next door to the resort which gave me a good reason to be thankful. Amidst his boisterous crowing, he'd mentioned many times that he owned a parcel of land in Dixon Holler where his house and gun range sat. The Holler that was named after Duke's family was located off Highway M north of Rock Creek's East Fork. To visit Joyce, Duke traveled around Turkey Mountain and crossed a lengthy bridge over Table Rock Lake to arrive at the resort. As the crow flies, I estimated the distance at four miles between the two places. In road miles, it was twelve

Duke was cordial having invited Joyce and me to burn gunpowder on his shooting range, but I hesitated to go. My inclination to shoot him would likely result in charges. I was also acutely aware of Joyce's aversion to guns. My immediate concern was if I accepted his invitation I'd get stuck alone with him for an entire day. Without a guarantee for his safety, I refused to set the stage for a tragedy.

As Duke sat down, he asked, "Tell us whatcha been doin' all the dang day, Stud?"

"Sheesh," I sighed. Was this the ordinary way people communicated down south? His irksome behavior I saw as meddling in my affairs.

Joyce had made Duke aware of my journalistic history. When opportunity knocked, I laid it on thick and let the testosterone flow freely. Politely I responded, "I met with a local newspaper reporter, Jay Landers, do you know him?"

Joyce's eyes squinted, and her eyebrows pulled tight but didn't answer. Joyce had introduced Jay and me. The question hadn't been posed to her. Minnie continued her lifeless stare at the porch decking near her feet while Duke answered, "No."

Unrealized by Duke, he'd given me an open door to raise havoc. "Landers asked my opinion and advice on how to cover the story on the murdered girl."

"That's wonderful, Walter," Joyce said. An air of excitement resonated from her loudly proclaimed statement. On the other hand, Duke didn't look happy at all.

Conflicts with Duke were not easily avoided. Of course, I hadn't tried either. Salt and a wounded ego didn't fare well together. "I've decided to involve myself with Landers coverage of the crime and lend him my expertise. Wouldn't it be a hoot if we can solve the crime?" It wasn't exactly a true rendition of how our conversation went down, but it was close enough. I was sure Duke saw it as competition since I'd made myself a person of importance in his view.

From his reaction, and the lack of anyone else apparently catching on to what I was doing, I tossed another slap in his face. "I think I'll take a part-time job with the local newspaper and stay right here, this town would make a great permanent residence." I didn't specify if I would be staying at Joyce's, but from the frown growing on Duke's face I surmised he'd interpreted what I'd said in the worst possible way. His like for me was about as superficial as mine for him, and I wasn't making it any better. He was a man with a plan, and I stood in his way. Although Joyce said he hadn't made a play for her and dismissed the notion as silly, I saw him as grooming her for the future, but first he had to get rid of me.

Minnie's face scrunched at the mention of the killing. I took it as a genuine surprise. Likely, she wasn't privy to the murder and probably the only person in Shell knob that didn't know. That revealed a lot about Minnie. Duke clearly had cut her off from the world.

Duke's reaction was not nearly so sincere. "I ain't heard nothin' 'bout no dead girl." His pasty white face contrasted sharply with his short cropped, coal-black beard that obscured his overall facial expression from being easily read. However, he wasn't able to hide the windows to his soul—his sinister deep-set eyes. There I focused my attention, and they told a different story. Duke had picked up on me as much as I had on him, but our actions significantly differed. He avoided eye contact and guarded his words carefully. I wanted to engage him in both. Either the girl's murder or the mention of me staying on his home turf had put him on edge. In the recesses of my mind, the word guilty screamed at me. I was wary of the prompt. It might've been nothing more than my disdain coupled with wishful thinking.

"Hon, would you like a glass of tea?" Joyce asked.

I've never been much of an ice tea drinker, but down in Dixieland, it fit like a hand in a glove. I gave her the thumbs-up sign and said, "Thanks, sweetie."

Duke had no problem controlling his eyes when it came to avoiding eye contact, but he lacked discipline when it came to a woman's anatomy. His eyes were glued to Joyce as she stood and turned to enter the house.

Boisterously he called out, "Bring that booty back here." If his crude words weren't enough, he followed them with a nasty sounding laugh.

Joyce looked at him the same way I'd seen her look at a cockroach just before she squashed it. With a wave of his hand, he said, "Go on, I'm just funnin' with you girl."

I didn't find Duke funny at all. He'd disrespected Joyce, his wife Minnie, and me all in one fell swoop. He had my blood boiling. If I'd pushed his buttons earlier, he had his revenge by pushing mine. Minnie lifted her eyes from her steady gaze of the porch floor briefly making eye contact with me. For a split second, I read into her expression an apology for Duke's atrocious actions. She passively glanced in Duke's direction then returned to her focal point on the floor. Duke hadn't seen Minnie look up. How could he, he was too distracted by Joyce as she opened the screen door.

Previously, Joyce had asked for me to overlook Duke's wisecracks. If the mood struck me, I was good at ignoring people, but therein lay the crux of the matter. Avoidance was not my style; confrontation was.

There was a way to bring his mouth to a grinding halt other than my intervention. Joyce had to confront him with an ultimatum. Why was she so passive about putting him in his place? She'd mentioned to me, more than once, that I was jealous because of the sexual nature of his comments. I assured her it was not the case. What I saw was a guy who was nothing more than a self-gratifying spoiler who didn't care who he hurt in the process of getting his way.

Joyce continued her indifference to Duke's comments, even though she'd become red-faced and embarrassed by his crude innuendos at times. I wondered whether Joyce still had an ember of passion for him or worse, she felt sorry for his marriage relationship. Regardless, I trusted that Joyce showed the same lack of concern for his shenanigans in my absence as she did when I was present. There were unexplainable vibes that prompted me to take a deeper stab at Duke whenever opportunity knocked. He was rotten to the core—my instincts have never failed.

"Landers had some great pictures of the crime scene. He said the Sheriff has substantial evidence. They might crack this case any minute," I announced.

What I said didn't have a shred of truth to it. I was on a fishing expedition, and I wanted to watch his reaction. Duke shrunk from cocky and brazen to a mousy bundle of nerves, either at the mention of Landers and the case he was covering, or the implication that the Sheriff had a strong lead.

Joyce returned with a tall jar of ice tea, bent over at the waist and set the glass on the rustic end table. I anticipated Duke's smart-mouth spew, but he didn't say a word and barely glanced at her buttocks. Not the kind of opportunity a baboon like Duke would've let slip by, not unless he were rattled deep inside. I watched Minnie as she cast a look at Duke; she'd noticed the change in his behavior too. Preoccupied, and without saying a word, Duke gulped down his jar of tea and signaled to Minnie to drink up. Moments later, Duke grabbed Minnie's half-full jar of tea and took it along with his empty mug into the resort.

I was amazed. Duke had taken the initiative to clean up after him and Minnie. When he emerged from the house, he moved quickly to the steps. "I've got an early day tomorrow. I gots to be goin'," he said. Stepping down off the porch and onto the stairs, he whirled back toward Minnie and yelled, "Come on woman!" There had been no reason for Duke to shout at her. Minnie was submissive to the point of unhealthy.

She stood and politely said her good-byes. As she turned toward the stairs, Duke barked a second set of commands. She looked back at Joyce and shame clung to her countenance. Without her uttering a word I heard her cry for help. As she turned to descend the steps, I watched her head droop. Pain swelled deep inside my being which I recognized that had risen within from a time, long past. The pain someone else had suffered, and I was compelled to shoulder it. To the prompt, I had to say, not today. It wasn't the path I wanted to travel.

Minnie wasn't petite although she'd been described that way. How I saw her was sickly, skinny, and frail. She wasn't one who displayed a lot of flesh for the world to see. Initially, I'd banked on the idea she was a religious zealot. Later, I came to realize it was all Duke's doing. What was visible below her vintage-style plaid dress was nothing but skin and bones for ankles. Not much else showed.

Minnie quickly shuffled across the yard to catch up with her husband. Duke fired up his pickup and backed out of the space. He'd allowed only enough time for Minnie to get the door closed before he slapped his old Ford in gear. The rig shot off with a clattering noise as it bounced through the driveway potholes, stirring up a cloud of dust.

Joyce and I sat quietly watching the dust settle on the driveway. I had to challenge Duke's behavior to change the situation, but persuading Joyce was easier said than done. "I don't like the way he abuses her."

"You think he abuses her?"

"From what I saw, yes. If I talked to you like that, wouldn't you feel abused?"

"I'd kick your butt!"

I laughed. "Yeah, yeah, you talk tough now, but you wait for later. Then we'll see."

A sly smile crept across her face. "You would let me and you know it."

There was no sense arguing about it. She was right.

"Just the same sweetheart, maybe we should accept Duke's invitation to visit. I'd like to see what it's like for Minnie to live there."

"It's not our business Walter."

I couldn't tell if she was naïve or didn't have a desire to know the truth. Her words were the same as what others had said that were in Minnie's life. It was a tough pill to swallow. If I was going to live a quiet country life in peace and harmony with my surroundings, I had to suppress the impulse to fix problems when I saw them. I'd taken an oath, and part of the oath was to rescue or defend the weak. How could I avoid conflicts? I'd trained my eyes to see them. It was that simple.

The vehicle in the driveway didn't bear the markings of a cop car, but it was obvious. The police cruiser had all the bells and whistles in the front and back window. Joyce and I watched from the porch as the driver slowed to a stop in front of the resort.

I had no interest in going out of my way to meet the local constables. I didn't see the benefit. It looked as if I was going to meet one today whether I liked it or not. The driver climbed out and leaned over the car's hood as he wrote on a notepad. He glanced in our direction then returned to his notes. Tall, slender, and dignified he was a class act for Shell Knob and looked out of place.

"Know him?" I asked.

Joyce looked the officer over carefully before she answered. "No."

Casually, the man strode toward the porch, tucking his notepad into an inside suit pocket. I watched his eyes shift left to right taking in the surroundings. He was searching for a particular person or object. "Hello, I'm Detective Simon Parker with the Barry County Sheriff's Department."

"I'm Joyce Farmer."

Parker extended his hand toward Joyce. His smile gleamed as they shook hands. Turning his attention to me, he said, "And you are?"

"Walter."

"Is that Walter with a last name or just Walter?"

"Walter Goe."

"Okay." Parker extended his hand. "I've heard of you."

I laughed under my breath, shook his hand, and said, "Nothing good I hope."

"Quite the contrary Mister Goe, it was all good." Parker continued the handshake. "Jay Landers spoke highly of you."

"That's because Landers doesn't know me well."

"Jay said you're a crime reporter and probably knew more about crime than anyone else around these parts."

"I'll have to thank Jay for his kind words. Yes, I was a journalist. A little tired of the crime beat. Took a break from the circuit."

Parker turned toward Joyce. "I'm investigating a homicide."

"There's been so much talk about it. How horrible."

Parker's eyes darted straightway toward me as Joyce answered. He was watching my reaction. "Joyce, I'd like to ask you a few questions."

"Sure, anything to help."

Parker spent the next few minutes tossing out questions concerning guests of the resort, especially people traveling through, one-night stays or unusual activity. It was interesting to listen to the side talk. Parker never came out and said it, but his interest was in the newest member of the Shell Knob community—me. I was familiar with side talk as a ploy. I had to remind myself that I hadn't committed the crime they were investigating.

Parker turned his attention toward me. "How about you, Mister Goe?"

"Call me Walter."

"Yes sir, have you seen anything out of the ordinary?"

I laughed, "Detective, I'm not from the south. Everything is out of the ordinary to me." Then I laughed again for emphasis.

Parker set the stage to mirror my actions with a hardy laugh. I was aware of that trick too. Parker offered a handshake as he prepared to leave. "Thank you both."

"Absolutely," I said.

Parker left as slowly as he had arrived. He sauntered toward his unmarked cruiser, breaking his casual stride with intermittent stops to take notes. He wasn't done yet. A sense of déjà vu came over me as if I was in a rerun of an old television episode, Colombo. Parker turned and walked toward the house making solid eye to eye contact this time. "You're not leaving the area anytime soon are you, Walter?"

"Not unless you're telling me I have to be out of town by sundown?"

Parker had looked me up and down before he answered, "We're down south not in the old west."

He was savvy, and I liked that. "No plans," I said, as Joyce stepped next to me, slipping her hand into mine.

Parker smiled. He turned toward his car and had walked a couple steps before he turned around to ask a question. "Do either of you own or drive a pickup truck?"

"Neither of us," Joyce answered.

Parker nodded, and once again headed toward his car. For five long minutes, Parker sat behind the steering wheel and worked on his notes. Finally, he backed out and slipped down the road out of view.

Throughout the evening, Joyce asked questions about the likelihood of Minnie's abuse. I could see she was interested. With each scenario recounted, the impulse to right the wrong grew stronger.

It would be great to live a life of innocence, but not one of naiveté. Too many victims started out naïve and ended up easy prey. Joyce's eyes had been opened to the possibilities. Duke wasn't the care-giving sort of guy he pretended to be. Under pressure, he could be tweaked, and his true worthless-scumbag nature would surface. Duke's personality paralleled Doctor Jekyll and Mister Hyde's. I would know—I had one too.

Back in my cabin for the evening, I checked my Palatini cell phone. I didn't need to carry the phone with me and had left it under my mattress where it was safely hidden. I had missed calls. Lead Palatini operative, Anna Sasin's, and our facilitator, Maximillian Karnage had left messages. Max had a fancy title, Society Palatini Grand Master, but he was mainly the go-to guy for all the knights. I called him first.

Max was a world traveler. There was no telling what country he would be in when I called so calling times were irrelevant. It was impossible to know his location. He might be in the cabin next to me, for all I knew. I rolled the dice and made the call.

As soon as he answered, I cut to the chase. "What's up Max?"

"I've had an inquiry if you're interested. An operative with a foreign engagement has asked for you by name. Are you game?"

"Is it Anna?"

"No, it's a mop-up operation in Paraguay. Do you remember Russell Gunn?

"Yes, I remember Rusty."

"He has asked if you were available." Max waited for a response, but he was met with silence. "What gave you the idea it was Anna?"

"I had a missed call from her; that's all."

"Are you presently engaged in a project?"

"No, I've taken some time to myself. I have an important agenda. You know, catch up on some fishing, and that sort of thing."

"Yes, yes, of course. I know we can count on you when you are ready. We have some enchanting places that would welcome you with open arms. Frankly, they need you."

"Thanks, I'll keep it in mind. Give my regards to Rusty."

"Keep in touch. It was good to talk with you again."

The next morning, I placed a call to Anna. I left her a cell phone message then put a call into Landers. I had plenty of time, and it was a good opportunity to touch base with him. When he answered, it didn't take long to get down to the nitty-gritty.

Landers voice dropped to a whisper, "Meet me at Whiskey Gulch. I need to talk."

"When?"

"It'll take me twenty-five minutes to get there from Cassville."

"Okay Jay, you can count on me."

I checked out with Joyce and confirmed she didn't have me committed to some domestic activity. I let her know I was meeting Landers again at his request. I was relieved to hear she didn't have an interest in tagging along.

I kept my weapons and bug-out bag in the trunk of the Avenger under strict lock and key. It was time to reconnect with my recent past. I fired up the car and drove toward the rendezvous location. A couple minutes down the road, I pulled over and retrieved my .40-caliber and paddle holster from the trunk. Concealing it carefully under my light weight jacket, I was careful to ensure Landers wouldn't be able to see it. The last thing I needed was questions surfacing about carrying concealed without a permit. I might have been over-reacting on the side of caution, but Jay sounded concerned. I'd rather be prepared.

Jay's car swung wildly onto the little dirt pad and alongside my Avenger. I focused my attention in the direction from which Jay had come for signs of a tail. With no second vehicle anywhere in sight, I rolled down my window. It was obvious he wasn't interested in getting out. Jay's window lowered as he sank back deep into the driver's seat. I glanced around once more for good measure and gave Jay a thumb up gesture. Confident we were alone he began, "Have you ever had an anonymous source give you information that was viable?"

"Yeah, sure. What did you pick up?"

"I got a call late yesterday in my office." Jay stopped and looked around before continuing, "She whispered, 'I know about the Alaskan girl found at Forbes place.' No one has called the victim Alaskan, not even the police. If it turns out to be true, the caller knows more about what's happened."

"No doubt. What else did you get?"

"My first thought was this lady is concerned about getting caught talking to me. I could hear the fear in her voice. She told me the girl was eleven-years-old and had been here about two weeks. Then the line went dead."

"Here means what? Cassville? Shell Knob?"

"I'm not sure, I think our area around Cassville. I'm going to sit at my desk and see if I get a call back. If my hunch is right, she'll call again. While I wait, I'll be scouring the missing person's reports, starting with Alaska."

"Jay, you didn't mention telling the cops what you picked up?"

"I'm not ready to get involved."

"Too late, buddy. The gal made that decision for you. Whether you like it or not, you are involved. What you do with it is up to you."

"I'm researching right now."

"Play your cards right with the information, and you could write your ticket out of Barry County. If you hand the information over to investigators, you could be a hero around here, make allies with the police, and still publish the scoop."

Jay relaxed, smiled and said, "Gotta go." I sat parked for a few minutes trying to figure out how a child from Alaska made it all the way to Missouri. It was bizarre. The most probable scenario was a kidnapping. If she had been in the area long enough for the anonymous caller to have seen her, it was possible others had too. While my thoughts drifted, I threw the Avenger in gear and headed south. I wanted time to think about Jay's caller.

The dead girl was not the key to the case. Jay's source was the ticket. In my mind, the witness was likely a local community member and not associated with a drifter theory. The caller had been specific. The girl was "Here" for a couple weeks. I hooked a right on Highway 86 and traveled west for a while. When I crossed over Table Rock Lake, I continued north to the confluence of Highway E. In Barry County there weren't that many women. One of them called Landers. She was a needle in a haystack, but the stack of hay had grown smaller. I took the turnoff to Highway E, which pointed the Avenger in the direction of Shell Knob.

I was traveling in a big circle. I didn't have a particular destination in mind, but I was being led by a prompt from my spirit. The road hooked to the right where I accessed Highway M. I wanted to keep my attention focused on the information Landers had received, but festering tensions with Duke were an ongoing issue and needed to be addressed. Confusion distorted my thoughts. I was near Duke Dixon's gun range and survival training camp.

I stopped the Avenger in front of Dixon Holler. There were no markings on the map. Most hollers, gaps, draws, and gulches hadn't been officially recognized. However, they existed in the knowledge of the local folks.

The only readily available landmark for the Holler stood twenty feet off the highway onto an access road. Spray painted on the four-foot wide weathered plywood sign read, "Dixon Holler Gun Range." Signage, down in Dixieland, especially those that have stood the test of time, have character—and bullet holes. A set of four mailboxes decked in various shades of gray and blue paint hung from a cross beam on top of a six-inch wide milled post, heavily soaked in creosote oil.

It was bone-dry weather for springtime. The usual cloudy skies had remained clear for weeks which led to cooler nighttime temperatures. I got out of the car and touched the red clay roadbed that led up the draw in a westerly direction toward Dixon's place. It was a powdery dust. Tire prints would readily show, and it was common practice to photograph tread marks. Plaster casts were unlikely, but forensic sciences might have a few new tricks. I caught myself. I was processing details as if I were on the hunt for a victim. I looked up the Holler and noted scrub brush and a diverse gathering of trees obscured the gun range and Duke's house from the highway. What was going on in my head? Old habits were tough to dismiss as irrelevant.

The prompt to look deeper at Duke's behavior was still with me. My Palatini oath had defined my mission to protect the weak and avenge the victims. Minnie was one of the weak that I'd sworn to protect. But was Minnie an easy excuse to knock Duke around because I didn't like the guy? I needed my Palatini oath to be my guide not my emotions. He wasn't a human trafficker or a pervert that needed killing. He wasn't like the types I'd taken out in the past. It didn't seem right; yet, it didn't feel wrong either.

Chapter 3

*"We the unappreciated must do the
unimaginable, to protect the ungrateful."*
—Unknown

On my return, crossing over Table Rock Lake, I soon pulled into the resort's graveled parking lot. Joyce was waiting on the porch with arms crossed. Not a good sign. My steps were brisk to the foot of the stairs. "Sorry, it took longer than I'd anticipated."

"You missed Duke."

"I'll never miss Duke," I smirked as I said it, but Joyce remained gloomy. "Okay, what did I miss?"

Two things I didn't like, Duke showing up at the resort unannounced and Duke turning up when I wasn't home. Home? This wasn't my home, so why did the thought pop into my head? A Freudian slip in my thinking? I wasn't sure, but the thought bothered me. I wasn't naïve. Joyce was a big girl and capable of taking care of herself, but she was buying into the deception that their relationship was strictly platonic as he insisted. And then again, perhaps I was naïve. Feelings from the past might be the reason she hadn't told him not to come around without Minnie. I didn't think so, but perhaps my thinking was a bit short on logic at the moment. Was I jealous? Apparently so—another thought that bothered me.

"He wants us to come to his place later this afternoon to visit. I said okay but, I let him know the final word was yours. I hope that's all right with you."

Joyce wasn't the shy type. She was forthcoming when she had something to say. This time, she wasn't saying boo. My thoughts shot off in a half-dozen different directions. If Duke had tried something I wouldn't like, she'd hesitate to tell me. The only way I'd get it out of her was to ask politely and then not overreact. The reaction could wait for a proper time and place.

I climbed the steps to where Joyce stood with arms folded across her chest. I wrapped my arms around her. The warm embrace calmed her fears. "It's okay sweetie. He wants something; let's find out what it is."

She nodded, wiped away a tear and said, "He's such a phony. I don't know what I ever saw in him." My concern lessened at Joyce's words. Duke tried to backdoor me, and Joyce slammed the door on his face. There was a light at the end of the tunnel for her and maybe Minnie too.

A three-thirty departure time would put us at Dixon Holler by four in the afternoon. I had an hour to kill before we took off. I kicked back lakeside to watch the fish jump for insects. Life was pretty exciting around Shell Knob, right on par with watching tomato plants grow. From a personal perspective, it was more relaxing than entertaining. I propped up my lawn chair and dozed off and on while I basked in the sun's intermittent rays. Clouds had begun to form on the horizon. It looked like we might be in for a storm.

My peace and quiet didn't last long. I'd placed my Palatini cell phone on vibrate, and now it danced in my pocket. All Palatini operatives changed phones regularly for security measures. Consequently all calls came up the same, "Unknown."

"Yes."

"Hi, Walter, is now a good time to talk?" Anna's voice was unmistakable. Her pleasant tone that I'd so frequently enjoyed resonated in my heart as much as it did in my ear. Regardless of the way it went down in Toronto, I would always have a fondness for her. "I always have time for your lovely voice."

"You are such a liar!" She followed with a laugh and so did I. "Are you working on a project?"

"Max asked me the same question. Are you two conniving to involve me in something?" I didn't give her a chance to answer, "Baby, I took some well-deserved time off. Right now I'm kicked back lakeside enjoying some of life's little pleasures."

"Life? That's a strange first name—how is she?" There was a mixture of jealousy and disapproval in her voice. I laughed, but it had a nervous ring to it. She joined in, but it wasn't the musical laugh I'd known in the past.

I changed the subject, "When we talked a couple weeks ago you said you were working on a project, how's that going?"

"It's in the bag. I wished you could have been here. The project would have gone smoother. We could have enjoyed the long, temperate nights together—working."

Mmmmmmm, I thought, tempting. For a moment, I raced back through time to our first kiss in Texas. She'd softly brushed my lips with her tongue, inviting me closer, and I'd tasted a sweet hint of heaven.

"You know I like it up close and personal."

I snapped back to the present. "Are you talking about targets or us?"

"Yes—I am."

Before I could meet her expectations I had to contend with reality first. "Maybe, one of these days soon...I can get back to Oregon, and we can, uh, talk, you know?"

Quietness was deafening in the moments before Anna answered, "Sure. One of these days."

I signed off with a promise to call more frequently, but I heard the hollowness in my words. I didn't want to burn any bridges with Anna, but by the same token, I had another iron in the fire. I would call as promised, if the mood struck.

Joyce stood under a shade tree near the parking pad. I was running late for our rendezvous. I could see she'd gone out of her way to look attractive. Her khaki Capri pants fit tight in all the right places and went well with her brown leather slip-ons. Her shiny auburn hair was pulled into a sleek ponytail. Joyce wasn't a "skinny Minnie," not by a long shot. Her white button up blouse dipped low in front and didn't have buttons enough to restrain all her curves. I would have problems with Duke for sure. If he got out of hand, I'd knock him down a peg—all six-foot-three inches of him.

"Let's take my rig?" I said.

I backed the Avenger out, pulled onto Highway 39, and cruised with the windows rolled down. It was wonderful to see Joyce with her dazzling smile again. She'd let herself worry too much about the visit.

"If Duke starts a fight, I'll take care of it," she said. "You're a lover, not a fighter."

"Don't sweat it, sweetheart, I can take care of myself."

"You're a writer."

Why was it assumed writers were wimps? But it was that stereotyping that allowed my façade to work in my favor.

As we passed over Table Rock Lake at Shell Knob she asked, "Do you know the way to Duke's house?"

I pointed at the road in front of the Avenger and said, "This way." I realized I'd made a mistake, and then added, "I guess."

She shook her head as if I were an idiot. "I'll show you." With Joyce's guidance, we made our way from one road to the next and zigzagged through the hills to Dixon Holler. As we approached the red-clay road that led to Duke's place, I slowed the Avenger to make the turn.

"How did you know where the turn off was?" She asked.

She'd caught me. Her look was one of puzzlement and surprise. I quickly pointed to the gun range sign, "I figured that was it."

"Wow, your eyesight must be fantastic. I don't think the sign was visible when you started to slow down."

"I couldn't read it, but I slowed to read it. When I saw it said gun range, I figured it was the right turn."

I wouldn't say she bought it entirely, but she let it go. She had something else more pressing on her mind, her concern for my behavior. She didn't know it, but she'd misplaced her concern. "What can I expect from you today?"

"Like what, how am I going to act?"

"Yes, exactly."

"Tell your buddy Duke, don't make a bad first action, and there won't be a bad reaction."

"Seriously?"

"No honey—like I told you yesterday, I'll watch my Ps, and Qs. Now it's my turn for a favor. I want you to talk with Minnie alone and get the lowdown on what's going on. I want you to talk to her as a friend. The kind of friends you said you once were."

"I don't know if she will talk to me about anything personal. I'll do what I can."

The Avenger climbed the draw's slight incline at a little more than an idle. I wasn't in a hurry; I was taking in the sights. In fact, I'd made a mental note of the terrain, landmarks, brush density, dried shale runoffs, wildlife, anything noteworthy. It was beginning to feel like an old habit.

Duke's redneck camouflaged pickup stuck out like a sore thumb. Most places I've been it would have been easily identified from a mile away. Not in this neck of the woods. I'd probably seen a dozen pickups, maybe more, painted in a similar fashion. Duke was parked alongside his house in the afternoon shade. I pulled up next to his rig and cut the engine. Feigning a stretch, I stood next to my car and surveyed his place. My base nature as a hunter was habitual. There was no sense trying to fight it. I'm a killer, and I would always be on the hunt for manifestations of evil. While I made mental notes, Joyce adjusted her blouse higher in the front. She apparently shared my unspoken concern for Duke's obnoxious behaviors. Why invite trouble. She stretched out her hand, motioning for me to join her. Out of the corner of my eye, I saw what had prompted her. Duke was hot-footing his way toward Joyce. I walked around behind the Avenger intent upon taking the hand she had offered. Duke swept her off her feet in a massive bear hug. The kind of hug you might expect from someone you hadn't seen for years or would never see again. Not from a guy you saw earlier the same day.

Making my presence known to Duke and standing next to Joyce, he landed her feet on terra firma and extended his right hand while holding his left arm wrapped tightly around her waist. In a dismissive manner, Duke said, "Glad y'all could make it, Stud." With barely a glance at me, he shifted his attention back to Joyce. Tension mounted.

As Duke spun Joyce around toward the house, she latched onto my hand and pulled herself from Duke's grip on her waist. For an awkward moment, Duke and I stood face to face. Joyce's hand wrapped around my arm to pull me back.

Duke extended his hand toward the house, "Come on, come on in. Minnie's excited to see y'all."

Joyce and I moved forward, hand in hand while Duke fell in behind us or at least behind Joyce. From the glimmer in his eye, his intent was evident.

The single-level house sat at the forefront of other buildings on the property. The red clay roadbed at the bottom of the canyon had changed to a light-brown color in the large circular driveway that wrapped around a small debris-filled pond. The house was a square ranch style cracker-box from the 1940s or 50s. I was filing notes away in my mind. How many bedrooms and bathrooms the house had was irrelevant to my interests. The absence of a screened front door or where other entry points were located in the home drew my attention.

The living room was warm and charming with two sofas, a recliner, and an old wooden rocking chair. Minnie barely greeted us before she shuffled off to the kitchen to fetch a couple beers as Duke had demanded. Joyce took a seat next to where Minnie said she'd been sitting. Duke invited me to sit in the nearby wood rocker, and then took the seat next to Joyce. While I considered how to break up Duke's action, Minnie returned with a pair of brews in hand. She stopped short of the couch and looked at where Duke sat. He stopped in mid-sentence, looked at Minnie, and said, "Give me a beer woman and sit your butt over there!" He nodded toward the recliner that sat across the room from where the rest of us were seated. Duke's abusive nature was poisonous to Minnie as he ran roughshod over her self-esteem.

Minnie had every right to be angry and embarrassed at Duke's behavior, but I didn't see that in her. She guarded her feelings well. I, on the other hand, was hypersensitive to Duke's actions, and it wasn't sitting well at all. The longer I stewed, the worse the tension grew inside me. I saw Joyce flash a look my way that screamed "I need to be rescued," but I'd made a commitment to her not to act brash.

"Duke, how's that gun range working out for you?"

If this was a passion of his, with his personality, he'd talk incessantly about it. So far, he'd only talked about himself and directed his comments to Joyce.

Duke knocked down his beer in four or five lengthy gulps. He looked at Minnie and commandingly said, "Woman, beer me." Minnie immediately hustled to comply. Without missing a beat, he belched, and then answered, "I got the house when momma passed away. I like workin' for myself, bein' my own boss, bein' my own man. The extra land behind the house ain't no good for farmin' none. I figured I'd make the land worth somethin' and turned it into a gun range and make money." Duke turned his attention back to Joyce.

In a vexing way, I threw another question at him. "I recall you saying you're a truck driver. How do you manage to run the range when you're gone?" If Duke hadn't been so egotistical, I wouldn't have taken advantage of his weakness and intruded on his game.

"Yeah, see Stud, I only do monthly memberships. Cuts down on a lot of work. I'm not sayin' if a newbie shows up with the cash and wants to shoot that I ain't takin' it, money on the barrel head y'know. Besides I got Minnie all trained up to take money whenever it's there. Ain't that right honey?"

Minnie handed Duke the beer she'd brought in from the kitchen and blushed at the mention of her name. "She's as good as gold to me. Ain't that right honey?" Again, Minnie said nothing, but a small smile emerged. She enjoyed the recognition.

Duke downed his beer in the same fashion as before and asked, "Why don't we take a look at the gun range?"

"Great idea." Whatever Duke was up to, it wasn't for my benefit. Since I'd interrupted his chitchat with Joyce, I had no doubt retribution was on the menu.

Duke said, "I'll be right back, get ready to hit the range." I looked at Joyce and shook my head. Alcohol and shooting don't mix. He returned carrying two black plastic cases. "Come on, let's burn some powder Stud." I was alert to the fact he had something up his sleeve. If I could figure out his angle, I'd best him at his own game.

"I don't care too much for shooting at paper targets."

Duke scoffed when he should've listened. He misinterpreted my entire statement. He mustered up his bravado and ran off at the mouth. "Joyce darlin' if your man don't shoot guns—you got yourself a girl-friend." He roared with phony laughter at his own joke then asked Joyce, "You're comin' too, ain't ya darlin'?"

"You guys run along and play."

"Come on, don't you want to see your boyfriend show off his so-called shooting skills?"

If Joyce held her ground, Duke would find himself between a rock and a hard place. He'd have to babysit me on the range, and that wasn't his plan. Duke was competitive and egocentric. He wanted Joyce to watch me shoot then he'd shoot in an attempt to embarrass me. Duke didn't respect anyone. He gave me no reason to believe he'd begin with me. He assumed I was a real dunce when it came to guns. That's why he wanted Joyce present to see if he could make a fool out of me. Once he'd bested me, he would strut his stuff and make a fool of himself. Mister Big was going to fall, but I'd let him have his fun before showing him the ropes on the range. Whether Joyce went or not, he was committed to take me to shoot.

Perhaps Duke had fears of leaving Minnie with Joyce. He'd never allowed them to visit alone since her return from Toronto. When they got together, Duke was there in the midst, and Minnie didn't say a word. Duke did all the talking, and the talk was all about him. There was a reason he kept her isolated. I wanted to know what he was hiding.

Duke hit his stress point, again. I loved to watch him squirm. His lips pressed together tightly in a slight grimace. As his face reddened, I turned up the heat.

"Let's go, Duke," I repeated it a couple times for good measure. Each time I said it louder and more forceful. "Come on we're burning daylight, partner." If looks could kill, I'd have been a dead man. Duke wasn't having fun and in his voice were signs of stress. It was pure torture for him not to get his way. It might've been as satisfying as shooting him. I'd have to wait to make the comparison.

"Come on, please, with sugar on top," Duke groveled. "Don't make me beg you."

He was too late and pathetic. For a two-minute stretch, his diatribe didn't change. Beg, beg, beg. What a sad display of a man. If Joyce's resistance didn't wear down soon, mine would, and the only humane action would be to put him out of his misery.

His woe-is-me attitude suddenly changed to anger. In a split second rage, he lashed out at Minnie, "You've got supper to get done. You don't need to be in here runnin' your gums!" Minnie took the verbal abuse but moved slightly to the side and away from Duke's wrath.

I nodded slightly to Joyce, who immediately responded to Duke with the answer he'd been counting on getting. Duke smiled ear to ear then hastened into a back room to fetch supplies for the range. I leaned over to Joyce and whispered in her ear, "Shoot, and then go back in the house to help Minnie."

She responded with a sigh and in a barely audible voice, "Okay."

Duke returned with a third black plastic case and handed it to me. "You're a big, strong stud. Why don't you pack it?"

With his hands free of responsibility, Duke tossed his arm over Joyce's shoulders as if they were old pals and led her through the kitchen, laundry room, and out the back door. I picked up the cases and followed. While Duke fixated his attention on Joyce, I concentrated on recon. How far was it from the back door? What kind of locks were on the doors? What, if any, does the house have for an alarm system?

The gun range was a short hundred yards from the house. Four lean-to sheds formed the front of the shooting line. They stood approximately twelve feet in length and spaced about the same distance apart. Under the sheds were gun benches made with roughed out lumber with plywood surfaces. Duke had me place the plastic boxes on top of two of the benches while he set up man-sized silhouette targets at a distance he'd estimated to be ten yards.

I didn't pay much attention to Duke as he gave the range instructions. He opened the plastic cases and removed handguns from each, grounding them on the table. The first weapon he loaded was a Herter's .22-caliber western-style revolver and handed it to Joyce. Duke had her step forward to the firing line and prepared her for shooting. He positioned himself behind Joyce as if he was sighting over her shoulder. When she lifted the pistol to shoot, Duke snuggled closer and brought both hands around, placing them on her wrists. Joyce stopped, wiggled away from his arms and said, "I can do this without your help."

"Sorr-ieee," he said with a smile, "Just tryin' to help y'know."

Joyce went back to the firing position, and Duke slipped behind her a second time, but this time he wasn't looking at the target. At least, not the silhouette that hung thirty feet away. To my surprise, Joyce was familiar with firearms. I'd misinterpreted her disdain for guns as ignorance of them. She fired six shots all striking the target. It was a loose grouping, but she apparently understood how to handle the weapon. Did Joyce, unbeknownst to me, harbor a secret life like mine?

She handed Duke the revolver who placed it on the mat that he'd removed from the gun case. "Try this one; it has more of a kick to it." Duke lifted a .38-caliber Smith and Wesson revolver from its case. Joyce interrupted, "Let Walter shoot next."

"Come on, Stud. Show us your stuff."

"Yeah. Okay. Which one would you suggest?"

Duke pointed to the .38-caliber he'd taken from the case. "That's probably too much gun for you," and placed the revolver back into the case. I opened the case again and removed it. "We brought it, let's shoot it."

I liked to sucker people. I stepped to the firing line, emptied the wheel gun, and purposely missed the target.

"Did I hit it?" I asked.

Duke was quick to laugh loudly and said, "Try aiming the pistol at the target."

I shot again winging the man-sized shape on the upper edge of the silhouettes shoulder. "That was better, huh?"

In Duke's condescending manner, he laughed and said, "Try shootin' with one eye closed or get closer…Like five feet away. Better yet, let Joyce show you how. Get off the line."

Duke turned to Joyce, "You're up."

She was ready and beat him to the punch. "Not right now. I'll give Minnie a hand in the kitchen." She turned and walked toward the house.

Checkmate!

This clown was stuck with me on the range, and I was going to milk the moment for all it was worth. The longer I kept Duke busy, the more time Joyce would have to talk with Minnie. How was he going to get out of this without looking like a fool? He watched Joyce as she approached the house then turned his attention to me. "You really interested in shootin'? I mean, you don't even know how."

I had no intention of letting him off the hook that easy. Besides, I was having too much fun—at his expense. I started to dig through one of his cases. "Hey—don't never be gettin' into another man's guns! You don't know what yur doin'!" His voice cracked as he wiggled his index finger in my face. Signs of frustration were evident. He'd come face-to-face with an issue he didn't know how to resolve. Maybe he thought the problem was Joyce being inside the house alone with Minnie and without his supervision. In reality, Duke had two problems, and I was about to make him aware of the second one.

"Come on, let's shoot!" I pulled a semi-automatic pistol from the third case. "What kind is this?"

The frown he wore looked like an upside-down funny-face, only Duke wasn't laughing, he was silent. The loud tapping of his foot was noticeable as he removed the magazine and began loading ammunition. "It's a Glock 9-mil," he answered. "Have you shot one before?"

"No. We carried revolvers when I was in the military, but I always wanted to shoot a semi-auto."

"Pay attention then." He stepped up to the firing line and peppered the target. I surmised he could shoot more accurately, but anxiety, impatience, and a short-temper had gotten the best of him.

To further aggravate the situation, I fumbled my way through loading the magazine and figuring out how to insert it into the weapon. Then I messed up and racked a round in the pipe twice while having my fingers slightly over the ejection port. The round stuck in the port, and I cleared the chamber, but accidently dropped the magazine to the ground in the process. I was buying Joyce time in a Duke-free zone. I blew on the magazine to remove dust and dirt that might have gotten in, then stepped to the firing line and shot a couple rounds purposely missing the target.

"Did I hit it?"

"Hell no!" Duke's lips pinched together. A strained tone filled his voice, "Give it up. Let's pack it in."

I shot a second time striking the target in the upper left shoulder and lower right hip. "You're all over the place," he said while I remained in the firing position. I unloaded two more rounds, this time reversing the order, striking the lower left hip and upper right shoulder. Duke stood quietly examining my shot pattern. Maybe he was a slow learner, but my hunch was it was sinking in little by little. If the target had been an adversary, he would've been lying on the ground, incapacitated, and every limb immobilized as he bled out.

"Wow," I said, "I hit the target good Duke!" He didn't share my enthusiasm or my opinion. I hadn't impressed him sufficiently, not yet; I needed to sign my name. Two more shots rang out punching holes side by side in the silhouette's head. Duke was quiet. A sign he understood I had a hidden talent. Perhaps the question in his mind was why I faked an inability to shoot. From my perspective, he'd learned all that I cared to teach him, for now.

We put the handguns back in their cases, and I picked up the brass casings. Duke tried to hurry me, but I drug my feet. We left the gun cases outside the back door as we entered the house. Duke didn't give me the grand tour of the place, but he did point me in the direction of the bathroom to wash the powder residue from my hands.

I overheard Duke demand of Minnie, "Woman, don't give me no sass. Beer me, and I mean now!" Minnie had been busy mashing potatoes with a hand masher when Duke snapped. She'd made the mistake of telling Duke, "I'll get it in just a minute." Duke rose to his feet from the recliner and started toward the kitchen. I intervened. "Whoa, Whoa, Whoa, I'm bringing the beers."

I'd walked into the kitchen to help Joyce transport the prepared dishes to the dining table when Duke started his tirade. Joyce looked mortified. All I could do was try to de-escalate the tension.

I handed Duke his beer which was met with a grumble. "Stud, beer fetchin' is women's work. You understand?"

"Not at all."

"Well, if you gonna make this little gal your woman; you'd better get her trained up right. You'll be a thanking me for my advice down the road a piece."

"Dinner will be in about five minutes," Joyce said. "Get yourselves washed up if you haven't done it yet."

I couldn't wait to eat. Not because I was hungry, but because I desperately wanted to leave. From the look of Duke's face, he wouldn't mind if I left either. My guess was Duke's soreness came from his evening with Joyce not having worked out the way he'd envisioned.

Duke sat at the head of the table and waited to be served. The smell of fresh baked cornbread permeated the air and enticed my taste buds. Minnie stood next to Duke and served his plate first. Joyce asked, "Hon, can I fix you a plate?"

"Nothing wrong with my hands, sweetie, I can get my own."

Duke piped up, "It's beneath a man to get his supper."

I laughed, and something that sounded like, "You're kidding," came out. But Duke wasn't laughing at all. He was serious which made it all the more laughable. This guy was getting his panties in a twist over someone's different point of view. While I tried to contain my sarcasm, I noticed Minnie stopped dead in her tracks. Shocked, Joyce was motionless. No one made brazen comments to Duke out of fear he'd retaliate. I couldn't have cared less how mad Duke got. If he wanted to dance, we'd dance. I could Watusi, and I wasn't shy about it.

Minnie offered to serve my plate after I'd declined Joyce's offer. It was a feeble attempt to placate the situation. I wanted this battle, and I didn't want Minnie anywhere near it. I laughed, loud and guttural. I scooped a pile of spuds from the large serving bowl in front of my plate as I flashed a broad, ivory smile at Duke. Minnie had sat the gravy to Duke's right side. I couldn't resist. "Hey Bubba, how 'bout you passing the gravy this way."

Minnie reached for the gravy.

"I asked Bubba!" Some people become fearful when an awkward moment follows a slap in the face.

Duke picked up the bowl, and with a shrug said, "Suit yourself." He handed Joyce the gravy to pass to me. Being the hospitable type I said, "Thank you."

Checkmate again.

Duke was a loose end about to unravel. Twice during our dinner, Minnie was made to fetch beer for Duke. He gulped them down almost as fast as she brought them to the table. After we had finished eating, we'd planned to move into the living room, but Duke made a surprising announcement, "I have to drive tomorrow. I'm gonna have to cut it short y'all."

One more poke before I left. I couldn't resist. "I have to go too. Landers and I are working that story on the dead girl."

Duke fired back, "We all 'round here heard 'nuff 'bout that there girl too."

Minnie, who rarely commented on anything, said, "I hope the family has found peace. Eleven is so young."

Duke's face flushed with bright redness, "Head on out now."

Duke, Joyce and I walked out toward the Avenger. Minnie would have joined us, but her loving husband had demanded, "Get the kitchen cleaned up now." I didn't have to ask Joyce her opinion of Duke—not anymore. Whatever Duke's agenda was, he'd miscalculated the effects on Joyce. I could only hope I'd had a small part in his self-destruction.

Joyce wore her feelings close to the surface. Duke tried to wrap his arms around her as he said, "Give me a hug Pooh bear." But Joyce would have none of it. Her face flushed a bright red, and with eyes narrowed, she crossed her arms tightly. Duke's brow wrinkled, as he turned toward me and with a wave of his hand said, "See y'all later."

Calmly I said, "I'm sure we'll see more of each other." I didn't bother to wave back.

Joyce and I rehashed the events of the evening during the car ride to the resort. Her talk with Minnie hadn't revealed as much as I'd hoped it would, but they had reestablished a rapport.

"I've misjudged her; I'm afraid."

"Don't beat yourself up over it; you only saw what Duke wanted you to see. You had no way of knowing he wasn't all he said he was to Minnie."

"She was beginning to open up to me when Duke came back from the range."

"I kept him occupied as long as I could. What did she say? Did she indicate he was abusive beyond what we've seen?"

"Minnie apologized for coming between Duke and me in high school. She said she liked Duke and was sorry; she hadn't meant for anything to happen between them. He had invited her to go boating on the lake with a group of friends, but no one else showed up. She didn't want to disappoint him, so she went alone."

I interrupted Joyce, "That slime bucket set her up."

"Minnie said they boated across the lake to a thickly wooded island where Duke wanted to swim. They never swam. She apologized again and said she hadn't meant to have sex on the island that day, but once they had, she couldn't turn back the hands of time. Walter, I think he might have raped her."

"It's pretty easy to believe he would. It's his style."

"She said Duke was good to her, and abuse was never mentioned. I don't know if she recognizes what he does to her as abuse. She talked about how wonderful everything was their first year of marriage. Duke wanted the baby, but it died. Things began to change after that. She blamed herself for losing the baby. I know she wanted to tell me more about what went wrong and would have if we'd had more time together."

"Maybe we need to make that happen?"

Joyce's eyes filled with tears, "After seeing how he treats her I'm concerned for her safety."

"What you see going on with Duke, has nothing to do with the baby's death. Whatever Duke is today, he's always been from the time his personality was formed. He could choose to submit to his desires and will to common sense and reason, but he chooses the lesser path of masking his identity. He knows what he is, which is why he presents himself as a great guy. He's a snake in the grass."

Joyce looked puzzled. "You learned that in journalism school?"

"I've studied behavior my whole life. I suppose in many ways it helps me do my job."

Joyce nodded. "I guess I've known all along what he was but didn't want to admit that I loved a man like him. After moving to Toronto, and starting a family, I'd forgotten about what had happened between the three of us. It was a long time ago."

Joyce fell silent. The night had been hard on her, and she needed a break. She sat back in the bucket seat; her clenched fist pressed against her lips.

We pulled into the resort's parking lot and coasted to a stop. Joyce's voice had penned up anger. "I want to get to the bottom of this. If he's hurting Minnie, he needs to be arrested."

Biting my lip, so not to sound too aggressive, I took a deep breath and blew it out slowly. "I can't agree more. What can we do?" I took another minute to feign my reluctance and followed it up with a hopeless look and tossed in a head shake for good measure.

"I need to talk with Minnie again—alone."

"Maybe I can help."

Joyce had confidence in me, and I didn't want to let her down. She reached over with her hand and softly stroked my neck, running her fingers through my hair along the back of my collar. I had a feeling it might be a later night than I'd planned.

Chapter 4

"The most damaging aspect of abuse is the trauma to our hearts and souls from being betrayed by the people we love and trust."
—*Anonymous*

An unannounced visitor was a rarity and especially late at night. Nonetheless, I answered the knock on my cabin door without my Glock in hand. The light from inside my cabin illuminated Joyce's presence. Her eyes were drenched in tears as she stepped over the threshold. "Can we talk for a while?"

"Sure."

Joyce recounted the day's event with Duke and Minnie mixed with her recall of the past. By midnight, she'd reclined in my arms and settled in for the night. I've never been in tune with a woman's need to talk but understood she didn't want to be alone. I enjoyed her company, and it served to keep the real me behind my false veneer a while longer. On the downside, it did nothing to further my goal of breaking off our relationship. I'd discovered it wasn't an easy task to accomplish.

Joyce and I had a bond based upon lies. That made for a bad foundation in my estimation. I was in a conundrum. She deserved a stable environment as did her children. I doubted she could find that with me.

Over the past few years, I've lived my life as if I were a feral cat. I've woken and slept at my leisure having no need for an alarm clock. Catnapping, as I did, was reportedly an unhealthy lifestyle for humans. But, I found it to be satisfactory to meet my needs. My life, day or night, was without a routine. I should've been the happiest man in the world, but Destiny stirred in my soul.

Dreams prompted me to awaken early and often. There was a paranormal calling placed upon my life, and it had to be answered or I would never know peace. I slipped out of bed without disturbing Joyce and brewed a pot of coffee to greet the morning sun. I poured the piping hot liquid into a large ceramic cup allowing the fresh aroma to tantalize my senses. I pulled the wood rocker from under the porch canopy. Glistening sunrays added a touch of warmth. In such a setting, I expected to find a sense of serenity, but I was disturbed. There was bad blood between Duke and me. Unbeknownst to him, he'd arrived in my dream world. It was not a friendly place for the likes of Duke.

My gut told me to mind my own business. I was free to ignore what I saw, but that's what other's had done. I wasn't other people. Besides—it was my business. I'd taken the Palatini oath for people like Minnie. If I didn't come to her aid, who would? Evidently the vigilance committee was useless to help. Duke was the president.

The sounds of movement from within the cabin pushed my thoughts aside and brought me back to the present. A door creaked, the familiar sound of the cabin's front door hinge. A hand slowly slipped onto my chest, and a gentle voice whispered, "Good morning, honey."

I put my hand on top of hers and replied, "Mornin' sweetie."

"What's wrong Walter?" There were times when my behavior was too transparent.

"Duke."

"I thought so." Joyce pulled in a deep breath then released it slowly. "Want some breakfast? We can talk afterward."

I nodded. Joyce and I could rehash the Dixon issue, but it was not the heart of the problems that occupied my thoughts. I've lived a shadowy existence hidden in this rural community for the past few months. I know in my spirit this way of life will never be mine. Duke wasn't able to rob me of my happiness in Shell Knob. He didn't have the power. It was the beck and call of a murdered young girl from her grave. Blood boiled up through the ground in my dreams. Her appeal has brought me out of the shadows.

I finished another cup of coffee while the sweet smell of maple smoked bacon lingered. Joyce was a gem. She'd brought out a tray table, and a folding chair, setting them near the rocker. She dashed back into the cabin and returned carrying two luncheon plates filled with bacon, eggs, and grits, dimpled with a pat of butter.

Duke required me to orchestrate behind the scenes while I kept my focus on the murder victim. I had to put Joyce in the driver's seat. "Do you still want to talk with Minnie?"

Joyce's face reddened, and the tone of her voice dropped to a whisper as she responded, "Yes—I want to know if he's hurting her." Any semblance of a long lost love for Duke on Joyce's part had vanished.

"Do you want to talk to her today?"

"How can we do that? Duke never leaves her alone."

"Sure he does. He said he was trucking today. We could take a sight-seeing trip, mosey by, and see her on our travels. We could get in and out before he got home."

Joyce leaned forward; her eyes aglow. "Where did you learn to think like that?"

"I'm not the warrior type, baby, I'm a reporter. Sneaky is the name of the game."

Joyce checked on her two young boys and made arrangements with her parents to cover for her while she was at Minnie's. It was a calculated risk, but early enough in the day that we'd miss Duke entirely. If he showed, we'd play the hand that was dealt.

A few minutes past ten we launched our mission. Joyce sat deep in the Avenger's seat, noticeably in a sour mood. "Hey, what's up with you?"

"It's not you, Walter. It's me."

"It's not you—it's him." Her jaws tightened as she nodded then looked out the window. Soon she slipped into a trance-like state. I focused on a more pressing issue. I didn't want to get out of the loop with Landers. He likely had new information, and I wanted to work it into the puzzle. We pulled off the highway onto Dixon Holler road and made our way up the incline to their house.

The circular shaped driveway provided parking with the nose of the Avenger pointed back toward the highway. Joyce collected her composure after a few moments of nostrils flaring and lips curling. She could hide the stress but not placate it. Engaging Minnie face to face on the issue was the only way she would have peace of mind. I was confident that Joyce's passion and sincerity would succeed to win over Minnie's trust to confide in her. I counted on it.

"Let's do this thing," I said.

Joyce nodded. By the time I had both feet firmly on the ground, Joyce had made a beeline for the front door. It wasn't unusual for Minnie to greet people at her house. She collected money from the gun range patrons, helped Duke with the survival camp, and had access to an old AMC Eagle to run errands. She had her means of escape, but she never made an attempt. If she had, I was sure he'd take it away from her. She wasn't entirely isolated from the world, but a social captive in Duke's control.

Minnie answered the door. Her eyes widened as she stood speechless. "We were out for a drive and thought we'd stop by to say hi," Joyce said.

Minnie cordially invited us in and served sun tea. We talked superficially about the drive and weather. I was bored to tears. If Joyce was serious about finding the truth I had to find someplace else to be while she dug up the dirt.

"Minnie," I asked, "When we shot on the range I noticed some other buildings in back. Is that the survival training camp?"

"Yes," Minnie answered with an eye-twinkling smile. The mere mention of Duke's accomplishment brought happiness to her countenance. "Y'all know he's the president of the Vigilance Committee. He uses the camp classroom for their meetings too." Again, she flashed the smile.

Minnie was a different person when Duke wasn't around to browbeat her into submission. She possessed a hidden personality that lived inside the shell of another human being. It wasn't healthy. According to Joyce, the Minnie we saw was not the old Minnie she'd known from her childhood. When behaviors are hidden, they spook me in an unexplainable way. I counted on a predictable set of actions, and neither Duke nor Minnie presented their true self. Which one was the real Minnie? I surmised—neither. Both personalities were smokescreens for surviving in Duke's world. There were likely more, and I attributed the blame to Duke.

"Think Duke would mind if I took a peek out there?"

"No, Duke has people out there all the time. He promotes the training camp whenever he can."

"Cool, I'll check it out." I pointed to the back door, and Minnie responded with a nod. Joyce stood and gave me a quick kiss on the cheek. "Don't get lost Walter. I don't want to have to come find you."

I headed through the kitchen counting the steps from the living room to the back door. Survivalists and doomsday preppers were a different breed of people. Some were sincere; others were money-grubbing fear-mongers. However, I'd found them an excellent resource for my vigilante needs.

I walked toward the gun range continuing my subconscious and occasionally conscious recon of the facility. I stood between the gun range that sat to the southwest side of the hollow and the training camp on the northeast side. Unlike the four shoddy lean-to sheds on the firing line, the survival camp had a single structure encircled by an eight-foot high cyclone fence topped with razor wire. The compound's primary two-story building had been respectable once but now was in need of paint and repair. An American flag fluttered in the light breeze atop the gabled overhang of the porch.

At the northern corner, a double wide vehicle gate stood open. I strolled inside the wire and around the camp structure, peeking through windows to grasp a visual layout of the interior. A row of windows across the south side of the building allowed for a look at an area much like a large meeting hall.

Climbing two steps onto the porch I made my way to a set of double-doors. A quick 360° scan turned up no threats of watchers. I had no idea why I felt the need for precautions I'd been given permission. I chocked it up to old habits. The prompting in my spirit warned of danger. Moments like these intensified without a weapon strapped to my belt.

I considered retrieving my bug-out bag from the Avenger. With a few of my simple tools, I would be inside the building in a matter of seconds. I reached for the doorknob and gave it a slight turn. The door had been left unlocked. I concluded with gates open, and doors unlocked, the fence and wire were more aesthetic than practical for security.

Inside the entryway was a small vestibule. From there, I saw a kitchenette on the right side, and a large room to the left. I stepped into what I believed was a makeshift classroom. Five rows of plywood topped tables mounted on sawhorses spanned the width of the room, leaving aisle space on either side of the rows. Each of the tables had three to four metal folding chairs lined up and facing in the same direction. A desk stood on the north side of the classroom with a padded chair, and a large dry-erase board next to it.

I walked the aisles around the tables and appraised a sweeping view of the layout. Between the rows of windows on the south side of the building, the wall space had been papered with topographical maps and prepper type news articles. Centered on the back wall hung a large white flag with a black circular symbol. Smaller Missouri State and Confederate Battle flags dotted the walls as well.

A police scanner perched precariously close to the edge of a wood shelf above the desk. It continuously emitted a high-frequency buzz through a pair of speakers mounted on either side. Hung on the north wall under the scanner was a large corkboard with Vigilance Committee emblazoned on the wood border. This facility doubled as the meeting hall for the committee. The VC, as the committee is known to locals, is reportedly do-gooders with an air of secrecy about them that I found unsettling.

I questioned the need for a police scanner? I doubted it had any survivalist purpose. To my way of thinking, a two-way radio communications, like citizen's band or ham were more viable for survivalists. Monitoring police broadcasts was far too limiting to be of any real value for disaster preparedness. It was most likely a tool for the VC to track law enforcement.

On the north side of the classroom, a short hallway led to a bathroom. Adjacent was a staircase that presumably led to additional rooms above the classroom. At the back of the classroom on the west wall was what appeared to be an exit door to the fenced area, but I distinctly remembered no such door visible outside. Along the hallway walls, an assortment of photos were taped and pinned to the wall panels. My buddy Duke was prominent in a majority of the pictures. Judging by the background terrain, they'd been taken at locations nearby. Weaponry was the common element; a slew of tricked-out AR 15s, AK 47s, and various sniper rifles were shown with notable pride.

At the head of the classroom sat a desk with a display of brochures. Dixon Holler camp was referred to in one flyer as the Missouri Alliance Tactical Training Center. Inside the advertisement was listed a range of features offered by Duke: Weapons training, armed response drills, escape and evasion, threat matrix, and membership to the Dixon Holler gun range. Minnie had mentioned Duke's followers were skilled in disaster preparedness. I questioned what sort of disaster they were preparing for where someone needed response drills and escape training?

I compared other brochures that lined the desk with the Missouri Alliance flyer. Some were "Urban" training centers that taught stockpiling long shelf life foods and how to pack a bug-out bag for a quick escape from a major city. Another camp focused on "Wilderness Survival" focusing their training on hunting, trapping, tracking, fishing, and foraging training. Those camps were more my speed. They sounded like vacation skills rather than training for a disaster.

The one notable commonality the camps shared were courses in weapons training. From the Louisiana Delta Alliance located on the Mississippi River bayous to the Alaska Arctic Alliance (AAA) head-quartered in the metropolis of some Podunk called Glennallen, they each offered unique specialties for their regions. There was an apparent connection between these survivalists although they didn't claim an affiliation.

As I looked through the various brochures, I had the deep impression there was something sinister at work—something hidden between the lines that wasn't written, but decipherable. I eased myself into the leather office chair at the desk and poured over the pamphlets. There was something here—I sensed it.

An hour quickly passed as I studied the various brochures. What I discovered most revealing had nothing to do with the survivalists, but with me. My dislike for Duke and his behavior had driven me to avoid him at every opportunity. Consequently, I didn't know who he was. I allowed my disdain to get in the way and cloud my vision. That was before I became cognizant of what he was—a violent wife abuser. Perhaps, he was more skilled than I'd supposed he might be. I would never again approach him passively. If I were required to intercede in his behavior, I wouldn't waste words.

I hadn't met anyone in Shell Knob, other than Joyce, who'd mentioned the Missouri Alliance. I would have assumed a local training camp of this kind would've had some influence on the makeup of the community. I had dismissed it as irrelevant.

I snagged a brochure from each of the camps, about a dozen in all, and stuffed them in my back pants pocket. I wanted to know everything I could about what Duke was into. I tidied up the desk and stepped out onto the porch. As I pulled the double doors closed, I heard Joyce call my name.

"Yeah." I didn't hear a response, so I made my way toward the house. Maybe Duke had shown up unexpectedly, and that spelled trouble. I quietly entered through the back door and into the front room. I didn't have a good feeling about what I'd walked into; in the quietness you could hear a pin drop.

Minnie sat on one of the sofas with her back toward me. Her head bowed low. Joyce knelt at her right side with their hands cupped together. Duke wasn't there. After a few quiet and uncomfortable seconds had passed, Joyce spoke. "Have a seat, Walter."

"Okay." I figured Minnie must have unloaded the goods. That would be good news. Talking was the first step. Nothing else could happen in a right sense if she wasn't willing to open up about the problems. I took a seat on the opposite couch.

Minnie hesitated to start. Tears welled up, and she sobbed bitterly. Finally, Joyce consoled her with a long hug. Shortly after that, she began, "Our love started out rocky, but grew. I got myself pregnant in high school right after Duke and I started going steady. In high school, it was a big deal to have a steady boyfriend, and I did what I needed to do."

I interrupted her, "You had to get pregnant to keep Duke?"

"No—that happened by accident. I didn't want Duke to get mad at me for not satisfying his needs." Minnie looked through the large front-room window toward the driveway leading to the highway as if watching for Duke to arrive. "I had to… It was only right. After he had found out I was going to have a baby, there was a lot of stress on him. He said he had to do the right thing." Minnie smiled. Her face reflected the bliss from her reminiscences, but they were lies. All conjured up memories from wishful thinking that had never existed, not with someone of Duke's low character. "During the first year, everything was wonderful. We had a new baby, and Duke had landed a good paying nationwide truck driving job. It was real hard on him because he didn't like to be away. He sacrificed for us."

"What went wrong?" Joyce asked.

Minnie buried her head in her hands. She took the time to regain her composure. Then she softly spoke, "Nothing." Minnie looked into my eyes, "Nothing went wrong. Duke loves me more now than ever before." Happiness radiated through the tears as she slipped deeper into her fantasy world of love.

Again Joyce asked, "You told me what went wrong, remember? You and I talked about it."

Minnie cast her gaze on a 5 x 7 framed picture of an infant. "It was all my fault. It had to be. When Jules died, there was no one else to blame."

"How'd the baby die," I asked.

"Duke couldn't understand how God would let something like this happen to him. I wasn't the mother I should have been. It's the only explanation."

I asked again, "How'd the baby die?" I'd suspected the child had died from abuse or neglect on Duke's part, but Minnie made it sound as if Duke wasn't there.

"The doctor told me that sometimes seven-month-old babies die. I'd laid him in his crib for a nap, and he never woke up again."

"How is it your fault?" Joyce asked.

"I can't explain, but it had to be me. Duke wasn't here when it happened."

Minnie paused for a minute and collected her thoughts. It was the kind of pause that might've lasted a minute but felt like an hour. "When Duke got home, I tried to explain what the doctor had said, but I couldn't; it didn't make sense, not even to me. I asked Duke to talk to the doctor, but he refused. He said if I'd been a better mother Jules would never have died. Duke was right."

It was the right time for me to interrupt and set her straight, but I didn't have the words. I didn't know if she'd been a good mother or not, she might have a screw loose or be a taco short of a fiesta plate. But, from what she'd said, it hardly sounded as if she was to blame.

"I didn't do well after that. Duke said I let myself go. I didn't want to see any of my friends. Some days I didn't get out of bed, and if I did, I didn't get dressed or brush my hair. Worst of all, I didn't attend to Duke's needs. He was spending more time on the road. When he was home, he was always unhappy. All I wanted was Duke to be happy after I'd let him down."

Joyce had been through her share of marital stress. She comforted Minnie with an affectionate embrace. Something I was incapable of. What I'd caught from Minnie was Duke, Duke, Duke, and that was a bad sign. Joyce might have broken through the ice, one-on-one, but there was now a chill in the air. In my book, it was a history lesson and added to a small degree my understanding. But I didn't hear the evidence I expected.

Minnie looked over at me and continued, "During the following year after Jules died, Duke and I argued—a lot. I'd failed in doing my part to keep the house clean the way he wanted. I was out of control; Duke had to keep me safe. Sometimes, he tied me up so I wouldn't hurt myself; other times he had to slap some sense into me. He didn't want to do it, but I made him. That's not his fault; I'm to blame."

"Is he mistreating you?" I asked.

"He never has; he loves me. Even when he threatened to leave me, I knew he still loved me. I could always tell. One time he accused me of sleeping around. He called me ugly, terrible names, but he was only trying to show me how much he loved me. Never in all my born days had I ever seen him so angry or jealous. He swore he would kill me before he'd let me go to another man." She quietly gazed out the window for a few moments then glanced back and forth between Joyce and me. "I think that shows how much he loves me, don't you?"

I wondered who she was asking. It was a waste of her time if she was asking me. Duke had mentally tortured her and physically abused her. She couldn't see it or didn't want to. She was a basket case of mental instability. Minnie stared into my eyes expecting a response, but I had nothing for her. The solution to her problem she'd never accept.

Joyce had choked up with emotion. I didn't share her feelings. As I listened to Minnie defend Duke and make a hero of him, I was sickened by her dialog. Minnie must have suspected I wasn't buying her bill of goods. Like any good salesperson, she quickly launched a second pitch.

"I thought he was wrong when I was restricted from seeing my old friends. I realize now he was right. They were a bad influence on me. When Duke insisted I cut ties with my family, it was hard, but he was right. All they wanted to do was lead me away from him. Duke was always right."

How misguided and brainwashed can a person be? Minnie had all the characteristics of a woman in the clutches of a traumatic bond. There was nothing that sounded healthy about her marriage relationship. Nothing. She'd made herself the scapegoat for Duke's violent acts and controlling behaviors. He'd belittled her in public, trashed her accomplishments, intimidated her with threats, beat her physically, and ignored her emotional needs. Duke's jealousy was a ruse, unfounded and without reason. Maybe she'd convinced herself that she was at fault for everything and Duke her hero, but I saw it differently.

"I went to the hospital. The doctor said I had a nervous breakdown. It was then I realized how much Duke had done for me. I'm so thankful for Duke. He is my whole world."

I'd become tone deaf to Minnie's verbiage. I'd been mistaken in my judgment. I'd given Minnie the opportunity to bare her soul, thinking she'd come clean. Instead, she'd elevated Duke's abusiveness to savior status. In my book, that made Minnie dangerous to Joyce and me.

It was a day of mistaken judgment. I'd hoped Joyce was the key to unlocking Minnie, but I was wrong. Whatever Minnie had confided in Joyce before I arrived back at the house, she was no longer willing to admit. Was it fear? Was it because of my background as a reporter? I'd picked up mixed signals from her. I couldn't put my finger on what I sensed, but I was sure other dynamics were in play. Rapidly, I became suspicious of her motives. Had Minnie put on the show for Joyce's benefit? Did Minnie feel threatened by Joyce returning to Shell Knob? There was more trouble at the root of the issue. I motioned to Joyce to cut it short. I needed to go.

I waved good-bye and walked. Joyce being polite hugged and shed another tear with Minnie. As we traveled back to the resort, my thoughts slipped out of my mouth. "There's no saving that girl from herself. All her health problems, depression, lack of self-esteem and self-confidence, are a result of Duke's abusive behaviors. It's just like Minnie said, Duke, Duke, everything is Duke. If she believes that, she doesn't stand a chance. I overheard her say the word love a few times, but I never saw it in anything she said. Someday. Maybe. She'll come to her senses and realize it's been Duke all along who was at fault. In my opinion, she'll never leave him." Joyce looked out the passenger window. I couldn't see her face, and I sensed she wanted it that way. I saw her brush tears away.

I've played my part well in Shell Knob. I've enjoyed living the life of a reporter without any responsibility. I'd entertained the notion of reforming my ways and setting aside my passion for killing, but that's not me. I don't belong in Shell Knob. However, leaving was impossible until police caught the young girl's murderer. If I skipped town prior to the capture, the manhunt would be on for me as a person of interest.

Late in the afternoon, Jay Landers pulled into the resort driveway.

"What's up Jay?"

"Where's the beer?"

A legitimate question for a friendly chat, I thought. There was nothing suspicious about Jay stopping by for a social visit. Except, it was the first time he'd stopped by to see me. "Around back on the porch in a cooler. I hope you like Harp Lager."

"Is it beer?"

"Irish import."

We walked to the lake side of the cabin. "Grab a chair." I pointed to a plastic lawn chair while I pulled up the porch rocker. Being the hospitable type, I would never make a man drink alone. Besides I wanted to hear what he had to say and what better way than over a beer or two. I grabbed a couple beers, cracked the top on one, and passed it to him. "So what's on your mind? You didn't come all this way for a free beer?"

"No." Landers chugged his beer empty. "I have an ulterior motive."

I cracked a smile and the tops on two fresh brews. "Does it have something to do with a murdered girl?"

Landers took a swig from his beer then said, "You're good."

"Elementary. You see, I suspect you have something you want to share, and you don't have anyone else you can do that with?"

"You forgot, "My dear Watson," after "Elementary.""

"Interesting point my dear Landers, except Sherlock Holmes never said those words."

Jay gulped his beer. "I'll check that out." Landers finished his beer and snagged a third round offering me one as well. "I told Deputy Delford about the anonymous call I'd received. He ran with it." He paused to wet his lips.

"And."

"Delford met me at Carole's today for lunch. He was probing for further information. He asked if I had any other contact with the caller. Of course, I haven't."

Jay took another swig, followed by an "Ahh," then continued. "Delford asked me to keep a lid on what he picked up. He passed on to an investigator by the name Parker the anonymous tip I had given him."

"Sounds like y'all are playing a game."

"So far it's a good game. This Parker guy acted on the lead, and they picked up a possible missing girl from Alaska. Delford said she fit the description. The facts are sketchy. But Delford believes the results will be positive."

"That's great."

Jay looked me square in the eyes, "The caller knew. There is nothing coincidental about what she had said. I find it hard to believe whoever was involved, lives right here amongst us." Landers shook his head. "It's hard for me to fathom."

"If Delford confirms the identification, you'll have solved the first equation within the puzzle."

"Delford said the missing girl was from Palmer, Alaska. The abduction took place while on her way home from school. One classmate witnessed the girl struggling with a man before she was shoved into a car." Landers sat back and gazed across the lake.

Resort guests, a man and woman, led a small procession of children to the water's edge, where they waded into the shallows. Soon the sounds of frolic echoed across the lake. Jay watched them intently. "How could she be abducted in Alaska and end up in Missouri? What kind of monster are we dealing with?"

The first question was answerable, but I didn't have one. I assumed the second question had been rhetorical. There was no rational answer.

"Jay, have you heard of a group around here called the Missouri Alliance? They're some doomsday survivalist group; best I can tell."

Landers shook his head.

"I want to know if they're legit. I'm thinking about doing a story, I find them kind of quirky."

"Can't say that I have." Jay's bloodhound nose kicked in at my question. "What are you thinking, Walter? You think they had something to do with what happened to the girl, don't you?"

"No, no, no, I'd run across some of their literature, and I was wondering if you'd heard of them. That's all."

"I can ask around."

I nodded. Landers was a relative newcomer to Barry County. I would've been surprised if he was aware of the preppers, but it was worth a chance.

In the Palatini line of work, less attention was better. People get the wrong idea about a guy if he asks too many sensitive questions. And I wasn't interested in people having the wrong idea about me. In fact, I didn't want people to have ideas about me at all. Yet, I had to ask questions. The wrong person asked the wrong question, and a lot of heat could come down on a guy in a small community where half the people are related by blood or marriage, or maybe both.

"What's the scoop on this so-called Vigilance Committee?"

Landers pondered for a moment, "I would call them a neighborhood watch program. They've helped the police locate meth labs, break up a local theft ring and chop shop. Rumor has it they've engaged in some alleged violence."

"Like what?"

"They've been in hot water with the Sheriff's Department. A few months ago they allegedly assisted an unsavory ethnic family to reconsider their decision to move into Cassville. Nothing has come from the investigation."

I reached in and grabbed another cold one of the cooler, "Some all-around good guys, huh?"

"They may have good intentions, but good intentions get carried away sometimes."

"No doubt." I took a long, refreshing drink. "If you pick up any more trivia, I'd like to know, okay?"

"I'll get back to you."

"Thanks buddy." I remained on the porch after Landers left. I pulled out the handful of Alliance brochures that I'd stuffed in my back jeans pocket and thumbed through them. I'd fallen prey to my prompts. My focus belonged on the dead girl's investigation, not on Duke. Finding the killer was my key out of Shell Knob. Strange, I thought, I vaguely remembered Minnie saying something to the effect the girl being eleven-years-old. If my recall was correct, how could she have known? The age hadn't been released yet.

Chapter 5

"The cat is obeying its blood instinct when it plays with the mouse."
—Agatha Christie

I have a suspicious mind. Maybe it was me looking for something that wasn't there, but I was puzzled by the Alliance. The Missouri Alliance had many common traits with 2nd Amendment patriot movements. I found the concept of a patriot militia appealing. Each brochure contained quasi-mission statements focused on the erosion of gun owners' rights and government conspiring to convince the public that guns in the hands of law-abiding citizens were responsible for criminal behavior. These were popular topics and had not gone unnoticed by me. If these were the causes for their existence, I could easily support them.

The flyer's primary purpose was to gain membership and buyers for their services. They had a large target audience and a useful tool to reach followers of their mindset. For those "believers" in coming catastrophic events, it was an easy sale.

Fringe elements of society, however, needed a hook to convince outsiders of their organization's value and validity. To accomplish this, the far-flung had to emphasize common features that the masses accepted, such as gun rights. But the hook was delivered when they promoted their secondary pitch. It made them stand out from the other salesmen with similar wares.

The Alliance geared toward doomsday themes. They offered "how to" guides and prepper courses for what to expect after the collapse of civil order. In their promotion, it was already a done deal. Not if, but when, so to be saved, you had to hurry to get in the boat before it sailed. The Alliance outlined their enemies in the post-collapse environment as street gangs and wandering bands of urbanites they affectionately referred to as zombies.

Doomsday predictions had a myriad of possibilities for what might upset the apple cart of humanity. For those who "believed," the event was imminent and already unfolding. The catastrophic events of biblical proportions outlined in the brochures were not as evident as they claimed. But such a compelling persuasion could be very lucrative. The Alliance had the snake oil and the passion for pushing it.

I found it interesting that in their core principles, there wasn't any mention of God or religious rudiment. They had the usual rights, liberties, and freedoms, but no God. Down in the hills of Dixie, it was hard to believe they'd left God out by accident. What these Missouri boys did have in their literature was the same circular symbol that was on the flag at the back of the classroom. Maybe what I'd stumbled across was a ragtag Aryan army but, that didn't jive with their affiliate Alliance brochures on display. Only one of the other advertisements showed the same circular symbol. Were they racists? Perhaps, but until I knew more, I concluded it was not a foundational element by which their movement had been allied.

My thoughts were interrupted by the clattering noise from a vehicle crossing the driveway ruts and potholes. Evidently it was another lead-foot who hadn't taken the time to read the posted warning sign that read "SLOW" in big block letters. I walked to the front of my cabin. To my surprise, Duke's unmistakable '69 Ford was parked cockeyed in the driveway. I took off running to the resort. As I rounded the front of the resort, Duke stood on the porch wagging his finger in Joyce's face and raising a ruckus.

With a sharp tone I yelled, "Hey! What's your problem?"

Duke glanced in my direction, but just as quickly, dismissed my presence as irrelevant. I saw the opportunity for an educational moment, and I had a lesson prepared.

I spun Duke around to gain his attention. His response was predictable. With his chest puffed up, and his finger in my face, he put forth a rambling series of threats. What I heard was blah, blah, blah.

Duke was used to people cowering in response to his intimidation. But I wasn't a run-of-the-mill kind of guy. I had to show him he'd bitten off more than he could chew. He said something foul-mouthed and indecent as I went into action.

He was a big guy with a bigger ego. He squared off face-to-face and tried to sound tough. I wasn't impressed; his mouth exceeded his ability. I sensed a lack of spine to back up his threats. In the seconds that followed, he made a futile attempt to back me off the porch with his size. Acting on a four-inch height advantage, he bumped his chest against my body. His ego wouldn't let him play it smart. He pushed against me again. I stepped back and gave him the confidence to step forward again. Once he'd committed to continuous pushing with his body, he'd given up any advantage he possessed in reach. Duke's tactics closed the distance between us. The element of surprise was in my favor, and I took the initiative. I snatched the finger he'd stuck in my face and gave it a quick wrenching twist. If it didn't bring him to his knees in pain, it would make it sore for a day or two. Duke bent at the hip to keep up with where his finger took him. When I let go, he sprang up like a jack-in-the-box. I grabbed a handful of collar and drove him backward. When we reached a wall, I slammed him against it. My forearm crossed under his neck and pinned him against the wall.

"I asked you nice once, and this is the last time I'm going to be civil about it. What's your problem?"

He momentarily struggled against my grip so I bounced him off the wall for a second time and for good measure slammed him against the same spot once more. Finally, Duke showed me the respect I deserved.

His deep-set eyes and piercing gaze displayed the intensity of his anger. But all he had to fight with were words. "You son-of-a—" He stopped in his tracks as I squeezed my free hand under his chin and pushed up until he was unable to form words or even breathe easily.

"I've had enough of your mouth. You either speak decently and learn to do it with respect or don't come around here. Do I make myself clear?"

Duke had pegged me as a wimpy journalistic type who was afraid of my own shadow. My façade had worked, and I had caught him with his guard down. He never expected a physical response. It had given me the drop on him this time, but it would never be as easy again. He nodded as best he could with his head pressed against the wall.

"Now, what's the problem?"

"Y'all don't have no business talkin' to my wife. Hear me?"

His body relaxed from the rigidness he had when he tried to free himself from my grasp. Slowly, I released his collar. I wasn't worried he might go off again. In fact, I welcomed it. I'd polish the floor with him if he acted out again. I let go of my hold entirely and straightened his crumpled collar. With a dramatic push of my hand he said, "Leave it alone. I can do it myself." It was a big show to save face, but otherwise meaningless. Any action he took was because I allowed it. I owned him.

Duke finished adjusting his clothing then piped up again, "I don't never need y'alls help, not with nothin'." His words had taken on a different tone and connotation. Joyce didn't catch on and wasted her time explaining our side of the story. "Walter and I were out for a drive. We happened to be in your area and stopped by to say hello. We weren't trying to start trouble." She'd lied. She knew the plan. It was a good sign.

"It don't sound nothin' like that to me. Sounds more like y'all were stickin' your nose in other people's business." Duke then turned his attention to me, "She never said you were even there."

I wanted to avoid Duke's comment, but I knew it wasn't going away. By Minnie not revealing I was with Joyce it might bring the wrath of Duke upon her. The only way forward was to be plain and simple, so Duke didn't misunderstand.

"You know what," I said.

"What's that?"

"If I see something wrong, I make it my business—then I take care of it. And I'm seeing all sorts of wrongs."

"Y'alls reporter crap don't fly none 'round here city boy. What goes on in my house is my business, not y'alls! I ain't askin', I'm tellin' y'all to stay out of my business and stay away from my house!"

I prayed for a sign from Joyce, so I could thump this big monkey.

"I don't understand," Joyce said. "We've been friends for a long time." Her statement was true, and Joyce's sincerity struck a chord with Duke. He didn't say a word, but stood motionless, and stared in her direction. Twice in a matter of minutes, he'd been bested. Manhandled by someone he thought was easily intimidated and then stymied by Joyce's passionate plea.

Joyce still didn't see the underlying behavior behind Jekyll's cloak. Duke's actions were the notorious Mister Hyde squirming to get free.

He was a caged animal and didn't like playing second fiddle to Jekyll. Duke's day-to-day life had hidden his real personality. The good people of the community saw only the Jekyll façade. But under stress, and challenged, he lost his ability to control the face he preferred to show to others. I'd discovered his Achilles heel. I could push his buttons anytime I wished and watch him dance. Duke didn't know it, but he'd handed over control of his life. It was mine whenever I wanted it.

Duke lit down off the porch without saying anything further. His long legs took rapid strides toward his pickup. Joyce called out to him, but he didn't stop. When he reached the driver side door, he swung it open. His behavior was ratcheting up. It would take a little provocation to set Hyde free.

He stepped back from behind the door into total view. For a brief moment, I thought he'd retrieved a weapon from his pickup but his hands were empty. Duke stood glaring in my direction. I started toward him. Another lesson was in order.

"Y'all stay away from my woman, or there's going to be real trouble," he shouted.

I picked up my pace.

Duke pointed at me, "You ain't wanted here, and you ain't stayin'."

I neared the front of his rig and slowed my advance. He could abuse his wife, he'd proven that. But if Hyde got loose what was Duke capable of? I wanted to know. I inched closer.

It was my turn to bump chests. I needed him to swing first. Then I was free to act in my defense and not incur Joyce's wrath. Stepping as close as humanly possible I gave him the opportunity to get busy and throw the first punch, but something stopped him. I surmised it was fear, for he reeked of it. I upped the ante. "I like it here—I'm staying." If a fresh challenge tossed in his face didn't escalate the situation, nothing would.

"It's too crowded round here for the both of us."

"In Shell Knob?" I laughed at my sarcasm. "Then you need to be leaving town."

Was I back in high school? Not that I fought all that much in those days, but an upper classman tagged me once during an arts and crafts class that resulted in a crescent shaped scar on my right eyelid. He was a bully, and I made every bully I came across pay for his transgression.

"Take your best shot," I said. He gave me a look that said he wasn't in any hurry to test my abilities.

"You can't scare me Stud."

"I beg to differ. You've been afraid of me from the day I arrived. Call me Stud again and I'll slap the hillbilly out of you."

He broke eye contact and looked at Joyce, who stood watching from the porch stairs. "I'd sure enough take you up on that—"

I cut him off, "Right now—let's finish it."

"I don't have the time right now." He turned and jumped into his Ford. The engine roared to life, and he peeled out toward the open road. When he hit pavement with the pickup's back tires, the rig fish-tailed until he let off the gas. Last I saw of him was a one finger salute. Since I was a polite sort of guy, I didn't wave one back. Next time, and I was confident there'd be a next time, I'd bend that finger all the way off and stick it in his nasty mouth.

I returned to the porch where Joyce stood, arms crossed and a scowl on her face. "That went well." She turned and walked up the porch stairs. At the door, she turned toward me, "I'm glad that's over." Joyce stepped inside closing the door behind her.

I stood on the porch and muttered to myself, "Ain't nothing over," but there was no one within earshot which was just as well.

I kept my eye out for Duke with a slight hope he'd changed his mind and sped back for round two. We could dispense with the verbal jousting and get down to business. I needed Duke's spousal abuse settled and out of my hair. I needed to devote my time and energy, helping the powers that be snag the Shell Knob murderer.

Joyce and I didn't talk the rest of the evening. I didn't know why. I hadn't done anything wrong. I'd handled the situation and subsequent physical intervention without getting too nasty.

Early the next morning, I fired up the Avenger and took a little drive. Alone. Typically, I would have asked Joyce along, or at least informed her where I was going, give her a hug and kiss good-bye, but not this time. I was on a mission to settle this mess once and for all. Duke wasn't going to listen to reason voluntarily and was evidently a slow learner too. He and I alone together might find a compromise to his bad behavior. I made a beeline to Dixon Holler.

The possibility existed that Duke was incapable of learning the lesson. I'd cross that bridge if and when it happened. I recalled a sagacious school teacher that had said to me, "The teacher hasn't taught until the learner's learned." I accepted partial responsibility for Duke, who under my tutelage, hadn't risen to the heights of comprehension I had expected. For me to rectify my shortcomings as an educator, I would double-down with one-to-one motivation. I didn't choose to be his teacher, but the way I saw it, there wasn't anyone around Shell Knob, who cared enough to lay it out for him. That left me.

One thing I was sure of, Duke knew how his nasty attitude and atrocious behavior affected the local town's folk, and he thrived on their reaction. Joyce had commented that Duke didn't care what other people thought of him. I saw it differently. He cared a great deal. That's why he continued his façade as a tough guy. He liked being that person.

I, on the other hand, wasn't one of the good ol' boys, and I cared a great deal how he acted. As a result, I was willing to lend a helping hand. He'd either straighten up or die while I was trying to help him. There wasn't another option on the table.

Admittedly my mood had grown dark, and for good reason. I'd set my sights on lying low and staying off law enforcement's radar. My work had brought plenty of trouble in the past, and I wanted to avoid those problems in Shell Knob. My desire to remain hidden forced me to "tiptoe around the bush" with Duke. That wasn't my style. I'd rather burn the bush to the ground. I wanted our meeting to be face-to-face, up-front and matter-of-fact. If he got stupid, I'd slap it out of him.

I pulled my Avenger to a stop directly in front of Duke's house. I didn't see his rig and assumed he wasn't home. Minnie's AMC Eagle sat parked in the morning shade. It didn't mean Minnie was home, but if she were, I'd hang out with her for a while, and rattle Duke's cage when he arrived. He'd go off half-cocked again, and I'd push his buttons into action. I'd convinced myself Minnie's life depended on my success. For a change, it would be nice to resolve a problem without killing it.

I knocked on the door jamb. No one answered. I listened for sounds from within the house then knocked again louder. With no response, I concluded Minnie was likely with Duke running errands. They were known to travel together frequently, especially around Shell Knob.

I returned to my Avenger, walking slowly while listening for sounds coming from the gun range, but there was a ghostly silence in the holler. My hackles rose. There were eyes watching my every move. I cranked the car engine and waited for the air conditioning to kick out cool air.

My binoculars had slipped from the center console onto the passenger side floorboard. I leaned to my right reaching for the binoculars' neck strap. The eerie feeling intensified. I'd had the "heebie-jeebies" before, and this was a sure case.

Quickly, I glanced toward the house. I wasn't sure what I saw in the window, but there was movement, and it struck me as unnatural. Possibly it was nothing more than a breeze filtering through the house, but a kitchen shade moved to one side. There wasn't any air stirring outside. I had a hunch I wasn't alone after all.

I turned off the engine, stepped out of the Avenger, and walked to the front door. I knocked aggressively leaving no doubt I meant business. I knocked twice more, still without a response. Country bumpkins were a lot like their city slicker counterparts—predictable. Urbanites and citified dwellers had a habit of locking doors. I could count on it whether they were home or not. But their country cousins rarely locked their doors. I reached down and turned the handle, and pushed the front door open wide.

"Hey," I called out to the empty room. No one responded. "I'm coming in!"

Suddenly, to my left, Minnie stood in the kitchen doorway. Her head bowed sheepishly, and her hands clasped together at her waist in front of her. Her behavior wasn't unusual. I'd come to expect it from her, especially when Duke was present. She had turned back toward the kitchen before she spoke.

"You shouldn't be here Mister Goe."

"No sense to be formal, Minnie. Besides, I didn't come by to talk to you. Where's Duke?"

She shrugged. "He left early this morning."

The submission gig played out to her benefit when Duke was around. I understood that. If Duke was here, her actions were on target, but according to her, he wasn't home. She was hiding someone or something from me.

I moved in close, I wanted to look her in the eye and put pressure on her to tell me the truth. With my hand, I turned Minnie toward me and lifted her head to where our eyes could meet. She was hiding someone from me—herself. You didn't have to be an Einstein to figure out she'd been beaten, and not long ago. Her facial bruising was fresh. The submissive act wasn't an act at all. She was ashamed. She'd been adamant one day earlier that Duke didn't abuse her. Now she was forced to admit the truth. It was a sorry way to get caught in a lie.

"Don't attempt to make any excuses for Duke this time," I snapped.

Minnie teary-eyed, cried out, "It's all my fault. I shouldn't have said anything to Duke."

I grabbed her by both shoulders, "Stop it! Stop it right now." My voice was curt with anger. "Stop making excuses for what he's doing to you."

"I shouldn't have told him that Joyce stopped by yesterday. I made him mad. I should have kept my mouth shut."

Minnie had been young and lovely once, and it wasn't all that long ago, but the years with Duke had taken their toll on her, emotionally, and physically. I took her by the hand and led her to the living room couch. She sat quietly and gazed at the floor in front of her. Whatever she was thinking caused her anxiety level to rise. She wrung her hands, which temporarily masked their shaking. I gently turned her chin with my fingers until our eyes met. I couldn't help feeling pity for her. She was too frightened and too wounded to make the right choice. Why should Duke be treated differently than a murderer? He'd killed all that Minnie had been, leaving only the shell of her former self. And he wasn't finished yet. Duke was working his way to destroying her physically as well.

"You need to get out of here. There is nothing right about the way Duke treats you."

"Duke is everything to me, and I know he loves me."

"You're lying to yourself. You can keep telling yourself that same old line, but it doesn't cut it. What he's going to do is kill you one of these days. Do you understand that? That's what wife abusers end up doing."

If fear worked to wake her up, I was willing to use it. But, Minnie's response was indecisive to my scare tactics. I went out on a limb and offered her my protection, but she refused to discuss the option. She was either sincere in her belief that Duke unconditionally loved her or she was an idiot. I didn't know which fit. If she honestly believed Duke loved her—she was utterly wrong.

"What's going to happen when you tell Duke I was here today? Don't answer—you know. He'll beat you or worse."

Minnie nodded, placed her hands over her face, and quietly wept. I waited with the hope she'd change her mind, but that hope faded rapidly. I'd been around and seen more than my share of horrible scenarios, but I'd never dealt with anyone like Minnie. I was baffled.

After a few minutes, I said, "Don't get up, I'm leaving." I walked to the front door and opened it. I was inclined to try once more, but I didn't want to look at her again. I had to cut all ties to my emotions, or they would rule my decisions. With my back toward her I said, "Do yourself a favor and get out while you still can."

I waited another minute. Thoughts bombarded me. Perhaps I was acting hastily by leaving with ideas unsaid. Time hadn't run out for her, only a chance to act while I was present. At the same instance, I saw her as a lost cause. You can't free someone from the shackles they hold in high regard.

Back in the Avenger, I slipped it into gear and idled around the pond before heading down the draw. I watched in my rearview mirror until the house was hidden from view. Minnie had made her decision.

I let the car roll in whatever direction it wanted to go. Maybe the drive would clear my mind. I went one direction, turned and went another. It didn't matter; they were all the same. One road flowed into another. I was lost in time, thought, and location. I passed an old fashioned road sign that read, "Cassville 6 miles." I hadn't planned to enter the town and skipped taking the exit. A moment later, reacting to an unknown prompt, I swung a right turn onto Mill Road, which led into Cassville. I pulled to a stop on Main Street and waited for the green light.

The turn had brought me to the city center or what there was of one. At two in the afternoon, there wasn't much activity. Not much different than any other time of the day. Part of the charm of a sparsely populated hamlet was the lack of crowded roadways. I let my Avenger drift through the streets while I kept an eye out for Duke. We had unfinished business. His abusive behavior and my Palatini oath were on a collision course. I promised to protect the innocent and I wasn't willing to let it slide any longer. Why should I turn a blind eye like all the others had done in Minnie's life?

I wanted to give Joyce a call and bring her up to speed on what I'd seen at Dixon's, but why bother. She wasn't on board with the idea of rough and tumble, and that's what it was going to take to get the point across. Victories are won in the will of the warrior's heart. Or, as one old sage counseled me, "You've got to have a want to." She didn't have what it took to defeat Duke at his game. I did.

I swung into a fast food joint to get a cup of Java. After I'd paid the cashier, I pushed the lid down tight for the car ride and headed toward the exit. That was as far as I made it. Jay Landers stepped through the door and immediately stopped me in my tracks.

"Wait up. Grab us a booth, okay?"

I slipped into a booth with my back to the wall. I let Landers sit with his back exposed to the entrance. When he joined me, he never noticed the seating arrangements. His mind was on what he wanted to say. For some reason, it bothered me. Someday, when he's gone through enough trials by fire, he'd develop the "Gunfighter syndrome." From then on he'd never leave his back exposed.

Landers brought burgers and fries to the table, enough for the both of us. I nibbled on the tasty morsels and sipped my coffee. Jay appeared to be in a hurry. With his mouth half full and between bites he said, "The Sheriff's Department received a positive ID on the dead girl. They're not releasing her name. She was twelve-years-old."

"From Alaska?"

"It was her." I could see Landers liked to be right. He leaned forward and whispered, "The abduction was reported eight weeks ago."

"Eight weeks ago. Why was she all the way down here?"

"Exactly?"

"Jay, that means your anonymous source was spot-on. Whoever she is, she has firsthand knowledge, and she wanted you to know the truth."

Landers sat back, stuffed a handful of fries in his mouth, and blurted out, "Weird, huh?"

"Listen, Jay, you and your source might be in danger. Whoever the killer is, he knows the person that called you. There's no other explanation how she knew the details. If you refer to a source other than police in your writings, the killer might figure out who squealed. It might be the reason you haven't heard from her since the initial contact. She might already be a victim. Whoever she is, she's in a perilous position."

"I can't help her unless she calls again."

"True." Landers had no idea I'd been struggling with a similar situation for the past twenty-four hours. Minnie needed help the same way his source needed help. Scenarios of this nature, left unresolved, frequently spiraled out of control. I've found it a difficult task to get people to see the only way out alive required them to take drastic measures. The sad fact in Minnie's case was she chose not to help herself when she had the chance. Now I had to do it my way. Landers source might not have had an option either. She too made a choice—a wrong choice. Instead of letting the cat out of the bag with a reporter, the right thing was to call the cops. But, she didn't. She wanted Landers to do the dirty work and bring out the story. That's the way I saw it.

"Does the Sheriff have any idea how this kid got to Missouri?"

"Detectives say they have leads, but I seriously doubt they have anything substantial. They are asking the public for help."

"You're aware a kidnapping and murder across state boundaries means FBI involvement?"

"Hadn't thought about that angle. It's becoming a bigger story."

"Play your cards right and you'll get national coverage."

We finished up, and I thanked Landers for the grub. At the exit, he turned toward me, "I'm heading to my office. I'm going to pray the caller is still alive, and God will put a bug in her ear."

"I didn't take you to be a religious man, Jay."

"I'm not, but it can't hurt to try."

"Don't forget to follow up the FBI angle."

He winked and pointed his finger at me as he walked backward out the double entry doors. Landers was out of the parking lot before I'd refilled my coffee. I climbed into the Avenger and set out on the hunt. The heat index had the makings of a dog day afternoon.

Chapter 6

"No plan survives contact with the enemy."
—Helmuth Von Molkte

Seated behind the steering wheel of my Avenger, I crisscrossed Cassville's streets in search for the reason of my unhappiness. With every turn of the wheels, my resolve to end Duke's reign of terror grew.

The main drag through town was exactly that, a real drag. The monotony wore on me, adding to my frustration with every passing second. The day was growing long, and I wanted to make things happen. Driving around wasn't getting the job done. Joyce had invited me to hang out with her old gang at a bar in Cassville. I'd declined but found myself wishing I'd paid closer attention to what she'd said. The name of the joint escaped me. Duke liked his beer and he liked to brag and run his mouth. Assuming I found the watering hole, I'd find Duke too. It was the best lead I had. I followed it.

It was four-forty-five when I spotted Dixon's camouflaged pickup parked on the 9th Street side of a rustic tavern. The hand-painted branch and leaf design didn't help it blend in well with its urban surroundings.

Whether this was the place, Joyce had talked about didn't matter. I'd found what I'd been looking for. I swung in and parked on the East Street side next to a chain-link fence. Above the Avenger stood a large neon sign displaying the bars name, "Two Steppin' Lounge."

Rarely have I had the opportunity to nip a tragedy in the bud. Vigilante operations typically involved after-the-fact assassinations to resolve a problem. What were the parameters of engagement I could employ to avoid further pain and destruction of innocent life? I was the sole interpreter of my Palatini oath. If it meant straining it to the edge of justification, so be it.

The bar's exterior, clothed in Western Red Cedar siding, showed its wear and tear from years of service. The entrance, located on 9th Street, had a narrow unimposing doorway. Windows lined the entrance side of the building. Each one nearly blacked out by alcohol and tobacco decals, posters, and an occasional neon sign. The East Street side had no windows at all.

Had this joint been located in Buffalo or Toronto, it would've been a gangster hangout. In Cassville, the place had redneck written all over it. Just the kind of place I would expect to find the likes of Duke.

I stepped inside the door and made my way up the inclined ramp leading to the main floor. It was everything I expected it to be, dark, drab and dreary. My first impression was I'd stepped into an unfriendly cavernous pit. I'd been in a dozen places like this old watering hole, and maybe some worse. If the need arose, I wasn't above being unfriendly too.

I've always tried to maintain a positive outlook, and I saw the good news here as well. Duke was bellied up to the well-worn, but once eloquent, mahogany bar with his back to the door, and alone, just the way I wanted him. To extract someone from a public place without making a scene was impossible. The key was fishing—not hunting. A skilled master of deception with a naturally cunning aptitude was able to walk a target straight out the front door under their volition. All the target had to do was swallow the bait.

I wanted to have our talk privately, but if Minnie had spoken with Duke, we'd likely rock-n-roll right here on the fifty-foot dance floor. My hands tightened into clinched fists. I stood at his right elbow and watched for a minute. He never looked up from his beer. From the lack of attention he paid to movement in his surroundings or entry into the bar, I surmised he wasn't waiting for anyone else to arrive.

Duke was a southpaw. To most people, such an observation was trivial. But, I'm not most people. Ingrained in my nature, I've habitually analyzed and evaluated those that have aroused my interest. I shook off my defensive posture and relaxed. Casually I slipped up to the polished bar which I guessed to be more than a hundred years old—it looked out of place in this Redneck setting. Duke sat to my left. If he reacted badly to my presence and tossed a sucker punch in my direction, he'd have to cross his body with his left to be effective. If he threw his right instead, it would be more like a warning shot that the fight was on. What he could do from a barstool didn't concern me at all.

"Barkeep, how about a round of drinks for Duke and me."

Behind the counter, a wrinkly skinned, white-haired old codger with gizzard jowls croaked out, "Whatcha drinkin' buddy?"

"Whatever Duke's having is fine with me."

The bartender brought two glasses of the cheapest draft on tap, set one glass in front of Duke and the other in front of me. His raspy voice strained, "That'll be two bucks."

I pulled out three Susan B. Anthony's that I wanted to get rid of, and slid the coins across the counter top.

"Keep the change, pal."

The old codger grumbled something, but my attention was on the seat next to me. I glanced over at Duke, who'd eyeballed me hard while I was ordering our beers. I stayed ready to react. I had my doubts he'd erupt into a full-blown fight, but I didn't put it past him to get mouthy and make a scene. With my beer in hand, I said, "I don't think we got off on the right foot. Maybe I don't belong around here." I waited for his response. Slowly, he picked up the fresh draft and took a healthy chug, downing nearly half the glass. I took a sip and pretended to like the nasty taste. I was only human. I wouldn't be able to carry out this façade for long. Not without switching to whiskey.

"You know I don't like ya none, don't ya?" It was apparent from his casual demeanor he hadn't spoken with Minnie or she'd wised up and kept her mouth shut about my visit.

"That's something we'll both have to live with until I leave." I threw out the bait. It was a tiny morsel, but enough to give him hope that I'd soon leave Shell Knob.

"Thought you were going to stay around here and work for the papers?"

"Nah, it was just talk. I like the bigger cities and the action they bring."

"So why'd you track me down?"

"I wasn't looking for you. I didn't know you were here. I'd met with Landers, the newspaper guy, and gave him a few tips on that murdered girl story. I ditched the ol' lady and ended up here. I'm a loner and need a break now and then. That's all."

A look of concern came over Duke. He stumbled with his question. I thought his uneasiness was about me, but it took on a different form. "This feller Landers, ah, he still be diggin' up lies 'bout that thar dead girl? I swear he ain't got nothin' else better to do than spin scary bogeyman tales. We knowed it were some city feller that dumped her off alongside the road then took on off. Landers just wants to sell papers. Bury it and her too. That's what I say." Duke stroked his short black beard with his left hand.

For a brief moment, while Duke spoke his opinion on Jay's motivation, my thoughts drifted to the blood that flowed like a natural spring from the ground. Suddenly, the blood burst into the air as if it were an oil geyser, filling the air with a red mist. I startled.

"Am I boring you?"

"No, I think I have low blood sugar."

"Yeah, well I want to be clear about something."

"Shoot."

"Joyce is my friend and y'all ar' together." Duke paused. His face grimaced. His words hadn't set well with him and had choked out slowly. "Like friends." Conflicted, he struggled to label Joyce and my relationship. Duke wasn't the kind of guy who chose his words wisely, but he'd made an exception. The hair rose on the back of my neck.

Regardless of how he described the bond Joyce and I had, it wouldn't meet up to his liking. He was between a rock and a hard place, and he knew it. He'd tried to influence our relationship, but he'd failed miserably.

"I can't do much 'bout y'all bein' friends. That's her doin', so I'm gonna overlook my feelin's 'bout you."

"Joyce will appreciate that."

Admittedly, at the forefront of my mind were thoughts of leading Duke out the door without anyone having noticed us together. To do so, I'd have to entice him. One of the great things about Duke was the immense size of his ego. Sugar coated words quickly attracted him. I bought another round of drinks and laid the sticky words on thick. "Duke, you're a standup guy. You spoke from the heart, and I want to compliment you on that." I found my presentation more difficult than I'd anticipated. "You've been a close friend of Joyce and that means a lot. From what Joyce has told me about you, you're a natural born leader in the community."

Over the next half hour, I expounded on what he was not, as if he possessed those attributes. His behavior toward me had become favorable as we made headway amending our rocky past.

My goal to walk him out the front door was within reach. Then his education would follow. Before we ended our talk, I wanted him to comprehend he was a worthless, wife-abusing, piece of human garbage that had manipulated, dominated and abused Minnie. His comprehension of how he'd failed as a husband and led to her destruction was paramount to the lesson.

"Ya knowed, we'd sure 'nuff got off on a wrong foot. I'd like to make it up to y'all. How 'bout I show you 'round my camp one of these days?"

My hackles rose higher than before. It was the opportunity I'd been looking for, but something didn't feel right. My motives drove my actions, but what had brought about this change in his behavior?" Tasty-sweet sounding words weren't enough. Remembering Duke's Jekyll and Hyde personality coupled with the insincere tone to his words brought caution to the forefront. Maybe it was his turn to fatten the calf.

I was a sucker for a good game. I put a smile on my face and mustered all the excitement I could. "That would be great."

Duke perked up, "Hell, ya ain't doin' nothin' right now, let's take a trip over thar way." He gave a nod toward the exit with his head and said, "I can show you the ropes." A feeling crept over me as he spoke the word ropes. It was exactly his intention.

I wanted to know more about the Alliance and Vigilance Committee. The only way that would happen was to get close to the source. I shared much of the same ideology as the Second Amendment Patriots and the prepper survivalists. From what I knew about the Vigilance Committee they, too, bore similarities to the Palatini. But, Duke's words were cheap and echoed with a hollow ring. He was every bit as insincere as I was, and conceivably as good at spreading lies. Maybe Duke thought he could make a sucker out of me, but he didn't know the real me. It was the Ace up my sleeve with whatever plan he was hatching. He'd tried to put my mind at ease, but had only succeeded in heightening my awareness to potential danger. The set up wasn't good. If things got out of control, I was without my weapon.

I wasn't buying what he shoveled in my direction, but I couldn't resist the challenge. I mentally overlooked the pun as I replied, "Sure, I'm game." Duke had set himself up as the hunter and hunters always feel superior to their prey. If I were Bambi and Duke the hunter, it would be true. Duke had plenty of deer heads, and antlers mounted on the walls of his house that proved he was capable. But he didn't have bodies in a bag. In our game, Duke had failed to consider that the hunter and the hunted were one in the same.

We finished our beer and left the bar. Once outside, Duke pointed to his pickup and said, "Jump in." Exactly the approach I would've taken if I'd planned to do him bodily harm. We backed out of the parking space and headed south.

If timing was everything, then the right place was equally important. Duke's rig wasn't a choice place to conduct business; neither was the compound. I'd have to endure his arrogance and constant self-aggrandizing until we were on the return trip to the bar. That would be the ideal time to hammer out our differences. The route to Cassville would take us through the same remote backcountry by which we'd traveled. The darkness of night would provide me with the perfect ally. All I needed was an excuse to stop. At that point, I'd kick around a few of my ideas with Duke and see where that took us.

First, I'd deal with whatever hair-brained scheme he'd hatched, which piqued my interest. He hadn't cooked his plan up during the past hour at the bar. It was an idea that had lain dormant in his mind for days or weeks then brought to fruition through opportunity. This new friendship pact he'd so quickly agreed to merely smooth the waters to carry out his plan. I wasn't paranoid; I was prepared. Duke had no way of knowing he wasn't the only one working behind the scenes.

While I waited for the right time and place, I'd ask questions about the Vigilance Committee. If they were a force for good as were the Palatini, I wanted to help them achieve success. Minnie was aware that I'd snooped through the training camp on the day Joyce, and I visited, but Duke remained unaware. Then again, maybe she'd told him. I had no way to be certain.

The compound was home turf. If he intended to unfold his plan, this was likely his best opportunity. There was a point to be made for holding the home field advantage. The cyclone fencing and concertina wire ensured our time would be uninterrupted. My gut clenched as I reacted to instinct. The prospect for an exciting evening was only starting.

Duke's setup would be simple because he was the product of a simple mind. I was poised to react when he launched his plan. I'd seize the initiative before he was able to bring it to fruition. Under no circumstance was I willing to allow him to demonstrate a weapon or display one. That's how accidents happen. An unexplainable weapons misfire and I'd end up with a hole in my head. Escaping the blame would only require him to convince a jury of his peers that he was innocent. I wasn't going to chance that happening.

We'd barely cleared the outskirts of Cassville when Duke started to rattle out the nuts and bolts of his survival camp operation. Most of what he said was old news. In a matter of minutes, Duke had gone from standard survival topics to weird. "You never heard 'bout the zombie apocalypse?"

I guarded my sarcasm as best I could, but zombies? I was at a loss for words. His IQ took a nose dive, and in my estimation, he couldn't afford to lose any points. Nonetheless, I shined him on. "Sure, who hasn't?"

"Well, it's a comin'." Duke's deep set eyes flickered from the reflection of dashboard lighting.

I took from his response that he was sincere. None of the brochures alluded to an imminent zombie invasion. He had an inside track on what most people didn't know. "Yeah, they're like half dead people or something, right."

Duke continued, "Most city folks don't know what I'm tellin' you, but zombies ain't dead nothin'. They be to livin' just like you and me."

His smile drifted up one side of his mouth and into an arrogant sneer. "Think 'bout this here, when the economy collapses, and everybody is fallin' part, what's people gonna do?"

"Starve."

"I don't think so. They'll turn into rovin' bands of parasites tryin' to escape starvation."

Duke did have a point and patiently waited for my comment. Through catastrophic events, the weak, elderly, feeble, sick, and very young were weeded out first. It was part of the cycle of Nature. The concept Darwin had put forth—survival of the fittest. Duke doubted that anyone caught unprepared would be capable of lasting until post-apocalyptic Nature preserved the remnants of the human race, but I intended to be one of them. "Then they'll die as scavengers and bottom-feeders."

"You be right 'bout that; they'll die alright. What's a gonna happen, hungry folks gonna empty out from big cities and into our areas, scavenging food, and water wherever they can find it. There'll be hordes at first. Soon they'll become like zombies, sick, diseased, and cannibalistic. They'll be a doin' anythin' to survive. That be where we come in."

"The survivalists are going to help the starving people?" Duke wasn't a humanitarian type of guy. He was all about Duke, and that didn't leave room for anyone else.

"Not exactly." He bit down on his lower lip as he paused. "Preppers ar' part of a bigger community of survivalists. We ar' prepared for when it begins with food caches, know how's to live off the land, and we sure nuff will protect all our loved ones from the infestation."

"Combating zombies, who would have guessed?"

"And tell you what, bein' a newspaper man and all ain't gonna keep you alive none. Armed survivalists gonna be the only ones to make it."

I pretended to ponder as he spoke. I wasn't about to let myself become entangled in his web of words and distraction. Duke's ego had become my most valuable tool to use against him. Preoccupied completely with himself, he couldn't stop pointing out his skills and abilities. The more questions he answered, the more condescending he became.

"We ar' teachin' and doin' survival under any situation. See, there's things y'all never think about until it be too late. Simple things, like how's to manage water. Most folks'll never think 'bout it, but what'll you do without no water? Y'all be faced with all sorts of contaminants and diseases. You better knowed how to get blood out of a turnip."

"Are you saying you can survive in any situation?"

"A sight better than most. I'll tell you that."

"I guess I'm destined to hunt, fish, and dig up grub worms, so I don't die when everything hits the fan."

"That there's what's wrong with y'all city fellers," Duke scoffed. "Survivin's only the half of it. There's more, a whole lot more." Duke lost his smile, and the tone of his words became terse. "I prepare fellers like you in my trainin' camp. Weak fellers that would die if they's didn't have me to help 'em."

I let the insult slide. "What do you teach, Duke?"

"All of it. But I'm sought after mostly to teach on weapons and tactical skills. I don't guess you knowed what that be?"

"No, I learned to survive with a pad and pencil."

Duke sneered.

We turned onto Highway 86 toward Duke's place. I was happy to see the turn into Dixon Holler. A sane person could only listen to Duke run off at the mouth for so long. We climbed the red clay ravine of the holler; darkness had already crept in. The moonless draw shrouded in trees had taken on sinister features, and shadows loomed. We followed the incline until the house came into view. Duke swung his pickup to the far right of the driveway and passed by the house.

"Are we stopping at the house? Joyce would want me to say hello to Minnie."

"Maybe some other time, Stud." Duke bit his words off tight.

Duke pulled his rig in front of the compound activating the motion sensor which lit a string of high-pressure mercury vapor lamps and slowly all quadrants of the fence line took on a ghostly haze. The partial illumination of the concertina wire woven to the top of the chain link fence resembled a World War II prisoner of war camp. This was the look Duke intended when he constructed the compound. Intimidating.

Duke opened one side of the double doors and held it open for me. "Go ahead." I didn't view it as a considerate gesture. Any other day of the week, Duke would've taken the lead position as a sign of his importance. He had something on his mind.

Absent was his cocky behavior. That wasn't Duke; that was Mister Hyde. The scenario was ripe. His actions and words convinced me he was up to no good, and he would likely make his play soon. I walked through the entryway, stepped to one side, and waited. I had no intentions of walking in front of a guy who had size on me. Besides, supposedly, I'd never been in the place.

Duke provided a superficial tour of the classroom to include pointing out each picture and article that contained his name or face on the walls. I sat on the corner of the desk with one leg hanging off the edge, and the other foot firmly planted on the floor. Duke handed me a Missouri Alliance pamphlet and recited a rehearsed section from the brochure.

Gibberish. What was he waiting for?

Duke forced eye contact and had the vernacular to sound authentic, yet duplicitous. Duke's piercing gaze intensified as he drew out his sales pitch for the survivalist's way of life. He no longer had my attention with his boring pretense. The question that burned in my mind was whether or not to crank the party up a notch.

"Duke, how's the Vigilance Committee figure in with the survivalist group?"

"It don't. The committee works with local law enforcement to maintain the security and safety of this here community."

Another canned answer.

Duke had been every bit as deceitful with me as I'd been with him. I had to give him credit for that. He hadn't disclosed his agenda with his usual boisterous display of ego. He'd exposed his fraudulent desire to befriend me. I was wise to him, and he knew it.

"Y'all been playin' me, Stud. I don't know if Joyce be in on it too, but you, you been in on it from the start, ain't ya?"

"Just like a fiddle."

Duke laughed, "Yer act's like you don't knowed how to shoot, but you be a lyin' for sure."

"I never said I didn't know how to shoot. What I said was, I didn't like to punch holes in paper targets."

Duke's coal-black eyebrows knit together into one elongated furrow. After a few long seconds of mulling over what I'd said, he replied, "You be a mystery, Stud. I don't like it none when a city slicker shows up out of nowhere and gets involved in my business."

"Old territory, Ace." I paused. I didn't owe him an explanation, and he wasn't going to get one. "I'm a mystery alright. If you're smart, you'll let it go."

Duke wasn't smart. His deep set eyes tightened. "I asked Joyce 'bout you."

"She filled you in, did she?"

"She don't know nothin' 'bout you."

I smirked at him. "I can't tell you how surprised I am to hear that."

"Yeah, smart boy, I had one of my boys run your name through a database. Want to know what they found?"

"Can't wait."

"He come up with nothin' neither." Duke paused as a smile crept across his face. "You ain't who you say's you is buddy-boy. Y'all be tryin' to pull the wool over our eyes 'round here. You be either a con man or a lawman?"

"Neither one, but you'd be better off if I were a lawman." I let that sink in for a minute. "But who I am, isn't what's eating at you, Duke? What bugs you is that I know who you are."

"Be doubtin' that."

"You weren't hard to figure out. Dirty—stinking—wife abusers rarely are."

Duke stepped forward unleashing a fiery outburst of vulgar obscenities. I rose to the occasion, and to my feet—toe to toe.

Of all the things I should've been focused on, what came to mind was how much I had missed the feeling of confrontation. I craved engagement with perpetrators of crimes. Violent criminals were my life and righting the wrongs my mission. Any other existence was meaningless.

"I already done told you, it ain't none of your business what I do with my wife," Duke shouted. "She be mine—my property—I own her. If I want's to beat her, I'll do 'er, and you ain't got nothin' to say 'bout it!"

"See, Duke, right there, that's your problem. You believe you're better than another person. You think you have the right to own Minnie and control her with beatings. Obedience or there will be pain, and that's not the worst of it, you loaded her down with guilt. You made her feel as if your violence and bad behavior were her fault. You're to blame. I see it in your eyes, you're scared. You know it's time to pay up for what you've done." I waited for Duke to comment, but he didn't say anything. Maybe I was getting through to him. "I've seen your type before, and it never ends well for them."

"You're gonna wish you'd never come to Shell Knob before the nights be done. I promise you that much."

I looked into his dark, deep-set eyes and realized the struggle between the two personalities, Doctor Jekyll, and Mister Hyde, was over. Only the evil Hyde remained. In a way, I understood how scary it was for Minnie to watch his transformation when Hyde prevailed.

I smiled. It was the kind of smile that had provocation written all over it. Duke had better sense than to try and intimidate me with threats and his ugly looks. He'd tried before and failed. He was a big frog in a little pond. All his croaking had worked for him in the past, and he had the corner on ugliness, but in reality he wasn't a badass and couldn't back his play.

For a moment, I suspected Duke was mimicking me with his smile, but it wasn't a smile at all. It was a snarl without a growl. He'd become too tongue-tied to speak or too furious to think. Maybe both.

It wasn't my plan, this was his, but it worked for me as well. We were on our way to having our issues on the table and ironed out.

I'd impugned his character and insulted his beliefs. He'd acted froggy but didn't jump. We should've been past the awkward moment when you've asked somebody to dance, and they've agreed, but nobody was rockin'-and-rollin'. He'd left it to me to lead.

I'd questioned whether the compound was the right place to sort out our issues. As it turned out, the classroom was apropos for the lesson. I needed no further incentive to polish the floor with this dirtbag, but I wanted him to have a taste of his behavior. When he was sufficiently humiliated, disrespected, intimidated, and beaten to a pulp, then I'd consider summing up my lesson.

Suddenly, Duke lost interest in what I'd said and broke eye contact. The unmistakable sound of a door creaked in the distance.

My heart sunk for a moment as I feared Minnie had arrived, and I didn't want her to witness what was going down. Duke turned to his left and looked over his shoulder as the mysterious door situated at the back corner of the room opened.

We weren't alone anymore, but it wasn't Minnie who'd entered the room. Three men quietly filed in, decked out in paramilitary garb, with their tiger-striped jungle pants bloused over black combat boots. It was all very stylish and impressive if you were part of the Aryan scene. Each man wore matching black T-shirts that read like a billboard advertisement, Alaska Arctic Alliance Survival Training. It went well with their black A-Team ball caps.

The visitors didn't say a word. They stood motionless against the north wall as if they were spectators waiting for a gladiatorial match to begin. Maybe they were. I didn't like the intrusion, but I wasn't going to let them interrupt the lesson. Duke turned back in my direction wearing a new smile, confident and cocky.

I assumed the worst—I'd underestimated my adversary. Duke was smarter than I'd given him credit. I'd let my disdain for him trump my usual cautionary approach. I'd been overconfident to think I was holding all the cards when it was Duke who had stacked the deck. I'd play the hand that was dealt and see who ended up with the chips— I had no choice.

"Pals of yours?" I asked. The question was intended to be rhetorical, but Duke wasn't the brightest candle in the camp.

"Close friends, you might say."

"What's the A stand for on the hat?" I asked. With these guys, there were a lot of possibilities for defining A. Right off the top of my head I only thought of one that fit.

Duke held all the cards in his hand but one—guts. His odds were favorable, but he didn't make his play. It was a sign. With all his advantages, he lacked what it took to make a move. Duke was a tough guy to his wife because he smacked her around enough, but that didn't take courage. His life experiences had taught him he could run his mouth without paying the consequences. People were intimidated and backed down because of his size, but it didn't take bravery to talk loud and ugly. What he truly lacked was nerve.

Starting early in life, big guys rarely had to fight. If they did, they rarely tangled with other big guys. They picked on guys half their size. On the other hand, smaller guys grew tougher and didn't let an adversary's size influence them. I was one of the little guys growing up.

Up until now, Duke's mouth and atrocious actions hadn't cost him much pain. He'd briefly tasted my swift response when I shut him down in front of Joyce. I wouldn't let him talk foul to her or let him intimidate me with his finger pointing.

Now, face to face with me again, he found himself in a predicament. If we danced, his buddies would see him get beat down. In the process, they'd also hear why.

"I think you be a scared little man," Duke said.

"You've thought wrong then. I've never been afraid of anything. Being scared doesn't serve a useful purpose. I'm not like you Duke—I'm no coward."

He winced. Evidently, truth does hurt.

Chapter 7

"The price of anything is the amount of life you exchange for it."
—Henry David Thoreau

With their backs to the wall, the A-team moved slowly in my direction.

"You here to watch?" I asked. The lockstep Nazi looking bunch didn't respond with words, but from the look on their faces I surmised they were more than spectators. As the Alaskans drew closer, I thought about something that I should've thought about before—alliances. Landers had questioned out loud, how could the murdered girl have gotten from Alaska to Shell Knob? I figured I'd stumbled upon the "how." If I pegged them right, I'd stumbled into a hornet's nest too.

I tossed out a word that started with "A" that would match their ball caps logo. I made sure they heard me, so I said it again and made it sound nastier than it had the first time. The lesson I had for Duke would have to be shelved for a newer idea that had come to mind. If I was wrong about the Alaskan crew being the connection, then I could revisit the education process with Duke at a more appropriate time and setting.

A prompt from my spirit told me to disrupt the showdown that had begun to take shape on their terms. I figured I'd sling a little mud around and see where it stuck. If my suspicions were correct, the A-Team would respond. If they'd killed the girl, they'd likely die before they let me leave the room. I wouldn't have it any other way.

I whispered to Duke, "Why'd you kill the girl?" He went stiff as a board and rapidly blinked. His behavior screamed of guilt. I repeated what I'd said to Duke, only louder for everyone to hear. The A-team stopped in their tracks. My accusation had caught them off guard. In shock and disbelief, their eyes widened, and mouths hung open. Guilt had taken up residence in their demeanor.

Shaken to the core, they lost their focus. It wasn't the way innocent men reacted. Their subtle communications through an exchange of glances had caught my attention. All eyes levelled on Duke.

But Duke was a natural born liar and quickly recovered. He shook his head ever so slightly providing a momentary degree of assurance for the Alliance, but their security was fleeting. The cat was out of the bag, and their situation quickly turned grim. Without a weapon, my only recourse was to exploit their guilt to my advantage.

"Duke, did you hear what I asked?"

Duke took a step back. His deep-set eyes narrowed. "You don't knowed near as much as you think you do."

"Wanna bet."

The fact was; I did know more about the case than had been released to the public. If I impressed the Alliance with my knowledge, I would have to deal with the consequences.

After the initial shock, a snarly look replaced Duke's cocky smile. He stood up big and tall, but his cowardice still showed. The way I had it figured, he'd get the Alliance to do the dirty work. To some degree, I'd helped Duke out with his plan. I'd scared the bejesus out of the Alliance with my spot-on accusation. If Duke's intention was to get them riled, I'd provided the catalyst to make it happen.

Up until this point, what I'd learned about the Alaskan Alliance was neatly inscribed on a tri-fold brochure. Now that I'd hit a chord over the dead girl I was in a position to gain first-hand knowledge of how they operated. So far, I wasn't impressed with what I saw. They were disorganized and without any clear-cut leadership calling the shots. I, on the other hand, was a strategist and tactician. When they moved closer, I played my hand.

The Alaskans lined up in a staggered row at Duke's left side. I looked at a fat pudgy guy and addressed him. "You look like smart guys. If so, you'd be interested in knowing where I picked up my information." I said it fast but spoke precisely. A slow expression of thoughts won't unnerve criminal types. You come off as unsure of your position. I wanted to impress on them that I was confident with my allegations.

I considered the possibility of the Alliance's loyalties becoming conflicted. But, I understood camaraderie. Whether they were right or wrong, in the end they'd likely stick together. Conscience might get a grip on one of them, but I couldn't count on it, and it wouldn't happen while they were grouped together. These were guys that had prepared to have each other's backs to survive. How would this situation be any different for them? Regardless of the question I asked myself, the conclusion came up the same. I was a threat to their survival. They had to eliminate the threat.

What the scenario had boiled down to was one of time and timing. I was buying time to sow seeds of fear, discord, and mistrust. I wanted their level of concern to inhibit their allegiance with one another, as much as possible. I wanted them in a state of confusion. The more time they gave me, the more I could create. I wasn't above lying to them either. In the end, it wasn't going to be a fight to win or lose; it would be combat—live or die.

The A-Team looked restless, so I threw them another bone to chew. "What I know came straight from the cops. I'd think that would be disconcerting—if I were the guilty party." They didn't move a muscle. Hardened criminals would've blown it off without concern. These guys were petrified. Guilt coupled with the idea of a felony rap weighed heavily on their minds and sent a chill to their core. For the moment, they were frozen in place.

"He's bluffing!" Duke's big mouth bellowed.

It was time to play another round. I was willing to show my hand, but the money on the table had to be right. I looked to the A-Team and said, "Sure, listen to your good buddy Duke. He'll steer you in the right direction." Then I laughed. "I'm sure he's been real helpful so far." I looked back at Duke and laughed again, louder.

If my hunch proved true, the Alaskan Alliance had the most to lose. I continued to play, "I know one or all of you are aware of everything that happened. Whichever of you that I'm talking to, you know the whole story of the dead girl."

"You is just talkin' in riddles," Duke said.

"The reason I know is because one of you is a snitch."

All eyes were drawn to Duke. I let my bet ride. I didn't mention it was a female caller. Why should I? I was running a bluff, and the Alliance was hanging on my every word.

"That's right—you've got a rat in your midst, and I know it was only one person that made the call." Duke's response to the crew was short and sweet. He only shook his head and said, "He's lying."

I was amazed that only Duke spoke up to refute my claim. "Deny it all you want Duke. I don't know who phoned it in or why. That's not my gig. I'm a reporter. I write the news and write it the way I see it."

"You're a joke," Duke said.

I looked over the crowd; no one was laughing. "One of you in this room reported the murder of the kidnapped girl from Palmer, Alaska. How's that for a lucky guess?" I let it take hold in their mindset. I'd levelled with them. I looked at Duke, "Who's the joker now?"

Duke stepped back, one step, then another. The A-Team's glances at Duke became piercing glares. He didn't have an answer this time. I was winning the battle without firing a shot. The Alaskans huddled together into a semi-circle and whispered amongst each other. It was the first sign of organization I'd seen amongst the Alliance. It wasn't a good sign either. I'd been operating fine in the chaos.

Eyebrows wrinkled as they looked in my direction and talked amongst themselves. One guy with a ponytail put his finger to his mouth and started gnawing on his fingernail. Next to Ponytail stood a stocky built guy with an old-fashioned flattop who had mumbled a few threatening cuss words toward me. The short, pudgy man, who could have passed for a fat pug dog on two legs, turned to me and cleared his throat a couple times. He looked as if he wanted to talk, but just stood there gurgling on his saliva.

What I'd been privy to was taking top billing with these guys. My guesswork had paid off. I'd gained the upper hand.

My attention focused on a game of death. I considered ways to play another round. I reached behind my back and acted as if I adjusted something at my waistline. It was enough to throw the room into a panic.

"What's he got there," Flattop yelled. Members scattered looking for cover and concealment.

"A gun—he's got a gun!" Ponytail shouted.

Duke barked, "He ain't got no gun." He measured me with his eyes. "He ain't man enough for that."

"Tough talk for a woman beater," I scoffed. "How are you with men?"

Fifteen minutes earlier, the only beef the Alaskans had with me was support for their pal, Duke. Now, I'd revealed myself as presumably dangerous to them. Duke motioned for the others to step forward. The A-Team regrouped but hadn't moved close enough to bum-rush me. Their hesitance empowered me.

I had no intention of letting Duke get away. I could hunt these Alliance clowns down at a later date, but I wanted Duke. Careful planning was preparatory to a mission. It was time for action. I stepped toward Duke as the aggressor. My action was confrontational and tactical. I'd put Duke's big frame between me and the wannabe Aryan commandos. Duke bowed up, ready to fight, but it was all show. If I had a pin, I could've burst his bubble. Adrenaline flowed. I had the position I wanted and stayed relaxed, allowing for a faster strike.

Duke and the Alliance were a clueless pack of amateurs. Without clear leadership emerging, the situation continued chaotic.

Duke acted confident I was unarmed. The Alaskan's were reserved. Ponytail evidently had a brain flash and cried out, "He's wired for sound. That's what he has, a transmitter." The A-Team responded and stepped back from the fight. Duke stood all alone. I couldn't resist the temptation.

I slammed a right cross into Duke's throat, and he buckled to his knees. A-Team members moved near Duke's left side in a diagonal fashion, Pug leading the way. More amateur moves on their part. If they'd known what they were doing, they would've spread out and surrounded me, but they didn't. I maintained a position to use their movement against them if they tried to come at me all at once.

Amateurs have a history of unpredictability. I've never found a way to know when or what tactical mistake an amateur would make. With these guys, I could expect a foolhardy move to happen at any moment.

The Alliance had practiced a bunch of canned scripts for some futuristic condition. Their training hadn't taken on reality. In contrast, I'd spent the past few years' actively stalking, hunting, engaging, and killing people in real-time. Even when I wasn't on a project, I found myself constantly on the prowl. As a natural predator, I watched and noted human behavior. At one point, I thought I'd developed a second nature. I was wrong. It was my only nature.

Fear had gotten the best of Pug, and he acted on it. He charged straight at me, but he was slow. Adrenaline dumped into my system, and I amped up with power. The added surge of energy set in motion a chain reaction of violence. I didn't have time to dodge Pug's attack. Instinctively, years of martial arts training surfaced. I struck viciously like a snake with an overhand finger jab into Pug's eyes and gouged when I hit. He sprawled on the floor. Duke had made it back to his feet and looked for a way to retreat. My façade had worked in my favor. The expectation of a mild-mannered columnist had been shattered. The viciousness of my attack left Pug injured and collapsed on the floor. The fight should have been thrust into full swing, but they were slow to engage.

I capitalized on their momentary hesitation and moved clockwise on Duke, leaving Pug covering his eyes with both hands. Bright red blood poured through his cupped fingers and ran onto the floor. If my jab had hit the mark, his vision, breathing, and thinking would be severely compromised. Blind and vulnerable was good. Mentally shattered was better.

I waited, but the Alaskans tended to their buddy Pug. Duke had the best shot at getting busy, but he tried to back-peddle out of the fray. The A-team tried to figure out their next step. They hadn't taken into account that I would be such a formidable foe. Ponytail angrily yelled something indecent while Flattop spouted a string of expletives. If they weren't all that gung-ho to dance before I stuck my fingers in Pug's eyes, they were quickly trying to psych themselves up now.

Duke tried to fade back from the frontline, but since he wasn't throwing punches, I wanted him right in front of me as a barrier. Limiting the number of attackers that could engage at one time was my strategy. I had to play it smart to beat these guys. The key to survival was combat control.

Ponytail and Flattop left Pug in pain and rushed in my direction. With all my strength, I unleashed an explosive swing into Duke's temple area, and he staggered clumsily. The two Alaskans tried to get a handle on me to grapple, but I wasn't having a wrestling match. If they wanted a piece of me, they'd have to throw down, not roll around. They shouted and cursed as they tried to get a hold on me, but their noise faded as I tossed punch after punch.

To keep the position in the fight, I back-pedaled but kept throwing punches. Flattop took a thump in the beak, and the blood squirted from his nose as if he'd been cut with a knife. I created more distance and kept the action one-on-one. Duke ended up too close, so I grabbed his jacket collar and dragged him with me. He still hadn't thrown a punch. My hands were sore, swelling and covered with blood. Ponytail swung wildly and managed to get in front of Duke, who slipped from my grip and retreated from the fight.

I stepped backward, unable to take over the offensive to attack forward. A flurry of fists flew. There was no way to block or duck to avoid all the punches pounding my face blow after blow.

My eyes swelled, and blood ran freely. I had trouble seeing. Duke finally stepped forward and threw a punch that missed by a foot. His swing left him wide open for a well-placed kick in the groin. He folded over and vanished behind the tiny pack. It was impossible to hit hard or effectively when stepping backward from a fight. A powerful blow caught me in the jaw. I fell back through an open door into an antechamber.

I threw everything I had back into the battle. Flattop went for a leg grab, and I kicked him in the chops dropping him to the floor. Duke bounced from side to side behind the Alaskans but never came to the front again. At some point, Pug re-joined the fray followed by Flattop popping back in too. As a last ditch effort, I used the doorway as a makeshift funnel for my assailants. The bottleneck didn't hold as they clobbered me again and again until they overpowered my position and physically pushed me further into the room.

It was quickly becoming a bloodbath. A red mist filled the air with each blow that connected. If I still had options, I couldn't see them.

I continued to dance on my heels until they had backed me up to a rickety staircase in the room. I lost hope of forcing the Alliance into one-on-one fighting. With three opponents in my face, I couldn't inflict enough damage to change the tide.

For a minute, I held my ground while we exchanged blows. Regardless of how blood-covered and sticky my hands had become, I continued throwing punches. Flattop tightly latched on to me with a headlock in an attempt to wrestle me from the staircase. But the slippery blood worked in my favor. I flipped him off, but lost footing and went down. Duke had either worked up the courage to get back in the fight or by sheer accident had ended up engaged on the front lines again. Duke reached for one of my legs. As he bent forward, I responded with a swift kick. He caught my boot. Not with his hands, but under his chin—full force. He dropped to the floor and didn't move.

The adrenaline had done all it could, but I was weakening. Vertigo loomed with every punch I took. Pug got his hands on one of my feet and pulled forward causing me to fall back. Suddenly, Flattop's face came into my blurred view. My foot connected with his groin, and he toppled to the floor.

Ponytail tried to latch onto my lower legs, and I saw the opening to secure a handful of his hair. With a swift pull, I dragged him forward onto me. Neither Pug nor Duke could get to me for a ground and pound with their pal in the way.

I never lost faith I would survive the fight. I remembered the words of my sensei, "There is always one more thing you can do." So, I acted on the only thing I saw readily available, Ponytail's ear. It wasn't a knockout blow, but my incisors fit nicely over the top of his right ear. I bit down hard and ripped at it with all the brutality I could muster. Ponytail let out a high-pitched scream as he jerked away. I spit the bloody piece of flesh in the direction of the others. I saw the look of horror on their face and heard the fear in their silence.

The mutilated chunk of ear lay on the floor and kept the Alliance at bay until the shock wore off. I rose to my feet. That's as far as I got. Flattop had gotten back on his feet and was taking short choppy steps toward me. It was his turn on the dance floor. I snapped a kick to his groin and chambered a roundhouse kick catching him in the stomach which put him to the floor. The fight went full bore, spitting blood and cussing between kicks and punches. One of the Alliance caught my foot as I'd jammed a kick which drew me into a tangled mess of their hands and feet. I fell backward to the floor. I tried to get to my feet, but they laid into me with their fancy combat boots, kicking, and stomping. Flattop straddled my chest and bludgeoned my face with the savage brutality of both fists in rapid succession.

The pain turned surreal. I no longer felt the blood. I drifted in and out of consciousness. My last thought was of Anna.

Chapter 8

"Luck often enough, will save a man, if his courage hold."
—Bullwyf, 13th Warrior

I wasn't comfortable lying in bed. I was hot one minute and freezing the next. If I'd been able to reach a blanket, I would've covered myself, but I didn't see one next to me. I felt around on my bed for any covering, but I wasn't sure my hands had moved. Drained of energy, I surmised the best course of action was to rest.

Mentally, I was wide awake, yet there was a strange feeling of disconnect from my body. Perhaps it was a temporary paralysis, but if it were, how could I have gotten in that condition? I struggled to move. A sense of confinement set in closely followed by foreboding. I was held a prisoner in my body and caught in a state of limbo. Maybe purgatory I thought, but wouldn't I have to believe to go there? Besides, what was visible to my minds' eye stretched the limits of reality.

I hovered above my body, watching. Time had no relevance. Had an hour passed, a day, or a month? I didn't know. I had no memory of how I'd gotten in the bed, or who had helped me? Where was the bed housed, and how long had my body lay in the bed asleep?

Destiny, my faithful spirit guide, looked as beautiful as ever. I was happy to see her. Even the scenery changed with her appearance. No longer was I the focus of my attention, only Destiny. Her beautiful bronzed skin glowed in the light of day. In all the years I'd known her, she hadn't aged a single day. I hoped to share her future in immortality. Her long blonde hair flowed down over her shoulders and onto her luminous white robe that shined with dazzling intensity. Most impressive were her eyes whose ever-changing color matched her mood. With soft pink lips, she appeared as a work of heavenly art. Angelic. Devine.

Destiny was once a troubled apparition that sought refuge with me. We'd formed a union together as one entity and set out on our Calling. We brought death and destruction to the vilest of criminals. Destiny had chosen me as a travel companion, having forever forged her place in my heart. We brought a sense of purpose and salvation to one another.

It wasn't everyone that had such a spiritual relationship. In fact, I didn't know anyone who admitted to having a familiar spirit as a close friend and ally. I felt honored and unique. We had a rich past. I mused on how unusual our conversations had been, not because she was an apparition, but because Destiny wasn't a big talker.

In my state of limbo, I contemplated our time together. Perhaps it was nothing more than the recollection of my dreams, but that was improbable. If it was only the compilation of memories, how could new thoughts emerge? Destiny extended her hand and lifted me from my place of rest and strolled onto a vast expanse of grassland.

At times, Destiny and I walked hand-in-hand and laughed. On other occasions, it was if I were a third person anonymously watching Destiny and me. I'd never had such a crazy dream if that's what I was experiencing.

Under a tree of antiquity at the edge of the lush grassland I rested. The Caledonian Pine, surrounded in white heather, cast a comforting shadow over where I laid. With arms casually crossed at my waist and eyes closed in peaceful harmony with my surroundings, I found tranquility. Destiny kneeled by my side and stroked the back of my hand with the gentle touch of her fingertips. "I'm awake," I whispered and peeked through one eye at her. She smiled and cupped her hands over mine. I'd found mankind's quest—paradise.

Destiny spoke softly, "Your sojourn in spirit will soon end. Rise from your slumber and carry on your pilgrimage."

An element of confliction plagued me. Regardless of the credence I gave her directive I could not bring myself to rise from my peaceful recline. I'd seen the cruelty of the world. I wanted no further connection.

"War rages," She urged.

"I've fought battles, and I've fought wars. Is there no one else willing to fight?"

"You are chosen."

"I answered my Calling and ran the course that was set before me."

"Blood of the slain call out for vengeance. The battle awaits the conqueror to arise."

I looked to the sky and saw a growing black mass of energy. Destiny held my hands tighter. "Crusader, you are a transient mortal. In time, you will come to the knowledge that you and I have always existed. Many times, over the course of history, we have intervened in the affairs of mankind. Do not fear. You have *One* who has called you to sacrifice. Hear me; no battle is won unless the will exists to fight. Go now and follow your Calling."

Gloomy, dark storm clouds whirled in the skies above, and an eerie darkness overshadowed the land. I looked for further guidance, but I was alone. I shut my eyes and awaited my fate under the old pine tree. A sudden bolt of lightning charged through my body. It brought with its strike an intense pain followed by a spinning sensation. A second bolt struck followed by another. The pain—unmerciful.

Small droplets of rain fell. I tried to open my eyes to seek shelter elsewhere, but couldn't. Involuntarily my body shivered and shook violently. My conscious state of paralysis did nothing to abate the torturous pain. The rain continued its onslaught, endlessly and without mercy.

Unexpectedly, there came a recognizable sound. Near my ear was the buzz of a winged insect—a sound that didn't belong in my dream world. I moved my fingers. At their tips, I could detect the softness of a silty loam mixed with wet grass. I tried to open my eyes but could see just a sliver of light. My head felt like it was jammed between the jaws of a vice and squeezed so tightly that every beat of my heart brought severe pain. I was a long way from Paradise and the refuge of the heather and Caledonian Pine. But each throb brought greater awareness that I'd been reunited with the mortal world, and I was thankful. The pain screamed that I was still alive.

I continued to suffer uncontrollable hot and cold flashes. I was determined to make my body move. I didn't know where I was, but my memory was sufficiently intact to know what had happened. After numerous tries, my right hand touched my face. Letting my fingers continue, they made their way to an eyelid and pried it open to barely a slit. The ability to focus was impaired but after a few minutes I could make out my surroundings. Struggling through the intense pain, I rolled my head to one side. Woodsy terrain opened up into a steep ravine.

I deduced the Alliance had dumped my body for dead as they had the Alaskan girl they'd murdered. The steep hillside suggested I'd been rolled or dragged to my resting spot from an upper location. No one had carried my carcass up from the valley basin. There was no other logical explanation for how I ended up in this place.

As the night fell, a distinct noise reverberated up the canyon from a distance. A truck's Jake brake had roared to life on the valley's decline. A roadway was not far away. Sometime during the night I'd rolled onto my side, the one that hurt the least, and pushed myself upright into a sitting position. At daybreak, I garnered my strength and stood to my feet. A simple undertaking if it weren't for such an unstable equilibrium.

The trek from the dump site to the road was daunting. I was determined to walk horizontally on the steep canyon, angling up or down only as necessary to meet the terrain challenges. Reaching the roadway was my immediate goal.

The rain hadn't been a dream world impression, but a double-edged sword. Cold and unpleasant as the steady drizzle was, it had helped to wash away the caked-on blood from around my hands and face. I'd taken inventory of the physical damage I'd sustained. Most of the injuries were above my waist. Every breath brought pain to my rib cage. Both my hands were badly swollen, and my jaw dislocated or broken. A persistent pressure throughout my head and neck was the cause of my greatest concern.

Daybreak had lit the canyon wall, and I started my climb out. I hadn't traversed twenty yards before I saw the telltale tracks where they'd dragged me down into the ravine. By following the signs back, I'd find the road. I stepped a few feet, rested, then stepped a few feet more. I repeated the process until I'd crested the edge of the roadway.

The Alliance deserved credit for learning from their mistakes. They dumped my body deep into the ravine. The heavily wooded terrain was ideal for hiding the presence of a body from the view of the road and wasn't likely discoverable through happenstance. A lesson they'd learned with their last victim.

The greatest proof these clowns were amateurs I found stuffed in my pockets. They hadn't picked me clean. They didn't concern themselves with my money or wallet. The attack was unplanned, so they hadn't taken into consideration their actions afterwards. Signs indicated they were running scared when they'd left me for dead. What went down hadn't fit their rehearsed scenarios, so they didn't know how to react. They had no contingency plan for body disposal. In their mind, when the day came for the zombie infestation, they'd be shooting at will with no need to hide bodies from the law.

My personal cell phone was the single missing item from my person. My Palatini cell phone had been left in a shoe box tucked under my bed at the resort.

On the opposite side of the road from where I'd climbed the embankment stood a natural brush hedgerow. I hobbled across the asphalt surface and took refuge. If the Alliance had any suspicion that I survived the attack, they might circle back and check on my status. I didn't see any reason to make it easy for them. Barry County's finest could sit this dance out as well. Palatini operators had no need for 9-1-1; we took care of our own rat killing. Our way.

I could see the road downhill a quarter-mile, but perhaps seventy-five to one-hundred yards uphill from where I'd taken sanctuary. The grade of the road coupled with its twisty curves slowed traffic speeds, especially uphill, where I had the best opportunity to choose which ride to stop.

I crouched behind a line of shrubbery to wait but doing so compressed my rib cage and increased the pain. I was forced to stand. I might've eased the pain by lying on my back, but then my view of traffic would be hampered. There wasn't a happy medium; standing was the only option. Over the next hour, I kept watch for traffic. Three vehicles had passed my location, all destined for the bottom of the hill. One pickup came into view traveling northbound in the right direction, but I hesitated to flag the vehicle down being unsure of the occupants. At the sight of a sedan making its way up the hill, I moved from behind the hedgerow and waited.

Two occupants came into view, and the vehicle slowed to a crawl when I stepped out onto the asphalt. They pulled to a stop alongside where I stood. My concern lessened as the travelers appeared to be teenage boys.

The passenger rolled down his window, but his look of shock explained why he didn't say anything.

"Thanks for stopping," I said in a garbled, hoarse voice."

The youngster seated behind the steering wheel reacted as I'd expected when he caught a closer glimpse of me. "What on God's green earth happened to you? You in a car wreck?"

I must have looked like death warmed over with my face battered, bruised and swollen. Remnants of blood and mud complimented my disheveled appearance. I appreciated their startled honesty, but I wasn't in the mood to reciprocate with the truth. "Uh, guys, I knocked off too many last night and it got the best of me." I shot them a cheesy, painful smile. They laughed.

The driver asked, "You weren't driving were yah?"

"Nah, I was riding with friends. I thought they were friends anyhow. Don't really remember the specifics, but I ended up holding the short end of the stick." I took a moment to look around then continued. "The truth is, I don't know how I got here. I remember taking a tumble down that ravine over there." I pointed across the road in the general direction of the valley.

"It's a good thing you weren't driving," the passenger remarked.

"You were a lucky man. You could've gotten yourself seriously hurt," the driver said.

"Well, I think I got the hurt part covered." Again, I tossed them a big, sheepish smile.

The boys had a chuckle at my expense. That was okay; I was happy to liven up their day as long as I got a lift back to town from them.

The guy behind the wheel said, "You need a ride to see a doctor, Mister."

"Don't think that's necessary, but a ride would be much obliged."

The driver asked, "Where you be headin'?"

"Back into Cassville"

The driver looked at me and said, "You're kiddin' right? We're a little ways from Eureka Springs."

"Never heard of it. I'm not from around here, but I left my car in Cassville." I reached into my pocket and pulled out a wad of cash. I peeled off a C-note and held it in the opening of the passenger window. "Would that make it worth your time to run me to Cassville?" The boys smiled a lot then.

The driver shouted, "Joe Don, get in the back. Let this man have a seat up front. We're goin' up to Missouri."

The passenger opened the door, stepped out, and politely invited me to take a seat. I handed the money to the driver and said, "So—we're not in Missouri?"

Joe Don spoke up, "No sir, you're in Arkansas. It ain't that far to go. Maybe an hour and then some."

"What's your name?" The driver asked.

"Walter. Yours?"

"Ricky, and that's Joe Don back there."

"Nice to meet you guys. You came along at the right time." I leaned my head back and closed my eyes. The boys were quiet and respectful, but the pain kept me from sleep. We made a pit stop once along the way. Ricky ran into a gas station convenience store and returned with a plastic bottle of water. He twisted the cap off the bottle and handed it to me. Ricky said, "You need this, you look pretty dry." He was right. Dehydration wasn't aiding my recuperation. Painful or not, I had to push past the soreness in my jaw exacerbated by the sales pitch I'd given the boys for the ride. I thanked Ricky for the water and took several painful sips.

A mile away from Cassville, Joe Don touched my shoulder and let me know we were nearly in the town. I provided Ricky with the general direction of the bar where I'd parked the Avenger. Once we were on Ninth Street, it wasn't difficult to locate the bar. We turned the corner onto East Street and parked next to the chain-link fence. My Avenger sat parked in front of us. In a joking manner, Ricky said, "You might want to stay out of the bar." I nodded.

During the trip back to Cassville, an underlying concern surfaced. What would be my next step if they towed my car? Evidently it had not been an issue for the bar. Duke knew I'd parked the Avenger at the tavern. It was unbelievable he hadn't disposed of my car. Rank amateurs.

"Hey guys, here's a little something for the road." Their eyes lit up when I handed each of them an extra Jackson for their trouble. "You guys are the cream of the crop around here, and I mean that." The boys were all smiles. "Hey, I'd appreciate it if you didn't mention this to anyone. It's embarrassing. It would be better if it didn't get out."

"No problem, Mister," Ricky said.

"What time is it?" I asked.

Joe Don looked at his wristwatch and said, "Five-fifteen."

With my hands swollen in pain, I struggled to operate the door handle inside Ricky's car. Joe Don patiently waited while I manipulated the handle to no avail. Finally, he opened the door from outside the car. I stood to my feet, got my balance, and said, "Thanks." Joe Don jumped in the front seat, slammed the door, and waved out the window as they drove off.

In Cassville happy hour started around four and went until seven. It looked as if the party was well underway. The parking lot was hopping. I moved as quickly as possible to get behind the wheel of my rig. I struggled to get my hand into my pocket. Touching the keys with my fingertips, I managed to catch the key ring with a finger and pull them out. I used my left hand, the one used least in the fight, to operate the key lock and door handle. Once inside I fumbled with the keys until the ignition key was inserted, and the engine started.

A fine dust that had covered the Avenger was a good sign it hadn't been disturbed. I looked the lot over for Duke's pickup; it wasn't to be found. Maybe I was too late for their victory celebration. I backed out and pulled onto the street.

I had a developing situation that worked to my advantage. Duke and the Alaskan's believe me to be dead, to the rest of the people in Barry County I'd vanished into thin air. Every rabbit had a hole to hide in, and I'd find one too. I needed to mend for a while.

At eight-thirty I checked into a small, low budget, motel on the outskirts of Springfield, Missouri. Upscale joints have security features I wanted to avoid and possibly question my appearance as well. Less expensive motels treat all paying customers with the same indifference. No questions asked.

I grabbed my bug-out bag from the car trunk and headed for my room on the first floor. Once inside, I pulled out my spare cell phone and activated it. I placed a call to Anna and left a message with my number for her return call. I placed the phone onto the nightstand and keeled over onto the bed.

I was still stunned from the registration clerk's words "It's Friday." I didn't have reason to doubt the clerk, except that meant I'd lost four days and not one day as I had supposed.

I slept throughout the night and until noon the next day. I struggled off the bed and battled to maintain my balance against the dizziness. I took off my shoes, pulled my dirty clothes off and tossed them in the bathroom sink to wash. I cranked the hot water on high and ran the stream of spray against the tub's sidewall enclosure. I left the plug out so it could run until the hot water ran out. I counted on the steam loosening the caked blood in my sinuses.

When the condensation cleared from the bathroom mirror, I surveyed the damage. What was commonly referred to as black and blue all over was an understatement. Every color of the rainbow was represented. Brown, red, yellow, green and orange spectrums all intermingled. The only notable improvement from the previous day was the deep purple facial swelling around my eyes had diminished.

Pulling spare clothes from the bug-out bag I struggled to dress. Naked was preferable, but out of necessity I got dressed. The motel had furnished a small ice bucket in the room. I wobbled to the first-floor laundry room and retrieved some much-needed ice. Using latex gloves from my bag, I made ice packs. The painful process to control swelling was underway.

When the cell phone rang, I cleared my throat to answer. Drainage of fluids and blood affected my voice box to sound raspy and old in years.

"Hi Walter, did I wake you?"

"Nah, I've been up since noon." I worked hard to pull my thoughts together to say what needed saying.

"Your call was unexpected."

"Listen, I'm kind of in a bad way right now. I could use your help." The lump of pride that had formed in my throat went down hard as I swallowed. Anna knew this wasn't me being a jokester. Joking around wasn't one of my attributes. I was a loner and disdained asking anyone for anything.

"What happened?" Her voice crackled with surprise.

"Do you have plans for the next couple weeks?"

"Are you in the same place as before?"

"Not exactly—but close by."

"All right, I'll call when I have my arrangements completed."

"Good. Use the east side major hub. It'll be closest to where I am."

Ten minutes later, Anna called to confirm her arrival time. We agreed she'd call after she picked up a rental to drive and was southbound on Interstate 44. I'd give her further details at that time.

I took advantage of having a fully stocked bug-out bag. There had been times in the past when stalking a predator I was unable to disengage to find an eatery or convenience store. I wasn't fond of meal replacement drinks and nutritional bars, but on occasion when I'd found them necessary, they were useful. I'd kept my bag stocked for such an emergency, and my present situation qualified.

I cracked the top on a can of Ensure and used the straw off an orange juice container. I drew the room temperature liquid meal through the straw but, in spite of my precautions, it was followed by a double whammy. Pain shot through my jaw and hammered me nearly off my feet. If that wasn't sufficient discomfort, I'd developed a sore throat making matters worse. But regardless of the pain, fluids and nourishment had to be consumed.

I put in place a routine of ice packs, hot showers, and frequent liquid food supplements. My bug-out bag was stocked with containers of Gatorade, Ensure, tomato and orange juices. I tried a relatively soft nutrition bar, but there wasn't a chance I'd be able to chew or swallow any size chunks. The attempt to crunch granola had produced another discovery. All my teeth felt loose. Lucky though, I hadn't lost any in the fight. It was one thing I could smile about, but painful.

Chapter 9

"A friend is a gift you give yourself."
—Robert Louis Stevenson

At five minutes after six I'd polished off the last of the Ensure for my evening meal. Anna had called earlier for directions, and I expected she would arrive soon. While I waited, my thoughts focused on Anna's willingness to help. In my book, she was a heroine. She'd answered the call and dropped everything that was on her plate to aid in my rescue. I hoped she'd stick around a while and nurse me back to health. I couldn't help questioning what my chances were to rekindle our relationship.

Late in the evening, Anna called. "I'm outside in the parking lot."

"Come on in."

The knock was quiet and discreet. I wobbled my way to the door with my .40-caliber in hand. Not that I expected trouble but smart habits don't die. I opened the door, and Anna stepped in quickly. She took a good look at my face then crossed to the dresser a few feet away where she laid her purse and a small tote bag.

I was mildly surprised that she hadn't commented on my appearance. Maybe I didn't look as bad as the mirror reflected. I kept my feet under me fairly well considering the challenge I faced with my equilibrium. Frequent lightheadedness produced a feeling of walking tilted. I thought it amusing until I lost my balance. Fortunately, I was able to grab onto a dresser and hold on until the feeling passed. Hitting the floor wouldn't be as funny as the feeling of walking at an angle on a flat surface.

Two double beds occupied the center of the room. Anna sat me on the edge of one and examined me from head to toe. "I want all your symptoms. Everything you're feeling, and then I want to take a close look at your injuries."

"What are you, a doctor?"

She didn't reply to my sarcasm. She didn't have to. But, the look she gave me wasn't warm and fuzzy either. I hadn't figured Anna for the nurturing type, but she was the only trustworthy person I had in my life that I could call. It took me back to a time when our relationship rocked; now it only felt rocky. I wasn't about to let her dictate the terms of our relationship. However, it was to my benefit to tread lightly. She was now my whole world.

I wasn't a pity party type guy, and I disdained whiners. What had happened was a butt whipping all right but I had manned up for the fight and I'd man up for the pain. I am a Palatini and know the dangers of the world better than most. Aches and pains were the least of my concerns. I would fulfill my Calling and Palatini oath even though there would be more pain to come. There was no escaping my Destiny.

"I just look like a mess; I'm okay."

"Sure you are. You look like you went through a meat grinder in the wrong direction."

Sarcasm aside, the tone of her voice said more than words about the way she felt.

"I need a little help for a day or two. That's all." I tried to soft-sell the idea I'd been pulverized, but she saw through my act.

"Why did you call?"

Fair question, I thought. "In a nutshell, I stumbled across a situation in Shell Knob. Unfortunately, I'm too close to the people involved. I wouldn't be effective at the legwork on the project."

Anna helped me up and steadied my gait by holding my arm as she led me to where the two wood framed tub chairs sat side by side. Anna moved the coffee table out of the way and eased me into one chair then moved her chair next to mine and sat facing me.

I hadn't paid attention to the condition of the motel room or its furnishings until now. I'd been single-focused over the last couple days. With Anna's arrival, I knew the accommodations were beneath her standards and questioned whether the arrangements were adequate for her needs—but they'd have to do for the next few days.

It wasn't so much the simple rectangle design of the room with its adjacent bathroom that was so unappealing. It was the 1960s vintage look. Out-of-date dark laminate wood furniture, coupled with dark-green shag carpet with olive-drab wallpaper, set the mood. Dreary.

Anna saw that I was uncomfortable and responded with gentle care. She removed the two throw pillows from her chair and tucked them in alongside my shoulders. She gave me a quick kiss on the forehead and sat back down. With folded hands on her lap she asked, "Tell me about the project."

"First, I'd like to apologize for the accommodations, funds were tight." Maybe it wasn't necessary to bring it up, but Anna was accustomed to finer living. On our first mission in Thailand, we stayed at a beautiful resort in Bang Saen on the South China Sea. From Thailand, we flew to Milan, Italy and traveled to Bellagio, on Lake Como. We spent a few days chilling out as guests at the Grand Hotel Villa Serbelloni, a luxurious five-star hotel. She hooks up with me and now finds herself in a Springfield dump.

Anna sighed, "That's foolish. Now, I want to hear about the project."

I left out most of the particulars concerning Joyce. I had an inkling it would be in poor taste and not warmly received. Instead, I concentrated on what would be considered a Palatini mission in Anna's eyes.

The hook in every project was the victim. Anna wouldn't pass up an opportunity to seek vengeance for an abused and murdered girl. All assassins of our creed believed rapists and murderers that committed such vile crimes would strike again.

Anna interrogated me until I had to call a halt to the questions for the night. I understood what she was doing; she was building a foundation for the project she had in mind. In my current condition, I had limitations. What I needed was tender loving care. I might've called the wrong person.

"Can you help me with these bandages? You don't have to know what to do, I'll tell you."

"I know what to do. I worked on an ambulance crew while I attended college. I haven't forgotten everything in twenty years." She paused and assessed my condition. Anna pushed and prodded in various areas, creating pain that I hadn't experienced prior to her examination. When she'd completed her assessment, she removed my clothes, placed me in the bathtub, turned on the hot water, and scrubbed me down. I wasn't sure I liked the treatment. Perhaps I was reading into it a level of punishment for my behavior toward her. Regardless, I refused to whimper no matter how much she hurt me, deliberately or not. She cleaned out the lacerations, applied antiseptic and bandaged the wounds.

"I have pain medication in my bag."

"For the love of God woman, you could have given them to me before you inflicted all that pain, are you a sadist?" She tried to hide the devilish little grin.

I have no doubt it was deliberate, and I wouldn't be surprised if she didn't enjoy it.

Anna handed over a small container that I checked out closely. "Where did you get Percocet?"

"I picked them up after I returned from Toronto."

I felt like a shmuck. On the Canadian project, Anna had endured her share of pain at the hands of mobsters, and I hadn't given her ordeal a second thought. I shook my head, "Maybe you need these more than I do."

"Nonsense. I have a strained back muscle. I get by fine without the pills."

"I'll bet you strained it carving a fat turkey."

To that sarcasm, Anna smiled. Maybe it brought back fond memories of Joey Naccarella. To escape his clutches, she'd stuck a steak knife in his back and throat, ending his career with the Abbandanza crime family.

Anna helped me to the bed. She fluffed up the bed pillows and covered me with a blanket as she helped me recline comfortably. "That should take care of you."

"Thanks. You're a lifesaver."

Anna gently picked up my swollen right hand and held it. She nodded and smiled.

"What are my chances?"

"I think you'll live through the night."

"I wasn't talking about my injuries." I looked into her eyes to read her response. "I was asking about my chances with you." I saw a tear form.

Anna's lips, soft and pink, parted slightly into a smile. "Better than fifty-fifty I would say." Her tone was warm and fuzzy.

"I'll take the odds." Anna dimmed the light over my bed and tucked me in. I was convinced then that I'd made the right decision by calling her. After having taken care of myself over the past couple days, I could see I wasn't the best help I could get.

By early morning, Anna had called my lost personal cell phone and the resort where I'd been a resident. According to Anna, when a man answered, she asked for me by name. "I ain't seen Mister Goe fer while now. I dunno where 'bouts he is. I can take your name and number to give it to him if I see him." Anna agreed and provided her name and number.

"Why all the calls?"

"I'm covering the bases. For now, you need to get your rest and trust me on this."

Constant jockeying in and out of bed and chairs provided little relief from the pain and made a long, challenging day. I continued my routine of fluids and nourishment and let time work its magic. At mid-morning Anna made a run to the store for supplies. When she returned, she kept herself busy putting together ideas for the project.

The following morning, Anna fixed coffee. I love the beverage anytime day or night, but jaw pain and my raw throat continued to rob me of this life's simple pleasure. Between noisy sips, I eavesdropped on Anna's phone calls. The first item of business was to fill Max in on as many details as she could. Max insisted on speaking to me directly after hearing Anna's version of the story. I was reluctant because I'd alienated him with my attitude.

"Hello, Max."

"I've spoken with Anna, and I want to say I am sorry to hear of your status. I wish you a speedy recovery."

"Thanks, I appreciate that."

"Scythian, Anna tells me you've come across a scenario that needs our attention."

"Yeah. There's a mess in Dixie that needs to be cleaned up."

"You have my full support with this mission."

"Thanks, Max. It might be a few days before I can get back in the saddle."

"Saddle? Yes, splendid, take whatever time you need. Anna has agreed to stay on to assist with the operation. Scythian, with your permission, I'd like to make an additional call for support."

I asked Anna, "Do you think we need help?"

Anna didn't have to answer. The look on her face gave her thoughts away. The operation would go smoother if she were able to concentrate on the bad guys without playing nursemaid to me at the same time.

"Make the call, Max."

"Too Cool is available."

"Excellent," I said and handed the phone back to Anna.

Max used my Knighted name, Scythian. That was a significant recognition. I was still in his good graces as a Palatini. Further, he pledged to support the operation. Every mission had a lead, and evidently Max wanted me in the lead slot. But, the icing on the cake was Too Cool. Thomas Orlando Kuhl, aka Too Cool, the Palatini crusader with a black ops background. For a team member on a project, I couldn't have asked for anyone more qualified. I'd garnered a great deal of respect for Kuhl on our last mission in New York and Ontario. We killed a lot of thugs and put a sizable dent in the Mafia's human trafficking ring.

My recollection of Kuhl had unintentional consequences. It brought to mind how harshly I'd judged Max and Anna during the final phase of the project and afterward when I turned my back on them. I was uncompromising, or so I was told, but I didn't see that necessarily as a bad thing. However, I'd decided to temper my attitude and actions, especially with those I respected. I'd told myself, whenever I disagreed with a call, I would make a conscious effort to agree to disagree, state my thoughts, drop it and move on. Ha, who was I trying to fool; this would be hard to pull off.

"Walter?" Anna had finished her conversation with Max. She looked eager to crank up the action. "We should designate this room as our safe house for the project."

"Okay."

Anna jotted something on her notepad. "I'm going to work on details. It's time for a hot shower." Anna guided me to the bathroom and assisted with undressing. Hot steamy showers had worked miracles to clean the blood and fluids from my sinuses. But each time I reclined the discharge seeped in and clogged my airway, and I'd repeat the process to clear the passages again.

I'd been in the shower maybe twenty minutes when Anna returned. "Thomas called; he's in Sheridan, Wyoming."

"Does he have anything going on?"

Anna swung back the shower curtain, "Says he will be here within forty-eight hours."

"Perfect."

"I'll make the arrangements for a room here."

"You're wasting your time honey. Kuhl won't stay here."

"Why not?"

"Because of the situation in New York, you didn't have the opportunity, like Bludd and I did, to watch his behavior. Kuhl asked for a separate location from us. I thought it was because of his bomb making, but that wasn't the reason, nor was it personal. His actions represent his training, a strategy geared to operational safety and security."

"I'll let him make his arrangements then."

I continued mending with repetitive hot showers, ice packs, nourishment, and fluids, which paid dividends in my recuperation. Although it didn't seem like much at first, I'd regained mobility in my joints and muscle groups. This progress allowed for the addition of stretching exercises to my routine for further gains. Most concerning was the development of an irritating high pitched ringing in my ears. It fluctuated but never went away.

I suspected one or more fractured lower ribs, but there wasn't any reason to confirm it with X-rays. Broken or not, it had to heal on its own. Unless additional complications developed, there wasn't anything a doctor could do to help.

The consequences of visiting a medical facility in my condition would've triggered a slew of questions about my injuries. Regardless of how well I lied, trained professionals would know differently. After the lawmen arrived, the real fun would start. I had to stay incognito. I had plans to take the lives of those responsible for the murdered girl. No matter what part they played from spectator or killer, I was intent on bringing a sense of justice.

Our two-day wait passed tediously. Anna busied herself with computer research and road trips to Shell Knob and Cassville to get the lay of the land. With each subsequent journey, Anna returned with new questions. The project was coming together, and we were almost ready to enter into the action phase, but I wasn't physically ready. Not even close.

"When Thomas arrives, he will expect a briefing on what we have covered and a discussion of the next step."

Had Anna read my mind or had she read my behavior? "What do you see as the next step?"

"Logically, the agenda is action. By the way, did you know you're listed as a missing person?"

"By who?"

Anna leaned close to my side and wrapped her hand around behind my neck. She leaned in and her lips brushed lightly against my ear as she whispered, "The other woman."

I drew a smile back past my eye teeth. "Jealous?"

"No."

Anna wanted to play. I could play too. "That's good, because you're the other woman."

"Oh, are you saying that Joyce is your main squeeze now?"

"No, I was merely responding to your comment. You were referring to Joyce were you not?"

"Yes, her. She hung flyers in Shell Knob, Cassville, and God knows where else." Anna stood and lightly patted the top of my head like I was a puppy dog.

"Publicity. I don't like it. If those Arkansas boys see a flyer, they're likely to tell someone. I need to stay a missing person until we get this job done."

Anna looked at me slack-jawed and uttered, "Augh—they are the least of our concerns."

My radar wasn't tracking. What could be worse for the project than me being identified alive?

Anna spelled it out. "What turned the heat on in Shell Knob in the first place?"

"The discovery of the murdered girl."

"Yes—and now a missing person. Think about it. It's Shell Knob, not the city. The Feds are going to tear this place apart. I'm concerned with the killers taking flight because of law enforcement putting pressure on the community. If they get nervous, they will either run or hide."

"Run or hide, they're not going to get away."

"All I am saying, Walter, if they run, it will present a difficult target. Where is home?"

"Are you talking about the Alaskans?"

"That's right. That's their home turf. We don't want to make that trip. It's best to settle this here. The sooner we get into action, the better." Anna's cell phone rang, interrupting the discussion. I sat back and thought. She was right. I needed to swallow any pride I had left and work with the Palatini operators to complete the project in Shell Knob. If I sat this round out and let the others take care of business, it wouldn't bring about the outcome I wanted—a piece of the action. I put my thoughts behind me and decided I would do whatever was necessary to finish this project.

I overheard Anna say, "Yes," and repeat it twice more before she disconnected the call. "Thomas is in Springfield. He will be over in the morning."

"Great, we can implement the plan right away."

"I will take Thomas on a tour tomorrow to orient him. We can discuss plans when we get back."

Thomas' arrival had a placating effect on my mood. Maybe I was capable of rising to the occasion and taking on a little action. I had frequent nosebleeds, and the discharge was problematic. The ringing in my ears continued to be bothersome but the worst pain came from the coughing which had increased in frequency. I still had a long way to go if I was going to run my AR 15 bolt. The more I thought about it, the more I realized that I wouldn't take someone in my condition on a mission. Neither would they.

I woke up early anticipating Kuhl's arrival. I hurried into the shower and was well into my routine when Kuhl arrived. He called Anna, as he'd said he would, from the motel parking lot. A moment later he was at the door. My vertigo had improved significantly, and I was on my feet when Anna let him in. As true comrades in arms, we exchanged hugs before we started. Kuhl pulled one of the tub chairs up to the coffee table and settled in. Anna had placed the small coffee pot on the dresser top for convenience. When I reached for the pot, Anna said, "I'll get that for you."

"Glad you called when you did," Kuhl said. "I was packing to leave my campsite in the Bighorn. I would have been on my way to Florida for a family visit with folks I hadn't seen in years."

"In the Bighorn on a mission?" I asked.

"No, I was living the dream. Nature, camping and fishing, all that."

Anna served the coffee, and then took a seat on the edge of the bed. "Thomas, are you free to accompany me today on a drive to the operational area? I'll brief you on the players and project status." Kuhl nodded, and the conversation turned to casual chat. I'd gotten the picture loud and clear; I wasn't invited along for the ride.

When it had become painfully apparent that Anna and Kuhl were ready to leave, Anna whispered in my ear, "Anything I can do for you?"

There was a lot that crossed my mind, but nothing I could say out loud. Besides, the time wasn't right. "Not right now honey, maybe sometime later." She leaned over and gave me a kiss on the forehead. The kiss was sweet, better yet, it came with a view.

Kuhl casually saluted as he walked out the door then stepped back in as if he'd forgotten something. "We need you on the mission so get yourself together."

I saluted him in return for the sentiment. "I'm hurrying buddy."

A few minutes after six Anna called from the parking lot. I was excited to hear what had transpired. She came in and perched on the edge of her bed directly across from where I was on mine.

"Thomas and I went to Dixon Holler. Afterward, we drove to the resort where you resided. We ate an early lunch in Shell Knob before finishing the day with a trip to Cassville. We checked out the bar where you ran into Duke. What a dive. However, I found something of interest on the entryway bulletin board—a Vigilance Committee flyer. There were a couple of them tacked up, so I removed one."

Anna handed me the flyer as she said, "It's a meeting announcement to nominate a new chairperson." Duke's name was absent from the notification.

I had scanned the flyer before I asked, "Did you see Duke's pickup anywhere?"

"No. It wasn't anywhere around, or we would have spotted the paint job."

"He's probably holed up like a rat at his compound. Maybe that's why the committee needs a new chairman."

"Why would he be hiding? You said there was no known connection between him and the dead girl, and no one was aware you had gone with him in his pickup when you disappeared. He should feel he's in the clear."

"Three things Anna: there is a local witness who knows what happened to the murdered girl and can finger the actors. If Duke hadn't known this before I revealed it to the Alaska crew when I implicated Duke as the snitch—he knows it now. Secondly, their crime has Fed's written all over it. Kidnapping of a child was enough to get the FBI involved, but with murder across state lines guarantees they are already engaged. Lastly, Joyce won't take my disappearance quietly. She'll suspect foul play. She'll hound the Sheriff for an answer. I'd bet she's corralled Jay Landers with her suspicions too. In the end, Duke will have a lot of fingers pointed in his direction."

Anna took a long moment to digest what I'd said. I surmised she was analyzing and evaluating the points I'd made. However, Anna caught me off guard with what she asked next.

"Why did you leave without saying goodbye to Joyce? You could have easily called her instead of me."

Why had I called Anna instead of Joyce? A tough question for sure, but I already knew the answer to why. Now all I had to do was figure out how to say it without sounding like a real cornball. "She didn't have a clue about me. How could we have had a relationship? I'm going to leave it that way and use the situation as a way out."

Anna cocked her head to one side and smirked. I hadn't answered her question, not yet.

"But that's not why I called you. The other night, when the fight was at its worst. My last conscious thought—was of you." I sat up tall for a minute and gave her a confident smile, "That's why I called you, honey. I realized how wrong I'd been and how much you meant to me."

"Why didn't you say that in the first place?"

"Because that's not me. I'm not a guy who can level with my feelings."

Anna rose from her bed and slipped next to me. She quietly reached her arms around me and squeezed tightly. Suddenly, she released her embrace and reeled back away from me. "Did I hurt you? I'm sorry."

"Not at all." But I'd lied. It was only a little white lie, but it bothered me.

"By the way, you mentioned Jay Landers. I have a meeting with him tomorrow."

Jokingly, I said, "Tell him hi for me," knowing that wasn't going to happen. I was a missing person. I intended to remain in that status. I concluded, my life in Shell Knob was over, outside of a few loose ends I wanted to bury. Soon, I'd return to my home in Oregon, settle back in, and kill some lowlife child molesters, just for kicks.

"What's Kuhls' agenda?"

"He plans an observation on Dixon's house and compound."

"Has Kuhl given any thought as to how he's going to hide a big four-wheel drive van with four antenna's protruding from the top? I don't think the van will go unnoticed in Shell Knob. There are too many people watching out for their neighbors."

"He's comfortable with the van."

"Okay." I was satisfied the project was in the hands of competent operators and progressing as it should without my input. I took my last shower for the night and was in bed by ten. Anna dillydallied for over an hour while she tended to her nightly details. Finally, she said good night and turned off the lights. Peace at last, I thought. But I hadn't counted on the effects of my earlier confession. There she was beside me. Not in her bed, but snuggled up next to me in mine. For comfort, I had laid on my back. Anna snuggled closer, careful not to press against my rib cage as she put her hand on my lower abdomen. Regardless of pain, her touch caused a rush of male appreciation and swamped my senses. A torch had been lit, turning into an inferno. I wanted her. Only a thin layer of night clothing separated our bodies. Still, she was close enough for me to feel heat radiating from her body. I moved my arm around her and touched the bare skin of her back. It was going to be a long, hard night.

In the morning, Anna prepared for her trip to Cassville. First stop on her agenda, the Sheriff's office. But before Anna made it out the door her phone rang. A second later she disconnected the call and alerted me to Kuhl's arrival, "He's five minutes out."

I sat in one of the tub chairs while Anna put on a fresh pot of coffee. It seemed less than five minutes when Anna answered the knock on our door. Kuhl casually strolled in smiling ear to ear. Under his left arm, he held two shoebox-size boxes. On the table before me, he placed one of the boxes and said, "Here." I leaned forward and removed the lid. Instantly, I recognized the contents as those items I'd left at the resort.

"I'm not even going to ask how," I said.

Kuhl laughed.

Anna had moved behind me and was softly stroking the back of my neck. "Did that make you feel better?" She asked.

"I feel a little more complete now that I'm in possession of my things again, thanks."

Kuhl piped up, "If that made you feel better, this will make your day." He placed the second box on the table and gestured with a nod for me to investigate the contents. I opened the lid, but this time I was baffled. "What the…" I didn't get any further with my question when Kuhl announced, "Happy Birthday."

"It's not my birthday Kuhl."

"It is now," Kuhl said with a smile.

From inside the box, I removed a Walther P99, complete with three magazines, a pancake holster, and a six-inch silencer. I lifted the weapon to eye level and ogled it.

"It's a .40-caliber. That's what you shoot." Kuhl said.

"Yeah, that's sweet," I said. I attached the silencer while I continued my admiration. It was a stunning work of art. Holding the piece close to my heart cradled in an affectionate, gentle embrace, I thought about something I hadn't thought about in a long time. I'd received a present from a friend. I couldn't recall the last time anyone had given me a gift. Palatini truly was a family.

As I sat mesmerized by the weapon's beauty, Kuhl remarked, "I'll be inaccessible for a couple days. Don't expect Situation Reports while I'm on point. You'll hear from me pronto if something urgent goes down."

"SitReps will consist of my actions until Thomas makes contact again," Anna said. "I will interface with Maximillian, so you don't have to carry the load, Walter."

"Perfect," I said. "That pretty much leaves me nothing to do."

Anna abruptly inserted, "But get better!"

Not being included in the batting lineup hurt. Worse yet, the game was being played on my home turf, and I wasn't invited to watch. It was bothersome being the lead Palatini asset and not being permitted to participate in the field. It must be what Max feels each time we take out a bad guy. It was my battle, and someone else was fighting it for me. Palatini assets had engaged as requested. I had no valid complaint. Kuhl turned toward the door and started to leave when I interrupted his departure with a simple statement: "Hey, thanks."

I caught Kuhl's reflection in the framed picture beside the door as he smiled. He opened the door and stopped short of the doorway. What he said next perhaps aided in my recovery more than any amount of antiseptic and bandages applied to my wounds. He turned back toward me and said, "We need you brother." Then he was gone.

Chapter 10

"Walking with a friend in the dark is better
than walking alone in the light."
—Helen Keller

Anna arrived back from her field trip earlier than I expected. I was anxious to hear how her meetings with Landers and the Sheriff had gone. She dropped her purse on my bed, turned toward me, and pulled me to her. With her body pressed tightly against mine, we kissed.

For a brief moment, I recalled an earlier time in our relationship. It was an intense experience in exploration and thoroughly enjoyed. I put my hand on her backside and held her. The kiss, however painful, was gratifying. Warmth swept through my body, followed by a deep pulsating bliss. Unexpectedly, and as abruptly as she had entered the room with unrestrained passion, she quelled my desire for more. Nurse Anna was back. She poked, prodded, and intruded upon my most painful body parts in her sadistic quest. I didn't buy her flimsy excuse to assess my physical condition. Besides, I liked the kissing better. I tried not to flinch but in the end I cried for mercy. She appeared satisfied.

My facial swelling had noticeably subsided. However, pain levels remained the same. Replacing the swelling was a spectacular palette with every color in the rainbow. Sharp pulsating pains in my neck had mysteriously vanished, but the same couldn't be said for my jaw. My teeth were loosened in their sockets and moved with the touch of my fingers.

I'd taken the time to research fractured ribs. According to the websites, I could optimistically expect a couple more weeks of babying them. I conveyed to Anna that the bothersome nosebleeds were less frequent. I didn't try to curtail them. They worked like a release valve allowing a small amount of drainage to escape and ease the pressure from the swelling. It seemed I'd grown accustomed to hearing the ringing noise in my ears which, at times, I subconsciously tuned out. But the high-pitched sound never stayed gone for long.

"Your recovery is going well."

"Yeah. I'll be at a hundred percent soon."

I sat opposite Anna in the tub chairs, eager to hear her account of the meetings. "I met with Sergeant Lancaster of the Sheriff's Office. He spoke as if he knew you, but you hadn't mentioned him by name."

"Haven't a clue, honey. I would've remembered his name if I had."

"I provided him with my Press credentials and informed him of our professional relationship. When he asked about any personal relationship we might have had, I let him know we were personal friends as well. He asked about your personal as well as your work habits. I had to laugh when he asked if you had any known psychiatric or mental disorders."

"That's funny. I guess you knew then he'd never met me."

"He was trying to lead me into saying something he could use. He asked specifically if you occasionally disappeared for lengths of time or were flighty and given to vanishing without notice. Of course, I told him no. He didn't ask about anything terribly intrusive other than your relationship with Joyce Farmer."

"Joyce is a sweet gal."

In a snappy curt tone she responded, "I'm sure she is." Anna paused, but I didn't bite. She continued, "The sergeant asked if I knew about your relationship with Joyce. I told him yes and that I knew you were staying at the family resort. It appeared to satisfy his interests."

"Sounds as if you had a busy day?"

"Did you know Joyce filed a missing person report?"

"No, but that explains the line of questioning."

"To some degree I suppose. A second officer joined us in the interview. He didn't speak other than to mention he had met you."

"Parker."

"Yes, Parker. He inquired how I had learned of your disappearance. I told him you and I were working a story together and I had called for your input. When I was unable to reach you by phone, I called the resort and spoke with the owner. He said he hadn't seen you for some time. I felt the owner was too vague, and wanted to see for myself what was happening. I drove to Shell Knob where I ran into a missing person flyer. They are on every telephone pole and bulletin board in town."

"What did he have to say to that?"

"He was aware of the handouts being posted."

"He bought it then?"

"He doesn't have any reason to check into my story. If he does, he'll speak with the resort owner perhaps, who might or might not remember that I called. If he does recall, he's not likely to remember when I called. It will only serve to verify my story and the reason that I was inquisitive."

"I suppose you're right."

"The sergeant asked questions concerning the nature of the story we had been working. He was looking for a possible connection to your disappearance."

"Yeah, they probably think I killed the girl and made a run for it. If they don't land on the truth soon, they'll be looking for a scapegoat to get them off the hook."

"That was not the impression I took away from the meeting. They focused on the report. They thought it was very strange. Joyce last saw you three days prior to her filing the report with the police. I saw the date on the flyers. They were in the same time frame. Why do you think she waited so long?"

"The cops might think Joyce is covering my tracks or giving me a head start. But, when you think about it, why did Joyce wait to file a report. She saw me every day. She had to know I'd vanished the following day."

Anna shot me a disapproving frown. I had tried to leave Joyce out of the picture. She wasn't any part of the equation. She was neither help nor hindrance to the Palatini process. We needed to keep our heads screwed on straight with a clear and concise focus on the problem. Anna interrupted my thoughts. "The sergeant suggested you might be on your way back to Oregon. He said you left abruptly, you didn't have roots in Barry County, and he questioned the stability of your relationship with Joyce."

"That's true on all counts."

"They are not considering you to be a victim of a crime or foul play. Consequently, there will be no expedited search or all points' bulletins issued. According to the sergeant, there are more than two-thousand missing person reports filed every day nationwide. You are officially a needle in a haystack."

"That's good. I can get done what needs to be done easier that way."

"Precisely."

"How'd your meeting go with Landers?"

"He is a weird little man. I gave him the same spiel I did the sergeant. According to him, he knew you had disappeared the day after you went missing. I don't know how he would have known that or why he hadn't reported it to the authorities."

"Wow, you have a conspiracy theory going. It would work better if I were dead, but hey, the circumstantial evidence is compelling. Jilted lover and a local news reporter worked together to get rid of little ol' me."

Anna had learned to overlook my rabbit chasing digressions. Now and then I'd go off on a tangent or get sidetracked and she'd have to rein me back to reality.

"He was incredibly guarded when I mentioned we had partnered in the telling of a story. He too, like Sergeant Lancaster, was inquisitive in respect to what we had been digging up. I related it was a human interest piece concerning a kidnapped girl. You were providing the background details, and I would write and publish the story. When I said that, he became fidgety and very anxious. For a brief moment, I thought I was going to have to tie him down to the chair. I don't remember the last time I saw someone that frightened—that I wasn't killing. Are you sure he isn't a person of interest in that girl's murder?"

"He's high-strung, that's all. He thinks I've been nabbed by the killer." Having known Landers personality type, I laughed loudly. It hurt but felt good at the same time. "I'll bet he thinks his head is next on the chopping block."

Anna chuckled, "He should be concerned. He's obviously a poor judge of character. If he knew what kind of friends he had, he would've been frightened to death."

Her tongue and cheek reference to Jay and my relationship as friends didn't go unnoticed. He'd been perfectly safe with me. I liked the little guy. He had a good heart, and maybe when this mess was cleared up, I'd drop the scoop in his lap as a reward. He'd have to receive the package anonymously.

"Get dressed for the outdoors. I'm taking you for a walk."

"I don't want to walk. Walking is painful. What if I'm recognized?"

"Being a bit paranoid aren't you? You're more than an hour's drive from Shell Knob and in a larger city. I'll be assisting your walking. Some people will notice your struggle to walk, but people who usually watch, don't look carefully. They wouldn't want to be caught watching. I think you're safe."

My equilibrium had improved. Not to the point where I wanted to do a hundred-yard dash, but I could rise to the challenge. Anna had picked up a Gambler's style straw hat. I pulled my shades from my bag and we ambled into the fading sunset.

"I'm going to devote tomorrow to online research and making calls. I want to see if any news is breaking on the Alaskan girl. I think I'll look into the Alliance and any affiliation with other groups."

"Like what?"

"Aryan Brotherhood, Neo-Nazi, the Klan, we need perspective on the big picture."

"Absolutely."

While outdoors, Anna kept a firm grip on my arm. Passers-by would've seen a pair of love birds on a stroll. Maybe we were. She linked her arm through mine in such a way she bore part of the load for my balance. We didn't have a destination, only a direction.

Cloudless and warm, I basked in Nature's picturesque setting and serenity of a roadside park. The scent of lavender beds mixed with the fragrance of sweet wild mint from a nearby field permeated the air. Weeping Redbud trees lined our walkway. Under the calm exterior, my thoughts ran rampant.

Hidden behind sunglasses and under the brim of the hat was a killer. I was doing what came most natural to me. I visualized many grotesque acts of violence as I daydreamed. Double tap, my signature kill, was far too expeditious for a man of Duke's caliber. Fast and merciful would not be my intention.

In my mind's eye, I imagined many pleasurable events to unfold. As with any serial killer, I dwelled on the execution. For some Palatini, it was about the mission. For me, I've always understood the underlying element is the excitement brought on by the kill. It didn't start that way, but the burden of righting wrongs drove me to kill, and satisfaction followed. My reliving of each slaying provided my psyche a genuine level of comfort, but only the prospects of another victim brought pleasure. Duke had become the object of my intention. Visualization produced a physical response of a pounding heart, the tingling sensation of excitement and breathlessness. Only reality at the point of death brought greater happiness and enjoyment.

Anna favored using the term "Palatini business" when she spoke of our previous assassinations. I didn't feel the same way. When opportunity knocked, I would kill Duke and share an equality between personal and business. How could it not be? It would be different from anger, but it would still be vengeful. I'd related to Anna my feelings as if I were a vampire. I didn't have a taste for blood; I craved its flowing. Not just any blood would satisfy, only guilty blood.

A small flock of blackbirds flew noisily overhead that caught my attention. Anna hugged my arm and smiled. "Isn't it beautiful," she said. I nodded and returned a smile. Then I slipped back into my daydream, slicing and stabbing Duke with my knife. It was, in fact, a beautiful day.

The next morning, Anna dug through the internet for information on the Alaskan Arctic Alliance. We hadn't heard from Kuhl, but it was still early in the game. I'd learned when he was in stealth mode; it behooved me to be patient. But patience was not one of my virtues. Pressure internalized and created a state of unrest.

I fidgeted as Anna read the press releases aloud concerning eleven-year-old Dawn Simmonds of Palmer, Alaska. The report included details of the earlier kidnapping and that she was found dead, the victim of foul play, three days before her twelfth birthday. "Taken so young," Anna commented. It reminded me of Minnie's statement at her residence in Dixon Holler. If my hunch was correct, Minnie was likely the caller that spoke with Landers.

"Unforgivable. I mean that Anna. I will not let this crime go unpunished."

Anna took it a step further and looked at additional criminal events that might tie in. Documents surfaced that were unsolved crime mysteries. Were they connected? If they were, would the evidence lead to the doorsteps of the Alliance?

Anna turned her attention from criminal events to the Alaska Alliance. Information was sketchy at best. The material she uncovered indicated they were a known entity to both the police and courts. Individuals belonging to the Alliance had accumulated minor criminal offenses that had tarnished their reputation. A weapons violations charge and game poaching seemed trivial in a place called the Last Frontier. But one case stood out apart from the rest. In the recent past, there had been a conspiracy to commit murder charge leveled against Alliance members. The complaint stemmed from a native village elder whose land in the Glennallen area had been encroached upon by Alliance members. Newspaper accounts weren't useful in determining what had transpired.

Frontier justice was a thing of the past in Alaska and its courts followed suit with the rest of the western states. It was strictly law and order, and plea deals. The Alliance members had racked up a handful of misdemeanor convictions through plea bargaining and a heftier felony charge of conspiracy to commit murder but never prosecuted.

Anna and I both saw project shaping up the same way. Perhaps the past provided the motive for the kidnapping. The Alliance might've targeted this girl in retaliation for an unresolved issue they had with the Alaska Native community. We wouldn't know until we had an opportunity to chat. If they were uncooperative with our questioning or their responses were evasive, I intended to use whatever means at my disposal to elicit their confessions.

Two more days passed while we waited for Kuhl. I occupied myself just twiddling my thumbs, and manipulating my new .40-caliber for action. On the other hand, Anna found there was nothing more to gain from our internet search. When Anna's phone rang, her conversation was short, sweet, and to the point. She said the sum total of two words, "Hello" and "okay." She disconnected with the caller, turned toward me, and spoke two more words, "Kuhl's inbound." Good, I thought, now we can crank up the action a notch or two. I didn't want to say anything out loud; Anna might be offended. She had worked her tail off.

Five minutes later, Anna answered a knock on the door. I stood inside the tiny bathroom doorway with the Walther still in my hand. Kuhl greeted Anna with a quick hug as he stepped inside the motel room. He appeared to be in a hurry. By the time Anna had closed the door, Kuhl was in one of the tub chairs motioning with his hand for us to find a seat. My anticipation heightened.

"I initiated recon soon after my arrival. I put a watch on Dixon's house and compound operation. Nothing, not a thing! No Duke and no pickup. Not even one person visited the compound or the gun range. Over a two day period, not one person. I had a giant goose egg to show for my time," Kuhl said.

"Sounds like he's on the lam," I said.

"How about Minnie, was she home?" Anna asked.

"Just by observing, I couldn't be sure. Consequently, I had to get creative," Kuhl said. "The next morning, I went to Dixon's house with my van, a tool bag, and a phony work order for her phone. A skinny little woman answered the door, and I laid it on her thick. I tapped the phone line and placed a bug on her coffee table. She sat on the living room sofa and watched while I worked on her phone."

"She didn't question the work?" Anna asked.

Kuhl leaned back in the tub chair and gestured by throwing his arms open wide, "If it's free they never do. I told her there was a problem with the phone lines in the area, and service tech's throughout the county we're making sure all the home lines were clear."

"She bought that?" Anna said.

"I think she had eyes for me," Kuhl jested.

"When you're over yourself, maybe you can proceed with the SitRep," Anna politely suggested.

Kuhl made a lopsided grin, "When I completed the install at the house, I was satisfied Duke wasn't home or going to be home,"

"Why's that?" I asked.

"Because she invited me back for a late dinner."

"Jeez," I moaned. "You must have gotten the wrong house. That's not like Minnie."

"Later in the evening, I slipped back–"

"Whoa buddy, don't know if I want to hear any more of this," I said.

"Let him talk," Anna said. "It's starting to get interesting."

I looked at Anna with a frown.

"As I was saying, I slipped back into the compound and dropped a couple ears in the place. Since then, here's what I can tell you. I haven't picked up on any unusual noises or seen anyone at the compound. Duke hasn't been to his house during the recon. I recorded all phone calls in and out, and there weren't many. No calls referenced Duke, and there were none placed to or received from him. There is something unnatural going on there."

"Sounds like a dead end," I said.

"It's more of a blind alley than a dead end. They are working together. She knows where he is, and she wasn't worried he was going to drop in on her when she invited me over."

"Minnie's IQ has dropped in my estimation if she thinks you're a catch, buddy," I said.

"Okay," Anna said, "Minnie has involvement on some level, that's clear. Where do we put her in the project?"

I butted in, "Minnie's not part of the equation here."

"How do you figure?" Kuhl asked.

"My take—she's a victim of this tragedy too," I said. "She's gotten herself mixed up in this mess involuntarily. He's given her a song and dance about what happened to the girl, and told her to keep her mouth shut. She follows his orders to the letter, so it looks like she's running cover for him. Remember, Minnie thinks she loves this bum, and she'll do anything for him."

Eyebrows lifted as the team shared glances. I hadn't been overly convincing.

"Would you say she loved him to the extent she would cover up a murder for him?" Anna asked.

"Like I said—unintentionally—yes. But, I don't think you could convince her he's a murderer."

"And if she did know?" Anna persisted.

"If she's the caller, I'll take it into consideration. I don't think she's capable of making the right decision with a situation like that," I said.

"We can't rule her out then," Anna insisted.

Anna was right. I found myself not wanting to believe that anyone treated as badly as Minnie might be part of a cover-up. It was unfathomable. Still, her behavior toward Kuhl didn't make sense. He wasn't that irresistible.

"Let's leave her out of it. I see her as naïve, and not a guilty party to the kidnapping, abuse, and murder of the girl. I'll review the situation if more comes to light," I said.

The reaction was cold and predictable. Finally, after a few moments, Kuhl continued. "Duke had a lot of irons in the fire. He was a truck driver by trade, head of the local Vigilance Committee, President of the

Missouri Alliance, gun range owner, operator, and survival instructor. He was a busy man and a little old school. He either didn't know how or didn't like the computerization of his records. He had paper trails for those irons, and receipts sorted into the files. He was very detailed."

"Alright, that's good to know. Duke was a good business man," I said.

"That's right. All his paperwork is in order," Kuhl said.

"Spit it out. You're beating a dead horse," I said.

"Most of what I found related to the gun range. One folder caught my attention, his fighting tactics, and survival skills course. Inside the folder with the receipts were pre-registration forms, contracts with attendees, and—" Kuhl waited for Anna and me to fill in the word he was leading us to say. We hit the same wavelength simultaneously, "Names."

"That's right—names." Kuhl pulled a folder from the small leather satchel that had accompanied him. He flashed the tops of a few forms as he'd described what they were then neatly laid the file on the coffee table.

Anna hadn't meant to reinjure me when she bumped me out of the way as she took possession of the folders, but a sharp pain coursed through my rib cage. I sat back and let her dig in; she'd include me eventually. I was the leader.

Kuhl sat quietly and watched until Anna abruptly stopped her review. Anna validated what Kuhl had discovered. She winked at Kuhl and said, "These three here are Alaskans."

"Check the dates," Kuhl said.

"I already have. They were registered to attend class at Dixon's four weeks ago," Anna said.

I piped up, "They were still here a few days ago too. I can vouch for that,"

Anna looked in my direction and read the names off of the registration forms, "Brady Woolf, Jake Boury, Hayden Leigh."

I gave a casual shrug at the names. Etched in my memory were the three guys I remembered as Flattop, Pug, and Ponytail. Anna waited for me to weigh in on what she'd read off. "Duke didn't introduce us formally," I said.

Kuhl added one more piece of fuel to the fire, "In Dixon's folders was a folder for the Vigilance Committee. An open record makes them less secretive, but I suppose any shenanigans are not recorded. I did, however, find in the meeting minutes where the three Alaskans showed up as members-at-large and attended a meeting at the compound while they were here."

"What do we know about the Vigilance Committee?" Anna asked.

"They advertise themselves as a friendly Neighborhood Watch Association whose members keep an eye out for crime and report it to the appropriate authorities. That's the aboveboard version. From their mission statement and articles of belief, they have all the hallmarks of a conservative movement with core family values and work ethics. That's the face they present to the public. I would venture to say, they're all respected pillars of the community too. I imagine the group is very attractive to the locals," I said.

"The Vigilance Committee meeting notes that I briefly scanned tells a different tale," Kuhl said. "They are united by a common conviction in their supremacy to rule. They blatantly profess intimidation, terror, and violence as justified when it's in the best interest of their destiny as a whole. They are Aryan or Ku Klux Klan like, perhaps an offshoot. They call themselves simply VC. On their paperwork, they don't display any Christian symbols or profess any religious affiliation. I think that eliminates them from affiliation with the Klan. More like homegrown vigilantes. The Alliance might act as a front for the VC," Kuhl said.

"Okay, Anna, here's the question. Might these guys be a white supremacy organization? Evidently it's difficult to separate the membership of the Alliance from the Vigilance Committee. Maybe there is no separation. The Alliance may be a recruitment tool. They've shaped a worldview where nothing is what it appears to be. They've created the need for a pseudo-military apocalyptic army to survive the future. They seem to be effective attracting the locals. Let's work it," I said.

"I don't want to sound too radical, but this might end up a large-scale project. Of course, that depends primarily on what we uncover about the individual actions of each member," Kuhl said.

Anna worked the names Kuhl provided through the power of the Internet. We needed positive identification on each person and any available background. Kuhl had hung tight for another hour before he cut out.

"I need to run additional reconnaissance," Kuhl said.

As he was leaving, I said, "Stay out of Minnie's bedroom. There's nothing there for you."

He smiled, which he didn't often do and said, "Beg to differ with you, buddy."

The lack of contact between Duke and Minnie was perplexing. Knowing Duke barely let Minnie out of his sight, it was a red flag that had to be investigated. As usual, we'd managed to create more questions than find answers, but it was the only way forward.

Chapter 11

"I am part of the power which forever wills evil and forever works good."
—Mikhail Bulgakov

In the darkness of the room, it caught my eye. I'd awakened before dawn to the reddish hue of the alarm clock's neon display. Barely five in the morning sounded like a good time to start my morning routine, but an unexpected issue arose. I'd fallen asleep during the evening while Anna continued to work on the files well into the night. Had Anna not fallen asleep next to me, I would have started my routine early. I could have aroused her if I desired, but instead I chose to relax in this appealing setting she'd placed me.

At eight o'clock we officially started our morning together with a cup of extra strong Java. Nurse Anna looked out for my best interests and stuck a yogurt in my face. "Eat." Her tone was commanding. I found Anna provocative and alluring with her assertiveness and power. I mused on the many attributes of her desirability.

"What's on the agenda?" Anna asked.

Finally, I thought, my cohorts have asked me to step in and provide the needed leadership. "Let's pool our Intel, evaluate the data, and execute a strategy. Let's table-top the Intel. Sweetie, this is your forte. You analyze and process quicker than anyone I know."

Anna smiled. I wasn't putting anything on her she didn't already want to do and was knee deep in as well. For my ego's sake, she let me sound bossy as if I were in charge—I appreciated the gesture. Unlike my façade as a reporter, Anna had an active career in journalism. She'd developed over the years in the writing business many friends and professional resources. Anna placed a call to a friend she referred to only as Marla, who operated an investigative database service in Portland, Oregon. Many times in the past, Anna had utilized Marla for background facts with her human interest articles. Her request would not be unusual or a reason for concern. The service wasn't free, but it was discreet. Anna gave Marla the information garnered from the pre-registration forms of the men in question and waited for a callback.

Two hours later, Marla was back on the phone with Anna. I moved close to where Anna sat scribbling notes on the yellow legal pad she kept close by. Waiting to be briefed on the call was one option, but so was eavesdropping on the conversation. I looked over Anna's shoulder as she jotted notes. One note read, "All three check out." Under that Anna had written, "Names legit. Alaska residents." From there, the notes became indiscernible. Later, Anna translated her chicken scratch into the parameters of the search.

"Depending on who the person is, the database records show everything from professional licenses to criminal records."

"The gamut."

"We have some good hits in property records, addresses, and assets that will be particularly useful."

Anna arranged four folders on the table, one for each of our project targets. No names or labels distinguished one from the other. It wasn't necessary. The target list was short. Anna placed the pre-registration forms in the folders and drafted the appropriate notes for each person on our list. When she'd finished, she addressed the folders individually by their initials.

"We have some discrepancies to sort out," Anna said. "On their registration forms, they listed a Glennallen post office address, but they have different residential addresses."

"What about the training camp address?"

"It's a post office box too."

"With their apocalyptic mindset, paranoia might've driven them to hide from society as much as possible. I suspect the post office box served to disguise their locations."

"Records for last year showed Leigh and Boury with Anchorage residences, and Woolf with property in Moose Pass."

"What about specific brushes with the law?"

"They have records, but nothing major on Leigh or Boury. Woolf was one of the men charged that was never prosecuted in the Glennallen conspiracy case, but there is something of interest here. Hayden Leigh has a 1990 Ford motorhome registered in his name."

"What are you thinking? These clowns drove here from Alaska with the girl on board? How'd they get across the border with her?"

"I'm sure it's possible. The Canadian border is very porous."

Anna was right. Over the last year and a half since the World Trade Center attack, border crossing security measures had tightened up. But tourism was still big money in Alaska and the remote Canadian provinces. With the world becoming increasingly dangerous for westerners, Alaska tourism had boomed. Every day, by the droves, motorhomes crossed the border. Economics coupled with low threat levels made it an attractive journey.

"Anything on employment?"

Anna pointed to a few references she'd written down. "Numerous construction type jobs. All three had employment in the past year. With the type of work they do, they might be working under the table too. That would explain how they've gotten by during extended periods of time without recordable income."

Kuhl telephoned Anna late in the evening. He was inbound. When he knocked, I let him in, and we kicked off the powwow. Anna presented her research followed by Kuhl, "I intercepted a brief call from Duke today. It wasn't the type of casual conversation a husband and wife usually share." Kuhl removed his ball cap, placing it flat on the bed nearest the tub chair where he was seated. "He told Minnie he was in BC and still had two more days of travel before he arrived."

Anna slapped the coffee table with the palm of her hand which was a departure from her ladylike presentation and leaned forward in the chair. "Ahh, we were right! He *is* with the Alaskan trio on his way north!"

"BC is British Columbia?" I asked.

"Has to be," said Kuhl.

"I can tell you this for certain; the call didn't take Minnie by surprise. She was aware he was traveling, and I'll bet she knows where he's going. Whatever their plans I can guarantee you this; those two had conferred before he lit out. Not once, did he have to explain anything to her. She apparently knows what he's doing."

A long moment of reflection followed. I surmised we'd all come to the same conclusion. "All right, are we ready to wrap up here?" Anna asked.

"I could talk with Minnie before we follow Duke north. Perhaps she can be persuaded to tell me what she knows," Kuhl said.

As lead Palatini on the project, it was my call. Kuhl brought up a viable reason to look closer into Minnie's involvement. I'd come to know Minnie on a personal level. Whatever she'd gotten herself into was driven by misguided love. I didn't expect the others to see it the same way. "Leave her out of it. I think she's been through enough."

All eyes were on me, and they weren't smiling eyes. "Listen up," I said. "If it turns out she is involved with the girls murder, I'll take care of it." The question now was whether or not they trusted me as a man of my word.

Kuhl picked his hat up from the bed and stood to his feet. "Let's pack it in."

"We need to move our base out of the area, I'd suggest we use Portland and plan our trip to Alaska," Anna said.

"Do it," I replied.

We jumped through hoops preparing for our departure. Pulling up stakes in twenty-four hours wasn't easy. Anna made flight arrangements while I called Max and briefed him. Kuhl and Anna surprised me with a tow dolly for the Avenger. Once we had it loaded on the dolly, Kuhl strapped the ratchets tight on the dolly and hooked up the security chains. "Do you need anything from the car?" Kuhl asked.

"Already done," I said.

Kuhl cloaked the Avenger with a car cover he'd bought and cinched it tight. "There," he said. "No one can see it."

We set a tentative plan for daily check-ins with Anna and said our good-byes to her. Kuhl expected the trip to take us three or four days to cover the two-thousand miles to Portland. Anna would be there in a matter of hours and would work out our Alaska travel plans.

My ribs were still tender, and my inner ear rang non-stop, but overall I considered my recovery to have taken leaps and bounds over the past few days.

Kuhl and I traveled quietly with little conversation for the first leg of the trip. As night crept in, Kuhl mentioned he was hungry and asked what I wanted to try eating. We saw a line of trucks parked at a greasy spoon just off the highway. "That looks good," I said. We hung a right at the next exit and worked our way back to the diner.

It had been a couple weeks since I'd eaten a real meal. If I never saw another cup of yogurt, it would be too soon. As we entered, we scanned the diner to locate a suitable seating arrangement. The empty booth at one end of the joint was the best option. It wasn't ideal, but Kuhl could effectively cover my back while we ate.

I ordered a two-buck plate of fries with brown gravy, and it was heaven on earth. Mashing the fries didn't take away from them in the slightest and I ate every bite. I contemplated another round of fries, but the food didn't settle as well as I hoped it would. I didn't understand the dynamics, but when you haven't eaten anything but yogurt for a couple weeks and scarf up a truckload of greasy foods it wreaks havoc on your digestion. Throughout the evening, I paid the price for my indiscretion. Kuhl found it inconvenient too. By necessity, we made frequent pit stops and, although he disagreed, in my opinion the meal was still worth it.

As we traveled north, I napped. A couple hundred miles into the trip, Kuhl took the Interstate Highway westward. We kept our eyes peeled for a motel that kept its light on for us. Interstates throughout the Midwest were populated with motels, and it didn't take long to find one suitable for our needs. We pulled in and bedded down for the night.

The next day our trek took us deep into America's breadbasket. The lackluster landscape coupled with an endless flat horizon soon bored me. If we chewed the fat, time would pass less noticeably. "Do you ever think about your military time on the special forces teams?"

"That was then," Kuhl answered. His words hung on their abruptness. Maybe he thought it was none of my business or it brought back bad memories he'd rather leave buried. Regardless of my motive for conversation, my question was sincere.

What I knew about Kuhl I'd seen firsthand. My Palatini pal, Seymour Bludd, had laid out a string of hearsay on Kuhl prior to meeting him in New York. What I wanted from Kuhl was his history related firsthand. "From your clandestine skills, your military training must've been intense?"

"We trained non-stop."

When it came to his past, talking with Kuhl was like pulling teeth. You had to yank on it. Sure, our kind of work made for isolation and loneliness, but when we're on a project together, it paid dividends to be social. I found myself less at ease around Palatini that didn't offer their experiences. "Well, at least you made the training pay off. How else would you have picked up the skills to get on the diplomatic security teams? The civilian market makes a lot of moolah."

"I was never civilian; it was the government. One day I was a commando; the next day I was a non-military security operator. It was the same thing, except the government could deny military boots on the ground in hostile territory with our organization."

"I can only imagine how fascinating it must've been. I spent my life at a foundry pouring aluminum oxide into smelting pots and heating the dry ore to a thick and soupy molten metal. Other than losing my fear of hell from the heat, I didn't learn anything valuable."

Kuhl continued quietly behind the steering wheel. His lack of response gave the impression he had other things on his mind. Perhaps he was waiting for another trivial question, but his occasional glance out the driver's side window told me he wasn't interested in the conversation. I had no intention of carrying on talking to myself. I'd let it go.

"Don't sell yourself short," Kuhl said. "I've known many warriors over the years. What they had in common was not their skill sets. The very best military operators of my day were my instructors. Absolute legends—and I had the opportunity to learn at their feet. What made them the best was what I was determined to learn."

"It would've been helpful to have had some training."

"You've trained your entire life for today. You've nurtured your natural skills to be at the pinnacle of success on a mission. Skills you can't learn from a book. You have made yourself a weapon against evil, and possibly the toughest fighter on the field to beat."

"I sure don't feel that way."

"It's not about what you feel. It's about applying what you know to what you do with devotion to the mission in mind."

Kuhl flipped up the center console and pulled out a cigar box. With his hand outstretched to me, he lifted the lid with his thumb. "You want one?"

"Not me."

Kuhl sat the box on top the console, slipped out a cigarillo and let the lid close. He wedged the little cigar between his teeth on the left side nearest the window. I've never found smoking pleasant, but for the sake of camaraderie I'd overlook my pet peeve. Smoking was unhealthy, and that was a sufficient reason for people not to indulge. But, my reason differed. Smoke destroyed the sense of taste and smell. Both of which I used in stalking my prey.

I waited for Kuhl to light up. It was odd that I hadn't picked up on the cigar scent or the odor of smoke. Most smokers carry the evidential scent and pallor. Usually, personal vices were the first things discovered. I gave him credit. He'd done an excellent job of masking the smell. He hadn't smoked when we were on the last project together, but we were separated a great deal of the time. He never lit up when he was around me.

"Still," I said, "I would've liked to have been in black ops."

"You can have it," Kuhl replied abruptly. His nose curled up into a snarl, "I'll tell you what you would have been part of—nothing. We trained every day. When a mission came up, they were quick to send us into harm's way. None of us asked for recognition. Why would we? We were shadow warriors. All we wanted was support for our mission. We wanted to get in and back out, successful, and with all our people accounted for. But politicians had their own agendas."

With one hand on the steering wheel and the other hand holding his chin, I saw he'd plunged deep into his memories and had gone a long way into his past.

"I'll tell you what the problem is—we lost operators and no one cared. That's why I say politicians have no business in military affairs. Political appointees, who had never carried a weapon in a battle or stood their ground in the face of an enemy, had no business handling security for our country. They're liars and backstabbers. They play political games with our missions and ultimately our lives. We were nothing more than pawns at their mercy. I hold them personally responsible for our failed missions and lost brothers. That's what I learned in black ops. Maybe you would have fared better."

It wasn't long before I forgot about the mundane drive, and miles rolled by without notice. Our conversation turned to Palatini operations and the current venture we'd undertaken. Kuhl and I found we had working chemistry.

We knocked off for the night at another nondescript motel. In the morning, we launched out early with a plan to eat breakfast on the road. We pressed forward with every attempt to put as many miles behind us as possible. Soon, the terrain showed signs of change. As we entered the Rocky Mountain foothills, the drive turned more to my liking. One more night on the road and we'd be in Oregon.

We traveled through mountain passes and across high plains until we reached the home stretch along the Columbia River. I'd had the question on the back burner since we started our trip, and it was time to find the answer. "Last couple days, you and I roomed together."

Kuhl laughed, "You find that odd?"

"Maybe. I was led to believe you never stay with other Palatini. Why the exception to the rule?"

"No exceptions made, brother. It's dangerous to lump our assets altogether. In Springfield, you and Anna were in one motel, so I chose another. On the Mob project in New York, you and Seymour had a place together. I stayed in another. I call it mission first. Other than for brief meetings to shape our projects, I don't think it's wise to lump all the assets together. That goes for traveling as well. We don't all use the same plane or vehicle. Something happens—it can be as simple as an accident or natural disaster. It doesn't have to be a 40-Mike-Mike that claims our lives. The point being, our mission would die too. If Palatini assets remain separated a majority of the time, we have a contingency element to continue our project. Remember what happened in Toronto?

"Mobsters grabbed Anna."

"More than that, you carried the project forward. If you two had been together, the whole project might have been terminated. By my actions, I limit the possibility."

"Good. When we arrive in Portland, you can stay at my place."

"Maybe I don't want to stay with you, you're no prize to sleep with you know. You make horrible noises when you snore."

"Don't sweat it. We'll have separate bedrooms." We laughed.

Nine-thirty in the evening, Kuhl pulled his rig to a stop in front of my 1972 Brookwood mobile home. First order of business was to call Anna.

"We're here safe."

"Let's meet tomorrow at ten for breakfast. I have more details to pass on."

I'd placed one last call before we disembarked from the van. My residence in the suburbs of southeast Portland had been maintained by a neighbor lady named Shelly. I'd sent money orders monthly for my lot rent and utilities, and paid extra to have the place looking 'lived in' and the yard freshly watered and mowed. Nothing said 'security' like a well-maintained place. Shelly answered, and I let her know my plans to leave again soon. She remained agreeable to the terms that we'd previously established, and I called it a day.

The porch light was lit as usual. When I approached the storm door, I noticed a small business card wedged into the frame. Imprinted on the front of the card was the name Brandon A. Ware, Private Investigator.

"Ooh, you have a cop on your tail," Kuhl said.

"He's only a PI. Nothing to worry about."

I remembered Ware as an old-fashioned, hard-nosed detective for the Multnomah County Sheriff's Department. That was before he retired. I had respect for his work as a homicide detective and was happy to see him depart the force a year ago. Written on the back of his card was a message, "Give me a call." I wondered what he wanted, but I wasn't going to lose sleep over it.

By ten the next morning, we found the joint in West Linn where Anna wanted to meet. As neighborhood restaurants went, it was dinky. We'd driven past the place twice before we spotted it squeezed between a couple of specialty stores in a strip mall.

Kuhl and I were a couple of peas in the same pod in many ways. If a meeting began at ten, we wanted to be there fifteen minutes early. To arrive at ten was late. Although late by our standards, we were first to arrive. I stepped inside and with my eyes swept the width of the room. The counter ran the length of the right side, and six pub tables lined the left side. The kitchen extended across the back, open to the restaurant via a serving counter where waitresses picked up orders. The only other people in the place were a teenage girl behind the front counter and an old man sitting at a table. Both were employees.

Kuhl led the way to the back table, and we positioned ourselves with our backs to the corner walls. The old man put a bead on me like I was trouble, so I stared back. In some way, perhaps he'd recognized me. Not so much by name or face, but a connection in spirit. What followed was a prompting. It was Destiny, and she didn't like him either. There was an evil about the old man. I didn't know the specifics, but I was sure if I delved into his past, I'd discover his filth. It's always been the case. Destiny, my companion and spirit guide, had never led me astray.

The old man mumbled something under his breath as he slipped into the kitchen. Maybe his foul spirit had prompted him likewise.

Anna arrived a quarter past the hour. The girl behind the counter put away her cell phone and politely took our order. The old man tossed a couple of glances at me from the kitchen. I didn't trust the situation. Whatever had crawled up his backside wasn't coming out on my plate. I called out, "Hey" to the waitress. She returned to the table wearing a smile.

"Can you cancel my portion of that order and get me something else?" I asked.

"No problem. What would you like?"

She had a good attitude, and her tone was pleasant. It wasn't her fault she had to work with the old scumbag. So I said, "Sure, bring me one of those bagels with cream cheese off the counter."

I watched the waitress enter the kitchen and scratch something off the only order the cook had in front of him. The old man said something foul that he shouldn't have said to the young lady and wrinkled his face in disgust. Anna heard it too. She patted the top of my hand and said, "Chill, there's not enough time in a day to right every wrong you see."

"It's more than that," I said. "This guy is no good. I can feel it." Anna exchanged a glance with Kuhl that said "weird" more than "doubt," then proceeded with the meeting.

"We'll leave for Alaska tomorrow. Are we all in agreement this is what needs to happen?"

"Probably a good thing," I said, as I tossed Ware's PI business card on the table. Anna examined it for a moment and said, "Tomorrow then?"

Kuhl nodded, and I shrugged. We'd been off the road less than twenty-four hours. It wasn't going to be easy to roll out again. However, it would buy more time for my body to mend.

"I've rented a motorhome with a tow dolly for the trip," Anna said.

"I'll need my van," replied Kuhl. "I can sleep in it too."

"Good," Anna said. "We'll tow Walter's car."

I nodded.

Anna slipped an envelope across the table to me. When I'd opened it, there was a crispy, new driver's license inside. Walter Eloy Goe had an additional piece of legitimate looking documentation. I looked it over closely noting the photograph was the same picture as on my phony passport.

"That looks pretty good for fake ID," I said.

"It's not a fake."

"What do you mean?"

"You are in the Oregon State system. Nothing false about it."

"The passport and all the paperwork was bogus."

"At the time, the documents were falsified to obtain legitimate documentation. The real you vanished—only Walter exists."

It was a tough pill to swallow and I faced an odd sense of loneliness. My true identity shelved for a new one. I preferred being Walter, if I hadn't, I would've spent more time outside my façade. Anna's actions changed who I was forever. Anna had recognized my desire to live as Walter and connected the dots so I could be Walter.

Walter existed for a particular purpose. She hadn't taken into consideration I'd avoided being tracked by police and government systems by being Walter, who didn't exist. Everything about him was false, and I'd spent time and energy to make him that way. Now, I was back in the system. The business cards I'd handed out that weren't traceable now had a real person attached to the name.

Anna continued, "With your passport and driver's license you can open bank accounts, transfer money from your old accounts, and conduct legal transactions under your new identity. With these, you can phase the old you completely out—the old you has vanished without a trace."

I didn't like the surprise, but I'd made a commitment to play better with others.

"How are we going to handle our weapons to cross the border?" I asked.

"I can take them," Kuhl said. "I have a false top in the van. It will hold a few rifles and handguns."

Kuhl was a true black bag operator. He wasn't going to part with his gadgets or bomb building supplies.

"What about the explosives?" I asked.

"I'll take the necessities. Everything else stays at your place."

When we closed the meeting, Anna left first while Kuhl and I stood by the diner door to watch. The young waitress came from behind the counter to bus the table when I caught her attention. Speaking in a soft tone, "Listen, you know the guy you're working with pretty well?"

"No, I've only worked a few shifts with him."

"A word of advice, if he offers you candy, a ride in his car or wants to show you anything—walk away fast,"

"Do you know him?"

"Let's just say I know him well enough." Kuhl motioned it was time to go and headed out the door. I looked back at the waitress as I left, "Keep yourself safe."

We hustled through the rest of the day to complete our preparations. Anna had reserved a motorhome for the trip. When she arrived with the coach, I was impressed she handled the thirty-foot rig like a pro.

"Nice, is it new?"

"2001," She said. "Is that new enough for you?"

"You know I only travel in first class accommodations."

She uttered a sound resembling "huh," but delivered it with a sardonic "yeah, right."

Kuhl stayed busy prepping his van while Anna and I worked on making the RV comfortable for the trip. The last item loaded was my new Walther P99. I was naked without my handgun. But we weren't defenseless in the motorhome. Anna had her tactical knives, and I had my Kabar.

Kuhl took off the next morning at eight sharp. Our departure time was staged for ten. The two-hour lag time was one of Kuhl's security measures. Anna drove while I rode shotgun as we pulled out onto Interstate 5 heading north. We'd planned to rendezvous with Kuhl at three points along our route. Otherwise, it was Anna and me, traveling at our own pace. We crossed into British Columbia at Sumas and cleared customs without a hitch. A couple of hours later we passed through Hell's Gate and then continued north along the scenic Frasier River.

Watching Anna at the wheel left me in a daze at times as I dreamed of what might have been and might yet come to be. As her curve-hugging skirt rode up the taught muscles of her thighs, it was difficult to keep my eyes on the road and my mind on the mission—I didn't even try. The mission was still primary, but I had the strange sensation that we'd just embarked on a tryst and thinking about the potential outcome drove any other rational thought from my mind.

Chapter 12

"Is evil something you are? Or is it something you do?"
—*Bret Easton Ellis, American Psycho "*

Mid-summer on the Alaska-Canadian Highway was a dream some people waited a lifetime to experience. Harsh landscapes of volcanic pinnacles, steep slopes, and vastly forested hillsides reminded me of my roots in Oregon's Mount Hood territory. Our route through the Canadian Rockies brought back those feelings I once enjoyed. Few roads and fewer inhabitants had pushed into the impenetrable wild of this country. Mile after mile, sprawling tree covered mountains, barren upper slopes occasionally crowned with glacier horns, and mighty rivers with their tributaries gorged the canyons and made up this vast wilderness. Perhaps no other twenty-five hundred-mile road trip equaled such spectacular grandeur in North America.

The farther north we drove, the longer the sun hung in the sky. As planned, we'd made our first contact with Kuhl at a campground near Fort Nelson. He'd parked and waited on our arrival. We parked on the opposite side of the campground, and invited Kuhl over for dinner, and a quick meeting. Anna was on deck to cook. Watching her as she carved the chicken into parts with a small kitchen knife, I couldn't help but notice her smile. It ushered in memories of Anna's ability to work a blade on a man's throat. She had minced few words in Thailand when she sliced a "Colombian necktie" on a guy. It was a work of art with a tactical blade. In Toronto, she was forced to perforate her abductors back with a common steak knife. The nature of a kill with an assassin's knife required up close, and personal engagement that was slow work, and rarely preferred amongst those of us that kill.

Engaging in small talk after dinner, the three of us chewed the fat recalling sites we'd seen thus far. Always below the casual surface chat were ideas about our mission. They remained unvoiced. Anna had brought up a more generalized question that made food for thought. "Do you ever wish there was another way?"

"Another way to do what?" Kuhl asked.

"To make a change," Anna remarked.

"Tried already," I said. "Nothing else works. Maybe someday when the world gets away from the psychobabble kick of thinking everything can be cured, and address the real problem of personal responsibility for the choices made. Maybe then the government will step up and take care of business rather than trying feel-good classroom theories that always fail at the expense of more victims."

"Got that right," Kuhl said, pointing his finger as if it were a handgun.

The following day, before breakfast, Anna and I stretched our legs in the crisp morning air. We stopped by Kuhl's van to invite him over for a bite, but he'd broke camp and was gone. We'd delayed our departure longer than intended. Spontaneous passion had interrupted our plans and moved us to explore new boundaries—we were picking up our lives where we'd left off.

Anna had planned the trip using her MilePost travel guide. When we crossed the Laird River Bridge, she looked for a campground to take a break. We weren't more than a mile and a half past the bridge when Anna spotted the place she later referred to, as her idea. She swung the motorhome into the RV Park.

Anna rested her eyes while I explored the camp area. From the motorhome, I saw a plume of vapor that rose skyward above a cluster of trees a short distance from where we'd parked. A boardwalk trail worked its way through a patch of conifer trees toward the vapor column. A quarter mile trek and I came upon a body of water. The posted sign read natural hot springs and the proviso for usage.

For a few minutes, I watched other people lounge in the hot springs. One or two were by themselves while others clustered into small groups. The outside temperature was warm, but a far cry from hot, and served as encouragement to get in the pool. I sat on one of the benches the park provided, kicked off my tennis shoes and stuck my socks inside. I checked my pockets for anything I didn't want to get wet then waded in thigh deep. As I walked around the pool, water temperatures varied from scalding hot at the head of the spring to the average temperature of a typical Jacuzzi at the lower end. Unbeknownst to me, I'd been followed. "You look silly in there without swim trunks," Anna said.

"Well honey, thirty years ago, hippies bathed in these same pools without a stitch of clothing. Would you rather I take my clothes off entirely?" I couldn't help myself. With a wink and a lascivious grin on my face, I continued "Come on in if you dare. I can feel things heating up."

Lacking a bathing suit didn't deter Anna. Not at all. She saw my reply as an invitation to play. She spotted my shoes, slipped hers off, and aligned them next to mine. Dressed in body-hugging designer jeans and a silk tank top, she slipped into the pool. She leaned back in the waist deep water dipping her hair beneath the surface. I loved the wet look. When she sat forward, the silky top clung snugly to her ample breasts. I needed no further encouragement. Our bodies drifted together. Anna's soft skin and delicate jawline begged for my touch. And touch I did. She responded in kind with her fingertips as she lightly traced my emerging goatee.

We whiled away the time, long enough that I suggested we spend another day at the hot springs. Anna agreed on the condition that it was for therapeutic purposes. Her heart was set on my full recovery.

Sweet girl.

We walked hand in hand back to the motorhome. Once inside, Anna threw a smile my way that promised everything. Slowly she stripped off her clinging wet jeans, then slipped out of her top which captured my full attention.

"We need to rinse off Walter. You don't know what might be in the water."

"Good idea, sweetie." Anna kicked her wet clothes into a pile and helped me get out of mine. She took me by the hand and led me the ten steps to the RV's shower. "You first, or me?" She asked.

I smiled and said, "Together of course, as good citizens it's essential we conserve water!"

She laughed, but then as I looked at the toilet with the shower head above, I mused, "That's going to be hard for the both of us."

"Hmm, perhaps harder than you think," and with that Anna turned the water on and adjusted the temperature. I took the seat while Anna straddled my legs facing me. It was quite a while before we noticed that the water finally ran out.

Our extra day was therapeutic for our mending relationship but didn't prove to be that conducive to my recovery.

At Whitehorse, Yukon Territory, a community of nearly twenty-thousand, we restocked our supplies and filled the motorhome's duel gas tanks. Two days later, just past Beaver Creek, we crossed into Alaska. A hundred miles further west, we took the Tok cutoff toward Glennallen.

We contacted Kuhl by cell phone, apologized for our day delay, and arranged to meet at the intersection of the Glenn and Richardson Highways. Kuhl was waiting as planned. After we had refueled, we picked up fresh supplies and backtracked five miles to our camp destination on the Gulkana River.

The image of a campground I had in my mind was one of peace and solitude. What we hadn't factored into our plan was a campground during the middle of the salmon season. The place was packed. Tents, trailers, and motorhomes filled the camp. Four-wheelers hauled anglers up and down the slopes to the river, while droves of fishermen lined the banks.

At the camp entrance, I disembarked the RV while Anna went to the makeshift office located in a twenty-foot travel trailer. I watched one young boy's face, filled with excitement, as he landed a fish and added to his memories of a lifetime. One guy climbed the embankment carrying a large trash bag with a noticeable outline of fish.

"Hey buddy," I said, "Looks like you did pretty well."

The fisherman set the bag on the ground and displayed the contents. With a brimming smile, he said, "We're slaying 'em today." It was music to my ears. I'd come to slay 'em too.

Anna finished the registration process and motioned for me to return to the motorhome. "Problems?" I asked.

Anna laughed. "No, they didn't require ID, only money. So I registered us under the name, Mr. and Mrs. Smith."

We pulled into our designated site and took care of the RV hookups. The large number of people in the camp area appealed to me. I didn't care for the social contact, but being lost in the crowd had its advantages. People were coming and going at all hours of the day and the portion of dusk to dawn that passed for night. It wasn't likely anyone would notice us as we blended into the backdrop of humankind.

We uncovered and backed my Avenger off the tow dolly and made her ready to use. Discreetly, Kuhl outfitted us with the weaponry that he'd transported. Once we'd finished settling in, he made plans to return to his camp area. He'd selected a campground three miles farther north.

"Is zero-eight-hundred good for everyone?" I asked.

"Breakfast will be on the table," Anna replied.

Kuhl nodded and took off. He'd arrived in the target area two days before Anna and me and had taken advantage of the downtime to conduct area reconnaissance. He'd mentioned there was a large gravel pit located a short drive north that might come in handy during the project. I wanted to waste gunpowder with the newest addition to my arsenal.

At seven forty, Kuhl pounded on the RV's front door. I'd misunderstood Anna from the night before. I'd interpreted her promise for a hardy breakfast to mean she'd intended to cook. I was mistaken. Her idea of breakfast was yogurt and a bagel. I took the initiative and tossed a half-pound of bacon into a skillet on the cooktop, popped some canned biscuits from the fridge into the oven, and fried the eggs in the bacon grease. Anna found the process unhealthy and totality disgusting. Kuhl, however, was appreciative.

"Cell phone reception is poor in the area. Hit and miss at best. Don't rely on coverage," Kuhl said. "I have two-way portable transceivers we can carry. Keep in mind range will be limited by terrain."

"Kuhl, we need a reconnaissance of the training camp. We need to know if there are people living there. How much time do you need to complete the mapping?" I asked.

"Three days from today," Kuhl said.

"Anna and I will recon our target's physical residences. That means a road trip for us. Let's get a bead on where these guys supposedly live."

Anna laid her files on the table and opened the covers. "These are the pictures I obtained from my investigative source in Portland."

I pointed to the first picture, "This guy here, Jake Boury, is the muscly A-team member I named Flattop." Next to Boury's folder was Hayden Leigh's file. I put my finger on his picture and said, "Ponytail. He's missing a piece of his right ear." I moved to the last folder, picked up the photo of Brady Woolf and examined it carefully. "This guy is heavier now, but he still looks like a bug-eyed Pug on two legs."

Kuhl's sardonic grin narrowed as if he'd bit into a crabapple. He fingered through the folders and with a harsh tone said, "Dead men, all." The room fell silent. I liked the way Kuhl thought.

I clapped and said, "Three days then."

Kuhl headed south toward the Richardson Highway. In less than a half hour, he'd be at his destination. He had a big task ahead, and three days wasn't much time. We believed from the inception of the plan that the project's success would hinge on Kuhl's powers of observation and detailed mapping of the training camp, the best place for the kills. We needed weak points identified on which to capitalize. If possible, put eyes and ears in the place, and wire it with explosives.

Unlike Kuhl, Anna and I would eat up our time traveling. We were up against a two-hundred-mile road trip to Anchorage—one way. If we traveled on to Moose Pass to recon Woolf's place, we'd add one-hundred-fifty-miles to the trip. The importance of our observations depended significantly on how well the project came together at the training camp. If we had to scrap the Glennallen idea, we'd have to engage our targets where they were most secure—their homes. As we travelled south we picked up cellphone service. Anna called ahead and snagged a room at the Golden Lion Hotel in Anchorage.

I was capable of driving my car, but Anna asked for the responsibility. I conceded. After two hours of hilly curves, doglegs, roadside overlooks, and steep descents into valley floors, the road emptied out into the Palmer flats. I knew our location immediately. Suffering and sorrow hovered over this place like a canopy. The loss had broken many hearts, and I felt their pain.

A voice deep within whispered, "Revenge me." I recognized the voice as a reaffirmation of my Calling and not the beckoning from a ghostly being; although I've never known for sure. Palmer was home to Dawn Simmonds, the young native girl murdered in Missouri. I was here solely to collect on the debt.

An hour later we arrived in Anchorage. I'd grown hungry for the taste of retaliation. We checked into the Golden Lion and set up our agenda. Hayden Leigh's house sat only minutes away from the hotel. We wasted no time and traveled toward the Chugach Mountains on 36th Avenue for a block, then hooked a right. We'd passed four streets before we spotted Ponytail's driveway.

Leigh's house, a 70's style two-story with the garage directly under a large bay window, sat fifteen yards off the beaten trail. I'd hoped to see Leigh's motorhome in the driveway—it wasn't there. Did he still own it? Had they returned to Alaska or had they left again? The fact was, without putting an eyeball on his RV, it remained a missing piece to our puzzle.

We made a loop around the block, turned around and came back up the street from the opposite direction. With Leigh's work history, I had to question how he could afford a house in this middle-class neighborhood.

"Start mapping. There's no place to set up," Anna said.

"Do another loop." We went around the block and pulled the car to a stop. "No matter where we set up, people can look out their windows and see us. We can't take the chance of being seen. Let's map it on the fly." Fieldwork was my talent, not Anna's. Her forte was the internet, fact building, and execution. Anna drove a loop twice more while I quickly scribbled details and drew outlines. We pulled into an empty city transit bus stop and made distance estimations and recommendations for target extraction from the home. Then we drove the loop again until I was confident we'd picked up enough critical information to initiate a home invasion if necessary. I closed my notebook and said, "Let's check out Boury's lair."

Anna cut a U-turn and cruised back toward 36th Avenue. "Besides the motorhome, Leigh is the registered owner of a silver, 1990 Ford F250."

"Wow, I'm impressed. How about Boury?"

"A red, Jeep Cherokee."

Back in front of the Golden Lion Hotel, we turned south onto the Seward Highway making our way to the Dimond Boulevard exit. We hooked a right on Dimond and followed the map to Jewel Lake Road, where we turned right on West 84th Street and into a housing maze. Boury's shanty, a 50's style box house, was located one space from a corner lot. Again, no vehicles were present at the address. Kitty corner from the target location, we set up observation in a parking lot of an apartment complex.

Seedy neighborhoods rarely took notice of two people parked in a car. Drug deals happened all the time. Unless we'd landed in an ethnic area, as Caucasians we'd be overlooked by locals.

I mapped the street accesses, observation points, and house details of Boury's residence while Anna kept an eye out on the place. The weak point was immediately apparent. We'd be able to drive directly to the rear of the house via the driveway. With no outside light fixtures, and partially hidden from view by a six-foot tall wood fence, it was inviting. However, Alaska in the summer has an additional issue to consider. It is the land of the midnight sun. That meant we were unable to rely on the cover of darkness. In this neighborhood, people might be up and about throughout the night. A home invasion would be an absolute last ditch effort.

Activity at Boury's place was easy to watch. Without a garage on the property, everything was in open view. We'd be able to photograph visitors and have an accurate body count before we fired a shot. We didn't see any movement in or around the house, but that didn't mean there wasn't anyone home. We hadn't been on location long enough to determine that.

As it approached five o'clock, traffic flow increased to an uncomfortable level. Ordinarily, Palatini developed project plans over a span of time to ensure a positive outcome. We'd placed ourselves in a time crunch, and the current phase had to be shortened if we were to get a visual on the three target locations. "Let's go back to the hotel," I said. "We can use the time to make preparations for the trip to Woolf's place in Moose Pass tomorrow morning."

Anna fired up the Avenger, backed out of the parking spot where we'd concealed ourselves in plain view and pulled out onto the roadway. At the first stop sign, Anna cranked the wheel to the left to retrace our steps out of the housing maze. We cruised the block between cross streets and slowed for the stop sign.

An older model red SUV caught my eye as it made the corner, passing directly in front of our vehicle's path. Three people were in the car, two in the front seat, and the other person in the back.

"There! Right, there!" Anna probably thought I'd gone nuts as I dramatically pointed at the passing car. Anna had already taken notice.

Admittedly the unexpected surge of adrenaline had taken control of my reins. I was fit to be tied. It had been too long since I'd been dowsed with exhilaration. I recaptured my cool and readied for action.

"Got it," Anna said in a pacifying manner. She'd taken note of my reaction to the rush. I'd gotten a good look at the driver, and was sure it was Flattop. But it was the guy in the front passenger seat who stole my attention. As the SUV completed the corner, I spun to take a second look, and that's when it hit me. The passenger riding shotgun was Duke—and he'd turned to look back at me, too.

Even with our increasing distance, our eyes met. I was sure the element of surprise was lost. If any doubt lingered whether Duke recognized me or the Avenger, it immediately vanished.

The adrenaline that had kicked in by our surprise encounter continued to course through my veins. My Walther P99 delivered to my hand like clockwork from its holster. Anna looked at me and started the car forward. I slipped the silencer in place and jacked a round in the pipe.

"Their brake lights are on. Are you ready to do this now?" Anna asked.

The temptation to end this here and now played on my mind, but there was no sense interrupting the quietness of the neighborhood. If an unplanned shootout was avoidable, it was the right choice. "Roll-on out and we'll play it by ear." Anna continued forward and made a turn to the south.

Playing on my mind was the loss of the element of surprise. Catching these guys out in the woods in a training camp ambush would likely never happen. They'd have to be morons to believe I'd followed them to Alaska and didn't know the whereabouts of their training center. Their camp was more than two-hundred miles away. The saving grace of our run-in would be if they reacted and hightailed it to Glennallen for safety.

Still spurred on to make something happen, it wouldn't take a lot of effort to set up an encounter. All we had to do was pull the car over on the road's edge and wait. They would take care of the rest. We simply had to lead them out of the populated areas.

As we passed by the corner house, I had an unobstructed view through their backyard to the street where the SUV had turned. The window of opportunity lasted just long enough to catch a glimpse of the Jeep as it completed its turnaround. Seconds later it barreled past the stop sign, barely slowing down as it went through the intersection. I alerted Anna, "They're coming."

We were in five o'clock traffic. Anchorage, like most cities, crowded the roadways at rush hour. We caught the light and turned left into slow moving traffic on Jewel Lake Road. Still, we were better off than the SUV that had become stuck at the traffic light. Anna yammered out her thoughts as they rattled around in her head. "There were three people in the Jeep. You said Boury and Duke for sure. Who is the third person? They may be innocent."

She was thinking out loud, but I tossed in my two-cents worth free of charge. "People are free to choose who they associate with but are never free from the consequences of their choices. I won't kill an innocent person except in self-defense. If the rider engages me, he's no longer innocent. He made his choice. Besides, it might be Woolf."

We hooked another left onto Dimond Boulevard, worked our way through the intersection and picked up speed eastbound. Flattop would've had to jockey his rig through traffic to have caught us. That didn't happen, and now the SUV had vanished.

Flattop didn't know the Avenger and didn't look as if he'd gotten a good visual on us. I counted on Flattop questioning his pal Duke's level of sanity. Maybe it was all a figment of his imagination. After all, they had left me for dead.

"Get our map out, Walter. Locate where we are and let me know when larger roadway intersections come up. We will keep our speed up that way and get the distance between us and them. Once we've lost them for sure, we can make our way back to the hotel."

Thirty minutes later we found ourselves on Lake Otis Parkway, heading in the direction of the Golden Lion. We crossed over the Tudor Road intersection and north to 36th Street. We sat in the parking space and waited a few minutes to see if we had any unexpected visitors show. Anna headed for the room while I placed the car cover over the Avenger and tucked it in for the night.

Plans were still on the table to check out Pug's place in Moose Pass. Now that the A-Team learned of a possible threat, I expected a sense of heightened security would follow. Kuhl's recon might result in disaster unless we notified him of the change in conditions. Anna called and left a message on his cell phone to contact us pronto. It was bothersome to leave it open-ended, but it was the only option available.

I watched the local news at ten while Anna completed her nightly routine. My thoughts drifted between memories with Anna and the close encounter of the day. I felt conflicted. Anna was the perfect lady for me. If things had gone as planned in Toronto, we would've left on vacation and laid the groundwork for our future together. But, it didn't go as planned and I ended up in Shell Knob without Anna.

Odd, how fate causes paths to crisscross in life. Anna and I were destined to be together. The haunting question was, how? Were we meant to be romantically involved or were we yoked together for the sole purpose of maintaining an assassination league. The one thing I was sure of was our paths had crossed again, and we were hot on the trail of a pack of killers.

The hotel had provided a beautiful third story view of nothing beautiful at all. The only window in the room overlooked a dimly lit IRS building. But my attention wasn't looking out the window. Anna had climbed in on one side of the king sized bed and whispered, "We should get some rest." I looked toward the couch, but Anna patted the bed next to her and asked, "Don't you want to sleep here?" I slipped my T-Shirt off, laid flat on my back, pulled the covers up over my bare chest, and exhaled a deep breath in hopes of relaxing.

Anna, being female and intuitive, honed in on my feelings. In the most roundabout way she could take, she tried to get me to open up. "Are you familiar with Yin and Yang?"

"What? I saw it in a couple of Bruce Lee movies."

"Yin and Yang is a Chinese philosophy of opposite forces. Very ancient."

As we lay in the dark room, the midnight sun peeked through the edge of the window shades to add a bluish hue to our surroundings. Anna snuggled up under my arm and continued, "The Chinese believe there is a connection between seemingly opposing forces, like darkness and light, or life and death."

We were going somewhere with the conversation, but I didn't have a clue where until she asked, "Do you think we have a similar connection, a yin-yang, with the people we kill?" Anna wasn't trying to be funny. I could hear the sincerity in her words.

"I don't know if I'm tracking here or not sweetie, but I'd say what we're doing is about as yin-yang as it gets. It's a blood vengeance."

"Blood vengeance?"

"Yeah, you ever hear of the Hatfield and McCoy feuds? They were opposites. The government called it a blood vengeance. Local law enforcement had chosen sides, and in order to quell the violence, the Fed's enacted martial law to gain control of the area."

"Sounds like they were the same thing, not opposites."

"Not if you asked them. One was right, and one was wrong, depending on which one you asked. There's your yin and yang. The Alliance and Vigilance Committee portray themselves as guardians of the people. Similar to what we say as Palatini. But we are opposite forces. They are kidnappers, rapists, and murderers. We are vigilantes, assassins, and executioners of justice. Not exactly a popular notion and some would say we're just as wrong as the Hatfield and McCoy's. Ideology lends itself to acceptance for what has been done. Our ideology does too."

"Walter, about what happened in Toronto–"

I cut her off midstream, "Sweetie, it's behind us—leave it there." My words might not have sat well with her, but that's where I needed it— in the rear view mirror. It was obvious she wouldn't be satisfied until we talked about what went wrong, but for me, now was not the time. I had to steer the conversation in a positive direction.

"Do you remember the first time we worked together? When I dropped that victimized girl off to you in Portland."

"That wasn't the first time we worked together. That was the first time you dumped your problem on me to fix."

"Well, you sic'd me on that creeper like I was a trained attack dog." We laughed. She knew I was right. I continued, "When did we work together before that? Are you talking about that lawyer I'd planned to take out, but you whacked him first?"

"We never worked together on that operation. And as I recall you had given up on the idea."

"I didn't give up, just making sure of my target's guilt."

"You didn't know another hitter was in the field, and I doubt if you would have ever hit him. You didn't know the depth of his child pornography. The first time we worked together was the religious cult leaders you shot at the hot springs, remember?"

Anna was able to lift my spirits when I was in a funk. She brought up my accomplishments and patted me on the back. Even attack dogs liked to be petted and appreciated.

"Yeah, I remember. I wanted to protect you and not get you involved. Wasn't I the idiot?"

"Well yes and no. It's probably a good time to tell you. I didn't stay in the car as you had instructed me to do. I'd checked out the area earlier and knew where you would set up, providing you possessed a logical mind. I gave you time to get comfortable and become confident that you were alone as you readied your ambush. Then, I left the car and made my way further up the hill so as not to attract your attention and worked my way to within ten feet of where you lay hidden."

"Why'd you do that?"

"For two reasons, one was to cover your back. The other reason was to evaluate you for Palatini candidacy."

"I briefly detected your perfume but discounted it as part of my fantasy—you were on my mind, even back then, in ways you never imagined." Anna's soft body pressed against mine as she ran the tips of her fingers lightly across my chest. "The point was, Palatini go after large scale operations. Like our trip to Thailand. We rescued those kidnapped children and gave them their lives back. Remember? We disrupted an entire chain of organized sex slavery crime."

"Yeah, that was wild."

"You followed up by joining in the assault against a Brazilian child pornography ring. You, Seymour, Rusty, and Donnie cut off the legs of their criminal enterprise. I remember Maximillian saying we don't have an accurate count, but quite possibly, you saved hundreds of lives by what you did."

"Donnie bought the farm on that project," I whispered. The room was silent for a moment.

"I know you don't want to talk about Toronto, but I want you to let me say one thing without interrupting."

"Okay."

"You performed amazingly well under the stress and circumstances you were under. You saved hundreds more women and children who were being trafficked by the Mob and those that would be enslaved in the future."

Lying at my side, Anna couldn't have seen my smile, but it was there, hidden in darkness.

"I wanted you to know that I support you in every way on this project. This is the first time I've seen Palatini devote so much time, manpower, and finances to a project that will bring justice to only one victim."

"What I'm going to say won't make a lot of sense, but I'm going to say it anyway." A brief pause had served to highlight my awkwardness. "I was shown the 'what' and 'who' of the crime committed against that little girl." Again I paused. "I don't want to make it sound weird, but I've been chosen to act on Dawn Simmonds behalf. I've been Called, by 'who' or 'what' I don't know, but her blood has made an appeal."

Anna's hair brushed across my face as she moved on top my chest. It was dark, but not so dark I couldn't see her eyes as she studied my face. "I don't think it's weird at all." She'd led me to the exact place I wanted to go. She nestled deeper into my embrace. "I believe whatever you say, Walter." I'd shed the reserve I'd felt earlier and allowed my errant hands to stray for the moment and walk down memory lane.

Chapter 13

"Fear is a reaction...Courage is a decision."
—*Sir Winston Churchill*

The night had been long and sleep short but rewarding. No contact with Kuhl remained a chief concern. We pressed forward with our plans to head to Moose Pass and recon Brady Woolf's place. We grabbed a quick bite at the hotel before departing.

"I have an idea I want to discuss before we leave."

"What's up sweetie?"

"Duke or Boury may have called Woolf and warned him to watch for you or your car. Even if they weren't positive, they might have considered notifying the others."

"What do you have in mind? We already agreed not to call off the trip."

"We need Woolf's place mapped. I think we should pick up a rental and drive it until we leave for Glennallen."

"Good idea, make it happen."

One thing I've learned about Anna, she loved to make the arrangements. She had a head for details, was a quick organizer and liked all the Is dotted and Ts crossed. While we finished breakfast, Anna made a call and found a car to pick up. The extra run-around cost us time but ensured our anonymity. It was a smart move.

With Anna behind the wheel of our newly rented Toyota, we made tracks south on the Seward Highway. We hadn't traveled fifteen minutes before we were out of Anchorage and cruising along Turnagain Arm with Cook Inlet in our rearview mirror. The Inlet waters turned tranquil a mile past Beluga point where the current of the tidewaters had been noticeable. I wished the same were true about the roadway. Although still early in the day, there were numerous motorhomes and travel trailers lumbering along like railroad cars on the only access route to the Seward Peninsula. We weren't going to make up lost time on the drive.

For most people, the view was scenic and relaxing. Even with pressing issues on my mind, I'd found myself trying to spot mountain sheep on the rocky outcroppings where the road had cut into the mountain side. Not far from Anchorage, a small pod of white Beluga Whales rolled and fed at the edge of the receding tide.

An hour south, the road ascended Turnagain Pass. Green, lush, picturesque beauty surrounded us. The slow moving traffic quickly got on my last nerve. Tourists in RV's hogged the road and hampered posted driving speed. When we hit the passing lanes, we gave the Toyota all she had but in the end it didn't matter how many we passed. We ended up stuck behind another RV or trailer.

We took the turn-off toward Seward and a hundred miles south of Anchorage a small sign appeared at the edge of the road that read Moose Pass. You didn't want to blink, or you'd miss the sign and the town. Moose Pass was similar to Shell Knob in some aspects. Small, isolated and spread along the roadway, hemmed in by the mountainous terrain to the northwest and the Upper and Lower Trail Lakes on the opposite side.

Pug had an old 1988 Champion 12' by 56' mobile home registered to his name. In an area that housed a little over two-hundred people, I didn't figure it would take long to find his place. We slowed the Toyota and hooked a left off the Seward Highway when we spotted several loosely clustered mobile homes.

"This is it," Anna said.

Nestled in the park, she knew which space was his. The lots were spacious, with yards and roads well maintained. Trees accented this neighborhood. Clearly visible were less than a dozen mobile homes, encircled by a gravel road in front of the spaces. The trailer park had one unique feature. A row of RV and travel trailer hook-ups bordered the park's edge nearest the highway. Every space was filled with fifth-wheel trailers and motorhomes that hadn't found their way to the roadways to menace other traffic. Eventually, they would.

On a hunch, I asked Anna to drive by the motorhomes and see if Leigh's RV was there. None of the rigs matched up to the description Anna had, so we turned our attention to Pugs trailer house. We crept along the gravel drive keeping a close eye out for Woolf's White 1980 International Harvester Scout.

We located Woolf's aluminum-sided palace where the map had indicated it would be, but there were no vehicles parked in the stubby driveway or under the attached carport. I mapped the area quickly, then we high-tailed it for Anchorage.

Kuhl had not returned my message. There was no way of knowing if his cell phone received a signal where he'd stayed. From not knowing his status, a sense of foreboding and anxiety set upon us. Given the distance we had to travel, and the quietness of the ride, a guy had time to think about the 'what ifs' and I didn't want to verbalize any of them. It would only serve to heighten the level of our concern.

We swung into Anchorage, dropped the rental car off, fired up the Avenger and hit the road for Glennallen. We were halfway across Eklutna Flats when I told Anna about an auto wrecking yard that we'd passed on the way to anchorage and that I wanted to pay them a visit. I needed to outfit the Avenger with local license plates.

The Oregon license plates the Avenger wore were registered to the new me and legitimate. That meant the new me was traceable. For the project, the legal plates needed to be shelved and a set of local non-traceable plates mounted in their stead. I asked Anna to watch for the junkyard as we entered Palmer.

It was four-thirty when we arrived. The two-tone dilapidated wood fence stood easily over seven-foot high in places and less in others, effectively hiding the mangled vehicle graveyard from public view.

"Wait here unless you want to stretch your legs."

Anna looked over the ratty storefront exterior and said, "Enjoy."

"I'll make it fast."

As I stepped from the car, I grinned back at Anna and said, "You sure you don't want to stretch your legs, sweetie? I'll bet the crusty old geezer that runs the joint would like to see them." With a wry look, Anna merely pointed toward the front door. I closed the door and hoofed it to the entrance. A red and white sign that read "Closed" hung by a wire and floated on the evening breeze. In the window adjacent to the entry door was a plastic sign. Stuck to the glass by a suction cup it read

"Business hours" and showed five o'clock daily as their closing time. I cupped my hand against the window and looked inside. A row of overhead fluorescent lights faintly illuminated a long counter. I didn't see anyone moving around in the place. I figured the old coot probably closed up early to beat the Palmer traffic rush to the nearest tavern. I reached over and pushed down on the vintage lever door handle. It opened. A chill came over me. Looking over my shoulder, I saw Anna watching through the rear-view mirror. The door opened smoothly and without so much as a squeak. As I stepped through the entrance, I placed my gun hand on the butt of my Walther. As I crept forward, there was a rustling noise somewhere in front of me. I didn't need to walk into a crime scene or criminal act in progress, but it was the first thing that came to mind.

He startled me as much as I had him. Behind the counter was a young man kneeled on the floor rummaging through a box. Quick to his feet, the little guy practically jumped out of his skin when a breeze caught the entry door and slammed it shut.

Sixteen or seventeen years of age, he appeared to be the boss, or at least for the moment. "You the man in charge?" I asked.

"Yes, Sir."

The shack was nothing more than an old log cabin piecemealed together with plywood. It had all the earmarks of a one-room warehouse that had been renovated a long time ago. The insides matched the outsides, dingy and dirty. Stacks of auto parts helped form aisles and dismal lighting hung over the showroom heaps. Shadows stretched into the corridors that harbored an accumulation of dust.

"I'm a visitor to your state and I'm looking to add a couple license plates to my collection. I hang them on the walls of my private bar. They always make for a lot of conversation among my friends."

"You looking for some real old ones 'cause I got some."

"What I'd like are current plates." I tossed out a laugh. "That way I can remember what year I came to Alaska."

The boy said, "Wait here, I'll be right back." He walked behind the counter that doubled as the stockroom and disappeared. Occasional clunks and clatter emanated from the backroom which assured me the kid was still digging. I passed the time by redistributing piles of dust in a bin filled with vintage tools that had caught my eye. The percussion of metallic jangling on the counter broke the spell of the old tools. I made my way back to the front.

Brushing my hands off on my pants I approached the counter and asked, "What are they running?"

The boy hemmed and hawed for a moment. "We don't get a lot of call for these, how would ten dollars each sound to you?"

I looked the stock over, paired up two sets, one of which had tags that were current. "How's fifty bucks sound for both pairs?"

The kid snapped up on it, "Yes Sir." He bagged the plates, handed them across the counter. With an exchange of thanks we parted. Anna and I were back on track.

Our prearranged meeting with Kuhl was scheduled for the following morning. If we hadn't heard from him before then, and he was a no-show for the meeting, our operation would take on a defensive posture.

We arrived back at our RV late in the evening. First order of business was to change license plates on the Avenger. Physically, I was getting around pretty good by now. The pain had ceased to rule my activities, although I was still careful with my ribs. I could sufficiently chew food with my teeth solidly attached. Even the rainbow coloration of bruising that had covered most of my head and neck had faded into a light brown. The only issue that persisted was the tinnitus. Since I hadn't noticed any notable change in the ringing sensation, I assumed there was permanent damage.

Anna and I turned in for the night. She had given me the bedroom at the rear of the RV while she'd taken the loft over the cab. Vaguely cognizant of the overhead cabins light dimming, I closed my eyes and waited. In time, sleep would overtake my thoughts. In Alaska, during the waning days of July, nights tend to be dusk rather than dark for the few hours the sun rested on the horizon. Consequently, Anna had placed aluminum foil over the windows to guard against a too early sunrise. Still, whispers of light crisscrossed the cabin of the motorhome. Particularly vulnerable to the light was the loft Anna had chosen for her bed.

A fresh rose fragrance wafted in the air and awakened my senses as I felt Anna's hair brush against my face. She whispered, "Walter. Are you asleep?"

"Yeah, what's wrong?"

"I thought you might like to work on your chances?"

I assumed the question was rhetorical, but she came to the right place for the answer. Without another word I took her into my arms. She slipped the bedcover aside and as our bodies touched, we entwined. Her soft, wet lips parted on contact with mine as she sought my tongue with hers. My hands roamed up her bare back heightening our senses. The rhythm of my heart picked up until it thundered against my chest and I could feel her heart pounding in sync with mine. Anna was a woman who liked to be in the driver's seat, traveling hard and fast with her hands firmly on the controls. My mind slipped into blissful oblivion as my body buckled up for a wild ride.

At seven in the morning, I awakened to Anna's eye-twinkling smile followed by a nudge to my rib cage.

"Hey girl, take it easy on the ribs, will ya."

Any expectation of sympathy was short-lived. "You're fine. You didn't complain about your ribs hurting last night."

I muttered under my breath, "That might be the reason they're sore today."

Anna held me in a close embrace, her lips nearly touching mine. She whispered softly, "It's time to get up and get going."

"Sweetie, I've got a better idea. Why don't you get up and make us…" Kissed into silence, my lips moved to her neck, then under her earlobe, seducing her to my powers. How could any woman resist such passion?

Evidently, it was easy. Anna abruptly rolled from on top of me and into a sitting position. With an excited, wide-eyed look, she exclaimed, "That's a magnificent idea, Walter. You can make us breakfast while I'm getting dressed!"

The enjoyable few minutes had passed too quickly for my liking. "Yeah, that's what I was thinking all right." It was wasted sarcasm.

"Come on." Anna tugged at my arm. "Thomas will be here soon and I would like to be dressed when he gets here."

Reluctantly, I nodded. Far be it from me to spoil Anna's morning plan. Besides, she was right. With any luck, Kuhl would arrive soon. If he didn't, we had a new ball game to play.

Having been reared a farm boy I had a different take on breakfast from that of my city-dwelling counterparts. Yogurt and English muffins were for hippies. For three long weeks, yogurt had been the staple of my diet. As long as I'd been tasked to produce breakfast, it was strictly bacon and eggs.

When Anna finished showering, she opened the tiny bathroom door and leaned out, "Put an English muffin into toast, will you honey." To show my willingness to compromise with my fellow Palatini, I conceded. Anna finished drying her hair as the aroma of toasted sourdough permeated the RV cabin. Muffins added a touch of class to an otherwise bare bones breakfast entrée of scrambled eggs. Maybe I was trying to impress Anna. I wanted to show her I had some degree of culture and wasn't a complete Neanderthal. She hadn't given me a reason to have felt lesser than her in any way, but it was obvious she was better educated and more sophisticated. On the other hand, my caveman qualities might have been what she found attractive.

Loudly I said, "Grubs on," as if I was feeding a small army. Pot holders lined the center of the table and were soon covered with skillets of eggs, bacon, and potatoes O'Brien. I opened a jar of Apple Butter and started another set of muffins toasting.

Anna stopped at the refrigerator and removed a yogurt before she joined me at the table. I shook my head.

Four distinct taps with a set of keys alerted us to Kuhl's presence at our door. Anna answered the knock. Kuhl placed a black canvas bag on the seat opposite from where I sat, turned and gave Anna a big hug. I'd risen to greet him with a handshake, but he took the extra steps to give me a hug too. Assembled on the corner of the table was a stack of paper plates and plastic wear ready for use. I pulled the hot muffins from the toaster, put them on a plate and said, "Don't be bashful, dig in," as I handed it to him.

Kuhl loaded up with plenty of bacon and eggs then drenched a muffin with Apple Butter. I kept the toaster going. Kuhl struggled to swallow and talk at the same time, "How did it go for you guys?"

"We mapped the residences, but it didn't go as planned," Anna said.

"Did you get our message?" I asked.

"No." Kuhl pulled his cell phone out and looked to see if there was a message. "No reception this far out." He closed the lid on the flip-phone and slipped it back into his jacket pocket. "Go ahead."

"We mapped Leigh's place first. No vehicles and no motorhome. We went to Boury's place next and mapped it. Again, it didn't appear anyone was home. When we left his house, we pulled out onto a side street and ran smack dab into Boury and Dixon," Anna said.

"I'm sure they got a look at me," I said. "They tried to follow us through traffic, but Anna lost them. The next day we rented a car and drove to Moose Pass to map out Woolf's mobile home. As far as we could tell there wasn't anyone at his trailer and no vehicles parked near his place."

Kuhl nodded and finished his last couple of bites. Ritualistically, Kuhl wiped each finger spotless with a wet towel followed by a paper napkin to dry them. I wondered what was going on in his mind. The element of surprise wasn't an element to relinquish to our enemies and we'd lost the edge.

"So, they know you're here?" He wadded the paper napkin into a ball and tossed it on his plate.

"My gut tells me they do," I said. "I've never known my instincts to be wrong."

"It's of little matter," Kuhl said as he pressed the fingertips of his hands together. "Often in Covert Ops, the enemy knew we were coming. They didn't know when, where, or how but they knew we were gunning for them. They never stopped us, and these guys won't stop us either." Kuhl's demeanor reminded me of a therapist as his fingertips mimicked the pattern of his words. "Keep in mind, they may think you're here, and Anna too since you had a driver, but they don't know about me. Surprise is still an element."

Kuhl was incredibly cool and confident which brought strength to our conversation. Anna, who'd been sitting forward during the SitRep, leaned back against the seat and appeared relaxed.

"We have more legwork to do," Kuhl said. "From my experience in similar situations, it is paramount we follow the information trail wherever it leads. Once we engage, there will be no time for recon. We must be relentless and persist until it's over."

It was my turn to nod. "Last killer standing—wins."

"Something like that," he said.

I shrugged and said, "I like it. How about you Anna?"

"What did you find at the training camp, Thomas?"

"I was able to enter the compound easily. Essentially, they are without security on the compound. They appear to rely extensively on no trespassing and warning signs. I counted a dozen or more posted on everything from trees to buildings. They make it an unfriendly place to wander into. In the way of real security, they have simple bolt locks on the two doors." Kuhl pulled from his black bag a small folder with drawings inside. "There is a series of mock buildings, some are nothing more than props used for training. It's very similar to what we used in the military for urban warfare training. Only the training camp is on a miniature scale from military operations."

"How large of a place is this?" I asked as I looked over the drawings.

"The mockup training area is spread out over a fifty-yard circumference. We should try to stay out of it when we bring these guys down. It's a risky environment because it's their home turf."

Anna and I both nodded while Kuhl continued, "The main building is the meeting hall and it sets separate from the training area. As you can see on the map, it's the first structure you would encounter from the highway. The driveway length is approximately two-hundred meters long and makes for easy access."

"Tell me about inside the compound."

"The amenities are pretty straightforward. The power plant is a small generator outside the back door. The latrine is a double wide outhouse located twenty yards from the rear corner of the building. No well or potable water supply. A singular propane furnace in the larger room probably takes the chill out of the air in the winter months, but that's about all. Most importantly, a one-hundred-gallon propane tank is attached to the building on the driveway side."

"Why is that significant?" Anna asked.

"You don't want to be anywhere near it when it blows. If we get in a shootout, find something else for cover." Kuhl laughed, "Just fair warning."

"The meeting hall is unlike the Dixon Holler compound. It doesn't have a second level; the design is simple with the one large room connected by a hallway to four smaller rooms. The small rooms look like poorly organized storage facilities for doomsday preppers. It's a hodgepodge of blankets, medical supplies, water containers and canned foods. The door lock sprung open quickly with the use of a pick set."

"There aren't any alarms in the place?" I asked.

"What they have are a couple of motion-activated cameras. They weren't hooked up and I suspect they are intended to intimidate visitors."

"What good does that do them?" Anna asked.

"None," Kuhl said. "You can tell this is a low budget operation. Everything in the place is old or used."

"Did you get completely through the place or do you need more time?" I asked.

"I had as much time as I needed. Not a single person showed up while I was there."

I noticed Kuhl's smile, so I pointed it out. "Your lip is creeping up the side of your face again. What's up your sleeve?"

"We know the Alaska Alliance is a proclaimed pseudo-paramilitary organization operating under the guise of survivalists. That's the front for their phony operation. Inside the meeting hall is a calendar with two of the weekends blocked out. I believe these are gathering dates for their group. Any legit militia would have muster or drill schedules, but I suspect it's a ruse of some sort. There is something deceptive going on. I haven't been able to get a handle on what the scam is, but it's coming together piece by piece. That's why we need to follow the information trail. There's more to what we see than what meets the eye."

"I'm not following," Anna said. "Are you saying the Alliance is not a militia of sorts?"

"Exactly," Kuhl said. "On one of the walls inside and again on their calendar is a circular symbol called a Black Sun. The same symbols Dixon had at his compound. I am vaguely familiar with its use in the occult and Nazi Germany." Kuhl paused to retrieve another folder from his bag.

Anna was my go-to girl for clues to solve a mystery. With her worldly travel and Internet investigations, I expected her to chime in and expound from her wealth of knowledge about the Black Sun but she didn't. She was in the dark, too.

"The symbol on the calendar is small, maybe two inches across but the symbol on the wall is easily three or more feet wide. They intend for it to be noticed. However, it is rarely seen and when it has been discovered, it's been displayed by social neo-Nazis."

"Maybe these guys are a pack of wannabes. You know, Heil Hitler and all that crap," I said.

"I don't see where they're politically aligned with Nazism," Kuhl said, "neo-Nazis are, among other prejudices, heavily anti-Semitic and they make no bones about it. We see nothing of the sort at the compound or in their flyers. No propaganda literature, no pictures of Hitler, no swastikas or other paraphernalia. And here's the thing, if they were for real, we should be seeing other signs of neo-Nazism besides the Black Sun. I think it's window dressing for another purpose."

"With these guys, one of the idiots could have seen a Black Sun symbol, thought it was cool and decided to use it for their logo," I said.

"That fits," Kuhl said. "Everything I've seen leads me to believe the Alaskan Alliance is a sham. We already know they're up to no good, but I'm leaning toward organized crime as the basis for their alliance."

"If you think the Black Sun relates to a criminal organization, then we don't know enough about our enemy," Anna said.

Each of us sat quietly for the next few minutes contemplating the possibilities. Then Anna piped up with a suggestion. "Conduct an interview with one of the targets. That should bring clarity to the issue."

"Whoa, whoa, whoa," I said. "I've seen your interview techniques in Thailand. It's hard for them to talk to you."

Anna bowed up. "People talk easily to me!"

"Not with their throats slit and their tongues hanging out the opening, they don't!"

Anna's lips pulled back into a smile. "They gave me the information I was after—and quickly."

"Yeah, well we'll never know for sure because you carved them up like a Thanksgiving turkey."

"Stop whining. You enjoyed flying first class."

"Leave the interviews to Kuhl and me."

Kuhl's lip curled up. A sign he had more to tell. "Not much else of value in the building. I exited the main building through a rear door at the end of the single hallway. Outside the rear egress is a four-foot tall mini-octagon arena made from eight wood and wire panels, six-foot-long."

"What?" I said in disbelief. "These guys fight?" I thought back and as I recalled, they weren't skilled fighters at all.

"Not people. They use it for dogs."

Anna immediately moaned in disgust. I shook my head. Over the years, my research of people that abused animals or allowed dogs to fight were frequently the same people who mercilessly hurt innocent people. With spousal abusers and child molesters, there was something depraved in their character that excited them by cruelty, in general.

"Any animals at the compound?" Anna asked.

"Yes. Four dogs hooked on chains and in small kennels. They appear malnourished and have combat injuries. They're not pit bulls or breeds commonly used for dog fighting. My guess, they have been used for training other dogs to be aggressive. I've seen it before and I don't like what I saw," Kuhl said.

I nodded, "I grew up on a farm and I killed a lot of animals, but I was never mean to a critter for the sake of being mean. I don't understand dog fighting at all."

"It would be good to get the dogs out of the compound area before we clean house," Anna said.

"We could do a grab and go," I said. "But I think we're getting the cart before the horse. We came to take care of business first."

"I'll see if I can find an animal rescue organization in Alaska. We could turn the dogs over to them with the understanding of anonymity," Anna said.

"We'll have to move quickly. Their next weekend gathering is coming up," Kuhl said.

"Anna, see what you can find out about where the animals will go. What else do we have?" I asked.

"It keeps getting better," Kuhl said. "Remember Leigh's 1990 Ford motorhome?"

"It's there?" I asked.

"Oh yeah and it was easier to get into than the building. From the condition inside the RV, I'd say they parked it when they returned from their trip and haven't touched it since. It's a mess inside. I'd call these guys pigs, but it would give pigs a bad name."

"If it hasn't been sanitized, it will be loaded with forensic evidence, assuming they had Dawn inside," Anna surmised.

"It's loaded all right," Kuhl said. "Like Walter said, these guys are a taco short of a fiesta plate when it comes to covering their tracks."

"What? I never said that. I don't even know what it means."

"My point is they aren't very smart." Kuhl placed a set of latex gloves on and reached inside his bag. This time, he retrieved a gallon-sized plastic bag containing a small stack of photographs. "Don't touch these," Kuhl said, as he laid the prints on the table. It took Kuhl a minute to arrange the twenty-six photographs into two groups. "These come from a Polaroid Spectra 1200 which is an instant film camera."

"Wow, that's amazing you know the type camera by looking at the photos," I said.

Kuhl grinned. "A drawer in the motorhome has the camera stashed." He continued, "As you can see, we have pictures with more than one native female victim in them. I suspect these photos represent trophies in some manner for these guys."

One photo caught my eye almost immediately. I pointed it out and said, "That's Duke Dixon and Ponytail."

"Is that Dawn?" Anna asked.

I compared the girl in this picture to my memory of the ones Jay showed me of Dawn. "I'd say it's her."

The graphic nature of the image and the appearance of pain on Dawn's face made my blood boil. The prompting by Destiny, the visual image of her torture, and the blood's appeal in my dreams, made a strong impression. Killing Duke would be easier now than before. Kuhl isolated another picture from the stack only this time Pug was the principal actor. With any photographic evidence, it can only tell you so much. In this case, it spoke plenty. Pug was sprawled naked on top of a young native female who looked unconscious. Was he having sex? I didn't care. She looked to be underage and unconscious; he'd already crossed the line. Another photograph showed Pug with a leather belt in hand and a different native girl cowering naked in a corner of what appeared to be a bedroom. Two things were now certain, the pictures weren't all taken in the motorhome and there was more than one victim involved.

"One guy is missing from the pictures," I said. "Flattop."

"Maybe he's the cameraman," Anna said.

"That's good work, Kuhl. The brutality I've seen in these photos is as bad as I've encountered on any project," I said. "Anna, you've done this once already, but I want you to go through your notes, use whatever means necessary, to check for other missing or murdered children in the Glennallen area. Then expand your search along the entire road system. Dawn was from Palmer and these guys lived in Anchorage and Moose Pass. Check everything that fits."

"I'll have to travel to one of the cities for internet and telephone service," Anna said.

"Take the Avenger and go. Now that we have pictures, I want to take them down before they have another opportunity to strike. No more victims," I said. "Let's rendezvous here tonight at ten. I'm going to hop a ride with Kuhl and check out this compound for myself."

"Don't forget about the dogs," Anna said.

With a resounding, "Roger that" from Kuhl, we started a weapons check. Anna prepared for her road trip.

Chapter 14

"As I walk through the valley of the shadow of death,
I shall fear no evil. For the shadow is mine and so is the valley."
—Unknown

Kuhl slipped behind the wheel of his van while I took shotgun. Literally. Kuhl handed me his new tactical Saiga-12 semi-automatic 12-gauge. I tingled all over and could hardly wait to give it a whirl. We'd traveled south for less than a half hour when Kuhl pointed to a driveway on the right that led to the training camp. We crossed over a small stream that ran under the roadway at the bottom of the ravine adjacent to the dirt access road. When we crested the knoll, Kuhl pulled the van off the hard surface and onto the road's shoulder before he stopped.

"Let's put our ears on." Kuhl made his way to the console in the rear of the van where he kept his electronic gadgetry.

"You planted bugs?"

"Only two on their phony cameras. There are no telephones or computers so we can't run wiretaps. It's a bare bones operation inside. The wireless voice transmitters I planted are our only monitoring devices. The scope and range are limited."

"At least we have something."

"They have a pick up range of approximately thirty-five feet in the open areas of the building. They are passive until it senses noise. At that point, they are good for less than eight hours continuous activation. In the event the Alliance has their gathering this weekend it's conceivable we'll only be able to monitor the first half of one day."

I stepped out of the van to get my first impression of the area layout. The camp lay hidden from view underneath an impenetrable canopy of trees and thick underbrush. The Copper River Delta was a never ending maze of rolling hills that spanned an area the size of West Virginia. The vastness of the valley was spectacular. Seeing the terrain answered a gnawing question I had as to why the Alliance had gone unnoticed by law enforcement.

The people of the Copper River basin were fiercely independent when it came to government control. Both the Feds and State officials had a keen interest in the region. Properly developed, there was money to be made from minerals to tourism. These were opportunities the government wanted to share with locals, but development of the area was slow and not the reason most inhabitants sought refuge in rural Alaska.

Copper River locals were self-reliant. Survival was a way of life. I hadn't found any indicators that residents in the Delta Basin were anything like the trio representing the Alliance. The fact was, the Alliance weren't area residents and they had nothing in common with the people.

With the salmon run in full swing, vehicle traffic was plentiful on the hardtop arteries. It suited me fine. Blending in with my surroundings was an art I practiced—chameleon-like. I was adept to the customs and behaviors of rural living. However, engaged in our present operation, it wasn't the people of Copper River I needed to imitate, it was the hordes of visiting fishermen. Locals knew their Copper River neighbors. What they expected to see in a visitor was visitor behavior.

One side of the van's back door cracked open. I turned to see Kuhl rapidly gesturing with his hand. "C'mon—quick!" He had my attention.

"Someone is at the compound." I waited while Kuhl continued to listen through his headset. Out the back window of the van, I could see the driveway where it intersected with the pavement. I grabbed a set of binoculars and trained my view on the access road.

Minutes passed slowly causing anxiety to build. Suddenly I caught a glimpse of color dodging in and out through the tree covered access road. I alerted Kuhl, "Movement!" I adjusted the focus to a crisp view as the object emerged from the dense coverage. By this time, Kuhl joined me with a set of binoculars; a white four-wheel drive vehicle had emerged from the thick growth at the edge of a highway.

"It's a Scout. I'm sure of it." Not many vehicles on the road looked like an old International Scout. I had firsthand knowledge of Scouts having owned a '66 version and there hadn't been much change in body style. The vehicle turned north on the Richardson Highway. Kuhl looked in my direction and said, "Should we go?"

"Pug had a white Scout. Let's put the tail on."

We hurriedly took our positions in the van, spun it around and rolled northbound.

"Let's not tag too close."

Kuhl laughed. "Thanks for the tip," and curved his lips into a smile and laughed again.

At the Glenn Highway, the Scout pulled into the only gas station at the intersection. Unofficially the juncture was the central hub for traffic in this neck of the woods. Kuhl circled the van around next to an eatery in a corner of the gas station.

Kuhl leaned back and using one barrel of his binoculars read the license plate aloud, "Alaska, GOR 622."

I scrambled to look up Woolf's vehicle registration in Anna's files. "It's a match," and read the plate number back to Kuhl.

"Roger that."

We could see a man refueling the Scout. We weren't able to identify him until he entered the Mom and Pop store at the station—it was unmistakably Woolf.

Less than ten minutes later, Pug had jumped into his Scout and pulled out behind a tractor-trailer rig. When he'd driven passed us in the lot, we confirmed he was traveling alone. We waited a minute and allowed two other vehicles to pass in front of us before we continued north behind our target. We loosely followed for miles, catching little more than a glimpse of the Scout on the winding hills of the delta.

Travelers hauling trailers and driving motorhomes caused an accordion effect in the traffic flow. Thankfully, Pug's Scout was caught behind the road turtles as frequently as our van. An hour into the drive, Kuhl asked, "How far are we taking the tail?"

"Like you said, brother, follow the information trail."

Kuhl had said, in a roundabout way, we needed more depth in the project. He wanted a better understanding of what we're dealing with and who were the players. After the photographs had turned up, all I wanted was them dead. Any dismantling of their organization had to occur one target at a time.

Two bars were showing on my cell phone, enough signal to place a call to Anna and let her know we were on a tail. Anna had easily made Palmer and would have better reception for the call.

"Hey sweetie, we might be late for dinner."

"What have you found?" Her voice crackled with excitement. Every Palatini wanted to be involved with this leg of an operation.

"We're tracking a Pug."

"Sounds sporting. Keep me updated when you can."

Ninety-plus miles north from where we'd started the tail, Pug pulled off and parked his Scout at the Paxson Lodge then went inside. Paxson was a touristy joint at the intersection of the Richardson and Denali Highways. He was safe here.

Kuhl and I tossed around the idea of a grab and go. What better way to shake things up than snagging our target at a remote stop. An Alliance member's disappearance, coupled with their recent sighting of me near another member's house, might create a healthy level of chaos. For the time being we watched and waited for the opportunity. I could hear it knocking.

Daylight, combined with a high traffic area like Paxson, stacked the odds against us for action. A half hour passed before Pug pulled back out onto the road. We were poised to continue following him north on the Richardson Highway. To our surprise, he took the "Y" onto the Denali Highway, a route that had little notable traffic compared to the Richardson Highway.

In one sense, we saw our wish come true for an isolated work environment, but it also created complications. We found ourselves having to fall back further on the tail, or he'd pick up on us for sure. The road climbed through a couple miles of brushy, low-lying hills and onto a lengthy flat without a tree in sight. We dropped further back. I kept Kuhl's fancy shotgun close at hand. If he pulled over anywhere on this stretch of road and the coast was clear, we would 'jack' him.

Kuhl and I hadn't figured out what game Pug was playing. Maybe it was a fishing trip, but it was hard to believe he'd travel a hundred miles for a salmon when they were in the stream next to the camp. With the minutes ticking away, I'd become interested in knowing his reason for the long drive on a road with only a few insignificant settlements. What was his agenda? I loved the mystery of the unknown.

From Paxson, we drove a twenty-one-mile leg of broken pavement and frost heaves before coming upon an Inn at Tangle Lakes. Pug's Scout was already parked in clear view when we pulled into the lot.

Pug and I had been too chummy when we'd met the first time. It was likely he'd pick me out of the crowd in a heartbeat. This was especially true if he'd been contacted by the others with the possibility I'd followed them to Alaska. Kuhl, who Pug hadn't seen, was elected for the recon duties.

Kuhl geared up to go inside the Inn. He gathered a few of his electronic gadgets together. I was sidetracked by Kuhl as he methodically hid items in his clothing. So much so, I barely caught the Scout's movement from the corner of my eye. Pug's rig pulled out of the Inn's driveway, crossed the road and barreled down the dirt access to the lake. Upper Tangle Lake was the largest body of water in a chain of lakes that were connected by streams and a popular fishing area.

Kuhl and I hadn't paid much attention to the floatplane as it touched down on the lake. When it taxied toward the dock where Pug waited, we became very interested. Kuhl used binoculars to read aloud the tail number, which wasn't on the tail at all but inscribed on the fuselage. "Looks like a Cessna," he said. "It's white with a two-tone blue stripe on the side." It was enough to give Anna for a research project. I looked at my cell phone signal; I had nothing.

"I'm going to hop out and use a phone in the Inn to call Anna while you keep an eye on the situation." We knew Pug was up to no good, which meant whoever he was meeting was up to no good. Pug had waved a big red flag, and my gut instincts reacted. Why would a guy have driven out to the middle of nowhere to meet somebody? There were dozens of lakes a floatplane could land on near Glennallen. The only thing that made sense was someone on board didn't want to be seen in the Glennallen area with Pug. I didn't blame them. I wouldn't want to be seen with him either.

Inside the Inn, the woman behind the restaurant register pointed out the single payphone in the joint. Hanging on a wall between the men's and women's restrooms was a beat up black telephone—it wasn't exactly private. With my back to restaurant diners and a lowered tone of voice, I placed the call.

Anna was eager to sink her teeth into fresh meat and what I gave her was enough to satiate her lust for the time being. I hung up the phone and turned around in time to see Pug holding the door open for a man I hadn't seen before. I quickly stepped into the men's bathroom and locked the door. Now that I'd trapped myself, I looked to my cell phone to get me out of the squeeze. I batted a thousand with bad luck. No signal.

Pug's visitor, a gray-haired man, dressed in business attire including a dark suit and tie, looked out of place for Tangle Lakes. He and Pug shared a remarkable resemblance in height and weight, but that's where the similarities ended. I'd given them a moment to get settled at a table before I unlocked the door and scanned the dining area. Pug was seated with his back toward the restrooms and against a window to my left. Chances were good that I could walk straight out of the restaurant, but I had to play it smart. The first step was the hardest but once committed, the next step came easily. As I passed by where Pug sat, I looked toward the service counter on my right and waved to the waitress. She didn't know me, but nonetheless smiled and waved back. I didn't want a big scene. Casual would do nicely. I thanked the woman at the register as I passed. Reaching the door, I didn't look back. I walked around to the front of the Inn where we'd parked the van. To my surprise, the vehicle sat unattended and unlocked. I climbed into the passenger seat, waited and watched.

Minutes later, Kuhl opened the double doors at the back of our rig. Without any explanation as to where he was or what he'd been doing, he climbed in, gathered a few electronic gadgets and hopped back out.

"I'm going in—wait here."

"I've got your six." The van doors closed and Kuhl vanished.

I'd lost track of time, but not of my target. Although initially out of view, Pug's Scout crept from the Inn's parking lot with a passenger onboard and across the paved road toward the airplane. With my binoculars focused on Pugs vehicle, I jumped with surprise when Kuhl opened the van door.

"Edwin Snuth is the old guy with Woolf. I picked the name up off mail in the aircraft."

"I wondered where you'd run off to earlier."

"I didn't have much time at the plane. Boaters approached the dock, so I walked."

"What's his claim to fame?"

"He's a businessman that's found his way to the top of the food chain."

Kuhl recounted his steps, "I took a table with a view just like they had by the window. The table I picked put me directly behind Pug, back to back. Kuhl's lopsided grin showed.

"What happened then?"

"The waitress brought the coffee, of course."

"What could you hear them saying?"

"For the most part they kept the volume low-key. But I placed my ball cap and a recorder on the table next to me. With only a foot between Woolf's back and mine, and Snuth facing Woolf and my back, I was close enough to make a recording of their conversation." Kuhl pulled out a small video camcorder and said, "It's all right here."

"Sweet."

"The recording might be rough and scratchy at the beginning. But, once I had checked the wireless screen viewer I had in my front shirt pocket and adjusted the angle slightly, the view of Edwin Snuth was spot-on. I checked audio with an earpiece when I was satisfied with the reception I left it alone to record." Kuhl pushed play and we listened.

Snuth said, "We've played this game too long…(Garbled and background noise). I have my people with the state ready to move on the mineral claims…(Garbled)…the Interior Department and BLM are lined up with their rubber stamps to let this through. These tribal leaders are driving me crazy with their delays. These natives want me to take all the risks and do all the work and they get all the profit. We talked about this, you and your boys were supposed to make life miserable for them. Soften them up. I told you I wanted them harassed to no end. They have to want to leave their tribal grounds. They need to be persuaded to sign the lease."

"Okay, Okay, I'll get it handled," Pug said.

"I don't want any more screw-ups. You were hired to do a job and I want it done. No more delays. It's in your best interests that it gets done fast."

"I'll put more pressure on the Elders and get the results you're looking for."

"I don't care how you do it. I don't want any witnesses. Do you understand? No more kidnapping girls so you can have a fun time with them. If you grab one of them, I want you to make it look like a drowning accident. I don't know what you were thinking taking that girl outside Alaska. Stupid move. You're going to have to do better than that."

"I get the picture, boss. I have some fresh ideas straight out of the south that's worked for them to keep problems under control. I have this guy, Duke—" Snuth interrupted Woolf, "Listen, I am not interested in the details. I want you to get it done."

Kuhl switched off the tape. Pug's Scout had crested the hill not fifty yards in front of us and turned toward Paxson. Kuhl asked, "What's the plan?"

"Like you said brother—follow the information."

We gave him a long lead. Unless we missed our guess, we knew the direction he'd be traveling. The sky had darkened and thick clouds masked the sixteen-thousand-foot peaks of the Alaska Range to the north. Bands of clouds swept rain across the delta. We turned south on the Richardson Highway and drove directly into the fast moving storm.

Vehicle traffic became fewer on the highway. I surmised the midweek weather had caused anglers to hunker down for an early evening. Pug's vehicle speed was affected too. He'd slowed his rig down to where we closed the distance to within eyeshot. Standing water collected on the asphalt surface and made driving treacherous. Pug had wisely exercised caution and slowed his speed allowing us the same opportunity.

The Scout swung into the parking lot of the Mom and Pop store by the Glenn Highway intersection. We refueled at the nearby service station. We figured if he got a head start on us, he'd be heading to the training camp only a few miles away. We'd easily catch him but, to our surprise, Pug pulled out heading west on the Glenn.

"He's either going home to Moose Pass or he's Anchorage bound," I said. "Moose Pass is a long way. I'm leaning toward Anchorage."

Kuhl nodded and said, "Where do you want to take him down?"

"Soon. Whenever the opportunity presents itself."

As evening fell, the storm-darkened sky gave the appearance of night. The thick mass of clouds showed no sign of breaking up the lock it had on the horizon. We'd driven thirty miles across the flats and passed Gunsight Mountain's tiny airstrip. Hemmed in by a cloud bank on either side of the Pass were jagged mountain pinnacles that peeked through like dark shadows. We could see the terrain changing as we headed down into the Pass.

Kuhl pointed out a set of vehicle taillights in front of us that had flashed rapidly. The driver had pumped the brakes and I counted two blinks from the right-hand turn signal before it disappeared from the road. Kuhl slowed the van as we approached the area where the vehicle had turned off. We could see Pug's Scout at the crest of a knoll. We looked for a turnaround.

Our target had parked on a three-hundred foot long pull off. Road signs marked "Trailhead Tahneta Pass" sat at either end of the pull off. The Scout was the only vehicle visible in the lot. Rain was coming down heavier and steady, the wind was picking up and temperatures were steadily dropping. The unseasonably cold conditions played to our favor. Had the climate been more conducive to hiking, the parking lot might have had a higher level of activity.

"Let's have a little chat."

Kuhl's eyes lit up and a smile stretched his lips tight. In the dim lighting of the dashboard, he had taken on a Guy Fawkes appearance without the mask. We traveled another quarter-mile and broke the crest of the hill before we swung the van around on the hardtop. We cruised back past the west trailhead entrance and turned into the lot where the Scout had entered, cutting our lights as we pulled onto the access road.

The Scout wasn't visible from the entrance. The rise in the road surface, trees and bushes had masked our arrival. We quickly geared up with ski masks, gloves and weaponry. We hoofed it to the top of the knoll and crept closer. Pug had cut the headlights off, but the engine was still idling. Kuhl used a set of Mil-Spec night vision goggles to verify Woolf was inside the SUV.

Kuhl gave the thumbs up and we advanced. Kuhl moved left from the vehicle and out of view of the side mirrors. Effectively, he was moving up in the driver's blind spot. I slipped into the brush on the right side of the vehicle and continued to close the distance on the rear of the Scout. Ten feet away, another step and I was eight, now six.

I startled. The noise I heard was indistinguishable. My P99 responded to a ready position. I instinctively squatted under the plane of the Scout's windows. More noise. Struggling sounds. A momentary tremulous voice—silenced.

I quickly took a position at the left corner of the Scout. Without hesitation, I spun the corner with my weapon prepared to destroy anything in front of the muzzle. The Scout's door stood wide open. Pug lay face down on the gravel, Kuhl's shotgun stuck in the back of his head. I was late for the party.

While Kuhl held our target at gunpoint, I slipped a pair of stylish nylon bracelets on his wrists. The style you'd find at a hardware store. I stood Pug up and dusted off the front of his clothes that were mostly wet from the rain-soaked gravel. I spun him around and put three more cable ties together then cinched them around his neck like a dog collar. I pulled his wrists up behind his back and fastened them to the noose with additional ties. Struggling or working his wrists free would cause the collar to tighten like a noose.

With my ski mask in place, Pug hadn't recognized me. He made two or three attempts to ask why we were jacking him up. We intensified his concerns by saying nothing. At one point, Kuhl laughed when Pug asked who we were. "You must be some kind of stupid. Our masks are to hide our identity. You think we're going to tell you who we are? Don't ask anything else until we say you can talk."

Kuhl pulled the shotgun sling to one side, turned Woolf around and said, "Wait here." With a slap on my shoulder, he trotted toward his van. I searched Pug for weapons and removed everything from his pockets. Besides a handful of change I took his wallet and cell phone. A check of his call log showed he'd placed a call recently. I put his belongings in my jacket pocket. Kuhl pulled up alongside us and said, "Put him in the back and put tape on his mouth."

Pug flew pretty well when I tossed him in the van head first. Finding a comfortable spot to sit was a challenge not easily overcome. However, he squished into the corner behind the driver seat nicely. I slapped a piece of polyethylene tape across Pug's mouth.

"What about the Scout?" Kuhl asked.

Clutching a flashlight that Kuhl kept handily within reach, I hastily looked through the Scout. A small pile of papers scattered on the back seat were the only items of interest I found. I quickly bagged them for Anna, who enjoyed digging through junk drawers and people's personal belongings. I turned the Scout's ignition off, took the keys, locked the doors and made my way to the van.

"Is that what you want to do, leave it parked out here?"

"No sweat brother. Vehicles park here all the time. No one's going to notice."

A half hour later we'd pulled up to the highway intersection at Glennallen. "Want to make a party out of it?" Kuhl asked.

"Why not? Let's pick up the little lady."

"Roger that."

There had been occasions when my thoughts have come back to haunt me and this was one of them. Countless times I'd told myself that cell phones were nothing more than electronic leashes. But I was wrong. They were valuable tools in our trade. I wanted to contact Anna and the Glennallen phone tower had the strongest signal in the area. But it was of no use. Located on the river's edge, the RV Park had poor reception. We would surprise Anna when we showed up with Pug.

It was late in the evening when we arrived at the RV. Pug had ridden quietly having chosen not to agitate us. He must've understood there wasn't any benefit in it for him. Anna was waiting with her coat on at the door. Quickly, I interjected, "I tried to call but I couldn't get an answer. There wasn't enough signal." I was puzzled when I saw she was ready to go. "How'd you know we were en route?"

"Women's intuition?" Anna patted my cheek like I was a child.

"That's what women always say."

"Relax, I didn't know. Do you feel better now?"

"No—because you were ready to go."

"I know you. You couldn't resist the opportunity to take him, and you knew better than to leave me out of it."

She had me pegged.

Anna fired up the Avenger and waited for us to pull out. Adherence to Kuhl's travel wishes for the mission's sake pleased him. I climbed into the van, pulled off my mask, turned to Woolf and said, "Remember me?" He had plenty of time to get a good look and I made sure he could see me. Confused, he nodded his head.

"Sit back and relax. You and me—We're going to have a talk. Man-to-man."

"Head north away from Glennallen," I said.

"What's north?" Kuhl asked.

"Nothing, I hope."

Camping areas were densely populated along the tributaries of the delta. I'd noticed on our trip to Tangle Lakes the farther north we'd traveled the less camping, fishing, and fewer people were near the highway.

"The road map shows a Trans-Alaska Pipeline crossing and an access road that veers off to the right. Look to the left side of the access and you'll see a large gravel pit. It's worth checking out."

"Gotcha." Kuhl liked the idea.

It was after midnight when we arrived at the pit. The clouds hugged the mountain peaks around us while the sky above cleared. Usually, I would have said weather conditions had improved. But the chilly wetness made being outdoors for any length of time miserable. I helped Pug out of the back of the van. I didn't want him to hurt himself. Kuhl upended a five-gallon paint bucket and helped Pug get situated.

I leaned toward Pug so we were face to face. "I need answers." Pug stared me in the eyes. I reached up and slowly pulled the tape from his mouth. "You tell me the truth and everything goes smoothly."

"The whole thing in Missouri was an accident. We didn't know who you were or nothing."

"Who is the Alaska Arctic Alliance? I want to know who's who?"

"Like what?" The smirk he showed displayed a level of disrespect I wasn't willing to tolerate. I'd rather he shook in fear than sneered.

"Anna, can you make our guest more comfortable and cut the cable ties holding his arms against his back. Leave the wrists tied for now," I said.

Anna moved behind Pug and with a flick of her folding tactical knife the blade snapped open. Momentarily I could see in her eyes what I'd seen before. Cold. Steely-blue. Pug had no idea how close he was to an angel of death. I'd seen Anna in action. Skilled. Lethal. Willing.

Anna slowly slid the knife blade from the bottom of Pug's left ear to his clavicle. I caught her attention with a nod. "Just the cable tie, sweetie."

"Are you comfortable now?"

Pug nodded.

"I don't want any song and dance this time. Answer the question."

"We're survivalists."

"Too bland. You've got more going on than a training camp. You'll have to do better," I said.

Pug shrugged.

The cold, wet, night chill bit at us until Anna, Kuhl and I put our fleece jackets and gloves on. Pug was not afforded the same luxuries.

After ten minutes of listening to myself talk, I kicked Pug off the bucket and kicked him about the head. I distinctly remembered Pug tap-dancing on my head with his boots not long ago.

I grabbed him from the ground and slammed him onto the bucket again. Gone was Pug's smirk. Only a grim expression of fear was left.

"You're nods and shrugs aren't the answers I'm looking for, but you know that. Who's bankrolling this outfit?" I asked.

I'm the kind of guy that prefers truth above silence and silence above lies. But Pug wasn't cracking. Perhaps it was me or maybe my style. I didn't see how it was possible that I hadn't asked the right question. "Who's Snuth?"

"Snuth?" Pug was a challenge to interview and I hadn't figured him for that. But, in all fairness, I'd been gentler with him than I had with most others. Usually, I convinced the target I wasn't fooling around in the first few seconds of our meeting. If the answers didn't start flowing, I'd have to use more persuasive means to get what I wanted.

"I'm not going to ask you again. You don't have any bargaining chips on the table. You tell me who Snuth is, or I'll make your death drag out for a week or more."

Pug was smarter than he looked. "Mister Snuth owns a mineral exploration company that I work for once in a while."

"What kind of work?"

"I clear obstacles out of his way."

I didn't see Pug as a problem solver for Snuth. He and his Alliance buddies might be good for harassing the locals, but they were more valuable as fall guys. They were too stupid to see the situation. If something went wrong, Snuth could disavow any knowledge of the Alliances activities while they did his dirty work. It was a wise investment on Snuth's part.

"Why does Snuth need you? He's a fat cat with deep pockets. He could buy off his obstacles."

"Money don't buy everything. He's a businessman and sometimes people hold up progress on his mining claims."

There are those persons who have a hard time looking at themselves in a mirror when they know what they've done. Not Pug. He put a spin on his guilt, so he didn't have to look at the reflection. In fact, he was proud of who he was. I wanted him to get a better look at himself. "Were those Alaskan natives a problem too?"

"That's right."

I took his cell phone out and asked, "Who'd you call?"

"Nobody."

I gave the phone to Anna. "Check the numbers."

"What was in Missouri for you?"

"Duke and Jake are family. We got the idea for an Alliance from Jake. Duke's helped us along the way."

"So what have you taken care of for Snuth?"

"Small stuff is all."

"What kind of small stuff?"

"We put a little pressure on people. We never killed nobody or nothing like that. We stole those natives fishing nets and wrecked a boat or two. Small stuff, you know."

"I know. I also know you've done a lot worse."

"Not any of us. It's all minor stuff."

"So when they didn't cave into your demands you upped the ante with kidnapping?" Pug was silent. His eyes searched for a way out of the question. I handed him his escape if he wanted it. "Did Snuth put you up to it?"

"I don't know what you're talking about."

I played a portion of the tape. While he listened, I put two and two together. In Missouri, I'd called him out on the girl's murder, but now I'd become convinced that Snuth was the one calling the shots. "The girl that was killed, she was the screw-up Snuth talked about on the tape, wasn't she?" I asked.

Pug stared bug-eyed; fear gripped his vocal chords. His words stuttered as he turned ghostly pale. I let him think about his answer for a long minute before I interrupted him. "Her name was Dawn, but you knew that. What I want to know is, why her?"

His eyes cast downward as he unconsciously shook his head.

"It's obvious it wasn't a random grab. You had your eye on her for a reason?"

"Her grandfather is a tribal elder. We were going to hold her hostage until granddad signed off on the lease. Mister Snuth said we could force the native leader to come around to his way of thinking." Still slightly shaking his head, he continued, "He wanted a guarantee the tribe would cooperate." Pug's mouth hung open as he searched my eyes. "She accidentally died," he muttered.

"Accidentally? Really? She was murdered."

"That wasn't the plan. That was never the plan. She ended up dead, but it was accidental."

"Did you take her to Missouri accidently?"

"No, we were only holding her for a while."

"How did you get her across the border without the border agents seeing her?"

"We took the ferry in and out of Bellingham, Washington to Whittier, Alaska—no cops or customs."

"You're the one who killed her? Was it you that choked her to death?" I walked a circle around Pug while I waited for his response.

"No. No way. I was sticking to the plan Mister Snuth had laid out."

Pug tried to keep an eye on me, but when I circled him a second time, I grabbed the cable ties around his neck and twisted. The plastic cut into his neck as he struggled in pain. I released the stranglehold and came around face-to-face.

"Whew—you just avoided an accident. You almost got choked to death. My guess is you felt like someone was trying to kill you on purpose and not accidently."

The deer in the headlight look works for a while, then it gets old. "Let's get on the same sheet of music. She didn't die accidently. She was innocent of any wrongdoing and you killed her."

No response. I grabbed the plastic zip ties, twisting them tight.

"I didn't do it," Pug gurgled.

"You didn't stop it either. You sexually tortured her and when you were all done with your games, you killed her and dumped her body like trash along the road."

"It ain't true. That's not what happened."

"Who killed her?"

"I don't know—but, uh, I heard maybe, who did."

"Don't give me your babble. I want a name and I want it right now."

Sobbing he said, "Jake, Hayden and me were on the range when she died. Duke was the one who told us she was dead." He squeezed the words out. It was an easy story to believe. I figured Duke was to blame.

"If you were holding her as a hostage, it doesn't make sense to harm her."

The cold had set in and Pug shivered. Choking out a whisper he said, "We had a little fun and that's all it was with her. It didn't hurt her any."

"You didn't hurt her? Is that what you think?"

"She's a girl like all girls. She might have been ashamed of what she did, but it didn't kill her."

"Ashamed of what she did. You amaze me, Woolf. Accidental murder and now she's ashamed of what she did. No doubt she was shamed. But, it was by something she had no control over. To top it off, you're an expert on what girls feel when you're done raping them. I guess it's not your first kidnapping and rape was it?"

"I've never done it before. I've only heard others talk about it."

Anger was building. "Let Woolf see the photos." Anna removed the plastic baggie of pictures Kuhl had obtained from the RV and held them in Pugs face. He couldn't hide his reaction. He recognized the photos. He knew they came from the motorhome. While Anna held the baggie, I removed one that I found interesting and held it for Pug to see. "Who's that?"

"Hayden and Duke."

"Really. You don't see anyone else in the picture?" I turned the photo toward me, then Anna and back toward Woolf.

"The girl," he said.

"The girl! She had a name. Say it."

"I don't remember."

"You sexually abused her for weeks and never learned her name. She was a person, a human being. She had feelings and a family that loved her." Pug didn't respond. Only his lips tightened into a grimace.

I showed him another picture. "This one is my favorite." Sarcasm hung on each word. This time, he was center stage with an unconscious native girl. "How old was this kid?"

"Eighteen, I think."

I looked at the photo and acted dramatically surprised. "More like fourteen, wouldn't you say. Did you kill her too? Did you know her name? She looks native to me, was she a relative of one of the elders too?

"I don't remember."

"Is that it? You can't tell me if you killed her?"

"I never killed nobody."

"Never killed anybody? You left me for dead in the ravine."

Pug was silent. He knew the truth. Anna searched through the baggie for another picture. I reached over to the bag and stopped Anna's search.

"You look uncomfortable Woolf."

"I'm cold."

I kicked Pug off the bucket and onto the ground. I pulled my Kabar and cut every stitch of clothing off him, ripping and tearing until he lay naked on the wet ground. His eyes bugged out. He screamed like I'd cut his flesh.

Maybe I had.

Anna flashed a picture. I looked at the image, another native girl, different from the other photo's I'd showed him. Pug with a belt in his hand and the frightened, crying face of the child. "I'd show you the picture, but I think you have fond memories of the times you've whipped girls bloody with a belt."

Pug was silent.

"You're the strong manly man type aren't you? You like to be rough and tough with defenseless little girls." I shook my head and handed the photograph to Anna. Reaching for the pile of clothes, I removed Pug's belt. "I'm going to teach you a lesson."

Three or four lashes into the beating, Kuhl stopped me. "Where are we going with this?"

"Extracting a payment. He owes a lot more than this."

"Let's talk for a minute?"

We walked several steps away from where Pug lay on the ground. Kuhl wanted to know that I had an objective. I nodded in acceptance. My comrade was right. We clasped hands and smiled. Suddenly, a howl reverberated through the darkness. Kuhl and I responded, prepared for battle. I saw a black figure twenty feet before us. Silent. Motionless. My hackles rose.

I moved toward the silhouette until the outline took form. It was Anna.

"He slipped his cuff and tried to get away," she said.

"Of course he did," said Kuhl.

I stood quietly and looked at the grisly carnage. Anna had made quick work with her blade. Pug lay dying. Kuhl touched my shoulder, "I'll take it from here." I took Anna gently by the arm and led her to the Avenger. I turned to Kuhl, "Is he dead?"

"If he's not, he doesn't know it."

Chapter 15

After a short shower and a tall whiskey, I climbed into bed. Four in the morning wasn't that unusual, but this was the first project since my injuries and I was dead tired. Anna cuddled up next to me although I was unaware of her presence until I woke at noon. I might have slept longer if it hadn't been for a dream. A pleasant fantasy, filled with passion, had brought me out of my slumber. I would have awakened Anna as well, but it wasn't her dream.

Anna stirred in bed as the aroma of coffee permeated the RV cabin. I put the rolled oats on to boil. Twenty minutes later she sauntered from the bedroom. Wiping the sleep from her eyes, she shared a smile and a good morning kiss. After her shower routine, she was met with a hearty breakfast.

"What's on the agenda," Anna asked.

"I say we kick it until Kuhl shows."

The day had warmed nicely, jumping up into the mid-sixties. The cold snap had passed for the time being. I placed a camp chair outside the RV door and soaked in the rays. The shade would have been inviting if it weren't for those notorious Alaskan mosquitoes that shunned direct sunlight.

I sipped on a glass of Jamison's over ice until late in the afternoon. Around five in the evening, Anna pulled up a camp chair and we watched the fishermen and families come and go from the Park. Dozens of jubilant children cavorted through the campground. Parents or adult chaperones accompanied some while others ran freely. Kids at play were thought-provoking. They were the reason I was a Palatini.

"Do you ever miss the simple life?" I asked.

Anna tossed a look at me as if I lived in an altered state of reality. "I haven't a clue what you're talking about. My life has never been simple."

"I miss avenging one of these little ones on a personal level. The Palatini ways are about numbers. Don't get me wrong, I see the need. But I miss the one on one contact."

"This project was about one victim. Then it became about the victim and you—a second victim. We find the pictures in their motorhome, and that raises the stakes higher, maybe another half dozen victims. The problem of avenging one victim is we find out the target has a deeper history of behavior."

Anna picked up my empty whiskey glass but before she entered the RV to get a refill, she gave me something to contemplate. "There is no such thing as one on one. Predators engage in networks. Those people you've killed were part of the bigger picture of child pornography or other vile acts."

"You don't think they were lone actors."

"Not at all. They appeased their depravity within a network of filth that operates for predators and by predators."

Anna returned with a tall, cold drink. "Kuhl's pulling into the campground."

"About time."

It was too beautiful of an Alaskan day to waste on an indoor meeting. I didn't sense that the vacationers and hardened fishermen had paid any attention to what went on at our RV. Besides, my charming smile and superficial waving satisfied our campground neighbors. Kuhl quickly settled into a camp chair and pulled the huddle in tight.

"Any problems last night?" I asked.

"I questioned whether we'd picked Woolf's brain for all we could get," Kuhl said.

"With our time and location restraints we did the best we could," Anna said.

"It matters little," I said. "We picked up new information to work with and a better understanding of these phony survivalists."

Anna added, "The information you had on Edwin Snuth was correct. He is a pilot. The plane he flew to Tangle Lakes is registered in his name. It is under private ownership, not corporate or company assets." Anna showed a picture she'd copied from a news article. It was the man we'd seen with Pug. "He's big time. He secures contracts with the State of Alaska for mine development. He has two prominent gold mines in operation that I'm aware of," she said.

"At first, I thought a weak fascist ideology ruled Alliance thinking. They want to rule the future, and that's what the supremacy and social regimentation was about. But that's not it at all. What they're engaged in is old-fashioned organized crime."

At this, their heads tilted slightly as they cast me inquiring looks. "These guys added Snuth's hatred to their greed," I said. "Hate is cheap and weak. But, it has also made their greed more volatile. Without their greed, we wouldn't have understood the purpose behind their actions. We would've continued to believe the crime committed against Dawn was sexually motivated. When, in fact, it was driven by greed."

Kuhl sat back from the huddle, pulled a tin of canned meat from his bag, inserted the key and twisted. With each twist of his wrist, I was drawn back in time to Toronto. Some images had taken up permanent lodging in my subconscious and emerged unbidden with the simplest visual or spoken cue. I took another drink of my libation.

"Any ideas on Snuth?" Anna asked.

Kuhl fired from the hip, "He was aware of what his henchmen were doing." The tone of Kuhl's voice turned crisp. "He's not going to jail. He's going to hell."

"He's the kingpin!" Anna said.

I turned my attention to Anna, "Get a hold of Max and let him know about the development with Snuth. See if he has any insights or knowledge of this guy."

Anna jotted down some quick notes. "I may have to drive into Glennallen for the cell phone to work."

"Take the Avenger," I said. "What about Pug?"

"He was dead when I loaded him in the van. I didn't have to take him far to find a final resting place. Fishing activity was at a lull because of the storm that blew through. Even the diehards were sitting the weather out. I took him north and dropped him from a bridge. The water was moving fast, it's possible somebody will find him, but I have my doubts. No access roads were east of the highway in that area," Kuhl said. "I burned his clothes at my campsite."

"Are there any issues concerning my killing him?" Anna asked.

"I think we already covered the biggest concern, that of Intel. I believe we can move on," I said. "Last night, I grabbed a pile of papers from Pug's Scout. Anna, I'd like you to sift through them and see what you can find." Anna's eyes lit up.

"I've reviewed the call log on Woolf's phone, wrote down the names and numbers and included his contact list to our file. There was a missed call on the phone with a voice message. With the reception being what it is in the area, I suspect it's normal to leave messages. We are unable to listen to it unless we get higher ground for a better signal," Anna said.

"Take it with you when you call Max. Download the message then get rid of the phone," I said.

Kuhl piped up, "I'll take it with me."

"It's late in the day. Let's set out in the morning to run surveillance on the Alliance compound. They are supposed to have a "gathering" this weekend. Tomorrow is Friday; I want to be in position before our guests arrive," I said.

"I'll be out of the area for a while this evening," Kuhl said.

"Roger that. Let's plan on camp surveillance at noon tomorrow?"
Anna and Kuhl nodded.

"I'm going to make the phone calls before it gets any later," Anna said.

"Guess I'll mind the fort," I replied.

Both Anna and Kuhl headed out on their missions. I relaxed in my camp chair and watched the Park patrons scurry up and down the river bank, some with fish and others not so lucky. A young couple came by, waved and said "Hi." Meaningless behavior to most people but to me it meant a lot. It was the toddler who marched along behind the young adults that caught my attention. I understood clearly; I was called to make the world a safer place. If I didn't answer the call, this joyful little tike might fall victim to a perp. If not him, it would be another inno-cent child. I had to kill the slime of humanity.

To remain hidden from the world has been my cross to bear. If I were revealed, society would find my existence repugnant. They wouldn't appreciate my labors and would abhor my judgments. My only satisfaction was the parade before me in the toddler that played safely on the riverbank.

An hour had passed when the Avenger pulled into the RV Park. Anna sat beside me while I related my feelings to her. I was taking a chance. I find life more comfortable guarding my feelings than talking about them. Anna looked at me with sad puppy dog eyes, "Don't I make you feel valued?"

I was smart enough to know there was only one right answer to her question. "You make my world go round, sweetie." I reached and took her by the hand. She reciprocated with a smile as she said, "We can only rely on our appreciation of each other for what we have accomplished in the shadows."

She was right. Anna followed up by saying something about putting a smile on my face and insisting on turning in early. I was game.

By five in the morning, I was awake and out of bed. I hadn't had much sleep. I checked gear and refreshed my bug-out bag. While I was rattling around in the RV, Anna crawled out of bed, made coffee and put the oatmeal on to cook. Shortly after six-thirty, we'd eaten breakfast and completed our preparations for an extended outing. We lounged in the camp chairs and sipped another cup of Joe.

Kuhl wasn't late when he arrived at ten minutes before eight. Anna had a fresh cup of coffee ready to hand him as he sat down next to me. "Breakfast?" Anna asked. "It's a bacon and bagel day."

"I'll pass," Kuhl said. "I retrieved the message from Woolf's phone last night when I went to Anchorage."

"You went to Anchorage?" I asked.

"Yeah," he said. "I couldn't see any reason to take a chance keeping the phone. A government agency might trace a signal. I gave it a healthy toss from the Eagle River Bridge. Only the rapids know its whereabouts."

"Anchorage?" Anna asked.

"Yeah, you remember, you located the address where the float plane of Snuth's was berthed? I wanted another shot at it."

"Was it there?" I asked.

"Yeah and it had little in the way of security. It was easy to access." Anna cut Kuhl off, "What did the message say?"

"Leigh called to tell Woolf that he'd meet him at the clubhouse around noon."

"Clubhouse?" I said. That term didn't ring a bell and set my mind to wondering what kind of Mickey Mouse operation these guys were running.

"That's what they called it. He also said Boury wouldn't be able to make it until late in the evening." Kuhl looked toward me and said, "No mention of Dixon or anyone else showing up."

"I hope Dixon didn't fly the coup," Anna said. "I'd hate for us to make the trip back to Missouri to finish the project."

"If he was sure he saw you, he might be running scared," Kuhl said.

I pondered the information for a minute. "Let's greet Ponytail. Brother, I need you in the van. I want everything recorded. He might say something to help us track Duke down or take out that fat cat Snuth."

Anna looked puzzled. "We are hitting Snuth then?"

"Our project is evolving," I said. Kuhl's lip had curled when he spoke of having accessed Snuth's plane. Something told me he didn't leave empty handed. "Did you do more than look at the plane?"

Kuhl's lip curled again. I knew I was right. "It's rigged to rock-n-roll," he said.

"Pug might have lied about who killed Dawn," Anna said.

"That's a given. It was to his benefit to blame someone else. But if he didn't kill her, I want to find out who did, and Ponytail is next on the agenda," I said. "Anna, you'll stage on the hillside. I want you on point as a lookout while I'm in the camp."

"But I'm not a long-range shooter."

"That's okay. I don't want you shooting him. Two-way communications will be your primary function. We have portables that will work fine for the short distance we're spread out."

Anna drove the Avenger toward the camp and pulled off by the bridge of a large tributary. She was fortunate to find a place to park the car. Dozens of fishermen and their vehicles crowded the small lot that had been carved out by years of usage. When Kuhl and I passed over the bridge, I saw the Avenger squeezed between a pair of pickup trucks. "That's a good idea, ditching the car in plain sight. Considerably better than searching for a remote area to conceal it from view," I said.

Anna faced a hike. We passed her jogging across the bridge. To insiders, it might have looked callous on our part not to stop and pick her up. Frankly, that was too chancy. As long as she remained in view of the fishermen, we couldn't make contact. Anna was a shapely woman.

I'd counseled her against wearing the jogging attire she'd chosen. "It's too tight on the bottom and too loose at the neckline."

"It's the only appropriate clothing I have to wear."

"Well, wear a light jacket. One that hangs down past your butt."

"That's crazy. It's going to be a warm day," she said. "Thomas, what do you think?"

"I think you look beautiful like you are," he responded.

I fixed my gaze on Kuhl, "Thanks a bunch, buddy."

A quarter-mile from the south end of the bridge, Anna entered into a sweeping right-hand curve. Kuhl pulled the van over and waited. Anna momentarily rested in the van while Kuhl outfitted her with radio communications and rangefinder binoculars. She'd previously taken the time to prep the .308-caliber rifle with the variable scope. I held the weapon until she was ready to travel.

The timing was critical. Anna crossed the road with the rifle in hand and climbed the barren hillside until her progress was hidden by the dense spruce.

Kuhl and I would lay low until Anna contacted us that she had an advantage point where the rangefinder provided a view over the training camp.

We drove to the same location we'd initially used to eavesdrop. My plan was to travel on foot along the access road to the compound. Kuhl slipped his ears on, and we waited. My heart jumped when the two-way radio crackled alive. "Line of sight acquired, one-hundred-twenty-seven yards to the compound—negative tangos."

Kuhl handled the communications, "Comm copy. Clear path." With Anna in place and no one in sight, I grew antsy. Kuhl turned to me, "Relax, let's listen and see if we pick anything up. You watch the road."

The next thirty minutes ticked off slowly. Anna had checked in twice and her reports were the same, "Negative tangos." Kuhl responded after Anna's second transmission, "Boots on the ground," and flashed a thumbs-up in my direction. I popped the rear door of the van. No bag of tricks this time. The clothes on my back, handgun, and a knife would be the total of what I carried. I slipped on a black tactical vest with pockets that held my leather police gloves, face mask, the .40's silencer and the pouch for the P99. I attached my Kabar, pummel end down, under the vest. It was my turn to jog. My trek was downhill until I reached the ravine. Then a slight incline to the compound.

When I reached the dirt road, I radioed my position. Anna responded, "Negative tangos."

"Copy. I'm moving up."

I moved quickly along the edge of the driveway past four distinct signs. The first, a simple red and white "Private Property" sign. On the opposite side of the access road was another sign that read "No Trespassing." No more than ten feet farther toward the compound hung two more signs. Each approximately the same size and had "Warning" at the top. "Trespassers will be shot. Survivors will be shot again," read the sign directly in front of me. On the opposite side of the road and written above the silhouette of a handgun read, "We don't call 911." I don't know how effective the signage was, but it made me laugh.

Recent rains had left soft spots on the road surface that would have showed footprints exceptionally well and had to be avoided. "Any noise inside," I radioed.

"Negative."

When the compound was visible through the thickets, I slowed my approach, working through the brush toward the back door. The dog pens were set adjacent to the back of the building and none of the animals had alerted at my presence.

I reached the small porch at the top of three stairs. I pressed my left ear to the door, hearing nothing more than the sound of my heartbeat. I had the feeling of being watched by something other than penned up dogs. Hayden Leigh's motorhome remained parked where Kuhl had drawn it in on his map and not farther than twenty yards from the back door.

The dogs were unsettling in one sense. Their eyes followed my every move. A yellow dog wagged its tail and appeared to have a gentle spirit while a second dog, covered with a rich black coat of fur, trembled. Two animals remained motionless but watched intently.

The cages that held them captive were small and filled with feces. The rain had filled their water bowls, and the small barrel-like containers of dry food had turned to mush. The animals needed to be removed but until I was able to report the compound was clear it would be foolish and dangerous to attempt to extract them. I turned my attention back to the porch.

We'd gone into planned radio silence as a precautionary measure. The last thing I needed was an inopportune radio transmission that inadvertently gave away my position. I turned the door handle and to my surprise it was unlocked. Kuhl said he'd left it locked. He wouldn't have made the mistake of leaving a door other than how he'd found it. Likely it was Pug who'd left it unsecured when he drove to Tangle Lakes.

"Entry," I radioed then pushed the door open slowly. A high pitched squeak emanated from the hinges. With the silencer attached, my Walther P99 took the lead. Kuhl wasn't kidding when he said it was a plain Jane building. One glance at the lengthy hallway and I didn't like it a bit. I was without cover or concealment for movement through the corridor. My weapon responded to high guard. My only cover would be suppressive fire. I moved forward. Kuhl had described the room doors having been locked, yet each room was wide open to view. It took less than five-minutes to clear the rooms. I stepped into the main meeting hall. I was alone.

I transmitted, "All clear."

Kuhl repeated the transmission, "All clear," and added, "Negative activity." An indicator from his advantage point the status had not changed. Anna likewise responded, "No change—all clear."

One of the dogs let out a howl that resonated as if it were a painful moan. It had a chilling effect. The main building was clear, but it wasn't time to relax. The motorhome and other outbuildings still had to be cleared.

"I'm checking out the RV," I reported.

"Comm copy."

I walked past the kennels and alongside the motorhome listening for noise. I tried the door handle; it too was unlocked. I kept my gun aimed at the door and opened it quickly. Not a sound. I stepped in ready to shoot. I walked the length of the motorhome and back to the front, stepped out and transmitted, "RV—clear."

"RV, kennels and back side of the building are not visible," Anna radioed.

"No worries," I said.

Two German Shepard crosses lay in their pens while I dumped the bowl of mush out and replenished their bowls with fresh, dry food from a covered food barrel. I had a soft spot after all. Next, the large yellow mutt, who appeared genuinely friendly, licked my forearm just above my gloved hand. I chocked it up as a sign of gratitude for feeding him as I poured food into his bowl. I was leery of entering the last pen. The animal's behavior bothered me. The large black wolf or wolf hybrid nervously paced in its cage. Finally, gathering my courage together I slipped into the cage, poured the food and stretched out my hand toward the animal that quickly withdrew and returned to pacing. I didn't blame him, from the looks of what he'd been through at the hands of men, he had every reason to not trust my actions. The scars he bore on his face were testimonies. He had been abused, and his trust of mankind fractured. Abused children reacted much the same way—often they were irreparable.

I took off my gloves and returned to the cage of the big yellow dog. He smelled me, looked me in the eye with his chocolate colored eyes. Big Yeller understood why I'd paid the compound a visit. He didn't know me from Adam, but he looked past the fact I was a human and gave man another chance to gain his trust. I wasn't going to let him down. I slipped my gloves back on.

Back inside the clubhouse I dug through one of the survival stockrooms. I'd taken the silencer off my P99, put it back in the vest pocket and stuffed my .40-caliber in the vest as well. We maintained radio silence until one of us picked up movement.

The Wolf let go with a low, throaty howl mimicked to a lesser degree by one of the other dogs. I walked the hallway toward the back exit to check on the commotion and try and quiet the animals. Perhaps a second round of food was all they needed. I opened the back door directly into a panicky shout and a gun waving in my face. "Stay right there!"

Slowly, I stepped backward in the hallway and away from the door. Ponytail followed. He'd been presented with an option as I'd defied his order. He chose not to shoot. How many more mistakes would he make?

The look on Ponytail's face was priceless as he realized who he had at gun point. Tremulously he uttered, "You." I kept stepping backward luring him further inside and under the microphone Kuhl had planted. Any time that I bought was good for me and bad for Hayden Leigh.

Looking disheveled, Ponytail pointed his small bore subcompact handgun with his arm extended all the way out. Frightened people tend to scare me. They might pull the trigger accidently at any moment.

"What do you have there?" He quickly gestured to my vest that hung loosely open exposing my new Walther.

Cornered, there was less reason to respond verbally and more reason to act instinctively. My inner beast awakened and was hungry to feast on his blood.

"Take it out slowly with two fingers and place it on the floor. Then kick it over to me, do it now. Two fingers. Dump everything out of your pockets onto the floor."

Kick my new Walther across the floor? Unthinkable! That was no way to treat a new weapon. From where we stood in the hallway, Kuhl would overhear our conversation. All I had to do was keep him talking long enough for the others to engage. I removed my P99, laid it on the floor and kicked it down the hall toward him. I took the two spare magazines and kicked them hard enough to bounce off the walls past him. I took my radio, turned the volume down low and sent it sailing past him too. "Is that it?"

"One more thing."

"Slowly," he shouted, as sweat beaded on his eyebrows and started to run down his neck. He wasn't handling the adrenaline well.

I took the silencer and rolled it down the hall toward Ponytail. It caught his attention. Ponytail stepped back further maintaining a lengthy distance between us. I suspected his next move would be to search, but he'd have to close the distance. I'd take him if he moved within arm's reach, but he didn't seem inclined.

Silence hung in the air. Ponytail blew out a chest full of air, "Why are you here?"

"I didn't get enough of you the first time."

Ponytail took his fingertips and rubbed them across the remaining piece of ear. "Why are you in Alaska?"

I let him see my smile. "Tell you the truth buddy, I needed a vacation. That last job nearly killed me."

He glowered at my response. Ponytail thought I was his problem, but he was shortsighted and mistaken. His problem—he was an open book and easy to read. "What's your name?"

"Rude of me, I apologize. I have many names. For your purposes, Walter will do."

"You still have a smart mouth. I remember, Duke saying you were a reporter."

"Reporter? Yeah, currently I'm not gainfully employed in the journalism racket. I've done a few jobs around, but they've led to dead ends. Didn't Duke or Jake tell you I was in town?"

"Never mentioned it."

"Evidently you're not significant enough to be kept in the loop."

"That's none of your business."

"I heard y'all fixed up a clubhouse for Mickey and his pals. I wanted to see it for myself. By the way, do you have a cute pair of those little Mickey Mouse ears hanging on the wall?"

"You're real funny. Maybe you should write comedy."

"The only joke around here is you, my effeminate friend."

Ponytail was slow on the uptake. However, I appreciated the honesty of his facial expressions. After a short tirade he grumbled something unintelligible under his breath, cussed and said, "Duke's wife snitched, didn't she?"

"That's none of your business."

"She didn't like that girl." Ponytail measured me with his eyes, "I smell cop all over you. You're outfitted with a handgun and a radio; you're not a reporter. I don't know what you are, but we're going to find out this time. No mistakes."

Ponytail didn't handle the confrontation tension well. Anxiety had internalized and built to a crescendo. His gun hand quivered uncontrollably, and he became breathless as he spoke. I surmised he was confused as to what course of action to pursue. The rational thinker would have questioned who was on the other end of my radio.

"The guys are going to be excited to see you."

"I don't know why. Your pal Woolf wasn't excited about seeing me."

"You're lying." Ponytail stepped into a supply room and motioned for me to walk past and toward the back door. "Keep walking," he said as he stepped into the hall behind me.

I took a couple steps toward the exit and stopped. "So what are you going to do to me when I step out the back door?" I wanted Kuhl to overhear which door we were exiting.

Ponytail was fed up with my slow compliance and from behind he pushed me forward with the muzzle pressed against the back of my neck. He had closed the distance. "You may want to think this through before you step out that door."

Ponytail was easily distracted and prone to error. The mere mention of considering another course of action required his IQ to process the information. It was not the time to be inattentive. He should've watched more carefully what I was doing with my hands in front of me.

He pressed the muzzle against the base of my skull. When it touched, I spun with a cross block causing the weapon to fire against the wall and dislodge from his hand. He started to yell something, but my Kabar pierced the soft tissue under the bottom jaw and drove straight up through the tongue and into the roof of his mouth. It was only a matter of time until he died.

Ponytail collapsed to the floor, gurgled blood and shook. He reached for the handle of the Kabar, and I gave it a swift kick driving it up into his brain. I opened the back door and booted his gun down the stairs. There was no need to touch it. I walked back to where my items lay scattered in the hall. Picked up my radio and transmitted, "Tango down, repeat, tango down." Then picked up the remainder of my personal effects to include my KaBar.

"Comm copy. Threat eliminated."

I walked out the back door, leaving it ajar. The light breeze against my face smelled fresh compared to the hallway. I smiled at the dogs; they seemed to smile back. Anna blasted out over the airwaves, "Inbound." She had taken a position in the window of a mock building to snipe Leigh, if necessary.

"It's unfortunate I didn't have a chance to pick his brain."

Anna nodded, "Maybe next time. He was pretty low on the food chain."

"He did say something about Minnie not liking that girl. I believe she was Landers caller. Poor thing was caught up in that sordid mess Duke made. She was probably scared to death they'd kill her too."

We walked on the grass covered edge of the dirt road to the end of the access road for our extraction.

Chapter 16

"Hunting and playing is all the same game to a cat."
—Odin Wilde

Although the highway was only a hundred-yard jaunt from the compound, the sweeping S-curve coupled with dense brush hid our rendezvous point from view. When Anna and I made the last bend on the road, we spotted Kuhl's van. He'd hastily pulled to a stop at the edge of the driveway minutes earlier with an expectation for action. Kuhl had been itching to try out his new Saiga-12 street sweeper that he'd recently modified with a hellfire trigger. Ponytail failed to provide the live fire opportunity he'd hoped would happen.

"It's over. Put the gun up and let's move out," I said.

Kuhl rendered a hand gesture resembling a salute. I climbed into the front passenger seat of the van while Kuhl cleared the shotgun. I grew concerned after a few minutes had passed, and the back of the van hadn't opened. I bounded out and walked to the back of the van. Anna was nowhere in sight, only Kuhl stood there gripping his shotgun.

"What's the holdup?"

"Anna wants to evacuate the animals," Kuhl said.

I shook my head. "You know better than that. We're knee deep in an operation." In the pit of my stomach, I wrestled with my discontent and the promise I'd made to work with my associates without copping an attitude. When I did open my mouth, I wasn't happy. "Great— that's just great."

Kuhl's lips drew tight. A slight smirk crept up the side of his face. Finally, he let loose with a shrug. "We might as well give her a hand, brother."

"I'll go," I said.

Kuhl drove to the crest of the hill to await my radio transmission for pickup while I hoofed it back up the slight incline to the compound to join with Anna. Together we'd bring the dogs out to the main road. I would've preferred Kuhl to have driven to the compound, but we'd leave well-preserved tire imprints and now wasn't the time to leave the forensic evidence with a dead body in the building.

I radioed Anna as I approached the building. We hooked up at the rear corner nearest the fighting arena. "What are you thinking?"

Anna didn't answer.

"You took off on your own, and the timing sucks on this."

She nodded. I'd hoped for more of an answer. Anna was a smart cookie. Few persons exercise good judgment and common sense. Anna had them both. "This is going to strap us down. Seriously, we need to be able to move fast on our targets."

"I agree."

Her response was quick. Too quick. We were doing it her way. She flashed me a smile and followed it with a wink. She picked up two leashes that lay draped over the arena fence, handed one to me and pointed to the yellow mutt without uttering a word. There was no sense arguing the point. She agreed the timing stunk, but it wasn't the deciding factor to action.

"I did what you asked. I made calls to an animal rescue center that agreed to take them—no questions asked. I can drop them off, and they'll receive veterinary care."

I looked at Yeller and had to do a double-take. I'd never seen a dog grin. Evidently, he'd picked up on Anna's cues and was ready to make tracks. This dog was by far the easier of the two animals to handle. However, he had a peculiar drawback that slowed his progression to freedom. Being male, he'd found a need to claim as his, every tree and twig along the way. I hadn't noticed how densely forested the roadway was before leading Yeller to the highway. Thankfully Yeller ran out of making fluid, and we picked up the pace.

Anna hooked the leash to one of the German Shepherds and off they trotted, zigzagging down the road. I had radioed Kuhl for the pickup before Anna made it to the asphalt. As it turned out, his timing couldn't have been better. He'd swung the van in, threw it into park and helped Anna load the first animal. When I emerged with Yeller at my side, we bedded him down in the van and shut the doors. I patted Kuhl on the back as he climbed in behind the steering wheel. Kuhl waved as he headed back to his roadside turnoff to wait for the next transmission.

At the compound, Anna hooked up the remaining German shepherd that appeared to be an adult animal, emaciated, with infected open wounds. The stench gagged me. When Anna walked him out of the gate, I noticed his grossly exaggerated limp.

Anna set a slow pace toward the front of the building. It was my turn to get the last animal. As far as the animals went, the wolf was in the best physical shape. Although difficult to tell, I guessed him to be an adult and weighing between eighty to one-hundred pounds. The look in his almond-colored eyes indicated he'd been socialized and possibly raised as a family pet. But the traits of a wolf stem from deeper DNA and his behaviors were rooted in what he was born to be, a wolf. I'd determined that when we exited the cage if he were to escape, I wouldn't hinder his progress. Of all the animals we'd taken custody, he stood the best chance of survival in the wild. He didn't fight the leash as I had anticipated, but his skittishness made him difficult to direct.

When I reached the front of the building, I was surprised to see Anna not far in front of me. I'd expected her and the shepherd to have traveled farther than she had, but her dog had laid flat in the parking area and didn't respond to her prompts. I traded leashes with Anna. I gently lifted the animal to his feet. His eyes were sunken, and his bottom jaw hung open.

The look was familiar to me. I'd seen it on the ranch. Sick and injured animals often had the identical look to them when they'd given up the will to live. Although survival is one of the strongest traits possessed by all creatures, sometimes it's easier to die than live. I'd seen the same lack of will to live in abused children. Many lacked trust in any adult to shield and protect them. Often they later committed suicide.

"The only way he is going to make it, is if I carry him." I bent down, lifted the dog into a cradled position and firmly held him against my chest. He barely squirmed. I spoke in whispers and promised him freedom. All he had to do was live. Anna had been right. The time had drawn short for this dog, and he wasn't out of the woods yet.

We hid in the brush line to await our extraction. Anna made the radio call; I had my hands full. The few short minutes we waited were the last moments of the shepherd dog's life. Perhaps the stress of his escape had been too much for him to bear. If he had remained at the camp for another day or two, likely he would've been baited in the training of another dog. It would have been a savage site as he was bitten and ripped apart, unable to defend himself. In my book, the book of Walter, it was one more reason to extract pain for payment. These low-lifers, the Alliance, had amassed a hefty bill.

The lifeless animal had accepted death and freedom at the same time. The filthy conditions of his rusted cage, the torture and the pain from dogfights were all in his rearview mirror. Dying—I couldn't argue the point.

I packed the dog's body down the embankment to the small stream on the valley floor. I spotted a soft grassy mound and laid the body to rest. He would have enjoyed the openness after his life in a cage.

Anna and Kuhl took it upon themselves to load the wolf in my absence. Evidently a task easier said than done. Anna's tangled hair and flushed face; along with Kuhl busy dousing his lower forearm with Isopropyl alcohol, told the story of a struggle. "What did you do, get bit?"

"We put the wolf in the back," Kuhl said.

"I don't think he took kindly to being lifted up by his midsection and into the van," Anna said as she blew strands of hair from in front of her face.

I climbed into the back and left the front seat for Anna. I squeezed between Yeller and an empty five-gallon paint bucket that had become wedged against one of the rear doors. I reached over and petted Yeller. The wolf didn't take his eyes off me. I liked that. I was of the same nature.

Anna said something, but I'd tuned her out. The predator sitting across from me captured my focus. I had great respect for wolves. Lions and tigers were larger and more powerful beasts that have for centuries been trained to perform in the circus but never the wolf. It was with this nature I had my kinship.

Anna's plan had moved to the front burner. I didn't like the interference, but it wasn't as if we had a well-thought-out agenda scripted for the project. Before we continued with the mission, we'd have to rid ourselves of the animals.

We gave Anna a lift across the bridge where she'd parked the Avenger, pulled over and let her out.

"Stay close," Kuhl told Anna. "Follow me when I pull off the road."

We waited on the shoulder of the road until Anna had pulled out on the highway. We had traveled less than five minutes before Kuhl turned off onto a lengthy overlook.

"Now what?" I asked.

Kuhl, as his manner was, squeezed into the back of the van and dug out his private stash of canned meat. Anna had climbed into the passenger seat and was doing her best to help empty the Spam onto paper plates. "Too much of the fatty meat might make them sick," I said.

"You're probably right. Their stomachs may not be able to handle it. We'll start with small portions on individual plates," Kuhl said.

We could control the amount each animal ate, but we couldn't control the speed by which they devoured the offering. The animals, less than satisfied with the sample, would have to wait for another helping until we arrived at the campgrounds.

From this point, Anna led the way. No one discussed what we were going to do when we rolled up on our RV. Anna unlocked the motorhome and stayed inside while Kuhl hooked one of the leashes to Yeller. "I'll be back in a minute for the next one," Kuhl said. I continued my stare at the wolf that'd risen to a standing position. There wasn't a threat in his eyes, only a seeking to understand human behavior. We had bonded telepathically and I saw his nature alive in me.

Kuhl returned for the second dog and asked, "You going to bring the last one inside or do you need help?"

"I got it."

Kuhl had accumulated a few nasty scrapes on his forearm from the wolf. Most animals would have struggled if an unknown person picked them up and loaded them into a van. Kuhl caught a loose paw—unintentionally. He was lucky it hadn't turned out worse.

I laid my arm over the paint bucket and let my hand hang loosely in front of the wolf's nose. He leaned back but couldn't resist the urge to take a whiff of my fingers. Then he did it again. I leaned forward causing my hand to make contact with the guard hairs of his shiny black coat. He allowed the touch but only for a moment, then he shifted his body from my reach.

Anna stood at the motorhome door and waved for me to bring the wolf inside. I'd had time to think about my next step and without hesitation I gripped his collar. If there had to be a showdown over which one of us was the Alpha male, so be it.

The wolf lit out from the van on the run toward the RV. It wasn't clear which one of us was the lead dog. One moment the wolf was pulling me in the direction we needed to go, the next moment I'd have to redirect his path. But, we never stop running. Once inside the RV, the door quickly closed. We'd managed to shuttle the three animals into our motorhome without an incident. Before we sat down and put our feet up, we needed to figure out our next move.

"We need to bathe and treat their wounds," Anna said.

"Better feed them a light snack to calm their anxiety," I said.

"Good idea. Thomas, would you mind going to the store and buying some dry dog food?" Anna asked.

I looked at Kuhl and added, "You may want to give them a song and dance about why you need it."

He looked at me and gave me the goofy grin he reserved for occasions such as these, and laughed as he exited the motorhome. Anna was quick to action. "Let's begin with the big blonde dog."

"Anna, take a good long look at the shape of these animals."

Anna looked, but she didn't want to see. She wanted to save them but refused to admit they required more than shelter, food, and tender loving care. We didn't have the means to take care of all their needs. Professional medical assistance was a necessity.

I pressed the point with Anna until she agreed the best course of action was for her to run the dogs to Palmer leaving Kuhl and me to handle business. Anna confirmed her plans with a call to the animal rescue center. I prepared the Avenger for its cargo.

Kuhl returned just in time to assist with loading of the dogs. After we'd fed them we hurried to get Anna on the road and the animals to their destination.

The Mom-and-Pops store at the corner of the Glenn and Richardson Highways was bustling with business when Kuhl and I pulled into the parking lot. I'd sustained my energy, in part, by snacking on protein bars and jerky from my bug-out bag over the past couple days and needed to restock. Kuhl likewise had depleted his canned meat supply on the dogs. He'd be intolerable without his potted meats.

Kuhl asked, "Do you want to stay with the vehicle while I go shop?"

"Not a chance. I'm picky when it comes to health bars. I'm sure I can find the canned meat section without much difficulty."

"I'm picky too. I like Spam and those little weenies in a can."

I shook my head as I got out of the van, muttering to myself, "little weenies in a can. I am not going to buy little weenies. No way."

Inside the store, customers had formed two distinct lines. Those making purchases were heel-to-toe at the register while the second grouping of folks stood cross-legged near the bathrooms. I cruised a couple aisles getting my bearings on the layout. Near the end of a row of canned goods, I found a stash of canned meats. I cleared the shelf placing seven cans into a plastic basket provided by the store. Feeling pleased with myself having scored Kuhl's favorite cuisine, I walked around the end of the aisle and abruptly came face-to-face with Duke Dixon. His nostrils flared as he backed away. His body tensed and quivered.

An uneasy quietness developed as I studied his startled response to our chance meeting. His anxiety and shortness of breath rapidly morphed into anger incapacitating his ability to speak. Not that there was any possibility for meaningful dialog.

Contrary to Duke's reaction, my emotional state was unfazed. However, the beast awakened and had to be satisfied.

Terrified people usually act first, and Duke was as frightened as a person could get without wetting himself. "I knowed you." He puffed out his chest and put on a fake smile. Duke was a creature of habit and with any perceived threat, he responded with intimidation. "You didn't get enough the first time?"

I had an answer for him that would likely set him into a tail-spin and out of control, but that would draw attention to us, and I wanted to avoid the showdown in public.

"Maybe one of these days we'll talk about Missouri."

Duke stepped forward. Again, his intent to intimidate me had failed. He should have known his size meant nothing.

"You made a whopper of a mistake this time, boy. There're a whole lot of woods out here." I let him run off at the mouth with his meaningless drivel. The higher the smile crept up the side of his face, the bolder he grew. "That's right, boy. You be gettin' the idea. Better be runnin' 'long now."

"See you soon."

"Y'all ain't nothin' too smart about it for bein' an educated man."

Silence has a frightening effect on cowards. Duke's deep set eyes squinted as I intensified my gaze. I whispered, "Someone has to answer for the cold-blooded murder of Dawn Simmonds." With that, Duke slowly stepped backward as if we were in an old western setting, and a gunfight was about to break out. I maintained a constant stare in his direction. I wanted him to feel my eyes on him.

The guilt Duke had tried to escape in Shell Knob had followed him to Alaska. My presence was a stark reminder of his part in Dawn's murder. His guilt was made heavier by my haunting appearance when I should've been a rotting corpse. Weighing greater than guilt on a coward like Duke was why I'd trailed him to Alaska. He could only conclude—revenge.

Duke hesitated as he exited the store. He'd avoided eye contact over the past few minutes, but he glanced in my direction as he turned and pressed his shoulder against the door. I nodded and glared. There was no misunderstanding on Duke's part. We would meet again soon.

I watched Duke climb into the red Jeep wagon with Jake Boury aka Flattop behind the steering wheel. Kuhl had parked at the edge of the lot with his van diagonally facing the store's entrance. I called his cell phone and tipped him off about my encounter with Duke. I collected a few items for my bug-out bag and hurried to the checkout line. When I reached the exit, I could see the Jeep Cherokee still parked near the store's exit with two people inside. In my estimation, they were waiting to see what I was driving. I wasn't going to make it easy for them.

I didn't worry about safety when I stepped out of the store. Engaging in broad daylight with witnesses didn't benefit either of us. I stood for a moment on the top step of the stairs hoping to draw Kuhl's attention. My adversaries hunkered down in their rig. Duke flipped me the universal sign of affection. A childish gesture of cowards and not a behavior I respected.

Instead of continuing to the van that was parked to my left I went to the right. A short distance from the Mom-and-Pop's was a fresh fruit and vegetable stand set up in front of a refrigerator van. I moseyed over to the fruit and bought a few items. The red Jeep pulled to a stop in front of the stand. Kuhl picked up my cues and understood I needed to slip these guys. I saw the van make a wide sweeping motion moving slowly toward the gas station. I walked across the lot like I owned the place in the direction of the van. I came to the front of the gas station and glanced back at the Jeep, it hadn't moved. I figured they were comfortable with their view. Where would I go? The lot was relatively open, and no vehicles could exit from the north side of the lot. But, Kuhl had moved his rig behind the diner. I walked to the east corner and then behind the station and cut across to the cafe.

I was losing respect for these guys. They weren't keeping up with the game. They either couldn't or didn't know how to make a plan on the fly. Amateurs. Weren't they watching for additional players? They knew it was game on, and they were falling further behind every minute we played.

They remained on the southeast corner of the lot. At this point, I was completely hidden from their view as I slipped behind the diner and into Kuhl's van. We exited the lot at the northeast corner of the lot and onto the Richardson Highway.

"I'm done with the cat and mouse routine."

Kuhl nodded, "Let's do it."

We drove to the crest of the hill where Kuhl had previously set up to monitor the compound.

"They may bolt on us," Kuhl said.

"Where are they going to go? The compound is the safest environment they'll find."

Kuhl handed me a pair of headphones, "Here, listen."

Excitement welled up inside as I anticipated Duke and Flattop's reaction to Ponytail's demise. Kuhl's audio monitor hung strategically above the back door where Hayden Leigh lay caked in dried blood.

There was no sign of the Jeep Cherokee. Kuhl had taken up a position at the van's back window with binoculars in hand. There was no reason for Kuhl to keep the glasses stuck to his eyes, not until a rig turned off the highway onto the access road.

Time slowed to a crawl and excitement faded into uneasiness. Kuhl put the binoculars up to his eyes and leaned forward until his little finger and edges of his palms rested on the densely tinted rear window to support his view. "You have a red SUV turning into the driveway of the compound. It looks like our boys."

The excitement was back.

As we waited for their arrival at the compound, I thought out loud, "Bet they've been trying to contact Pug and Ponytail."

Kuhl tossed in his two-cents worth, "Unless they used a clairvoyant—that call didn't go through but they might have gotten a hold of Snuth."

"They can call the entire Alliance militia for all I care—it's not going to change the outcome. They can't stop what's going to happen—their fate is signed and sealed, all that's left is for us to deliver."

Kuhl looked at me deadpan, "You sound confident."

"I'm going to kill them."

I put a hand up toward Kuhl in a gesture to stop all noise. He grabbed a set of headphones and held one side to his ear. A door creaked. From the placement of the audio pickups, it was impossible to determine if the entry had come from the front or back doors.

"Come on," a voice rang out. It was a good indicator there were two or more targets, and at least two were entering via the front door. Time stood still. Faintly came the words, "Looks okay." Then an eerie cry of anguish and indignation echoed through the audio pickups followed by a mournful howl. I had no doubt where they were in the building.

One man bellowed a tirade of profanity, followed by a second man spouting threats of violence mixed with obscenities. Kuhl looked toward me and said, with admiration in his tone, "You did well." I humbly acknowledged his remark with a nod and a wink.

The targets had moved far enough from our microphones that the words they spewed were unintelligible mutterings. "Are we going to wait for Anna?" Kuhl asked.

"No. They're in a state of shock and emotional chaos from seeing their pal laid out on the floor. Strike while the iron's hot. If we give them enough time, they'll muster forces and contact Snuth for sure."

Kuhl set his headphones on the makeshift workbench in the van and geared up for the hike. He function tested the two-way radios and concluded, "Range won't be a problem in this valley. I'll take my shotgun and a .45-caliber auto for backup."

"I'm getting the feel for my P99." I connected the silencer and admired the weapon's intimidating beauty. "I don't see the need for a long rifle. We're going to be up close and personal. It would only get in the way."

Kuhl shrugged, "Suit yourself."

The weather was uncooperative from my perspective. It had the makings of a warm and sunny evening. I preferred the dark of night or stormy skies to work my magic but with only a few clouds on the horizon, we'd have flat light conditions of dusk and dawn.

The small creek at the base of the Valley ran down alongside the compound's property and acted as an impassable border. In some areas where the stream widened out, the flow was shallow enough to cross. However, we'd be exposed to the openness for longer periods of time. Kuhl and I went over the steep embankment and hoofed it down the hill. Within minutes, we were hidden from open view of the road. At the bottom of the ravine, we walked under the bridge and then moved quickly into the brush a hundred yards from the training camp.

"I'm going to work my way up the creek to the back door."

"Roger that," Kuhl said, "I'll work up the hillside into the thick brush and cover the front door. We can use the radios to coordinate."

We bumped fists and moved in separate directions. Having recovered my physical abilities since the beating, I was able to cover the territory with ease along the creek bottom. I knew I would be in position before Kuhl traversed the brush-laden hillside. From where I stood, the rooftops were clearly visible. Utilizing the creek bank, I squatted and waited to hear from Kuhl.

The unmistakable blast from a rapid-fire weapon echoed throughout the valley. One burst—then silence. What had gone wrong? A misfire or maybe worse—they got Kuhl? I crept up the ridge from the creek toward the building. As I closed in on the back door, I saw a man running with a long gun in his hands. It was Duke, and he'd fled into the artificial town made of plywood and two-by-fours. I took cover at the corner of the building and took a quick glance around its edge. Squatted next to the red Jeep was Kuhl.

"What happened?" I radioed.

"You're clear, come on over."

When I reached the front corner of the building, I bent low and moved quickly to the Jeep. Duke was out there somewhere with a long gun. I wasn't taking the chance.

Next to Kuhl, Flattop lay curled up in a fetal position bleeding from a shoulder wound. "What happened? What went wrong?"

"They were in their vehicle and backing out. I made a decision to engage and keep the battle here."

"I saw Duke running into the mock-up buildings."

Kuhl nodded, "He's got a rifle with him. He grabbed it out of the vehicle and ran."

I turned my attention to Flattop and pulled him up to a sitting position. He acted as if the pain was killing him.

"Shut up, for once in your life act like a man."

Flattop whined and moaned.

"You can play all the kid games you want, but you're going to take responsibility for what you've done."

He groaned, "What?"

"I know all about the little games played for Snuth. Why'd you kill the girl?"

Jake shook his head as he drooped forward.

"You don't know who it was, or you're not saying?"

His words stammered as he pushed them out with gasps of air. "Duke."

"Duke killed her?" I asked.

Jake shook his head. "You have to ask Duke, I don't know. I think his old lady went crazy or something."

"Are you saying Minnie killed the girl?"

Again he shook his head, "Duke said that it was her fault."

"Duke's a liar. Minnie didn't rape and abuse that girl, and she sure doesn't have the strength to strangle her. Here's my guess, you and Duke killed her."

"I swear it wasn't me. Duke dumped her body at an old drunk guys place."

I'd noticed in the Jeep an unopened case of plastic water bottles. I tore open the covering, pulled three bottles out. I handed one to Kuhl and opened one for Jake. His left side had taken the brunt of the shotgun blast, but his right arm was uninjured. I handed him the bottle.

Flattop had sipped two or three times before I resumed my questioning. "What's your part in this Alliance?"

"We're just trying to make a buck. Duke said it was a money maker for him to have a gun range and the survivalists meeting at the same place. We had plenty of room here to do the same thing."

"You're an inside guy. In the know and all that. You handled some of the business dealings for your crew. What's Snuth have to do with it?"

"He's just a source."

"For what?"

"He leases the land we're on. Hundreds of acres up this valley and further. It's all his property."

"What's he get out of it?"

"We contract with his company for loss prevention and assets protection."

"Snuth gets his hands on the land to mine for minerals and has a pack of thugs to protect his assets. Did you kidnap Dawn for Snuth?"

"Yeah, we were helping him secure his assets."

"Here's what bothers me, these crimes you committed are behaviors, not security functions. Do you get where I'm coming from?"

His fixed gaze and lack of an answer spoke volumes. The Alliance was nothing but a criminal organization of pawns and cannon fodder. Snuth needed fall guys for his corrupt dealings, so he made them a cheap deal."

I stood to my feet and said, "I'm going after Duke."

"What about Snuth?" Kuhl asked.

"No question he's complicit. Through him and his money, these thugs had spread their torturous brand of evil." Anna had been right. Greed was the driving force behind their evil and once conceived, evil beget evil to form a union. Each one trapped by their own doing.

"Want me to take care of business with Snuth?"

"We will," I said. I took two bottles of water from the case and fit them into my tactical vest and walked from behind the Jeep.

I overheard Jake say, "I need a doctor."

I stopped momentarily to press-check my P99. I looked toward Kuhl, "Can you take care of Flattop's request?"

"Roger that."

As I walked toward the training maze, the sound of Kuhl's shotgun roared to life again. Flattop's last request had been granted—vigilante style.

Chapter 17

"The most powerful weapon on earth is the human soul on fire."
—Ferdinand Foch

I penetrated the training maze looking in, under, on top and behind every partial wall, room and structure in this make-believe town. Duke was a formidable opponent in such a setting. He had a tactical mindset, owned a gun range and taught survival courses. He was physically fit and had in his possession a long gun. I, on the other hand, was a hardened killer and a .40-caliber auto for weaponry.

My search was painstakingly slow. It was far too easy to ambush a guy in the mock-up. When I'd completed my sweep, I concluded that Duke's cowardice had forced him to run as fast and far as his adrenaline would take him.

Duke and I had been dealt a level playing field when it came to our knowledge of the local terrain. Neither of us knew the Copper River Delta. Of that, I was sure. How we each handled the challenges encountered might make a difference how the game ended.

"You there?" The radio crackled.

I adjusted the radio and keyed the microphone, "Go."

"Bugging out."

"Roger that."

"I'll continue to monitor the compound from the van in case our friend circles back. I've trashed the Jeep. Our two-way communications will likely fail at some point."

"Copy."

"After you tie off the loose end, transmit your position when you reach the compound. I'll be here for you brother."

"Thanks, see you soon."

At the northwest end of the maze, I focused my attention on the trails leading out of the training area. Duke had escaped. I trusted my tracking instincts to close the gap between us. It posed an interesting challenge to my naturally developed abilities versus Duke's trained survival skills. The Cascade foothills didn't differ much from the forested areas of the Copper River Delta. Duke would not be able to compare terrain in the same way to the Mark Twain National Forest.

Duke was a big guy with a bigger ego. He loved to wear cowboy boots because they added to his six-foot-three-inch frame and allowed him to tower over people. Those same boots made deep and distinct impressions into the soil and it wasn't difficult to see the heel strike on the soft wet trail that lead north into the wilderness.

A man with a long gun had ample opportunity to stage an ambush in open terrain. The wooded river bottom with dense underbrush cut into Duke's advantage. I'd traveled close to two hundred yards upstream from the maze and noted Duke's strides had become shorter. As long as he was running, he wasn't setting up any surprises for anyone following him. Another fifty yards upstream and the footprints had flattened out on the soft ground surface. A clear sign he'd slowed his pace. A short distance farther he'd come to a halt. His boot prints had turned sideways on the trail. An indicator he'd either stopped to watch the pathway behind or looked to leave the trail and enter the brush for safety. I stood where he had stood and looked in the direction he'd looked. I concluded it could only have been to see if he was being followed.

Duke's lead time was perhaps half an hour. There was no need to rush or make up the time. He wasn't going anywhere his footprints didn't go. He had two choices, go deeper into the wilderness or setup an ambush. It didn't matter to me, either way he was mine. I was close enough for the time being.

I kept an eye out for movement on the trail ahead. If Duke caught a glimpse of me at any point along the way I had no doubt, he'd attempt an ambush. I would. The path Duke followed had separated as the valley walls increased in their steepness. Duke had taken the lower trail. Why the lower trail? The long gun gave him the advantage in the more open and sometimes barren hillsides higher up. The lower path was well-worn and likely frequented by hikers and fishermen whereas the upper path was used by animals to traverse the hillside. It was natural for Duke to take the road that required the tiniest amount of effort. A lot like electricity; he followed the path of least resistance.

Additional footpaths broke off the main branch of the trail. Duke didn't alter his course or make any attempt to disguise the direction of his movement. I was confident he was unaware of my presence as he continued his walk in a straight line to nowhere. He had no plan, no provisions, and no way to escape. He was heading away from civilization and what lay before him was extreme wilderness. He bore the earmarks of a man running scared.

It was a rough estimate, but I guessed we'd traveled the better part of two miles into the valley when dusk set upon us. The rising hills coupled with a heavily forested basin restricted the evening twilight to near dark conditions. The shadowy blackness was my friend. I continued to move along the barely visible path. Any hope of tracking was lost.

I rounded a bend in the creek and squatted low. No further than fifty yards in front of me I'd seen a flickering light. I closed my right eye and kept it closed as I remained as motionless as any predator would that had closed in for a kill.

The flickering flames of a campfire became apparent. Having chosen my avenue of approach. I moved off the path and inched my way forward. The snapping of a twig underfoot or the noise from the friction of clothing against branches of a tree or brush would give my position away.

Holding my Walther with my right hand, and using my left hand to move the slide slightly over a half-inch, I reached up and touched the brass with my gloved middle finger. Locked and loaded and ready to rock 'n' roll. I crept closer. Slowly. Silently.

Looking in the direction of the flames with my left eye, I moved within fifteen yards, Duke sat cross-legged by the fire. In the event things went haywire and Duke ran off into the darkness, I would open my right eye and cause my vision to rapidly orient to the darkness. I squatted and allowed my excitement to settle.

I had to admit Duke deserved recognition for utilizing his Boy Scout survival skills to build a fire. Besides the warmth, he'd used green, moist bows to create smoke and ward off the mosquitoes. If the breeze had drifted in my direction, I would've smelled the smoke a mile downstream. He had the wind in his favor. It was a dumb idea for a guy on the lam but indicated his relaxed state. If he'd been concerned for his safety in the slightest, he would've dealt with the chilly night differently and suffered his choice of huddling at the bottom of a gorge beside a stream where the temperature was a good eight to ten degrees lower than it was on the upper reaches of the area he'd chosen to facilitate his escape. Duke leaned back and zipped his lightweight windbreaker to the neck.

As I watched, Duke's head occasionally moved from side to side, giving the appearance he was looking into the dark. His actions didn't faze me at all. He was vulnerable and at a disadvantage. The flames essentially blinded him and made him a sitting duck. I had a shooting scenario in mind, but first I had questions. Dawn had died at Duke's hands, but I wanted him to say it and accept responsibility for his actions.

Duke faced toward the trail with the campfire directly in front of him. I crouched low and stepped closer, followed by another step, then another. I'd purposely waited between each movement to ensure he'd not heard a sound. My P99 had risen, ready to engage the fight. I continued my advance until I had closed to within ten feet. My hands had grown sweaty inside my black leather gloves and the adrenaline had risen to a crescendo.

From my position, I could see Duke's long gun leaned against a small sapling that barely held the weight of the weapon. For Duke to arm himself, he'd have to cross the distance without sustaining a case of .40-caliber lead poisoning. His long gun was the only visible weapon. It didn't mean it was his only weapon. Duke liked to shoot handguns and had many to choose from in Missouri. It was unlikely he'd be without a belly gun even if he had to borrow one from his crew.

"Hello, Duke."

His reaction was instantaneous and chaotic. He yelled something indiscernible as he tried to stand then toppled onto his side. I moved a step closer. My eyes opened wide as I watched for Duke's hands to produce a weapon. He rolled to his knees and up on one foot. The shine from a black leather holster from under his windbreaker caught my eye.

Shuup... I unloaded my first round. He collapsed to the ground rolling and cursing.

Duke shouted expletives. I think he was comforted by his vulgar vernacular. Me, I wasn't affected by his behavior one way or the other.

However, I wasn't happy with my shot. I had intended to take out his left knee but ended up with a flesh wound five inches higher on his leg. Incapacitating injuries take the fight out of targets. When he'd ranted and hadn't displayed a weapon, I asked, "Where are your weapons?"

His multiple foul utterances interjected into his answer made him difficult to understand.

"On you, right now, what weapons do you have?"

"Nothin'."

I figured I'd caught him in his first lie of the evening. "Unzip that jacket and take it off. I want to see for myself."

Duke's face flushed with redness. Yanking and pulling at the jacket until it was off and tossed on the ground next to him.

"Where's the gun that goes in the holster?"

"I dropped it in the car."

"You panicked and dropped your gun. How stupid can you get?" It was a rhetorical question. Instead of answering, he cursed, ranted and threatened.

"Hey," I shouted, "There's no one out here to intimidate or impress. It's just you and me."

"What you want with me?"

"We have business to finish."

"You a sore Loser? Is that it?"

"Not really. I wanted you to know, Hayden is dead."

"Why? He never done nothin' to you near that bad."

"I suppose you're right but leaving me for dead isn't much different than leaving me dead. But, that's not why I'm here."

I could see a folding knife attached by a belt clip on his right side. "Throw your knife on the other side of the fire."

Duke reached into his front pants pocket and pulled out a tactical folder much like the one Anna carried. He'd given it a toss without looking where it went.

"The knife on your side."

He reached to his side and pulled the knife off his belt and tossed it on the opposite side of the fire.

"Woolf is dead." I gave it a moment to sink in. I wanted him cognizant. Too much good news too quickly and he might miss the reason we were here. "Boury is dead, too." He looked dumbfounded and in disbelief. He shook his head from side to side and repeatedly uttered, "That ain't right."

"Why did you kill the girl in Missouri?"

Shocked to hear the death knell for those he'd formed relationships with he was subdued as he answered. "I told you before; you don't knowed what you think you knowed. I didn't kill her."

Duke no longer manifested his Jekyll and Hyde personality. He'd been stunned by reality. What I saw before me was the shell of a defeated man with one foot in the grave and mercy wasn't a bargaining chip.

"I don't believe you, Duke. You have an honesty problem. If the truth doesn't fit your ego, you have to lie."

"I didn't kill her. I liked the girl."

"You mean you liked raping her."

"It was consensual."

"She was a kidnapped victim."

Duke collapsed into a sitting position and pressed down on his leg wound to slow the bleeding. I steered the interrogation away from the whodunit and temporarily avoided the inevitable showdown that was coming. I had other questions that I wanted answers to. "Tell me about Snuth."

"Never met him."

"You've heard of him?"

"Sure."

"What have you heard?"

"I'm supposed to meet him this weekend."

"Why?"

"Business opportunities. He figured I'd be able to help with the details."

"What sort of details?"

"Jake was working that out."

"Did Jake say what he did for Snuth?"

"Some."

"Some thug work?"

Duke's gaze fell to the ground in front of him.

"Yeah, I'm sure Jake told you the stories about kidnappings and intimidating people—and I think you liked what you heard."

Duke's stare at the ground intensified. Despondent. His lips pressed into a thin line.

"I know the mold Snuth was cut from—pure greed. He's a pressure squeezer, but he doesn't have the strength to do it himself. So he uses his money to buy people like Jake and Hayden—and you. He needs you to strong-arm people until they submit and relinquish their land for his purposes. He's a modern day carpetbagger."

"Jake said Mister Snuth had his eye on a silver mine in southern Missouri. He wanted to 'acquire' it. He was willin' to pay a good chunk of change for the right guys who could watch over his assets."

"Listen to yourself. Snuth needs a private force that'll commit crimes for him. He doesn't care how you get the results. Woolf kidnapped Dawn for that very reason. Snuth said he 'wanted,' and everyone on his payroll was willing to do whatever—to satisfy his lust."

Duke was an unprincipled man. He'd proven he had no foundation. Above all, he'd misled himself through bad opportunities and foolish choices.

"Who killed the girl?" I tried to blindside him with a hope he'd trip up and confess.

"I wanted to keep her around."

"You were just going to use her for a while."

Duke shrugged and said, "Yer so smart, you figure it out."

I didn't appreciate his snotty tone or the ugly look he threw my way. Rather than engage in name-calling and other childish behavior, I took the higher road and unloaded a hollow-point into his Durango cowboy boot. His foot was still inside.

When his lungs gave out from the howling and screaming I raised my weapon to gain his attention. "Duke, I know who killed Dawn."

Duke scoffed between sobs, "I doubt that. There ain't no witnesses to prove it."

I aimed my weapon at Duke's good boot and said, "We can do this all night. You have plenty more parts to shoot up."

Duke covered his good foot with both hands. I lowered the weapon and tossed some bait his way, "Minnie killed her." I didn't believe it; I wanted to see his reaction. If he admitted he'd killed Dawn, I'd put him out of his misery quickly. If he tried to lay that phony excuse on me like he had the others he'd suffer a long time.

Duke's expression went quickly from pain and agony to bewilderment. His eyes widened, eyebrows raised, and his jaw dropped open. He was as close to speechless as I'd seen him. Duke's reaction—was all wrong.

"I'm not sayin' nothin' no more. You're just gonna kill me like ya did the rest of them."

Duke wasn't a chivalrous kind of guy. He could have taken the bait and said Minnie did it but I suspect he clammed up because he didn't have it in him to accept responsibility for Dawn's death?

I pressed the issue with him, but he wouldn't talk. I threatened him with more lead and shot him once in the hand, but he wouldn't talk.

With no one feeding the campfire, it faded to a few smoldering embers. Daylight had crept in amongst the gloomy shadows, cast by the spruce and hemlock trees that dominated the basin's landscape.

Duke's head bobbed and his eyes closed for short periods of time. He'd grown lethargic. A loss of a couple pints of blood does that to a guy. Our interchange was over. I stood behind him for a moment and waited for his reaction. He showed no sign of concern. I've always believed a man faced with an end-of-life scenario chooses to end his life quickly rather than continuing to suffer.

Shuup…

A pink mist blowback filled the air. I took a step toward his shoulder and took aim at the back of his head a second time.

Shuup…

Bone fragments and brain matter splattered onto the ground. Double tap—a signature kill. I preferred to end all my hunting trips in that manner.

Dixon's body lay sprawled along the edge of where he'd crafted his campfire. Forest scavengers from bears to fox and ravens to a myriad of insects would take their toll rapidly on Dixon's flesh. Alaska's wilderness being vast and remote would not quickly yield his body to discovery.

If ever.

I picked up my brass, counted them against the number of times I'd fired my weapon and placed them in my vest pocket. I located both knives he'd tossed across the fire pit and into the dirt. The folding belt clip knife was a Kabar Warthog. I found it fit nicely on my belt and looked better than when Dixon wore it. The second knife was a high-quality Kershaw speed assisted automatic. I thought I'd give it to Anna as a gift. She would appreciate its value. Dixon's long gun, an SKS, was a substandard junker in my opinion. I tossed it into the water to let it return to nature.

After a quick search of the body, I'd found only his wallet that had any form of identification. In his front pants pocket was a wadded up ten dollar bill. I tossed his wallet in the river, but there wasn't any sense throwing good money away when it could be donated to a charitable cause.

I retraced the same route that I'd taken when tracking Duke. I covered the distance in a quarter of the time. At the training maze, I stopped to make radio contact. The level of commitment and excitement that had spurred me on through the night had wavered. I was exhausted.

"Comm, inbound."

I waited and listened. Nothing. I repeated my transmission.

The radio crackled, "Go for Comm."

I breathed a sigh of relief. Kuhl's voice was crisp and clear. "Comm, pick up."

"Roger, en route."

I walked through the training maze keeping a sharp eye out for movement. There was potential to encounter other members of their militia. This was the Alliance weekend for their drill. According to Duke, Snuth was scheduled to arrive for their meeting.

I passed Boury's charred and burned out Cherokee at the edge of the parking lot. I didn't bother looking at the body. No other vehicles were in sight. I entered the brush behind the compound and worked my way to the road. Kuhl was parked at the edge of the Richardson Highway at the compound access road. It was as if a fifty-pound weight had been taken off my shoulders.

When I opened the van door, Kuhl immediately asked, "What about Duke?"

Sarcasm stuck in my craw, "I'm okay, thanks for asking."

"I can see how you're doing. What about the other guy?"

"He won't need a ride."

Kuhl slipped the van into gear and pulled onto the highway northbound. We pulled into the RV campground and alongside the Avenger. I knocked to awaken Anna before I entered the motorhome. When she answered the door, she didn't look like she'd slept at all. I stepped inside and closed the door. My bug-out bag hit the floor as Anna fell into my arms. Her head tucked tightly to my chest. She whispered, "I missed you."

I repeated the words back to her. When the embrace began to loosen, I said, "I have to shower and get cleaned up."

She took me by the hand and led me down the short hall to the bathroom before she let go. "I'll be waiting," she whispered.

The words were pleasant to my ears. She might have expectations of more than I could deliver. Once I'd showered I stepped into the bedroom and as promised Anna was waiting for me—fast asleep. That's what I called getting lucky. There was still time for a power nap.

Late in the afternoon, Kuhl arrived for the powwow. Anna recapped her delivery of the animals to the rescue center in Palmer. "As promised there were no questions asked. I also made a substantial cash offering to ensure the animals found a good home."

"Well done," I said.

"You need to get those Alaskan plates off your Avenger right away," Kuhl said. "Those animal rescue staffers might have captured your license number."

"They're not traceable to my rig."

"You're right with one exception. As long as they are attached to your car you run the risk of being connected to our events. Dump the plates."

"Good idea."

The next half hour Kuhl and I recapped our target acquisition and their terminations. Kuhl mentioned that Minnie's name came up as the killer.

"I find that hard to believe," Anna said.

"Her personality is all wrong. I don't think she has it in her to be a killer," Kuhl said.

"Boury believed what Duke told him. That's all," I said. "In the end, Duke was unable to accept responsibility and confess."

"What's our next step?" Anna asked.

"Snuth," I said.

Kuhl closed his eyes and lifted his eyebrows, "I don't think anybody disagrees he is the root cause of all that has happened." Anna acknowledged Kuhl's statement with an assenting nod.

"He's supposed to meet with Duke and Jake this weekend," I said.

"I'll need to set up shop with a visual on his plane. Once he's airborne, I can track by GPS then notify you with his direction of travel. In order to do that, we have to improve our communications ability."

"We'll spend a couple days in the RV near the Glennallen phone towers," I said.

Kuhl took off for Anchorage. Anna and I broke camp early in the morning and drove into Glennallen and staged. We checked our cell phone signal and placed a call to Kuhl.

"Good timing. Snuth is at Lake Hood and appears to be pre-flighting the Cessna.

We sat for the better part of an hour waiting for Kuhl to call back. When the phone rang, Anna answered, and with a simple "Okay" disconnected the call. "Thomas said Snuth is driving east out of Anchorage."

"He's full of surprises."

"Thomas said he's alone in a beige Cadillac Escalade and that he is running a loose tail. He'll update us when he has something."

It was a long forty minutes before Kuhl made contact. "We don't have Intel on where the meeting was taking place, correct?"

Anna put him on speaker. "Right," she said.

"He's stopped at King Mountain Lodge. I'm going inside."

"If you think he'll be there a while, we'll roll that direction. It might have been selected as the meeting site."

"He's coming out, stand by."

Ten minutes later Kuhl reported, "There is a row of small cabins on the south side of the lodge's parking area. He's pulled his Caddy over to the end cabin farthest from the lodge."

"We'll travel. Where to?"

"A mile or so south of the Chickaloon turn off. It'll take you a couple hours to get here, and you'll lose cell phone capabilities through some of the passes."

"We'll be there."

Chapter 18

"If money is the root of all evil, then greed is the seed."
—Unknown

At Milepost Six just north of Chickaloon, I put a call into Kuhl. "What's our target's status?"

"Rats in the hole. What's your locale?"

"Chickaloon turn off."

"I've positioned my ride at the east end as you enter the AO. Pull your vehicle directly in front of the lodge, parallel with the highway. Go into the lodge and get a drink at the bar or order food. Give it an hour or so, then take a stroll alongside the highway in my direction to hook up."

"Got it."

We swung the RV in as planned and shared a plate of nachos chased with beer. After an hour, Anna and I made our way through the parking lot and onto a dirt trail next to the highway to Kuhl's van. I made the call that we were inbound. As I reached for the handle, the vans rear door cracked open.

Inside we pulled up empty five-gallon paint buckets for stools. "We can't depend on the darkness of night to cover our activity," I said.

"He may not be here later," Kuhl replied. "He was supposed to be meeting with someone—nobody has shown."

"Then he's still alone," said Anna, "that's good."

Kuhl nodded and said, "There's quite a bit of action at the lodge. We can use the wooded area behind the cabin and move up without being noticed."

"Okay, I'll knock and Kuhl, you breach. Anna, I need you at our six on this one. Let's prep."

In less than twenty minutes, we'd prepared for the assault. We slipped into the wooded terrain and made our way about fifty yards to the small one-floor cabin. Kuhl and I moved up alongside the east side wall. Momentarily we would be exposed to the highway that ran parallel to the row of cabins and within eyeshot of the lodge that sat on the west side of the long parking lot.

I mounted the two steps onto the twelve-foot-wide front porch that ran the length of the rustic building—an awning covered the entire porch. Kuhl was close behind me but kept enough distance between us in case he had to react to unforeseen circumstances. With our light windbreakers over our tactical vests, we looked like a pair of religious zealots knocking on doors. Kuhl stepped to my right and opposite the hinged side of the door. Pulling his .45-caliber from his vest he held it tight to his chest. He nodded and flattened his back against the wall. I stepped slightly to the left to give Kuhl plenty of room to breach.

Thump. Thump. Thump.

A voice rang out from inside the cabin. "About time!" The door swung open wide, too wide to close it when Kuhl stuck his .45 in the guy's face. The man took a couple of steps backward. I followed Kuhl inside. By the time I closed and locked the door, Kuhl had already subdued our target on the floor. It took only a moment to insure we were alone in the one-room cabin.

"This a robbery?" Snuth nervously asked. We let him run off at the mouth as he repeated his question. Sometimes you can learn a lot about someone just by listening. In a subservient tone he said, "I have money. Cash. It's yours if you leave now."

Neither Kuhl nor I spoke.

Tension had gotten the better of him and a chill filled the air as he fixed his gaze on me. With a gruff tone Snuth bellowed, "I'm a businessman. I have friends in Alaska clear to the governor's office. I'm telling you I have very powerful friends, and unless you get out of here now, there'll be hell to pay."

"Hell will be paid in full," I said. "You can count on it." To let Snuth know the level of concern I had with his scare tactics I smiled and said to Kuhl, "Once we take care of business here, evidently, we need to pay the governor's office a visit."

Kuhl nodded.

Snuth looked at his wristwatch, "There are men on their way here— right now. They aren't the kind of people you want to have a run in with."

I glanced at Kuhl and said, "First he wants to give us money. Lots of money. He thinks he can buy his way out of his problems. And when we didn't accept his cash offer, he starts threatening us." I looked back at Snuth, "Is that how businessmen conduct business? Throw money at a problem and if you don't get what you want, you intimidate until you get it?"

"It works," Snuth conceitedly said.

"The native lands you wanted to mine up by Glennallen. Is that how you handled that business transaction? You tossed out some money to get it and when the elders told you to pound sand, you leaned on them?"

"That's garbage!" Snuth shouted. "Those are false accusations! Is that who you're working for, a bunch of stinking Indians?"

"No, Mister Snuth, we freelance in the justice system, and your moral principles have come into question."

"Hey, that was smooth. I'm impressed," Kuhl quipped.

"You think this is funny?" Snuth snapped. He looked at his watch and grumbled, "Some sort of big joke. I offered you a chance to make a buck and leave and now it's almost too late."

"You're wrong Snuth, it is too late. You're responsible for what your greed has wrought. Those henchmen you hired to put pressure on the tribe through criminal activity—" Snuth cut me off, "I had nothing to do with any of it. Nothing. And you can't prove otherwise."

"Prove? I suppose you're right. But like I told you, we're freelancers. We've come to right the wrongs you've committed on innocent victims."

"You act like what you do is somehow nobler, but it's the same thing I'm accused of by this pack of Indians. How ironic," Snuth said then glanced at his watch.

"They're not coming," I said.

"Who," Snuth asked.

"Boury, Woolf and Leigh."

"You got to them did you? Snuth asked. "Convinced them it was in their better interests to back out of their dealings with me." His smirk widened.

"No—I killed them."

Stunned into silence, Snuth's mouth gaped open in shock.

Then with a speed that belied his short, pudgy frame, he bounced to his feet and broke for the door. I body-checked him into Kuhl's arms who took him to the cabin floor again. I scrambled to keep a glove over his mouth while Kuhl pulled his knife and went to work.

Kuhl stabbed Snuth three times in the chest then stood to keep from being covered in blood. People don't die as quickly in real life as they do in movies. As long as the heart worked, blood pumped out the holes.

Snuth rolled to his right side, eyes wide open. Motionless. He tried to speak, but his words slurred. Soon he was merely silent.

Snuth indicated earlier that he had money on his person. Kuhl checked his wallet and collected the cash. "Two grand in hundreds," Kuhl said. "Plus some smaller bills."

Anna was our lookout at the cabin's front corner. I opened the door and motioned her inside. "The head of the snake," Anna voiced as she saw Snuth's lifeless body.

"Time to wrap up," Kuhl said. "You guys get going; I'll tag along in a few days."

We prepped for the six-hour drive to Tok and planned to cross into Canada the following day. We fueled the RV at Glennallen, paying cash as always. The practice of leaving credit card tracks was a sure way to get caught.

Arriving in Tok after eleven allowed us a chance to get off the road and out of the motorhome for the remainder of the night. Anna pulled into a motel off Highway 1 as we neared Tok's city center. Room accommodations weren't much to look at, but Anna told me, "If it has a bathtub it has everything I need." It had a tub, so we stayed.

Anna's routine never changed. I was able to time my bath after hers and still manage to be in bed before she'd finished. I stretched out in the queen sized bed and closed my eyes. A few minutes later, Anna nestled next to me. Her lips caressed my shoulders, neck, and chest. I'd fallen under her spell for sure. It wasn't a bad thing. We were meant for each other.

Before crossing into Canada, the Alaska license plates I had on my Avenger had to be swapped for my Oregon plates. Using my gloves, I removed the plates and tossed them in the motel dumpster. After we had grabbed breakfast in Tok, we topped off the gas tank and made a beeline for the border crossing. Whitehorse, Yukon Territory, Canada lay a little less than four hundred miles to the southeast. We expected to make it by evening and get a motel for the night.

The weather, warm with puffy white clouds toward the coastline, made for perfect travel conditions that brought out the scenic majesty. With Anna at the wheel, I leaned back and relaxed. I'd no sooner closed my eyes when Anna asked, "I thought we might find a house together."

"I opened my left eye and rolled my head in her direction before I responded, "What?"

"If you don't want to just say so!"

"Easy baby, I'm weighing my options."

Anna took a good long look at me then laughed, "Honey if you have a better option on the table, you better jump on it."

"I think we can work something out."

We'd driven the Alcan Highway slow and easy, enjoying each other's company. We shared ideas about how our life would be together. It was easy to focus on the positive, but we also had to be realistic. In some degree, we both were damaged goods, and our new life wouldn't be without its challenges. All the same, our relationship was worthy of the attempt.

Cohabitation wasn't that scary of an idea, but maybe it was taking its toll internally. I thought if we talked long enough about our plans, the developing uneasiness that twisted tight in the bottom of my gut would abate. It didn't.

We crossed the border from British Columbia into Washington. It was good to be back on home turf. One more days travel, and we could put this project to rest. Although, satisfied we'd made those responsible for Dawn's tragic demise pay for their transgressions, something continued to gnaw at my contentment.

"Before we get to Seattle, I would like to find a resort where we could stay for a day or two," Anna said.

"Sounds good to me. We deserve time to rest and relax."

Anna had spent a majority of her time behind the wheel of a rig during our mission. She was due for a hot tub and massage, but upscale resorts were too ritzy for my liking. Given my nature as an ambush predator, I was better suited for inexpensive and out-of-the-way motels that dotted the landscape.

We pulled off Interstate 5 in Bellingham, Washington and found a suitable diner. Anna telephoned a coastal retreat that she'd previously visited. Her eyes twinkled with the good news there was a room available.

"Where to?"

"We have reservations for tomorrow. Relax Walter, you will love it. It is a remote bed-and-breakfast with a breathtaking view out on the Olympic Peninsula. It's gorgeous."

"Yeah, but where to tonight?"

"It will be a surprise."

I wasn't fond of surprises, and Anna's choice of a place to stay wasn't what I'd expected when she swung the RV into the Walmart lot in North Seattle. My jaw dropped as I uttered, "Here?"

"You like to blend in with the people. Well, there is plenty of fellow travelers right here, so get out there and blend."

Anna had a sense of humor, but she wasn't very funny. She'd parked on the outskirts of the lot along with a line of other travel trailers and motorhomes. I popped the side door of the RV open, had a firsthand glimpse of my neighbors and closed the door.

"What's wrong, Walter?"

"I don't have a gun!"

Anna picked up her purse and patted me on the check. "Don't fret, I will protect you."

"Probably need to from the looks of that bunch out there."

"I'm going shopping for a few supplies. Do you want to go?"

"No, but I'll be ready after I switch shoes."

We turned in early to get a head start in the morning. Following the road signs out of Seattle toward Port Angeles, we stayed with Highway 101 as it turned southward toward Kalaloch. Shortly after five in the evening we arrived at our destination in Larkspur Landing. The Peregrine House, a three-story beachside inn, was atypical of other B&B's in the area. Strikingly picturesque, the guesthouse sat deeply nestled amongst a grove of red-barked Madrona trees.

Inside the entry, Anna and I were greeted by a middle-aged couple who owned and operated the B&B. While Anna took care of our accommodations, I focused on an aviary viewable through a large glass window from the home style foyer. The owner, Ted, pointed out a pair of rescued Falcons that stayed in the aviary. The female, according to Ted, was the larger of the two birds and nested near the top of the canopy. The male sat perched on a limb ten feet away from the viewing window. I looked into the eye of this predator species that sat motionlessly. Empathy for this magnificent creature flooded my soul. He longed to live, not exist. Regardless of what Ted provided for his complete care, there remained a void. His natural predatory behavior could not be supplemented. It had to be fulfilled, or he had no life at all.

Anna and I climbed the wood staircase to our suite. Once inside our room, Anna called dibs on the jetted whirlpool tub that sat directly under a three-panel skylight. I wandered around the living room until Anna was situated in her hot soak. Then it was my turn to stretch out for a catnap.

As I transitioned from wakefulness to sleep, I'd entered into the borderlands between the two states of being. At first, I drifted in blackness, aware only that I wasn't dreaming. Seemingly within seconds the blackness vanished, and thick whiteness appeared as if I were in the midst of a Cumulus cloud. I anticipated and prepared for the appearance of some creature or object that would ultimately require action on my part.

I'd no sooner finished my thought to prepare for the worst when the whiteness gave way to a burst of light followed by the cloud separating and drifting apart.

Amidst a dry, barren field, a gray, leafless, dead shrub stood alone, engulfed in flames. As I looked on, I marveled that the bush was not consumed. Surrounding the fiery vision, the bleached yellow prairie grass swayed in an otherwise undetectable breeze. My eyes were drawn to the ground in front of the burning bush as a small patch of soil quivered.

Through the crumbling layer of sod came a spurt of red crude, followed by a second ejection, then a third. The pulsating flow continued until the ground had been covered red with blood.

Awestruck, I questioned the meaning of this vision. Was I being summoned to another victim's right to justice? I pondered my question.

A dazzling energy of sorts, barely visible to the naked eye, appeared over the barren landscape. A child's voice thunderously echoed in the distance, "My blood is my appeal."

I shouted into the skies, "Have I not satisfied vengeance?"

The voice cried out again with a roaring intensity, "No peace without justice—no justice without truth."

The bubbling of blood produced by the ground prompted my action on Dawn's behalf, and five men paid the ultimate price for their transgressions. But now, there remained a hidden truth.

Anna's presence woke me as she entered the room where I slumbered. "The tubs all yours."

Perhaps I looked confused as Anna stopped in her tracks and asked, "Are you okay?"

"Never better."

"When you clean up, I'd like to mingle with the other guests."

It didn't make sense why she wanted to waste her time jaw jacking about meaningless gibberish. I'd learned at the aluminum factory nobody cared about the opinions of others. The economy, politics, and wars were small talk and insignificant. Thirty minutes later we were in the foyer area visiting with the owners and fellow patrons. I fielded most of the questions that came my way with yes and no answers. It didn't take long for the message to get around that I wasn't a social guy, and they backed off.

A half-dozen guests and the owners mingled until well past nightfall. When another couple left the group, I signaled to Anna it was time to bow out. We gracefully said adios to the group and turned in for the night. However, any idea of rest flew out the window when we got back to our room. We'd suddenly caught a second wind and, feeling fresh and energetic, we fell into bed to further explore our multifaceted relationship where boundaries have yet to be ascertained.

The night seemed much shorter than the nights I could remember before I'd met Anna.

At breakfast, Anna struck up a conversation with one of the couples that was preparing to leave. They suggested ardently that we would be doing ourselves a disservice if we didn't check out Ruby Beach while we were in the area. I thought a walk on the beach was an excellent idea. There wasn't anyone there we had to carry on a conversation with.

We wandered aimlessly along the soft sand, soaking in warm rays of the sun, and enjoying the fresh salt air on a beach otherwise void of people. Anna picked up the broken shell of razor-clam and said, "Let's look for a seashell that resembles a heart."

What I thought and what I said were two different things as I answered, "Oh boy."

"It represents our relationship."

We exhausted the afternoon on our hunt. When we'd turned up empty-handed in our quest, all I could do was hope it wasn't an omen foreshadowing our future together. Fortunately, on the pathway leading from the beach to the parking area, Anna spotted a small rock that had the general appearance of a lopsided heart and settled for that as our good luck charm. I was relieved.

The following day, we were met with a gloomy brume that had rolled off the ocean during the night. Coastal temperatures had shifted cooler as a storm front loomed.

"I'd like to come here every year, Walter. It can be our secret get-away." The sparkle in her eyes caught my attention as she spoke. I nodded my approval.

We headed south until we intersected with Interstate 5 that took us the rest of the way to Portland.

Anna pulled the RV into an outlet mall on the south side of Portland, and I unloaded the Avenger from the tow dolly. Anna's plan was to return the RV and take a cab back to her house. I made other arrangements for her. "How about I follow you to return the motorhome and give you a lift home."

"Why don't you spend the night too?"

"Okay, honey." I found myself easily persuaded when Anna made suggestions that affected our relationship. Was it weakness on my part, or was she my kryptonite?

I picked Anna up from the RV rental, put the Avenger in drive and threw on a blinker. I waited. After a moment, Anna turned and looked out the back window. "I don't see any traffic." It was an awkward moment.

"What are you waiting for?" She asked.

"I don't know where you live."

Anna snickered, "Want me to drive?"

"Just give me the address."

"It's in the Dunthorpe neighborhood. Do you know the area?"

"I know where it is."

"Then let's go."

We turned onto Southwest Riverdale Drive and followed the road to where it curved along the Willamette River. Anna pointed to a six-story condominium building and said, "That's it."

After a quick tour of her condo, I made myself at home. I threw off my shoes and propped my feet up on the sofa where I fell into a stupor. As I dozed off I could hear Anna clanging around in the kitchen, and I tried to say something, but I felt paralyzed. My mind was wide awake, but my body was not responding. I drifted deeper into oblivion and unlike any time previously, I experienced a true to life nightmare.

Detective Brandon A. Ware, Multnomah County Sheriff's Department, was out of retirement and hot on my trail. In the dream, he stalked my every move and discovered forensic evidence at a crime scene that linked me to the murder. He had proof that I was the vigilante he had hunted over the last years of his career. It was only a nightmare, and I knew it was, but my subconscious played into the dream and emotionally I felt the threat.

I woke up in a sweat, looked about and saw Anna making dinner. "How long was I asleep?"

"Five minutes, maybe."

"Man that was the longest five-minutes of my life." Anna continued in the kitchen and hadn't paid any attention to my comment.

The next morning I planned a trip to my place in Portland to check on things. She insisted on tagging along. We took her ride, the Lexus— she drove. We might've been in a deep romantic relationship, but she reminded me she was an independent woman.

We walked to the front door where Anna pulled a business card from my screen door that had been wedged into the metal frame. "Don't worry about that. It's that old detective snooping around is all."

Anna read the card out loud, "Brandon A. Ware, Private Investigator."

"Anything handwritten?" Ware had come back around since I'd taken his card off the door before my Alaska trip.

"Nothing."

Perhaps my dream was a premonition but I didn't see the need to worry Anna with it. I played it off, "Persistent, I'll give him that."

"I've known Detective Ware for a few years. He's a tough cop."

"Was. He's not a cop anymore?" I didn't mind playing a game of cat and mouse like I had with Duke. But, I was in no mood to play pin-the-tail-on-the-donkey, with me being the ass. As long as Ware was in the game I was going to make myself small and hard to find.

Anna and I went through the trailer quickly. I picked up a few personal items to take with me then lit out before Ware knocked again.

Later in the evening, I leveled with Anna my feelings about the unfinished business in Shell Knob. We'd pulled together strong evidence with the photographs incriminating Duke in the murder of Dawn Simmonds. I'd promised myself to repay Landers for taking me into his confidence with a scoop for his newspaper. As of yet, no one was the wiser concerning Duke's demise. I wanted to capitalize on the time frame and get the packet to Landers. I'd chosen to drop it in the mail from a nearby post office, so it bore a local postmark. Using our normal precautions for handling material, we'd made sure none of our fingerprints would be found on the packet. It was certain to end up in the hands of the cops.

It was necessary to meet with Minnie and tell her what we'd discovered and that Duke would never bother her again. She deserved closure. It was a risky step. She might tell Joyce or perhaps the police that she'd seen me and what I'd said, but I wasn't concerned. I was a missing person. If I was considered a person of interest by police, the photos of the guilty party would lessen any focus on me. Also, I had my doubts Minnie would be a credible witness.

Anna's travel agent had hooked us up with airline tickets on the red eye to Dallas.

"Why Dallas?"

"Dallas-Fort Worth International Airport is a large complex with hundreds of flights daily. Less traceable is the best option. It will put us within a reasonable drive to Shell Knob."

"Makes sense. What about weapons?"

"Do you plan to shoot someone?" She jested.

"The killings are all done. Just some loose ends to tidy up."

"Also, I booked us a suite at the Marriott in Dallas for a week. We can travel as needed from that location. Shell Knob is about four-hundred road miles northeast from there."

"Why not get a little Motel 6? That's what I've always done."

"We can if you want but if the police get a lead it might spell trouble. The Marriott is large with hundreds of people coming and going daily. No one's going to remember your face. At a small motel, they might take notice of you. I think bigger is better."

I considered coming back with an innuendo, hoping for an ego boost but thought better of it, and I nodded in agreement. Anna had put a great deal of thought behind each move. She'd successfully planned other trips in the past; I saw no reason to distrust or question her judgment this time.

Booking the flight on short notice left Anna and me separated by three rows. I was the lucky one to get a window seat. But it had come at a price. Next to me sat a little squirt probably two years old with a snotty nose that stared at me for most of the flight. I hoped the little tyke would fall asleep, but she was kept awake by the crying baby her mother held. But they weren't the worst kids on the plane. It appeared that the airlines had hand-picked the back of the cattle car to house all the babies.

We picked up our checked bags and headed out for the shuttle bus to the car rental. Although early in the morning the temperature soon soared into the seventies and the humidity grew thick and muggy.

Anna and I squabbled over which midsize car would work best. There was a red Avenger up for grabs, but Anna didn't like the color or the car. Anna liked an Audi, but I felt it was too small. Finally, we agreed on a full-size Ford Taurus. It was a familiar everyday car, roomy and sporting a metallic silver color. I knew Anna would like the Taurus. It was similar to her Lexus in size and color.

We checked into the Marriott and headed to our eighth floor room. It was a little too ritzy for my blood, but Anna had been right; there were hundreds of people bustling about in the hotel. While Anna plotted a route, I took the elevator to the first-floor concierge desk. He pointed me in the right direction to pick up a complimentary newspaper. I sat in the lobby and looked through the want ads for a cheap throwaway pistol. There were plenty of them listed. It was Texas after all. Then a thought struck me that I should've thought of before. Duke had firearms in his house. If I needed a loaner, I'm sure he wouldn't mind.

We relaxed by the pool and dined at the Marriott. At seven twenty-five in the evening, Anna's phone rang. After she had said hello, I heard her say, "Just a moment," and handed me the phone.

Maximillian wasn't the kind of guy that tried to micro-manage Palatini assets, but he did like to keep up with the latest news. After briefly backfilling him on the project status, he asked about Kuhl's status. "We've had negative contact."

Max knew the drill. We never said more than was necessary over open airwaves.

"We're tying up a few loose ends."

"Good show, anything I can do for you?"

"Negative. We're inbound tomorrow to put a wrap on the project."

"Good luck. Keep in touch."

I turned toward Anna, "I want to leave bright and early. We can catch breakfast on the road."

We turned in early. I waited for Anna while she went through her nightly routine. I flipped on the television and that was the last thing I remembered doing. I woke up in the middle of the night covered in a cold, clammy sweat. Detective Sergeant Brandon A. Ware had fingered me, and I was on the lam. The faster I ran, the closer he came to putting his mitts on me. I'd escaped by waking.

Ware didn't scare me, at least not when I was awake. I could outfox him because he was in my world and a player in my game. Nobody beats me at cat and mouse because I'm not a mouse at all. I'm a chameleon. Ware had been a good cop and I could count on him being a good PI. If he continued to hound me, I'd have to give him the slip.

We pulled out of the Marriott parking lot at ten minutes till five. I was driving. We caught the city loop that brought us up on Highway 75. We took it northbound.

"We should be there at noon," Anna said.

"Let's make it one o'clock." I took the exit north of Plano and said, "Let's grab a bite."

The pancake house was fast with the service, and we were back on the road in less than an hour. I set the cruise control and let her roll. We made a pit stop at Muskogee, Oklahoma, refueled and tanked up on coffee. From there to Dixon Holler would be a maze of state highways and roads. We skirted the south side of Cassville and made a beeline for Thompson's corner followed by Bates corner. When we came up on State Road M, we hooked a right and proceeded to Dixon's turnoff.

In a bold move, Anna planned to drive straight to the Dixon residence and present herself as a State of Missouri crisis counselor for child and spousal abuse. Minnie didn't have the character or nerve to ask Anna for credentials. It was a calculated risk, but players like Anna knew how to be tough with her accusations. She intended to engage Minnie in a dialog concerning the incriminating photos of Duke. In my estimation, Minnie was the most likely candidate to be the whistleblower. Once she'd handled the photos we would drop them in the mail to Landers. When he opened them, the police would pick up her prints, and tag her with having made the call whether she admitted to it or not.

At the base of the road leading into Dixon Holler, I climbed into the back seat of the Taurus and laid flat. Once Anna was inside, she would engage Minnie and capture her focus. I would give it a few minutes then quietly sneak from the car to the back door located on the south side of the house.

"If she refuses to allow me inside, how do you want to handle the situation?"

"Keep her busy at the front door."

Anna was capable of doing it the rough-and-tumble way. She was physically more capable than Minnie in every aspect and possessed a tactical mindset. Not to mention she had a razor-sharp speed assisted Kershaw blade, compliments of none other than Duke Dixon.

Duke's pickup was parked next to Minnie's car on the south side of the house. Anna pulled the Taurus past the main entrance that faced to the east and parked directly behind the two vehicles. Anna spoke aloud, "Two target vehicles—no others in sight."

"Gotcha."

The gun range by Dixon's place wasn't a busy place, but we didn't want to drop in when she had company. It was early afternoon and the heat had become unbearable. Anna opened all four windows, stepped from the car and walked directly to Minnie's front door. I couldn't hear any conversation, but I'd heard Anna knocking. I took a quick glimpse through the back window in time to see Anna entering the house. I opened the back door nearest the target vehicles and slithered out not wanting to attract attention, I closed the door with barely a sound.

There hadn't been any noise coming from the range, and there were no extra rigs parked within eyeshot. I quickly made my way to the compound, entered and was satisfied no one was there. We hadn't scheduled a time frame but the sooner we tied up this end, the better.

The back door was open, as I suspected it would be. I turned the handle slowly and inched the door forward. As stealthily as a cat, I stepped over the threshold and into the utility room. I could hear a conversation and identified the two voices as Anna's and Minnie's. Anna was loud and demonstrative. It was a convincing act. I crept slowly through the kitchen until I stood in the doorway of the living room. Anna was seated in a lounge chair faced toward me. We made eye contact briefly. Minnie sat in the chair across from Anna and had her back to me. I called her name loud enough to command her attention. She startled and gasped for air. I moved to a position where I could get a good look at her. But it wasn't the Minnie I knew.

I'd described Minnie's appearance to Anna before they'd met. She must've been surprised when Minnie answered the door. With Duke out of the picture, she'd changed. Her hair was colored an Auburn shade and cut short to around jaw level and aligned close to her face. She had a hint of makeup and looked as if she'd spent time outside catching sun rays. She'd exchanged the Quaker style dress for the casual look of summer with a pair of hip hugger jeans and T-shirt. With a complete makeover, Minnie was a new person with a new lease on life. Judging from her appearance, she wasn't expecting Duke back anytime soon. Remembering Kuhl's comment about the Minnie that had opened the door to him and invited him back for dinner wasn't the Minnie I'd described.

"You're the one that tipped off Landers, aren't you?" I asked.

Minnie looked at me curiously, "I don't know what you're talking about."

"You don't have to play dumb with me. I know you're the one who called."

With Duke no longer around she didn't bow her head or kowtow. She was a different Minnie in more ways than one. She was able to look me in the eye and lie.

"Why are you here?" She demanded. "Why are you here with this government lady?"

Anna slipped on her gloves and collected the pictures she'd let Minnie handle. I pulled up the ottoman and took a seat near Minnie. What I had to tell her would be devastating but she had to know. Otherwise, she would never be free of Duke's bondage. While I waited for Anna to finish her task, Minnie became testy. "You're supposed to be a newspaper reporter, and Joyce said you'd vanished into thin air."

I kept cold, hard, eye contact. "It's not about me it's about you. All I want is the truth. Why did you contact Landers?"

Minnie started to rise from the chair. "Sit back down!" I had no intention of allowing her near the room where Duke stashed his weapons.

"Landers did what I wanted him to do." Minnie sat back deep in the chair, crossed her ankles, and clasped her hands behind her head showing off the new Minnie. But there wasn't much to the show. As she stared at me, I couldn't help wondering if this was the new Minnie or the old Minnie—or maybe the real Minnie.

"What was that?"

"I needed him to scare someone, and he did."

"Scared Duke too because he went with them."

"I didn't expect that, but you obviously know everything."

"Why didn't you call before the girl died?"

"She didn't mean anything to me." An eerie chill cascaded through the room.

Chapter 19

*"I am the punishment of God...If you had not committed great sins,
God would not have sent a punishment like me upon you."*
—*Genghis Khan*

Anna stood with the photos in the manila envelope tucked under her arm and walked to the front door. There she turned and said, "I'll be in the car."

I nodded.

Minnie spoke up, "Duke will be coming through the door at any moment."

"Yeah—I doubt it—and so do you."

"Why is that?"

"Your hair, makeup, and clothes tell a different story. You don't expect to see Duke any more than I do."

Minnie smiled. I read her response as an acknowledgment that I was right. However, Minnie didn't have a clue he was dead.

"You said you didn't care about the girl, but you did care. You cared what Duke and the other guys were doing with her?"

"Not the others, I didn't care what they did with her. They were sick, nasty animals."

"But you cared what Duke did, and he was doing it too."

Minnie's face flushed red. She leaned forward placing her face into her hands and cried. When she'd wept for a few moments, she looked through her fingers at me. Something phony was in the air. Slow to regain her composure, she hid her face partially behind her hands. She kept her face covered as she spoke. "She stole all Duke's love and affection from me. She went up to our room and in our bed. I couldn't stomach it any longer. She was getting what was rightfully mine."

"You mean Duke took her to your room against her will and repeatedly raped her?"

Minnie dropped her hands from in front of her eyes. "But that's how Duke shows his love."

"How dense can you get? It wasn't love or affection; it was a crime."

If Minnie believed what she was saying, she was severely messed up in the head. She was blind to the truth and couldn't see reality. I don't know when it happened to her, maybe when Duke took her on the beach that day. In her mind she justified it as love and had held onto it ever since.

With a piercing gaze through teary-eyed mascaraed eyelashes she said, "Duke wanted to keep her." Her cold stare continued, "I wouldn't let that little tramp come between Duke and me." I nodded as the picture she painted became apparent. "He said I would learn to live with it."

"You got a raw deal for sure. But I want you to know that problem is over now."

She continued her icy stare, "No it is not." Minnie closed her eyes, but instead of a sigh of relief she shook her head. "Duke bought me new clothesline cord. It was mine. He gave it to me." I nodded, but I had no idea where she was going with this. It sounded like pure craziness.

"But for her, he cut my clothesline in pieces and tied her up to play games."

I listened intently.

"When my husband and that whore were done, he wanted to shower and told me to watch her so she didn't wiggle out of the cord. She wiggled, but she never got out."

"You watched her struggle to get away?"

Minnie smiled, "I took a piece of my clothesline, put it around her neck and squeezed it until she didn't wiggle any longer." Minnie barely blinked an eye as her icy stare intensified, as if she was reliving the event.

"I'm not buying it, Minnie. I know Duke killed her and you're protecting him. You don't have the strength to squeeze the life out of anyone."

"You're wrong. I put a piece of strapping tape across her mouth and wrapped it around her head so it didn't come off. While Duke showered, I took the toilet plunger handle and tied a piece of cord around her neck then slipped the plunger into the loop and twisted the cord tighter and tighter. When that hussy stopped trying to get away, I twisted it tighter. When Duke finished showering and saw what had happened, he was angry with me."

Her bizarre coldness and attention to details were convincing.

"Duke showed how much he loved me. He didn't want me to get in trouble, so he took that thing and dumped it."

A chill rippled through my body as I realized Minnie's wiring had become so screwed up she wasn't capable of making a right judgment.

"Tell me again how you supposedly killed the girl so I can believe you." I picked up a six-foot extension cord that connected a floor lamp to a wall socket. Minnie passively sat smiling and looking out the window while I disconnected the cord from the lamp and then from the wall receptacle. With no apparent reaction from her I stepped into the kitchen and took the paper towel roll off the holder that hung on the wall and brought the roller back to Minnie.

"You took the cord and placed it around her neck." I demonstrated on Minnie with the electric cord." She assisted with the placement of the cord on her neck. "Is that the way it went?"

"Yes like that."

"All you did was place something inside the cord and twist?" Again, I went through the motions with the inch-thick paper towel roller inside the loop I'd made around Minnie's neck. I twisted the cord twice and it became snug on Minnie's neck.

"Yes, that's it." I tightened it only slightly more than snug. Minnie reached for the cord gasping, "Too tight."

I squeezed to test her theory. I twisted the roll tighter and tighter. Minnie dug at the cord with her fingernails, but she had been too late the minute I'd started. She sprawled on the chair, jerked and kicked until only muscle spasms were left. Minnie had been right. A physically weak person like her was capable of killing someone in the way she'd described.

The house had to burn. I hadn't intended to kill Minnie, only to let her know she was free of Duke. In one way, I'd freed her from his bondage forever. I saw no other option. Nonetheless, the house was loaded with forensic evidence. It had to be sanitized.

The compound could stand. I had gloves on, and there might be something of value for law enforcement tucked away in a drawer that would further connect Duke to criminal events in the community. I slipped my gloves back on and went to work.

As all good survivalists, Duke had fuel in reserve. I took a five-gallon Jerry can of gasoline from off his pickup and brought it into the house. I picked up the body and placed it back in the chair where she'd been sitting. I reattached the electrical cord and put the paper towel dispenser back in the original condition. Some might ask why the extra steps. I've always believed in putting the scene back together in the way it was prior to the killings.

I walked out to Anna, who sat in the Taurus with the air conditioning running. "She was the killer."

Anna nodded. "She was a victim as much as Dawn."

"Yeah, well now she's dead. I'm going to torch the house. It's dry, and the fire will spread fast likely destroying any evidence in the place and mask, at least for a little while, how Minnie died. The rural fire department will respond and any vehicle tracks we leave will be covered."

I went back inside and thoroughly doused the house with fuel and lit the accelerant. With Anna at the wheel, we made our way out of the Holler. The blaze wasn't noticeable as we drove away but at the bottom of the Holler we could see smoke rising.

We set course along the same route we'd taken from Dallas. Anna dropped Landers package at the Cassville Post Office then we continued along our route. Anna had a great idea to stop at a Texas-style roadhouse where the smell of charcoaled meat permeated the air. Searing meat drove my taste buds insane.

We traveled as far as Fayetteville, Arkansas before I'd given into hunger pangs. I topped off the tank at a gas station on the edge of town while Anna sought information on our quest from two of the attendants. When she returned, she had a hand drawn map to a local restaurant that they highly recommended.

It didn't take us long to find the joint. I was skeptical; I didn't see a line of people as promised. Our waiter assured us we'd come to the right place and fortunately for us, we'd missed the dinner rush hour.

After downing a tasty slab of beef, I climbed in behind the wheel to take on some of the driving. Anna acted like it was a surprise when I moved the car to the edge of the parking lot and dropped the windows an inch to let the cool evening air pass through the cabin. After a hard day's work, a good steak and some well-deserved shut-eye was in order.

"I can drive if you want to sleep, Walter. We should drive on to the hotel."

"I don't see why, it'll still be there tomorrow. Close your eyes and get some rest."

Anna hunkered down in the passenger seat and was sound asleep before I found a comfortable spot to rest my head. The two-hour power-nap passed quickly. I felt fresh and ready to tackle the drive. Anna remained asleep.

At eight fifteen in the morning, I pulled the Taurus into the Marriott parking lot; the hotel hustle and bustle was in full swing. We strolled through the midst of the people, none being the wiser to our affairs. We rode the elevator to the eighth floor and squeezed out between people with their luggage crowding on board for the return trip. Once inside our room Anna launched into her bedtime routine. I didn't make it any farther than the couch. I turned on the television and headline news was the last thing I remembered. I woke up five hours later. Anna was still in bed.

We were starting our day late but in reality, our day had never ended. Projects frequently ran one day into the next, until time became an indistinguishable blur. After showering and putting on clean clothes, I suggested it was time to contact Max. Anna placed the call. We had the good fortune to have Max answer; it didn't always work out that way.

Max and Anna jawed casually before the conversation turned to the business at hand. Anna sat the phone on the coffee table and turned on the speaker function.

"We're packing it in," I said. "All ends are tied off."

"Superb. Have you received any word from Kuhl?"

"Not to date."

"I would like to get his input."

"If we hear from him, we will relay your message," Anna said.

"Wonderful then, stay in touch soon."

We kicked around the Marriott the rest of the evening and hung out at the pool the following day. Two days remained on our reserva-tion and Anna and I were living the dream. I wanted to do something special, but it had to be the right something. I ordered a couple margaritas to be delivered poolside. I shot Anna a big toothy smile when they arrived.

"Look at you," she said, "What is the occasion?"

"I don't need a reason, I'm the romantic type." I lifted my glass. "To us." I took a sip; Anna followed suit. "For the record, I'm sentimental too."

Anna had extended her arm to place the drink on the glass-topped table that sat between us. She stopped midway. "Sentimental? Okay. Are you feeling alright?"

"Absolutely! I want to take you on a date tomorrow."

"Ooh, how exciting." Anna never made the table with her margarita. Her eyes locked onto mine as she took a long slow drink then placed the glass on the table. "Where, a crime museum?"

"No way baby, Corsicana! I thought we might pay the place a visit and recapture our first romantic moments."

"There's hope for you yet, honey."

The next morning we got an early start. Corsicana was a two-hour drive south. Our first stop was the park where we first kissed. There was something magical here, not in Corsicana itself but in seizing moments from my recollection. By returning to the places where romance blossomed, it not only brought back memories, it brought back an emotional connection to them.

Our day was filled with holding hands without the mention of missions, Palatini, or killing. It was a day dedicated to "us." That evening, during our return drive to Dallas, I believe I reached a point in our relationship that I had never known. The lingering question of mistrust—was gone.

We'd passed under the 635 Loop on Interstate 45 when Anna's phone rang. After answering she gestured a thumbs-up and responded, "Great, how are you?"

"We can," she said then directed a question to me. "It's Thomas, he would like to meet."

"Is he near Dallas?"

"He's in Washington."

"Tell him to hang tight in our neck of the woods. Two days from now I'll buy him dinner."

Anna relayed my message verbatim and ended the call. She followed up with a call to Maximillian and passed on to him that we'd heard from Kuhl and planned to stand down the project with a final meeting.

I'd managed to keep my mind off the rights and wrongs of Minnie's death. I felt right about my decision, but I didn't feel good about it. Dawn Simmonds had her revenge. My dreams could rest easy.

Lounging on our last day at the Marriott sounded relaxing but Anna found a new project to sink her teeth into. By evening, she'd put together a list of suggestions for me to prioritize upon our return to Portland. Number one on her list was my moving into her condo, followed closely by selling off my old double wide trailer. Talk and reality were coming together.

We left DFW International Airport in the early evening. Anna had succeeded in getting our seat assignments changed so we were seated together. The flight attendant made his canned announcement on how to properly kiss your butt goodbye in the event of an air tragedy. At the conclusion of his speech, I scanned the rows front to back. "Where are the crying babies?" I whispered to Anna.

"Stop."

I sat back in my seat, closed my eyes and enjoyed the quick and painless leg of our trip. When we arrived in Portland, we'd gained two hours traveling from east to west. At the airport, Anna put a call into Kuhl to set up for an early luncheon. Anna drove us to the condo. It was her car after all.

"We're home," Anna announced with a smile.

It was more of a Freudian slip than a conscious affirmation on my part when I said, "Your home." Anna tossed me a look that clarified how I was to interpret what she'd said and referred me to my "to do" list.

Our meeting with Kuhl was scheduled at ten-thirty in the morning. Anna thought it would be fun to grab a bite at the joint in West Linn where we'd met to plan the Alaska trip. I wasn't convinced it would be fun at all. There had been an old geezer working the grill that had rubbed me wrong. I'd just as soon not see him again, but Anna insisted.

I was up early the next day, drinking coffee and looking forward to our meeting with Kuhl. I felt naked without a weapon strapped to my belt. Anna had put the finishing touches on her makeup when I noticed a black subcompact automatic next to her purse.

"What? No knife?"

"I have that too."

I picked up the belly gun and gave it a once over. "Kel-Tec makes a nice .380." I kicked the magazine out and pulled the slide back to where I could get my finger into the chamber and felt for brass. The round was there. I picked up the magazine and slipped it quietly into the bottom of the handgrip.

"It's small and lightweight. Six rounds with a seventh in the chamber. It's not much firepower, especially with a small caliber."

I thought she'd be appreciative of my insight, but her response didn't bear that out.

"Tend to your own rat killing. It's only a backup."

The Kel-Tec was not her preferred weapon. She appreciated the cold steel of a tactical blade and its many applications.

We took the Lexus to the strip mall in West Linn where the little diner was wedged into the L-shaped corner of the building. We were fashionably late when we pulled to a stop next to Kuhl's van. Being the gentleman that I was, I caught the door for Anna, which allowed for a quick scan of the diner. Seated at the pub table nearest the back wall was Kuhl, facing the entrance.

I recognized the teenage waitress behind the counter from our previous visit. At the second table from the entry, two patrons were seated, and an old guy sat on a stool at the bar with his back to the tables. He shot a glance at us when we entered but paid no further attention. What caught my eye was the cook. I'd expected to see the crusty old man behind the grill scowling and cursing up a storm. Instead, a middle-aged woman with her hair pulled up in a bun was taking care of the orders.

Kuhl rose from his seat and gave Anna and me big hugs. Anna sat with her back toward the door while I'd taken the chair to the left of her. I was comfortable with my back against the side wall. Kuhl, with his foot, pushed a bag over next to my chair and said, "These are yours."

"Everything go as planned?" I asked.

"No problems on my end. I talked with Maximillian. What's the story with Minnie?"

"My purpose for the visit was two-fold and would tie up the loose ends. The picture evidence you had secured I wanted to be delivered to Landers. Before we dropped them from a local postmark, Minnie's fingerprints had to be on them. In my opinion, she was the anonymous caller who contacted Landers. Secondly, I felt I owed it to Minnie to let her know she was free of her abusive husband. I figured she'd say good riddance to him and thank-you to us after she looked at the photos."

"What went wrong?"

"I had a dream that a piece of the truth was hidden. A voice in the dream said, 'No peace without justice—no justice without truth,' but I didn't know where to find the fact that remained."

Kuhl nodded, but I knew he didn't understand. Neither he nor Anna had dreams like I've experienced.

"Minnie held the hidden truth about Dawn. She wasn't the same person that I knew. It came out when we visited with her that she'd strangled Dawn out of a perverted sense of jealousy. Duke had painfully manipulated Minnie through years of abuse into what she had become. I saw no recourse but to deliver justice for Dawn."

The young waitress made her way to our table with ice water and menus in hand.

"Where's the cook, the old guy that was here last time?" I asked.

She hemmed and hawed while searching for an answer. Finally she replied, "He's gone."

The tone of her voice and the change in her demeanor spoke to me louder than muttering of words before she answered. There was more to the story, and I was all the more inquisitive.

"Is he gone for the day or gone for good?"

Looking toward her order pad to avoid eye contact she sheepishly said, "Oh he's gone for good."

"What'd he do, get himself in trouble?"

"That's for sure," she said. "I'll take your orders when you're ready."

"Can we have a few minutes?" Anna asked.

The waitress said she'd be back and moved to the other table of patrons before slipping in behind the glass display case where the register was located. She picked up her cell phone, but that was as far as she got when she noticed me on the other side of the register from her. I whispered, "What'd he do?"

"I was told not to talk about it."

"Of course you were." I let a smile slip out. "But what did that old guy do to get himself in a jam?"

"Bad pictures of little kids I hear. I don't know if that's true and I don't want to know. He was creepy."

I nodded and said, "I've been around—my gut sensed there was something wrong with this guy, but I couldn't put my finger on it. Thanks for filling me in on what you heard. By the way, what was his name?"

"Olin Boe."

"Got it."

Too often I'd felt my thoughts and dream world were out of sync with reality, but confirmations such as this brought a sense of justification. Revelations of this nature allowed me to realize I was on target. In the event that Olin 'slime bucket' Boe gets off of the charges through a technicality of law or goes to jail for too few years, I'd be watching. If whatever power directs my path wants him dead, he'll end up as a project. I wanted to tell the others what I'd discovered, but it would appear as gloating.

Hugs and kisses were passed around our little group as we parted with fond and heartfelt goodbyes.

"I want to ask one more favor," Kuhl said. "Allow me a ten-minute head start before you and Anna take off."

Kuhl wasn't the kind of guy that dropped his guard because a mission ended. He lived every day expecting to battle enemies at the drop of a hat. We gave a quick wave and Kuhl exited the diner. He strolled out into the parking lot but not directly to his van. I watched as he backtracked to his van and moments later pulled away toward the frontage road.

"When we're done here I need to take a trip to my trailer and check things out."

"I have time to go with you."

"Not necessary. I need to call the lady I've had keeping an eye on my place and let her know I'm back in town. I'll grab some clothes and the mail then head back to your place."

"Our Place!"

"That's what I said, our place."

At Anna's condo, she gave me a gentle kiss and said there was more where that came from if I hurried. Noon wasn't the best time to travel across Portland. From the northwest tip of the city to the outer corridor to the southeast wouldn't be a fast trip. It was a long route regardless of the flow of traffic. I fired up the Avenger and edged out into traffic.

At one-fifteen I called Shelly from my trailer's driveway. She wasn't happy about the short notice but when I mentioned I was back and wanted to settle up, she said she'd be right over. I figured while I waited for her to arrive I'd round up my clothes.

At the front door, I was greeted once again by a business card from Brandon A. Ware. He must be checking every day. If that's the case, it's only a matter of time until we have a face-to-face meeting. I stuffed it in my pocket and went inside the trailer. I grabbed an old bug-out bag and filled it with my favorite casual wear then carried it to my car. After tossing the bag into the back seat, I was about to shut the door when the neighbor lady appeared across the trailer park road. Her walk was brisk. There wasn't a smile on her face. Under her arm, she carried a brown paper grocery bag.

"Walter, I have your mail."

"Thank you, Shelley, what's the bill?"

"You've paid me more than the agreed amount. Let's call it even."

She gave the impression she was in a hurry to leave or that something was terribly wrong. I re-engaged her to keep her from leaving abruptly. "I can't tell you how much that's appreciated. It was an expensive trip to Mexico."

Her scowl became more pronounced, "Where in Mexico?"

Shelley wasn't one to question my comings and goings in the past. Someone had put a bug in her ear, and I was the recipient of that ill will. I needed to come up with a good story to pacify whatever her concern. "I was doing research on the Yucatán Peninsula for a National Geographic piece. I think you'll enjoy it if and when it's published."

Slowly the corners of her mouth turned upward accompanied by a slight sigh. "There's been a police officer asking questions about you and canvasing the trailer park."

"Was it a guy named Brandon Ware?"

"Yes, that was him."

"You can relax Shelley. Ware is not a cop he's a PI and there's nothing criminal going on to worry about." I tossed out a chuckle to put her mind at ease. "He's been papering my door for weeks, maybe longer. He hasn't left me any messages, so I don't know what it's about, maybe details in one of the stories I wrote struck a chord with him. Like I said, I don't know, but I'm going to follow-up with him now that I'm back."

I pulled Ware's business card from my pocket and pointed to his title of Private Investigator.

"Thank God, I was worried you were in trouble."

"Quite the opposite. Ware is probably after my help."

I planned on paying Shelley an extra hundred bucks as a tip. I pulled a small wad of twenties I'd folded in half from my pants pocket, but she was adamant the gesture wasn't necessary. I remembered her mentioning on more than one occasion how much she liked my six tree-size yard planters. They were meaningless to me, and I'd never used them. They'd accompanied the trailer at purchase, and I wanted to get rid of them. I told Shelley I planned to sell the trailer and move out of state. If I bring those planters over could you give them a good home?"

"Thank you, I will."

I pulled my '57 Chevy pickup out and hooked up my travel trailer. I would be able to load the trailer with odds and ends I wouldn't be in need of for the time being until we found a house to move into. Portland is a city with many storage lots for RV's, fifth-wheels, and travel trailers. I'd passed a lot near the condo that had the appropriate level of security to meet my needs. I figured once the trailer was loaded I'd park it along with the '57 until we secured a home.

I separated items that I couldn't live without and loaded them into the Avenger. The next couple hours I boxed thousands of newspaper articles and research materials I'd collected over the years. Only occasionally was I distracted by a memory.

I'd begun the loading process, shuttling boxes into the trailer when a blue Chevy Impala pulled in behind the Avenger. The brightness of the sun's glare from the front windshield made seeing the driver impossible. However, my hackles rose. The Impala could pass for a cop car.

A heavy set man stepped from the car. I had to control my reactions. Brandon A. Ware and I had never officially met, but I recognized him immediately. If I wasn't careful, he'd see he was familiar to me. I put the box down on the porch and awaited his approach.

"Hello." His warm smile and friendly demeanor would not throw me off guard.

I responded, "I don't need any salesmen or religious door knockers."

"I assure you I'm not here for either of those reasons."

"I didn't mean to come off unfriendly mister, but it's my first day back and I want to get some of my junk cleaned up."

"I understand. I promise not to take up too much of your time. I have a couple questions that I hope you can help me with?"

"Shoot."

He extended his hand, "I'm Brandon Ware." His big mitt nearly encompassed my hand as we fulfilled the customary greeting.

"I'm investigating a cold case." Ware broke eye contact as he opened the leather bound notepad he had with him. I understood why Shelley might have thought he was a cop if he used the same language with her as he had with me. A person who drives up in a vehicle resembling a cop car, wearing a suit and tie and tossing out words like "investigating" sounds like a cop.

I decided two could play the game. "You a cop?" I wanted to hear him say it.

"No, I represent a private interest."

Anna had mentioned that Ware was notoriously difficult for the media circus to work with when he was with the Multnomah County Sheriff's Department. In my opinion, his no-nonsense dealings had earned him kudos. I admired many of the qualities and principles he'd displayed.

"You are a journalist, correct?"

"I'm a feature writer. What's my occupation have to do with your cold case?"

"History, Mister Goe. I want to have my facts straight."

I could see inside the notebook pad Ware held open with one of my business cards in the plastic sleeve. The only way he could have obtained it was from a project I'd worked. It was the only time I'd passed any out. He didn't make reference to it, but I was sure he intended for me to see it and gauge my reaction.

Ware had no authority to compel me to talk. I'd learned from the criminals to always shut up and lawyer up. I disdained lawyers, and Ware had a ways to go before I needed one. But I could shut up and make his job more difficult. "I don't have time for this right now. You can see I'm busy."

Ware looked at the trailer hooked to my pickup. "Yes, busy packing for a long trip?"

"Like I said, I'm busy right now."

"Next time then." His words were short and clipped and I felt certain from the forbidding look on his face, being friendly would no longer be an option when our paths crossed again in the future.